Praise for *The Innkeeper's Daughter*

"Schwarz launches her *Gentleman Spy Mysteries* series with an immersive and suspenseful Regency romance. The magnetic love scenes and enticing mystery will have readers eagerly anticipating the next installment."

— *Publishers Weekly*

"*The Innkeeper's Daughter* is a sumptuous, sensual Regency romance that teases the senses and recalls the golden age of romance novels."

— *Foreword Reviews*

"A gritty, steamy series opener full of dark twists and hot trysts."

— Grace Burrowes, *New York Times* bestselling author

"From the brutal opening pages to the tenderest of love scenes, *The Innkeeper's Daughter* took me on a ride of contradictory emotions. Sadistic villains paired with beautiful Regency details made this story unforgettable, but it is truly the characters who steal the show. Eliza is a delight, Sir Henry March has my heart, and our author, Bianca M. Schwarz, has me eagerly awaiting the next book."

— Amanda Linsmeier, author

"Historically well-researched with enthralling characters and excellent storytelling. Absolutely wonderful."

— C. H. Armstrong, author of
The Edge of Nowhere

THE GENTLEMAN SPY MYSTERIES

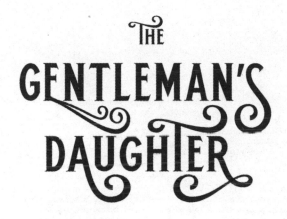

BIANCA M. SCHWARZ

central
avenue
publishing

2021

Published by Central Avenue Publishing, an imprint of Central Avenue Marketing Ltd.
www.centralavenuepublishing.com

Published in Canada
Printed in United States of America

1. FICTION/Romance - Historical   2. FICTION/Historical

THE GENTLEMAN'S DAUGHTER

Trade Paperback: 978-1-77168-240-4
Epub: 978-1-77168-241-1
Mobi: 978-1-77168-242-8

1 3 5 7 9 10 8 6 4 2

To the artists in my life who taught me how to mix watercolors on a palette and expel excess water from a brush with the flick of my wrist.

SETTING: LONDON AND BRIGHTON

YEAR: 1823 (PROLOGUE: 1820)

CAST OF CHARACTERS (IN ORDER OF APPEARANCE)

    SIR HENRY MARCH (AGENT TO THE CROWN AND CONCERNED FATHER OF EMILY)

    ISABELLA CHANCELLOR (PAINTER)

    EMILY (HENRY'S DAUGHTER)

    BERTIE REDWICK (EMILY'S COUSIN)

    MRS. TIBBIT (HENRY'S HOUSEKEEPER)

    ROBERTS (HENRY'S GROOM)

    WILLIAM (FOOTMAN)

    THOMAS (FOOTMAN)

    LADY GREYSON (ANN; HENRY'S GODMOTHER; LIVES ON BROOK STREET)

    LADY BROCKHURST (SOCIETY WOMAN, MIDFORTIES)

    SARAH BROCKHURST (LADY BROCKHURST'S YOUNGER ELIGIBLE DAUGHTER)

    MRS. WILDER (LADY BROCKHURST'S OLDER ELIGIBLE DAUGHTER, A WIDOW)

    IMOGEN TUBBS (CHARGE OF THE HEDGLEYS, COUSIN OF LADY CAROLINE)

    LADY JANE CASTLERIGHT

    LADY CASTLERIGHT, COUNTESS OF WELD (JANE'S MOTHER)

    EARL OF WELD (JANE'S FATHER, ONE OF THE DUNGEON CLUB)

    GEORGE BRADSHORE, VISCOUNT RIDGEWORTH (ONE OF THE KNIGHTS, ISABELLA'S CHILDHOOD FRIEND)

    BARON OSTLEY (ONE OF THE KNIGHTS; HUSBAND OF EMILY'S MOTHER)

    EARL OF WARTHON (HEAD OF THE KNIGHTS OF THE SNAKE PIT, OWNER OF WARTHON CASTLE)

    ELIZA BROAD (HENRY'S FORMER MISTRESS)

    ALLEN STRATHEM (HENRY'S FRIEND)

    LADY KISTEL (FRIEND OF RUTH REDWICK)

    MARY (BARMAID AT THE RED LION IN BRIGHTON)

    BARONESS CHANCELLOR (LADY CHANCELLOR; LYDIA; ISABELLA'S MOTHER)

    MAXIMILIAN WARTHON, LORD DIDCOMB ("DIDDY"; EARL OF WARTHON'S GRANDSON/HEIR)

    SALLY (ISABELLA'S MAID AND FRIEND)

    MRS. CURTIS (LADY CHANCELLOR'S FRIEND, ISABELLA AND HER MOTHER ARE STAYING WITH HER)

    MRS. TWILL (WIDOW OF EDMOND TWILL, WRITER OF GUIDES)

    BARON TILLISTER (WIDOWER, SUITOR)

    MR. WICKHAM (RAKISH SUITOR)

    SQUIRE GARDENER (SUITOR)

    BEN SEDON (EMPLOYED AT WARTHON CASTLE AND LORD DIDCOMB'S FRIEND)

    LORD JENNINGS (CURRENT DUNGEON MASTER)

    PATSY, MARIE, JENNY (LADIES OF THE NIGHT BROUGHT TO THE ABBEY)

    RUTH REDWICK, PRUSSIAN PRINCESS/DOWAGER DUCHESS OF AVON

        (GROSSMAMA, HENRY'S GRANDMOTHER)

    MRS. BENNETT (HENRY'S HOUSEKEEPER AT HIS ESTATE NEAR BRIGHTON)

❦

THE

GENTLEMAN'S DAUGHTER

PROLOGUE

JANUARY 1820, HAMPSTEAD HEATH

A GUNSHOT REVERBERATED DEEP WITHIN THE hillside and startled the servant in the sedan chair awake. The man jumped up, disoriented by the dark, cold night around him. But as soon as he remembered himself, he kicked his colleague, who slumbered under a heavy blanket next to the chair.

"Something's up, mate."

The other servant scrambled to his feet and straightened his wig just in time. Hurried footsteps sounded from inside the hill, and his partner opened the heavy iron door. Four elegantly dressed figures spilled out of the portal set into the hillside. They were all masked, and one roughly pulled the only woman of the group along with him.

Another new arrival, completely dressed in black, motioned to the man holding the woman's arm. "Take her away and make sure she talks to no one."

The man complied instantly, dragging the woman farther down the heath, where a coach waited by the side of the road. They got in, and the vehicle pulled away just as another gentleman emerged from the dark tunnel and stepped out into the open, leaning heavily on a carved ivory cane. He was bowed by age, but the mouth below the mask was harsh and unyielding. As the coach disappeared into the darkness, the old man ripped the mask off his face and threw it to the ground. Ignoring the servants, he fixed the other two gentlemen in a death stare, anger rolling off him in waves. "Let that be a lesson to you: arrogance leads to mistakes. March may act the fool, but do not underestimate him again. Astor is dead because he got careless."

He walked to the sedan chair and sank into it, some of the tension leaving his body. "As for you two, give me your rings and collect all the others. We won't meet during the customary mourning period. I'll send out the rings again when it's time to elect the next dungeon master."

From their pinky fingers, both men removed gold rings depicting two snakes hissing at each other, and handed them to the old man. They then pulled off their masks and stashed them in their pockets, and the young man bent to pick up the old man's from the ground. The one entirely in black stroked a weary hand over his face. He looked somber, even a little shaken, while the younger one trembled with barely contained anger. He was tall, powerfully built, and handsome; but there was a dangerous glint in his eyes. "I can't wait to get my hands on the meddling fool's bastard and show her that she's indeed the whore she was born to be."

The old man turned his unsettlingly bright eyes on the young man and pointed his ivory cane at him. "You have yet to be elected dungeon master, and there are at least three ahead of you who want the honor! Do not embarrass me by doing something rash; you just saw where that will lead. In case it has escaped your notice, we did not achieve our goal tonight. March may well be able to prevent the scandal we need to discredit the reform bill. Besides, young Emily March is only twelve and apparently still flat as a board. As far as I am informed, most of us still like our women to have tits and be old enough to appreciate what's being done to them."

The young man, properly chastised, hung his head. "As you wish, grandfather. I apologize."

The old man's eyes softened just a fraction. "Fiddlesticks, my boy." He gestured for the two servants to lift the chair so they could depart, then turned to the man in black. "Tell Ostley it will be his responsibility to retrieve the March girl when the time comes. And if he succeeds, he'll earn the right to be in the dungeon when she's broken in."

"It shall be done, my lord."

Both men bowed as the sedan chair was lifted and the old man waved his cane in a dismissive salute.

"It had better be. I will not tolerate any further mistakes. The Knights can't afford them."

The two men watched the chair until it was swallowed completely by the night, then the younger man turned to the older. "I don't understand why Sir Henry isn't one of us. His father was!"

The older man smirked and turned to head down the hill. "Ah, the older March was a true believer, having served Charles Stuart himself for a period of time in Italy. Sir Henry, on the other hand, hated his father, did well in the army, and may still be serving the crown. Besides, not everyone shares our sexual tastes, and we never could find anything sufficiently damaging to force him into the fold. His failings are all right out in the open for everyone to see."

The young man shook his head. "That's unfortunate; he is actually very clever."

The older man chuckled. "You have no idea. You were too young during the war. He's a formidable opponent. But fear not, we will break him through his daughter."

CHAPTER ONE

THE DAY WAS RATHER SPECTACULAR FOR LATE February. Sir Henry March, accompanied only by his groom, piloted his curricle along a small country road toward Upavon and his ducal cousin's estate. He'd taken his hat and greatcoat off some miles back to let the sun warm him. The dry and unseasonably warm weather had left the roads passable, the riverbanks painted in crocus yellow and purple, and the bare trees brightened with the first hint of spring. Sir Henry had high hopes the familiar beloved landscape in all its spring glory would cheer him, but so far, nature's exuberance had served only to highlight the melancholy holding his heart hostage.

It was out of character for Sir Henry to feel so low. At four and thirty he was in his prime, blessed with a considerable fortune and the respect of his peers. He enjoyed good health, and nature had favored him with a pleasing countenance, straight limbs, and the kind of charisma women found hard to resist. His eyes were blue and penetrating, his hair sandy blond and cropped short, and his smile engaging.

However, only three weeks had passed since he'd said goodbye to his lovely mistress, Eliza. There was no anger to carry him through the parting, since her sacrifice was as great as his own, and so he could only miss her. He missed her smell, her smile, the way she twirled her long dark locks around her fingers while she read. Most of all, he missed knowing she would be there when he got home. But Eliza had taken on the task of helping his friend and partner, Allen, who had returned from a foreign assignment with considerable injuries. And, to honor his agreement not to see Eliza for six months, Henry had to trust another agent to investigate the Russian threat and to keep Allen and Eliza safe.

Henry and his groom had just passed through a sunlit oak forest, bright with early whispers of green, and were heading up the last rise before the descent into the Avon valley. He pulled up his grays on the crest of the hill overlooking the river. His cousin's ancestral castle stood in the distance. The horses bent their heads to nibble at tufts of grass by the side of the road while Henry allowed himself a moment to take in the familiar vista.

The road ahead led down a sheep-studded incline and over an ancient stone bridge spanning one of the arms of the Avon River. It passed through the charming hamlet of Upavon and disappeared into the forests beyond. The calmly flowing river below was bracketed by willows and hazel, shimmering silver where the sun hit the water.

The scene was utterly peaceful. Not even the river had any sense of urgency, meandering here and there along its gently sloping valley, bordered by farmland and wooded groves. Henry took a deep breath, wanting the calm of this place to penetrate every cell of his being.

He let his gaze travel back up the side of the hill to the forest to his right and paused. There, some distance away, where the forest stopped and the grassland began, a woman sat silhouetted against the horizon. She was seated on a portable stool and leaned toward a spindly easel as she painted.

The woman was half turned away from him, absorbed in her work and oblivious to his presence. Henry found that circumstance most intriguing. It left him free to observe her, as she observed the landscape, and just like that, his love of the land was shared with another and his loneliness somewhat alleviated.

Her figure was pleasing, and she seemed too young to be sitting at the edge of the forest by herself. Even from where he sat, the look of concentration on her profile was unmistakable. Her dark hair was brushed back from her face and held together at the nape of her neck with a sky-blue ribbon. Curiously, there were also several brushes stuck in it, and some of the shorter, slow-curling strands were unceremoniously tucked behind her ear. She wore a rather dowdy blue dress, and a large green triangular shawl was tied around her peasant-style to keep her warm and her hands free.

But what held Henry's attention was not her youth, or her looks, but the way she painted. She blindly bent to wash out her brush in a preserve glass on the ground, then flicked it behind her to expel the excess water, while looking alternately at the scene before her and her unfinished painting. Then she dipped her brush into two different pots of paint, swiftly mixed the color on her palette, held the palette up to check the accuracy of the hue, and added a few self-assured dabs to her composition. She cocked her head to the side to check the effect, added one more dab, and moved on to paint the sky with a broader brush she pulled from her hair.

Henry couldn't see the watercolor from his perch on the curricle, but he was willing to bet it was good. Every movement she made proved she was put on this earth to paint, and seeing her embrace her purpose was very attractive. Perhaps if he could find a woman who had a purpose he could understand and respect, married life might not be so bad. Eliza was right: he had to open himself to the possibility of meeting a woman he could at least like, if not love. He would never even have contemplated such a thing if she hadn't insisted they go their separate ways.

Over at the forest's edge, the painter lifted her clasped hands overhead and reached skyward to stretch out her shoulders, inadvertently offering Henry a tantalizing view of the curve of her breast. But before he could wonder who she was, his attention was drawn to two riders emerging from the woods across the river and racing toward the old stone bridge. The flag of silvery blond hair streaming behind the female rider identified her as his daughter, Emily, who urged her dappled gray Arabian into a hair-raising full gallop, intent on winning the race. Impatient to see her, Henry pulled up the reins, set his team in motion, and promptly forgot all about the intriguing woman on the hill.

EMILY BEAT HER COUSIN BERTIE to the bridge and slowed her mare to a canter to cross it, having spotted her father driving down the hill. Coming to a halt, she kicked her boot free of the stirrup and slid down the side of her horse with practiced ease. She patted the mare on her rump to let her know she was free to munch on the tender spring grass, then pulled herself up to sit on the bridge's stone wall, letting her booted feet swing from under her slightly too short riding habit.

As Henry approached, he couldn't help but notice that not only had Emily outgrown the length of her frock but the material stretched tightly over her chest. With growing unease, he realized his lovely Emily—his treasured baby daughter—had grown breasts. No wonder the well-meaning matrons in Henry's life had deemed it necessary to impress upon Eliza the urgency of considering Emily's coming out.

Oblivious to his musings and her growing feminine allure, Emily sat there with the air of one who had patience with the male of the species, but only to a point.

Bertie reined in his big bay gelding just as Henry pulled up to the side of the bridge. But Emily's attention was still on Bertie, obviously keen to see his reaction to her win. At seventeen, Bertie was tall and lanky, and promised to fill out into a fine male specimen before too long. Right now he brushed his overlong dark-blond hair from his eyes and looked at Emily with a mixture of admiration and annoyance. "By Zeus, Em, how do you get her to go like that? She's barely bigger than a pony."

Emily's blue eyes sparkled, her silver-blond hair still wild and her face flushed from the exercise. "Maybe she just loves me and knows how much I love winning. Don't you, Adonis?"

Adonis lifted her head at the mention of her name and softly blew in Emily's direction.

Bertie, meanwhile, frowned and shook his head. "That name is just wrong. You should rename her, or stick to calling her Addy."

The horse moved to her mistress's side and nuzzled her neck in silent support while Emily glowered up at Bertie. "Adonis is her given name. It's not my fault that stupid Greek deity turned out to be male. I just liked the name and what's done is done."

Familiar with the ceaseless bickering between his daughter and her favorite cousin, Henry shook his head, tossed the reins to Roberts, and jumped down from the curricle. Taking her cue from her father, Emily hopped off the wall and stepped into his waiting arms. "Hello,

Papa. Do you want me to ride with you back to Avon?"

Henry hugged her close and grinned at her cheek. She may have grown up, but she was still the same incorrigible, gregarious, horse-mad tomboy she had always been. "Hello, Poppet! Yes, I would very much like your company, and yes, you can take the reins. Has Uncle Arthur been giving you lessons?"

Emily wrinkled her nose and rolled her eyes. Secretly the irreverent gesture delighted Henry, especially because it infuriated Hortense, his cousin's humorless, unbending wife.

"Hardly ever! Aunt Hortense doesn't approve of women driving, especially not teams. We have to sneak around so she doesn't find out—and you know how much Uncle Arthur hates sneaking around."

"That's not fair, Em. I've been teaching you at least twice a week. And I've incurred more than one lecture from Mama for it too." Bertie's righteous indignation fairly made him tremble, while Emily's eyes danced with amusement.

Listening to them, Henry wished Bertie would stand up to her. It was really too bad the boy let Emily run roughshod over him and that they both acted in all ways like siblings. They may have made a match of it, had their childhood love turned into romance over time. Obviously that was a vain hope now, a fact certain to please the duchess. Henry would just have to look for a suitably chaste and well-connected wife, reform his debauched ways, and launch Emily into society when the time came so she could find a husband she could love as well as respect.

Henry extended his hand to Bertie, who had not bothered to dismount. "Good afternoon, Bertie. My grays and I surely appreciate your efforts to teach Emily, even if she herself remains ungrateful.

When are you going up to Oxford?"

The young man beamed down at Henry and shook his hand enthusiastically. "September, Uncle Henry. Reverend Spittle thinks my Latin still needs work, but since I don't have the brains for law or medicine, and no inclination to join the church, I really don't think it signifies."

Henry nodded his understanding. There was another reason Emily would have been a good match for the boy: he loved the land, and the only way to get his hands on an estate was to marry an heiress. "Are you still planning on studying land management and taking over from Watson when he retires?"

Bertie huffed. "If he ever retires, you mean. But, yes, that's my plan until I can buy my own land."

Henry smiled at his favorite nephew. Perhaps he would do something for the boy if he proved himself. "Good for you. Stick to your guns and don't let your mother push you into the church if you don't feel a calling. There are more than enough mediocre churchmen out there already."

Grinning from ear to ear, Bertie announced, "That's what the good reverend said. He even went as far as to tell Mama so."

Both Henry and Emily gasped in mock shock.

"He did not!"

"Does the man have a death wish?"

Bertie chuckled. "I thought it was rather brave of him. Mama almost had an apoplexy though, and if Father had not agreed with him, Mama may have pushed to have poor Spittle excommunicated."

That statement sent Emily into a fit of giggles before she noted with a superior eye roll, "They only excommunicate people from the

Catholic Church, you dolt."

And off they went into their next enthusiastic round of bickering.

ON THE OTHER SIDE OF the stone bridge, a little ways down-river, stood an aging barn. Within its wide open doors stood two men, leaning on a broom and pitchfork respectively. They had been in the middle of a lazy afternoon chat when Henry met up with his daughter by the bridge, and now the two men watched the little group with interest.

The younger of the two men nodded his chin toward Emily. "That'un Sir Henry's?"

The older man slowly moved his head up and down in the affirmative while his eyes traveled up and down Emily's young, nubile body appreciatively. "Yep, that's her, Bob. Growing up fast, ain't she?"

The younger man grinned, revealing a large gap where his two front teeth had been knocked out in a pub brawl. "Sure is, Jerry. Just look at the jugs on 'er. Last time I saw 'er she was still flat as can be."

Jerry watched Sir Henry's daughter and the duke's youngest son argue good-naturedly. "Looks like young Lord Bertram noticed too."

Bob laughed. "Course 'e did. The rest of 'er ain't 'alf bad either."

Jerry rubbed his chin thoughtfully. "It's that blond hair I wouldn't mind spreadin' over me pillow."

Bob nudged his elbow into his friend and employer's side. "I wouldn't let the missus 'ear you talk like that if I was you."

They both laughed, and Bob took another calculating look at Sir Henry's daughter. Miss Emily growing up was news, and he knew Baron Ostley would pay good money to hear it. The only problem was getting back to Oxfordshire to deliver it.

Loading his pitchfork with hay, Bob headed back into the barn. "So how long's planting gonna take? I can't leave me auntie alone for too long. She's getting on, you know."

Jerry took up his broom and headed for the tack room. It was always the same with Bob; as soon as he got here, he started worrying about his aunt back in Oxfordshire. But he was a good worker, even if he was a bit odd. "I can spare you for a week at Easter, how's that?"

MEANWHILE, HENRY HELD THE GRAYS' heads until Emily securely held the reins, then climbed up beside her, while Henry's groom and Bertie rode off across the fields.

Blessed silence descended as Emily concentrated on controlling Henry's spirited team. But then, into that silence, Emily asked the one question sure to disturb Henry's peace. "Where is Eliza, Papa? I thought she was to come with you this time."

Closing his eyes for a moment, he decided to tell his daughter the truth. "Poppet, Eliza and I parted ways."

Emily was clearly shocked. "What do you mean, you parted ways?"

"I mean we agreed to not see each other for six months as I look for a wife. It wouldn't be fair to her, or me, or my future wife, for me to be with Eliza whilst I look over the debutantes."

Her response was almost desperate. "No, no, no! Papa, you love Eliza, and she loves you. You can't just cast her aside. This is all because of Grossmama's harebrained notion that you have to bring me out with a wife by your side so society will accept me, isn't it? Please, Papa, you don't have to marry some silly wigeon just because I'm illegitimate! Aunt Hortense can bring me out."

The horses started to react to Emily's agitation, so Henry steadied her hands and gave them a little squeeze for reassurance. "Sweetheart, she has four daughters of her own to bring out, and you know what she's like."

Emily wouldn't concede the point. "Then Grossmama and Aunt Greyson will do it."

Henry shook his head. "They will help, but they also think I need to reform my ways, and the easiest way to do that, in the eyes of society, is to marry a proper lady. They have decided it's time, and Eliza agrees with them. You see, she knows me well enough to know I would never forgive myself if I didn't do all within my power to ensure you can choose freely whom you want to marry."

He wrapped his arm around his now crying daughter. "Sweetheart, Eliza will always be our friend, and she will never want for anything. I promise you that."

Emily hiccuped, and Henry felt like crying right along with her. "Can I still see her?"

"Of course, darling. In fact, she is helping Allen right now and will still be working with Aunt Greyson, so you will see her every time you come to town."

Nodding slowly, Emily returned her attention to the horses and the road ahead. When she spoke next, it was with a calm and maturity that showed no trace of the bickering adolescent from just a few minutes ago. "I hate that you have to miss her because of me. Eliza made you happy, and I like seeing you happy."

Henry sighed and stretched out as far as it was possible in the sporty vehicle. "I do miss her, and she did make me happy. But you see, sweetheart, she taught me that I can love more than one person over the span of my life. So it is possible I shall love again, and so will she."

Emily didn't really understand what Henry was trying to say, having no experience with romantic love herself. But she knew he had loved her mother and still loved Eliza, and from what he said, it followed he could love someone else if he met the right person. She hoped with all her heart the salons of London this season would yield a lady her father could love. Emily felt comforted by the possibility and swore a silent oath never to be the one to stand in the way of her Papa's happiness ever again.

CHAPTER TWO

HENRY SPENT THE NEXT FEW WEEKS LETTING his relatives ease his loneliness. His cousin's large family was lively and entertaining, Emily enchanting if prickly, and his grandmother loving and supportive.

The Duke and Duchess of Avon planned to introduce their second daughter into society during the coming season, and Grossmama promised to come to town with them, so at least Henry wouldn't be alone in his search for a suitable wife.

By the time he said goodbye to his cousins and Emily in mid-March to begin the spring round to his estates, he felt more able to enter this new stage of his life, possibly even felt a small amount of excitement at the prospect of meeting a new woman.

Henry's first stop was the modest estate near Reading he had inherited from his mother. Oakdale was the smallest of Henry's holdings, but the fields were well irrigated and extremely fertile, and it was close enough to London for goods to be brought to market there.

Henry left the lovely Palladian manor behind a couple of weeks later. As he traveled through Reading, he saw a watercolor in the window of a small gallery. It looked like it had been painted from the very spot where he had observed the alluring painter on the hill above Upavon. Stopping on an impulse, and finding the painting to be of excellent quality, he bought it. The landscape was signed with the initials

IJC, giving no indication as to the painter's gender and fueling Henry's fancy of purchasing the very painting he had seen the lady paint.

But duty called, and a fancy was after all just a fancy, so Henry got on his way to Sussex to oversee the lambing. From there he went to Norfolk, where planting was underway, and then headed to his ancestral lands in Lincolnshire.

BY THE TIME HE GOT back to London in late April, spring was in full bloom and the season had already begun. The moment Henry entered the library in his house on Cavendish Square, it became abundantly clear his grandmother and Lady Greyson had sent word to the season's hostesses that he was in the market for a bride. His desk was literally overflowing with invitations to all kinds of events, from balls to musicals to Venetian breakfasts.

It took Henry an entire day to sort through and answer his mail. He was aided in this by a letter from his godmother, Lady Greyson, who had taken it upon herself to make a list of all the families attending the season with unmarried daughters. She included information as to each lady's age, how many seasons she'd had, her musical talents, and her other interests. Lady Greyson also furnished a brief description, in those cases where she had met the woman. But for the most part, the ladies were in truth girls under the age of eighteen, and Henry was tempted to exclude them on their youth alone.

There were only nine candidates over twenty whom Lady Greyson had not dismissed for one reason or another, and a handful of virtuous widows under the age of thirty. Since the widows were unlikely to host events, Henry would rely on Grossmama and his godmother to introduce him. But he matched the names of the nine older misses to his invitations and accepted all those from their families. Then he sorted through the rest and accepted all the invitations to balls, as he liked dancing. He also committed himself to a few musicals. Those gave the young ladies a chance to showcase their accomplishments, and he did wish for a wife with a purpose of her own. Not to mention he himself was fond of playing the pianoforte.

Henry's first engagement was a ball that very night. Having no desire to face the lion's den all by himself, he sent a message asking Lady Greyson whether she had need of an escort for the evening. Then he ordered a bath and went about the lengthy process of preening himself to the level of polish expected of a man in search of a noble-born wife.

Two hours later, Henry emerged from his rooms clad in an exquisitely cut dark blue velvet tailcoat with wide lapels and double rows of silver buttons. His silk waistcoat was the same shade of blue, but shot through with silver thread, and his satin breeches were a silvery gray. Light gray silk stockings brought out well-formed calves, and the dark gray dancing shoes sported silver buckles matching the buttons on his coat. A square-cut sapphire winked from the folds of his snowy white neckcloth, mirroring the color of Henry's eyes. He was freshly shaved, his sandy sideburns trimmed short and his nails polished. In short, Henry was the very picture of wealth and elegance.

Lady Greyson's note expressing her unmitigated joy at having Henry as her escort arrived during dinner and stressed he was expected to pick her up at eight. Groaning at the thought of arriving so very early, he called for his carriage without even inspecting dessert, earning himself an eye roll from his man, William, and a disgruntled mutter from his housekeeper, Mrs. Tibbit. Both knew the circumstances of Emily's birth and his need to marry a woman of good standing in society. But they'd become accustomed to the easy camaraderie in Henry's household and missed Eliza, almost as much as Henry himself did. No doubt they were apprehensive. His new wife, once he could bring himself to choose one, would come from a respected family and would naturally expect the servants to behave like servants and keep their opinions to themselves.

Heaving a sigh, Henry concluded he would have to reassure his two most senior staff, both also friends of long standing. "Will, why don't you help Daisie write a letter to Eliza? That way we can all find out how she fares. After all, I'm the only one who isn't allowed to contact her for the time being."

William, broad shouldered and square faced, handed him his hat and gloves, then met his eyes. "We already did that, and she is well enough. Worried about Mr. Strathem and you, but well enough."

Mrs. Tibbit chimed in, "We are mostly worried about you, sir."

Henry smiled, knowing her concern was genuine, but also conscious of what the "mostly" signified. "It'll be all right, Tibby! I promise not to marry a harpy."

His housekeeper, round and maternal, looked like she wanted to swat him, but returned his smile in the end. She and William nodded their understanding before Henry walked down the few steps to the sidewalk and stepped up into his carriage.

"LADY GREYSON, HOW WONDERFUL OF you to grace us with your presence." Lady Brockhurst was a comfortably rounded matron in her midforties, decked out in a ruby-red ball gown with matching ostrich feathers in her hair. Diamonds winked from her bosom and her hair, competing with the twinkle in her eyes. "And you brought Sir

Henry with you. How absolutely marvelous."

Henry bowed over her hand as she turned her attention to him.

"I hear you have finally decided to look for a wife, and since I have two unmarried girls on my hands, I doubly welcome you to our house."

A Miss Brockhurst was in fact on Henry's list of debutantes twenty and older, so he assumed she had a younger sister, but only one of the young women next to his talkative host wore pastel pink. The other young woman appeared rather somber in midnight-blue taffeta that did nothing to enhance her mousy coloring.

Lady Brockhurst was obviously excited to introduce her daughters to Sir Henry, so while her husband shook hands with their guest, she hustled her girls forward. "Since we have a moment, I might as well introduce you to my girls." She indicated the shy, plump girl in pink, who blushed profusely and sank into a deep curtsy. "This is my youngest, Sarah. She's in her second season, so feel free to ask her to waltz."

Henry felt bad for the clearly mortified girl as he bowed over her shaking hand and raised her out of her curtsy. But before he could ask her to dance, Lady Brockhurst continued:

"But if you don't fancy wedding an infant, this is my oldest, Mrs. Wilder. Her husband died a little over a year ago, and she is in need of another."

The young widow glared daggers at her mother and sank into an absentminded curtsy while Henry did his best not to laugh. "I would be most gratified to dance with both of your lovely daughters. Mrs. Wilder, your servant."

Henry bowed over the older daughter's hand but addressed the younger first. "Would you grant me the pleasure of the opening quadrille, Miss Brockhurst?"

The girl smiled a tentative smile and handed him her dance card. After he had put his name in the appropriate spot, he turned to the other. "And may I have the pleasure of your company for the first country dance, Mrs. Wilder?"

The young woman appeared less than pleased to have to dance with Henry, but finally managed a civil enough, "I would be honored," and handed him her card.

Henry filled in his name, stepped back, nodded to all three ladies, and offered his arm to Lady Greyson to help her into the still sparsely populated ballroom below. Once they had navigated the five steps and were out of hearing, Lady Greyson patted his arm and murmured, "Well done, my boy! Dancing the opening quadrille with the host's daughter is polite and firmly puts you on the market as a possible husband. I expect to be inundated with requests for an introduction. Now all you have to do is turn up at Almack's every Wednesday and there'll be no doubt in any of the matrons' minds that you're set on finding a bride."

Henry gave a humorless chuckle as he led her to a sofa along the wall, where they had a clear view of the new arrivals. "I'm just glad I didn't have to sacrifice a waltz to either of the Brockhurst daughters. I take it Mrs. Wilder does not approve of my lifestyle to date. I can only hope she doesn't decide to make it her mission to reform me."

Lady Greyson arranged her voluminous jade-green skirts around herself before she returned her attention to Henry. "Mrs. Wilder doesn't approve of many people, not even her mother, whom I like very much. I think it very unlikely this virtuous widow will set her cap at you, but don't be so quick to dismiss the younger girl. She may not be the prettiest of the bunch, but she has a sweet nature."

They were distracted by a flurry of new arrivals. The Earl and Countess of Hedgely had stopped at the top of the stairs to survey the activities below while their charges, Lady Caroline, a dark-haired, green-eyed beauty in a butter-yellow gown, and Miss Imogen Tubbs, a classic English rose in pure white, chatted to the Brockhurst girls.

Henry nudged his godmother. "I do hope at least one of them is on my list."

Lady Greyson smirked behind her fan as she watched the two beauties float down the stairs. "They both are, my boy. Miss Tubbs was a late debutante due to her mother's death two years ago. She was declared a diamond of the first water last season, but fell in love with a penniless viscount her father objected to. She's reportedly still nursing a broken heart, but her cousin and best friend, Lady Caroline, persuaded her to come back for her second season. Lady Caroline is in her third season and, as you can see, a beauty in her own right. However, she's been very vocal about her wish to wed a rich, as well as titled, gentleman. Since titles have been a little thin on the ground over the last few seasons and rich titles are downright rare, she hasn't yet caught one."

Henry shook his head in resignation and laughed. "How on earth do you expect me to consider anyone for my wife, and Emily's mother, after you just informed me she is as calculating as a Covent Garden strumpet?"

Lady Greyson rapped his knuckles with her fan but laughed right along with him. "Well, Henry, you of all people should know knowledge is power. I'm just helping you make an informed decision."

Henry's laugh held genuine mirth now. He rose and held out his hand to help his companion to her feet. "I do appreciate the information and your concern, Ann. Let's explore the refreshment table before it gets too crowded, and you can introduce me to the English rose so I may waste one of the waltzes on her. I do believe her viscount is one of my neighbors in Lincolnshire, and he has made great strides toward restoring his lands to their former productivity, so perhaps she should hold out for him."

Lady Greyson stood and smiled up at him. "Why, Henry! You've turned into a bona fide romantic! And you're right, Chelmsly is indeed her viscount."

She paused for a moment, then turned them so Henry faced the stairs again. "Coming down the stairs, the lady in blue, that's Lady Jane Castleright."

The receiving line had gotten busier, but Henry had no trouble identifying Lady Jane. The young woman's features were too sharp to be called pretty, and her hair was a rather lackluster dark blond, but her green eyes held intelligence and her figure was pleasing. Henry had never met her, but had heard the name. "Isn't she the one said to be able to cut a man in half with her tongue?"

Lady Greyson chuckled. "Yes, well, she can be rather cutting. But I think it may have more to do with the fact she just can't abide fools rather than that she is mean-spirited. She is very bright, extremely well read, and loves the theatre."

Henry smiled down at his godmother. "That certainly warrants a waltz. If that cutting tongue is used with enough wit, I might enjoy it."

As luck would have it, they were intercepted by Lady Jane's mother on the way back from the refreshment table. Lady Castleright rushed toward Lady Greyson, lavender skirts fluttering behind her, purple turban swaying dangerously, bringing a cloud of floral scent with her.

"Dearest Ann, so wonderful to see you here." She grabbed Lady Greyson's hands and air-kissed her cheeks, then sent a coy smile toward Henry, who surveyed the scene with bemusement. He knew for a fact Lady Castleright did not belong to his godmother's inner circle, so why the display of affection?

"And this must be the charming Sir Henry!" Lady Castleright exclaimed.

With an amused smile and a surreptitious wink at Henry, Lady Greyson gestured toward each in turn. "Lady Castleright, the Countess of Weld. Sir Henry March."

Henry kissed the air just above the countess's hand. "I am delighted to make your acquaintance, Lady Castleright."

"The pleasure is all mine!" The lady preened for a moment at Henry's attention, then pulled her daughter forward. "Allow me to introduce my daughter, Lady Jane."

The young woman, for there was nothing of a girl in her, sank into a polite curtsy and extended her hand. Henry bent over it and allowed his lips to actually connect with her gloved fingertips. "I've been looking forward to meeting you, Lady Jane. Would you honor me with a waltz?"

The quizzical look Lady Jane sent him indicated she was aware of her reputation, but her reply made it clear she didn't intend to curb her tongue. "As long as you can string a sentence together without tripping over your tongue or your feet, I have no objections."

She said it with a completely straight face, handing him her dance card while her mother gasped with mortification, and that was Henry's undoing. He burst into laughter, and Lady Jane's eyes snapped up to his, challenge written clearly in them.

"Well, my lady, that sounds like a challenge to me. Shall we make it the supper waltz so you can flay strips off my back with your tongue whilst I cut your meat for you?" Henry cocked a brow at her and she raised one of her own, but he detected a twinkle in her eyes.

"I do enjoy delivering a good set-down. The question is: are you a worthy opponent?"

Henry wrote his name into the space before supper, his eyes dancing with merriment. "Keep that up, my dear, and I shall have to call you Kate."

That got him a little chuckle and a clipped "Touché!"

ON THE OTHER SIDE OF the ballroom, a young man, dark haired, blue eyed, and average in every way, stepped up next to the Earl of Weld, a corpulent man in his sixties. They both watched Henry being introduced to Lady Jane.

"What possessed the countess to introduce Lady Jane to Sir Henry March?"

The earl sighed heavily. "Lady Jane needs to get married, and Sir Henry is looking." The earl turned to the young man. "What are you doing in a London ballroom, Bradshore?"

The young man drew back his shoulders, looking affronted. "I'm Viscount Ridgeworth now."

Completely oblivious to his companion's delicate feelings on the matter, the earl returned to the observation of his daughter. "Oh, right you are, I heard about the accident. My condolences."

The new viscount lowered his head, trying to tamp down his annoyance. "Thank you."

Henry's laugh carried over to them, prompting a sigh from Lady Jane's put-upon father and a headshake from Viscount Ridgeworth. "Warthon won't like this. He is still planning to avenge Astor."

The Earl of Weld sighed again. "Not to worry, nothing will come of it. And if, by some miracle, Jane doesn't put him off, it will be easier to get to March once they are married, don't you think?"

The newly minted viscount raised a superior eyebrow. "I doubt Warthon will see it that way, but I concede your point."

The Earl of Weld was obviously not very interested in his companion's opinion on the matter and changed the subject. "So do you still hold the living in Hove?"

The young man colored with annoyance. "Indeed not! The title comes with rather extensive lands and responsibilities."

The hapless earl waved his hand in apology. "Oh, right, right. I suppose Warthon is looking for a replacement?"

Remembering the earl had a son in the church and smelling a threat to his position with the powerful Earl of Warthon, the viscount hastened to correct him, but not before a furtive look around to make sure he was not overheard. "I remain ordained and am a full member of the organization now. I will be on hand to officiate at ceremonies."

Weld looked at him quizzically. "I thought you already were a full member since your cousin never joined."

The viscount colored again at the correction. "The title lends more weight." He obviously had more to say on the subject, but managed to control himself and bowed with feigned respect. "I better ask one of the young ladies to dance. I find myself in need of a wife."

The Earl of Weld only grunted and turned his attention back to where Sir Henry was now leading the younger Brockhurst girl out for the opening quadrille. The bugger was putting his best foot forward, and Jane hadn't handed him one of her famous set-downs yet. It was just like her to pick the one man with whom a connection would put a strain on his friendship with old Warthon.

BY THE TIME HENRY ESCORTED his godmother home at one o'clock in the morning, he had danced with seven of the nine candidates on his list of debutantes and four of the possible widows. He had liked three of the debutantes, one of his favorites being Miss Tubbs, in whom he inspired hope that she might achieve her heart's desire after all. He was summarily dismissed by one virtuous widow, and less than half an hour later propositioned by another.

It seemed high society wasted no time embracing Sir Henry March, but only Lady Jane made a lasting impression, with her sharp wit and ability to converse intelligently on many a subject. She did appear a little cold, but Henry thought her attractive enough, and she surely would always be an interesting dinner partner.

CHAPTER THREE

THE SEASON RUSHED BY IN A WHIRLWIND OF AC-
tivity. Henry danced with every wellborn woman of marriageable age
attending the London ballrooms that year. Miss Brockhurst was indeed sweet natured, and the nightly dancing did her figure a world of
good, but she had eyes only for Avon's oldest son, Julian. Miss Tubbs
was lovely in every way, but Henry couldn't bring himself to pursue a
woman who was so thoroughly in love with another.

The voluptuous and widowed Lady Chalmsford seemed a distinct
possibility, until she revealed she loved the freedom of being a widow
and had no intention of ever marrying again. She softened the blow
by taking Henry to her bed for a night and then wished him luck in
his search for a wife.

Convinced he had exhausted all other possibilities, Henry focused
on wooing Lady Jane. He danced two waltzes with her at every ball
and led her in to supper so he could converse with her. Lady Jane was
intelligent, well informed, and opinionated. Some of these opinions
bordered on harsh, but Henry considered that to be a symptom of her
youth rather than a sign of malice. So they danced and conversed and
rode in the park, and before long everybody in society, including Lady
Jane and Henry himself, assumed he would offer for her before the
end of the season.

On a balmy Wednesday in early June, Henry's grandmother summoned him to inform him of a measles outbreak at the ducal estate. The duchess was already on her way to see to things at Avon, but Henry decided to rush to Emily's side.

He penned a note to Lady Jane, explaining his absence from the Duke of Wentworth's ball that night, and got on the road. He was halfway to Reading when he was intercepted by a letter from his daughter. Emily confirmed the measles outbreak, but reminded him she'd had the measles already, and therefore there was no need for him to come and join the ranks of the infected. Having no recollection of having had the disease, Henry thought it best to heed Emily's advice and turned his curricle around.

Arriving back in town in time to attend the Wentworth ball, he decided to surprise Lady Jane. Wentworth House on Grosvenor Square was famous for its terrace spanning the length of the building and overlooking the gardens below. There was to be a full moon that night, and Henry planned to ask Lady Jane to be his wife right there, under the stars.

He dressed with extra care in a brand new plum-colored tailcoat and a gray-and-silver striped vest. Brilliant white diamonds winked from his neckcloth and cufflinks, and his mother's heart-shaped diamond ring rested in a little pocket close to his heart. Henry hadn't spoken to Lady Jane's father yet, but perhaps that, too, could be arranged over the course of the evening.

Arriving late, he slipped into the ballroom and located his lady on the other side of the dance floor, sitting on a sofa close to one of the open windows leading out onto the terrace. She was flanked by her mother and her aunt. People were milling in and out of the open

French doors not far away, but her corner was shielded by the palm fronds grouped in the area. The dance floor was crowded with couples swirling and swaying to the rhythm of a waltz, so Henry headed to the library and used the French doors there to get out onto the terrace. A few steps took him to the open window behind his prospective bride. He felt a moderate measure of excitement at the prospect of proposing to Lady Jane, but as he drew nearer, his ears were assaulted by the aunt's shrill voice.

"Well done, Jane! Sir Henry, eh? Who would have thought you would get to marry all that lovely money."

Henry heard Lady Jane laugh and realized he had never heard her laugh before. He had heard her chuckle, titter, and make a rather affected noise he had assumed was her laugh, but never an honest, spontaneous laugh. Unfortunately, Lady Jane's laugh had an unsettling harshness to it.

"Yes, I will be able to travel as I wish, and he is no fool, which has to be considered a bonus."

The aunt gushed, "Has he proposed then?"

"Not yet," Lady Castleright chimed in, "but we are in expectation of his visit any day now."

"Where is the good man today? I haven't seen him all night."

Lady Jane answered dismissively, "Apparently there is a measles outbreak at his cousin's estate where his bastard lives, and he felt the need to rush to her side."

Henry was quite sure the woman who had just spoken so derisively about his daughter was the same lady he had danced and conversed with over the past three months, but he could not recognize her. So he remained just outside the window, watching her, needing to know how she truly felt, especially about Emily.

The aunt leaned in as if to reveal some great secret. "Isn't the girl being educated at Avon with the duke's children? I cannot imagine Hortense Redwick being thrilled about that."

Lady Castleright shook her head in dismay. "I'm certain the duchess is not, but it appears the dowager dotes on the girl."

Lady Jane's aunt gasped in shock at the very idea and shuddered with the thrill of the delicious wickedness of it all. "I heard Sir Henry has decided to marry so his wife can bring out his daughter when she is old enough." She was breathless with excitement. "What on earth will you do when he demands you parade his bastard around society?"

Lady Castleright patted her daughter's hand reassuringly. "We will cross that bridge when we come to it, won't we, dear?"

Lady Jane laughed again, and to Henry's ears it was downright ugly. "Oh, fiddlesticks, Mother. I'll just make sure I fill his nursery in the next few years so he is too busy to worry about the girl, and when the time comes we will quietly find somebody who needs her dowry. He has more than enough money to bury that little problem."

The ice in Henry's veins quickly turned into hot, pulsing lava, and before he could think better of it he climbed through the window and rounded the palm trees to face the conceited woman he'd been stupid enough to think worthy of becoming his wife.

The moment Henry stepped in front of them, the storm clouds clearly visible on his face, the color drained out of the faces of all three ladies. He ignored the other two and addressed himself to Lady Jane only, barely containing the fury coursing through him. "My daughter's birth may be less than desirable, but she is neither cruel nor calculating, and nothing will ever displace her in my affections. You, however, are a lady in name only."

Staring down the woman he had almost proposed to, Henry ignored the attention their little scene was beginning to draw. Lady Jane, in turn, gaped at him in openmouthed astonishment, perhaps for the first time in her life lost for words.

Before she could find her voice, Henry bowed curtly. "Goodbye!"

As he turned away from her he added a clearly audible "Good riddance!" before he stormed out of the ballroom.

BEHIND A CHARMING DORIC COLUMN, up on the mezzanine, the Baron Ostley stood. The prominent lines on his forehead deepened into a frown as he tried to work out what was going on between Sir Henry and Lady Jane. According to Bob, Sir Henry's bastard daughter had finally matured into a young woman, and anticipating the hour of his revenge, Ostley had come to town to see what his nemesis was up to. The last thing he'd expected to find was the man courting a respectable plain Jane.

Ostley nudged his companion. "What do you make of this fracas, Ridgeworth?"

George Bradshore, Viscount Ridgeworth, former Reverend of Hove, watched Sir Henry cross the ballroom. The man's whole being radiated rage, the storm cloud on his face prompting the crowd to part before him.

"Trouble in paradise," Ridgeworth quipped brightly. "Looks like Lady Jane's cutting tongue finally drove Sir Henry off."

The older man's face twisted into a sneer. "What possessed Weld to let that man anywhere near his daughter?"

Ridgeworth shrugged. "He needs to marry her off, of course, Ostley. Sir Henry is eligible, wealthy, and generally well respected, despite the live-in mistress."

Ostley hissed at his companion, "Not in our circle, he isn't, you numbskull."

The new viscount looked like he might take exception to the name-calling, but then a sly smile crept over his face. After all, the good baron wasn't exactly the brightest light on the chandelier. George never could fathom why his former employer gave Ostley the time of day; he was volatile and rude. "Not to worry. It seems the courtship is at an end."

Ostley's eyes were hard and cold as he watched Sir Henry walk out the front door without acknowledging a single person. A deep satisfaction settled over him to know Sir Henry suffered. Not as much as he had suffered when Sir Henry made off with his pretty young wife, though, and no one would ever know the depth of despair he had felt knowing her belly was full of the cretin's bastard. He grimly promised himself things would soon get much, much worse for Sir Henry. It was time to find out where and when he could get to the girl.

He shook back his hair, which caused a sprinkling of dandruff to settle on his shoulders, and announced, "I will return home on the morrow. Give Warthon my regards."

Viscount Ridgeworth declined his head in farewell, but didn't offer his hand. "We shall expect you for the meeting in July."

Heading for the exit, Ostley only grunted.

No one, not even Henry's grandmother, would have blamed him if, after the debacle with Lady Jane, he had turned his back on society once more. Henry did, after imbibing copious amounts of brandy, contemplate going up to Oxfordshire to retrieve Eliza and leaving it up to the dowager duchess to lend his illegitimate daughter respectability. But those plans didn't survive sobriety and the clear light of day.

The attitudes he'd encountered in Lady Jane and her relatives proved beyond a shadow of a doubt he had to do everything in his power to ensure Emily had choices beyond the unfortunate circumstances of her birth. His daughter had beauty and wealth, and Henry would be damned if he stood by while society dismissed her, sight unseen, as nothing more than a bastard.

Of course the scene in the Duke of Wentworth's ballroom became the scandal of the season. Enough people had overheard parts of the exchange to piece together a version that came fairly close to the truth, and the story spread around London's salons like a wildfire. To Henry's surprise, the court of public opinion came down firmly on his side. He was lauded as a devoted father who had sacrificed his happiness for that of his daughter. Henry could only shake his head in bemusement, but his grandmother and Lady Greyson milked the wave of sympathy for all it was worth, saying it would do wonders for Emily's chances once she joined society.

INTO THE MIDST OF ALL this clamoring, Charlotte Eliza Pemberton was born. Her father, Robert Pemberton, Viscount Fairly, was Henry's oldest friend and former colleague. Since both Henry and Eliza had agreed previously to serve as godparents, they decided enough time apart had passed, and both traveled to Hampstead to attend the christening.

Lady Greyson and Grossmama had done their fair share of hand-wringing over the meeting of the ex-lovers, but Henry couldn't bring himself to feel anything but pure joy at the prospect of seeing his friends.

Henry made the hour-long trip with his cousin Arthur, Duke of Avon, and walked into Robert's sunny morning salon in the ducal wake. To his relief, as well as disappointment, there was no pang of awareness, no fireworks of attraction when he spied Eliza across the room holding her new goddaughter, just the warm sense of familiar-ity and gladness at seeing her looking so well. Allen stood beside her, his hand resting on her shoulder. Both cooed at the baby, and when Eliza looked up at Allen, there was no question they had feelings for each other. And for the first time since he had left Eliza, Henry knew he had done the right thing, not only for Emily, but also for himself and Eliza.

On the chair opposite the one Eliza occupied with the baby, the proud but exhausted mother sat leaning into Robert's side. The vis-count perched on the armrest, his arm wrapped around his wife and his other hand caressing her hand, which rested on his thigh. The hap-piness radiating from them stopped Henry in his tracks, and another thing became abundantly clear: He couldn't just marry some woman because she came from the right family. When he married he wanted it to lead to something approximating the blissful contentment he saw before him. He wanted it for himself, but also for his future wife and for Emily; and for that to happen, his heart would have to be involved.

Glad to have some clarity at last, Henry abandoned his observa-tion post. The first to spot him was Robert, whose hand Henry shook vigorously before he drew him into a half embrace. "Congratulations, my friend! A healthy baby girl, you're a lucky man. How is Stephanie?"

Robert beamed. "Thank you. Stephanie is tired, but well. She feeds the babe herself, so sleep is a rare commodity at present."

Robert led Henry to the group around the baby, where Henry greeted Eliza with a smile. "Hello, my dear! How are you?"

As she returned his smile, he could tell from her eyes that she felt as pain-free as he did.

"I'm well. Enjoying the country air and Allen's company. How are you?"

Henry held her hand between both of his. "Good. I still haven't found a bride, but I'm hopeful."

Allen clapped Henry's shoulder in greeting. "We heard about the debacle with Lady Jane Castleright. I'm sorry, old man."

A sigh escaped Henry as he let go of Eliza's hand. It was comforting to discuss these events with his friends. "I'm glad I discovered her true nature before it was too late. I'm disappointed because I liked her, but at the same time I'm immensely relieved I don't have to settle for a woman I don't love."

Eliza smiled her approval. "You deserve love, Henry. You should hold out for it. There's time; you will find the right woman. I'm sure of it."

At that instant, some of Robert's political associates were announced, putting a period to the intimacy of the moment. Robert moved forward to greet his guests, and Eliza returned her attention to the newborn. But Henry took the opportunity to take Allen's elbow and steer him toward the window seat at the other side of the room.

He had worried about Allen a great deal in the past few months. When he had taken him off the ship in Dover, Allen had been a mere shadow of his former self. Then Henry had handed over the watch over Allen, and the investigation into the Russian menace, so he could honor his separation from Eliza, who had been assigned to help Allen recuperate. Not watching over his friend himself had been hard, but it seemed all had worked out well. Allen walked steadily, his dark hair and his skin looked healthy again, and even his green eyes had regained some of their old sparkle.

"You look much restored, Allen! And you walk rather well too."

Grinning his boyish grin, Allen nodded to where Eliza conversed with Stephanie. "Eliza deserves most of the credit for that. She even worked with the cobbler in the village to make a boot to help me balance. She nursed me when I needed nursing, kept the darkness at bay when I was ready to drown in it, and pushed me when I needed pushing. And now she is teaching me to love life again. She is truly remarkable."

It wasn't so much what Allen said, but the tone of his voice and the warm light in his eyes as he looked at Eliza.

"I do believe you are falling in love, my friend."

Allen smiled ruefully. "Henry, I fell in love with Eliza the first time I met her in your breakfast room, more than three years ago. But back then you needed her, and I was not done chasing adventures, so I left as soon as I knew both of you were safe and you no longer had need of me."

Henry was a little taken aback by his friend's confession, but before he could say anything, Allen stopped him with a shake of his head and continued. "As I said, you needed her back then. And when I most needed her, you sent her to me. I will be forever grateful for that, but I am no longer content with a nursemaid, so I am giving you fair warning: I will do everything in my power to make Eliza love me back, and when she does, she will be mine forever."

Henry really looked at Allen then, noting how much he had grown up in the last few years. "I think you are well on your way to achieving your goal. I saw how she looked at you earlier. I wish you every happiness; you both deserve it."

Their tête-à-tête was interrupted by Robert announcing it was time to make their way to the chapel. The two friends walked out side by side and caught up with Eliza carrying the babe. They flanked her, steadying her from both sides as she walked down the front steps of the mansion. She smiled at them both, but asked Henry, "What will you do about your search for a bride?"

Taking his first good look at his new goddaughter just as she opened her eyes and blinked into the bright summer's day, Henry stroked a gentle finger down her rosy cheek and smiled. "The Old Man had a report from Brighton warranting further investigation, so I might as well see what the local hostesses have to offer."

Allen looked eager at the idea of a mission. "Well, let us know if you need any assistance. I'm recovered and quite frankly could stand a little excitement."

Nodding, Henry smiled at Allen's use of "us." He took the babe out of Eliza's arms and settled her on his shoulder. "You are quite perfect indeed, Miss Charlotte! You are number thirteen, you know. And that's a lucky number, in Italy at least."

Allen chuckled. "Seriously, Henry? You let twelve of your men talk you into godfathering their children? I suppose you're sending them all to school."

Allen spoke in jest, but that was exactly what Henry did for his godchildren.

Henry chuckled as they made their way to the chapel. "Yes, and if they show any aptitude, I even send them to university!"

CHAPTER FOUR

THE OLD MAN'S REPORT CONCERNED ANOTHER possible hellfire club. This one was said to be based on or around the Earl of Warthon's estates near Brighton. Henry had investigated a number of these organizations after Lord Astor's death in his Hampstead dungeon three years ago. He had taken a ring depicting two snakes hissing at each other off the dead man's hand. Later, Emily's mother, Cecilia Ostley, had reported more men had watched the horrific spectacle from a secret room, leading him to believe they were involved in some kind of secret society. He had first concentrated on the underground clubs and societies in London and Oxford, but had found nothing worse than scathing political satire and a few bacchanalian orgies.

Henry then scoured the best libraries in the country and found the image of the two hissing snakes on a number of ancient heraldic designs, including his own family's first English crest. But it wasn't until he spent some time in the library on his own ancestral estate in Lincolnshire that he found any mention of the snakes and what they might stand for.

Apparently, the snakes represented a group of twelve untitled, landless knights who had been fiercely loyal to William the Conqueror. Once crowned king, William had rewarded them for their services on and off the battlefield with large estates formerly owned by vanquished Saxon lords. Even after the land had been conquered and they had settled upon it, they had organized yearly meetings, which they later encouraged their sons to attend.

All this Henry learned from documents pertaining to his family history, but it was sheer luck and a gust of wind that brought him the one clue connecting the ancient knights to Astor and his dungeon.

In a strongbox, inside a long-forgotten alcove behind a threadbare wall hanging, Henry found a handwritten account of a meeting of a group calling themselves the Knights of the Snake Pit. The document wasn't dated, but had once been held together by a seal showing the two hissing snakes. It stated the brethren had been called together to protect their interests in the kingdom and to discuss undermining any monarch on the English throne who didn't favor them and their goals. They proposed to attract new members by offering unique sexual displays. Those same displays would also serve to ensure the members' silence and loyalty, since their involvement would spell social ruin if it were known.

Henry couldn't find a list of the names of the twelve knights, but he made note of the families whose coat of arms had once included the hissing snakes. Out of the seven crests he found, only his family and that of the Duke of Elridge survived, which left five more families, as well as the ones recruited later. Henry had no doubt the Snake Pit related back to the Norman knights. Furthermore, there was little doubt that the traitor Lord Astor, the Duke of Elridge's third son, had also been a member, and that the dungeon he had died in was used for unique sexual displays. But Henry couldn't prove the connection, so he kept looking and waiting.

The old Earl of Warthon was rather reclusive by all accounts. Henry remembered his grandmother describing him once as a "cantankerous old goat" who sported two left feet on the dance floor. However, he was one of Elridge's political allies in the House of Lords, had blasted Mad King George repeatedly for losing the American colonies, and had been rather vocal about his disdain for the new king during his Regency. But what was most interesting about this was the sexual angle of the report. Could Warthon be hiding a secret as dark as Astor's?

ALL THIS PLAYED THROUGH HENRY'S mind as he descended the South Downs, entering the city of Brighton just in time to watch a pale orange sun set into the silvery sea while the lavender sky turned indigo behind him. He owned an estate not seven miles to the east, but had opted to take rooms in town so he could attend the evening's entertainments and investigate the Earl of Warthon's estate.

Pulling up to the Waterfront Hotel in his curricle, Henry handed the reins to Roberts, and his overnight bag to one of the pages who'd come bounding down the front steps. At the hotel desk he found a distinguished-looking clerk presiding over the book. Henry always wondered where hotels, the world over, found staff who put their most regal guests' manners, bearing, and looks to shame.

Eyebrows rose in haughty inquiry. "May I help you, sir?" The man had the politely phrased insult down to a fine art.

Fighting the need to applaud, Henry granted the supercilious clerk his warmest smile and slipped a crisp ten-pound note from his billfold into the guest book. The clerk retrieved it without a blink.

"I am Sir Henry March. I anticipate being here for several weeks and would appreciate it if any mail arriving for me would be brought to my rooms directly."

The man's whole demeanor warmed miraculously. It was not an unreasonable request and he was being paid extra for it. "Of course, Sir Henry, I shall assign one of the boys to the task. You are in the Royal Suite on the third floor. Your man arrived yesterday and assured us you would appreciate the ocean views and not mind the stairs."

Henry smiled his thanks. "He is quite right, of course. I presume he is awaiting me there." He raised an expectant brow.

"Indeed, sir. You take the stairs to the third floor and turn left. The Royal Suite is to your left, right at the end."

That was precisely the reason William had chosen it. All the windows would face out to the water, and no one standing on the esplanade or the beach would be able to see into a third-story window. Since the suite was at the end of the corridor, he would have only one neighbor who could possibly overhear anything. Furthermore, Henry felt confident he would find a service staircase at the end of said corridor, leading to a door into the alleyway next to the hotel. Over the years, William had secured him many places to rest his weary head in comfort and safety, always with strategically advantageous entry and exit points.

Henry made his way to his suite and found William had opened the tall windows to let in the cool ocean breeze. In the bedroom, hot water for washing awaited him, and William presented him with a snifter of brandy.

"I didn't know what you wanted to do for dinner, sir. They serve a nice spread downstairs in the dining room, but I can bring you up a tray, if you like."

Waving a dismissive hand, Henry indicated the brandy. "Dinner can wait. Pour yourself one, sit, and tell me what you have found out so far."

William grinned and helped himself, effortlessly switching gears from proper manservant to trusted friend and partner, and returned to his native cockney in the process. "Well, I 'ad the pleasure of makin' the acquaintance of the maid accusin' the old earl over me pint last night. She ain't shy about talkin' about 'er so-called ordeal, but after the second pint she started 'avin' trouble keepin' her facts straight, and the locals just laughed at 'er. Lots of people around 'ere work for the earl and agree he's a surly old bastard, but they say she's makin' it up, at least the stuff about the gatherin's."

Henry swished his brandy in his glass. William hadn't totally dismissed the story, even if the locals had, so he prompted, "What exactly is this maid saying?"

Taking a healthy swig of his brandy, William settled into the depth of the armchair opposite Henry's. "Mary, that's 'er name, says the earl's a horny old goat and 'e likes to watch, especially rough stuff."

Henry raised an eyebrow and sat up a little straighter. "How rough?"

"She was told to pretend she was bein' raped. She also says the earl uses the ruins of the old abbey on the castle grounds and invites some of 'is friends for gatherin's there. She's never been to one, though. She was asked to 'ave at it with one of the footmen in the earl's private sitting room. She did it a few times, but then 'ad a falling-out with the footman, and when she mouthed off about it all, she was dismissed."

Henry drained his glass and relaxed back into his chair. "I'll see whether I can find something in the abandoned abbey, but I'm not sure we'll have anything there. She agreed to the act, so it sounds like sour grapes to me."

William nodded thoughtfully. "That's what I thought. But then I 'eard whispers about the earl's grandson. He's so scary some of the local whores won't go with 'im—likes to tie 'em up and take 'is sweet time apparently. When I asked if he 'urt them, they said no, but I also 'eard he offered two local girls employment up in London, and nobody's 'eard from them since. I'll go out later on and find out who those two are, and then tomorrow I'll see about visitin' their families."

Henry was pleased with William's progress so far. "Sounds like a plan to me. Where do I find Mary, if I decide to ask her some more questions?"

"The Red Lion. She tends bar there and lives in. I 'eard whisper she'll take ya upstairs if she takes a shine to ya."

Henry grinned—apparently William thought a quick romp might do him good after recent events in London. "She is attractive then?"

"I'd say so. She's got blond curly hair and lively green eyes. Nice tits, too. But 'er mouth could well get 'er into trouble."

Henry weighed that for a moment, then nodded. "Duly noted. I won't ask her any pointed questions till we are somewhere private." He rose and deposited his glass on the sideboard. "But first I'll change and go eat my dinner in the dining room. You never know what gossip the local gentry has to impart."

As it turned out, there was no local gentry present in the dining room to impart any gossip, but Henry ran into Lady Kistel, one of his grandmother's old friends. She was just as sprightly, opinionated, and fashionable as Grossmama, but wore her snowy white hair in a style reminiscent of the powdered coiffures of the preceding century. She immediately offered to procure invites to all the local entertainments for Henry, making him suspect she may have had prior notice of his arrival. Not that he minded; he liked the old lady a great deal.

The Red Lion turned out to be a comfortable establishment on Duke Street. Away from the misty waterfront, the night was lovely and clear. It always amazed Henry how intrigue existed in the most innocuous of places. The pub was lit by lanterns hung along the front of the building. Several of the patrons had opted to enjoy their ale in the balmy summer night on the benches there. The sound of laughter and conversation drifted through the open windows, and when Henry stepped inside, it smelled pleasantly of stew, pipe tobacco, and good ale. A large round table in the corner housed a friendly card game, and in another corner a few men had gathered to watch two of their friends square off at darts.

Two barmaids distributed drinks in large earthenware containers around the room, exchanging pleasantries and flirting with the regulars. A rotund matron delivered bowls of stew from the kitchen, and the publican presided over the lengthy bar at the back.

Henry easily identified Mary by the blond curls peeking from beneath her maid's cap, and headed for the left side of the bar where she had stationed herself after delivering drinks. He sat on one of the stools and looked expectantly in her direction.

She noticed immediately and bustled toward him, wiping the counter as she went. "What can I get ya, sir?" The girl's voice was soft with the lilt of the south coast.

Henry gave her his most winning smile. "A pint of bitter, please."

She took in his broad shoulders and the quality of his jacket and leaned closer. "A bit of stew would go well with that; or a nice piece of steak and kidney pie?"

Henry kept smiling. "I just had dinner, but how about you get yourself a drink and keep me company?"

Her grin revealed an even row of little white teeth. She was really quite pretty.

"Don't mind if I do." She picked up two tankards and went to fill them directly from the casket built into the back wall. She swayed her hips as she walked and bent over more than necessary to give Henry a good view of her nicely rounded backside. All the while she kept up the conversation. "What brings a fine gentleman like yourself to our 'umble pub?"

"I arrived this afternoon, and my manservant recommended the Red Lion. He said the barmaids were especially pretty here, and I must say he was right." She smiled brightly and blushed at the compliment, and when she placed his tankard before him, Henry slid a silver crown toward her. "Keep the rest for yourself."

Still smiling, she batted her eyelashes and bobbed a quick curtsy, then, using two fingers to highlight the act, she placed the coin inside her bodice, right between her breasts.

Grinning, Henry allowed his eyes to follow the coin and leaned forward to see more of her breasts, then raised his tankard at the same time she did. The pleasant bitterness of the ale lingered on his tongue, just as her eyes lingered on him. The girl knew how to flirt, and if she was as good between the sheets, this encounter promised to be enjoyable as well as informative.

"What's your name?"

She bit her lip and sent him a smoldering look. "Mary. And what'll I call ya?"

Watching her over the rim of his tankard, he took another sip from his ale. "Henry."

She leaned across the bar and dropped her voice to barely above a whisper so he had to come closer to hear her over the noise in the pub. "Well, 'enry, it's very nice to meet ya, but I've gotta serve that table over there." She indicated the card table where a man was trying to get her attention.

Henry grinned at her antics. "I'll watch you work, then."

She laughed, and as she turned to go see to her other customers, she threw over her shoulder, "I like a man's eyes on me." Then she sashayed across the room with an extra little swing in her hip, just for him.

Henry followed her with his eyes and wondered how long it would take him to get an invitation to her room. He itched to find out more about the Earl of Warthon and his proclivities, but the pub was full of locals, and two strangers asking questions about the earl two nights in a row would get reported back.

Henry made sure to wink at Mary the first time she looked back at him, then he let his eyes wander over the other clientele. There were several who had noticed his flirtation, and while most just seemed to be amused, a dark-haired young man sitting farther along the bar eyed him with some speculation. When Mary returned to the bar to fill her tankards, the dark-haired gent waved her over and said a few hushed words to her. She stiffened and hissed a response. Most of it was too low for Henry to hear, but the last words did carry to him.

" . . . tell 'im I talk to whoever I want." Then she turned to Henry, eyes still flashing with anger, and gifted him with a brilliant smile before she took her tray of tankards to the card table. The young man sighed, drained his ale, and made his way to the door with the air of a man who had done what he could.

The episode could have been about something completely unrelated, but Henry didn't think so. The next time Mary came back to the bar, he inquired, "Was that young man bothering you?"

Mary touched his arm and smiled. "Ain't you a lovely man." Then she took his empty tankard, refilled it, and set it back before him. "He works at Warthon Castle. The horny old goat of an earl up there doesn't like me talkin' about 'im."

This was confirmation. If someone was trying to silence her, then her story was true and there was most likely more to it than she knew. For her benefit, however, he made light of it with a laugh and a dismissive gesture. "Titled horny old goats tend to hate tales about their misdeeds. Trust me, I know, I have a couple in the family."

She laughed with relief and touched his hand again. But the young man's visit had made her nervous; she sent a furtive glance around the room and lowered her voice before she spoke. "We'll be callin' last orders soon. Stay behind and I'll tell you all about the old goat, if you like."

Beckoning her closer, Henry whispered in her ear, "I would love to spend a little time in private with you, whether you tell me about the old goat or not."

The girl blushed very prettily and giggled. "Oh, ain't you forward."

Henry sat at the bar for the next half hour, watching her hand out the last drinks and clear away tankards, while the landlord settled up for the night and then went to extinguish the lanterns outside. The other girl was helping in the kitchen, leaving Henry alone with Mary, so the next time Mary walked past, he grabbed her around the waist and pulled her into his arms. "When will you be done with your cleaning, fair Mary? I'm anxious to continue our conversation."

She felt soft and warm, and smelled gloriously of woman.

Giggling, she let him kiss her before she pulled away. "Not 'ere. My room's up the stairs right in back."

Henry couldn't help his triumphant grin. In this instance, he didn't mind the mixing of business and pleasure one bit. "Hurry! I'll be waiting."

CHAPTER FIVE

THERE WAS ONLY ONE DOOR AT THE TOP OF THE stairs, so Henry entered the modest bedroom and made himself at home. He located a taper and matches on the small table by the window, lit the taper, and finding it rather warm right under the roof, he opened the window and took off his jacket. No light illuminated the backyard from downstairs, and the night lay quiet and still below. Henry guessed they were above the woodshed and was grateful for the privacy this afforded.

He lit a cheroot and looked forward to kissing Mary again.

Before long, she entered with a smile, pulled off her cap, and took the pins out of her hair. Shaking out her golden curls, she sashayed closer to Henry, who watched her with appreciative eyes and patted his knees. When she was right in front of him, Henry put his hands on either side of her waist as she rucked up her skirts and straddled him.

Tapping her lips with her index finger, Mary directed considering eyes to the ceiling, looking like a naughty cherub. "Where were we? Horny old goats, was it?"

Henry laughed out loud. "Am I to be counted among them?"

Her eyes twinkled. "Goodness no! You're a manly man, nothing of the old goat in you . . . yet."

Loving her cheeky antics, Henry pulled her close to kiss her soft, eager lips. He enjoyed the fullness of her breasts against his chest and the heat of her groin over his, but before he could get carried away, he pulled back and chuckled. "All right, tell me about the titled horny old goat."

She threw back her head and laughed, exposing her throat, so Henry had to trail kisses up it and make her purr.

"Mmm, that feels good. The old earl got some strange ideas, all right, and 'is friends are no better."

"Oh, a horny old goat with friends! This gets better and better." Henry kissed the tops of her breasts where they pushed up over her bodice and let his tongue trace the valley between them.

Mary groaned with pleasure and raised herself a little to give him better access. "You've no idea. Five years I worked at the castle, was maybe thirteen when I started as a tweeny."

Her voice was breathy now, but she continued her story in between placing kisses all over his face. "Maybe a year ago I started goin' with a footman at the castle. He's one of the men who carry the earl about in 'is sedan chair when 'e goes out. He told me the earl liked to watch and pays well. My da 'ad just died and I wanted to put a nice marker on 'is grave, so I said yes."

Henry was busy undoing the laces on her bodice, but his attention was firmly on her story. "Do you still have family in the area?"

She sighed and leaned into his embrace. "Only me mum. Anyway, we did it a few times, but the earl likes it rough. He kept asking for things I didn't like, and when 'e started to invite the reverend from Hove to watch with him, it got really strange." She gave a little dramatic shudder, but it didn't stop her from helping Henry to take her dress off and push his waistcoat off his shoulders.

"He wanted to join in, and that's when I said enough's enough."

Henry brushed her hair out of her face as she opened the buttons on his shirt. "The reverend from Hove, you say? That's very strange. I would've expected more decorum from a churchman."

She giggled. "Them are the worst."

He chuckled along with her. "I suppose you're right."

She pulled his shirt out of his waistband and over his head. "Anyway, Edgar enjoyed draggin' me around by the 'air way too much. I like a 'ard fuck every now and then, but every time?"

Henry nodded thoughtfully. "I prefer a nice slow ride that builds in intensity."

"That's the ticket!" She rewarded him with a kiss and rubbed her now-naked breasts against his chest. "The last straw was the preacher sayin' it didn't look like a real rape, and he'd show Edgar 'ow it's done."

Henry halted kissing her neck and looked into her eyes, worried she had suffered through an actual rape. "Jesus, that's taking the role-playing much too far."

She shrugged. "That's what I thought. I ran out of the room and didn't stop till I was in the housekeeper's room and askin' for me last week's wages. She got all huffy 'cause there were guests coming the next day. Me leaving was gonna leave 'er shorthanded. Then the earl sent word through Edgar I wouldn't get a dime out of 'im either, so I left and started tellin' tales."

She looked up from playing with Henry's nipples, the light of determination shining clearly in her eyes. She'd been treated badly and she would make them pay. "The earl's grandson knows 'im well enough to know I'm not makin' it up, and 'e won't want me to keep tellin' them tales 'cause 'e's got them meetin's out at the abbey. He'll pay me soon enough." She nodded for emphasis and returned to laving his nipples with her tongue.

Henry wanted to know more about the meetings. "Naughty clergy and clandestine gatherings in an abbey! Sounds like a gothic novel."

Mary grinned conspiratorially. "It's all 'ush 'ush and the abbey's been abandoned for ages." She didn't elaborate any further, which made Henry think she didn't actually know much about the meetings, so he dropped the subject and busied himself with taking her petticoats off. She was prettily made and responsive to his touch. He wasn't going to let an opportunity like that go to waste, so he divested her of all her clothing and stood with her in his arms.

She let out a little shriek when he first stood, but then laughed and wrapped her legs around his waist. "Getting impatient, are you?"

Henry carried her to the bed, chuckling. "Time to get more comfortable, love. These pantaloons of mine are far too tight now."

She sing-songed, "I bet I know why."

Henry dropped her on the bed and retrieved the silk pouch with his French letter from his pocket while Mary busied herself with his placket. He sighed with relief when she pushed his pants off his hips and his erection sprung free.

Taking hold of Henry's member, she studied it before rubbing it up and down and smiling up at him. "That's quite the cock you 'ave."

Gathering her hair at the back of her head, he grinned down at her. She took the hint and bent to suck the head of his cock into her mouth, making Henry hiss with pleasure. He gently pumped himself a little further down her throat. "That feels so good."

She took a little more of him and hummed around his cock, until he had to stop her so he wouldn't come in her mouth. He took out the French letter, pulled it on and fastened the string around the base of his penis. The restriction the string created was the one thing he liked about wearing the damnable things, but worrying about the pox wasn't Henry's idea of a good time.

Mary lay back with a smile. "A French letter! You really are a gentleman."

Henry knelt between her legs, braced himself with one hand beside her right shoulder, and stroked her sex with the other. Finding her already wet, he positioned himself at her entrance and rubbed his nose along hers until his lips hovered right above her mouth. "Always."

She hummed her agreement and wrapped her legs around his hips to pull him closer. Kissing her, he swallowed the lovely noise she made when he pushed inside her with enough force to make her cry out.

She felt good around him, even through the French letter. Henry lost himself in the sheer sensuality of skin against slick skin, in the smells and sounds of passion. It was good to feel alive in this way again, even with a near stranger. He found his climax, but kept going long enough for Mary to find hers and then collapsed on the bed next to her. Cuddling into him, she closed her eyes with a contented sigh.

Henry let her rest for a minute before he asked the question festering in his mind. "What makes you think there are gatherings at the abbey?"

Mary's tongue was further loosened by sleepiness. "Great big dinner parties with all the guests stayin' the night, and all the guests are men except for the few ladies of the night they bring in from God knows where. No one's supposed to know they're there. I figured it out, though." She stretched with a self-satisfied smile. "It's the young lord bringin' them, I know. Well, at least it is since the really scary one stopped comin' about three years ago."

Henry digested that for a moment. A really scary man who stopped coming three years ago. He wondered if it was coincidence or if Astor had been to the castle. Had he arranged sexual displays for those meetings, and had the earl's grandson taken over after Astor's death? But when he turned to Mary to ask her whether she knew the man's name, she was fast asleep.

Henry knew the girl was playing with fire and wanted to let her know what he suspected she had gotten mixed up in, but William was right, her mouth had already gotten her into trouble and he needed to keep a low profile to investigate further. Besides, the damage was most likely done already, judging by the way she baited the earl and his grandson. One thing was for sure: it was not a good idea for them to be seen together again. William would have to keep an eye on the fair Mary.

Henry left a few coins on Mary's bedside table, enough for the post coach out of trouble should she need to leave town. Then he scanned the dark yard below before he climbed out the window. The stairs would have been more comfortable than the drainpipe, but it was best no one saw him leave Mary's room.

THE NEXT MORNING HENRY WOKE to the smell of coffee wafting in from the sitting room. Having no patience for crumbs in bed, Henry belted his dressing gown and followed his nose to the coffee pot.

Breakfast was set up on a little table by the window overlooking the glistening sea. William greeted cheerfully, "Good mornin', sir! I 'ope you slept well enough with them waves makin' a racket all night long."

Henry good-naturedly slapped his old comrade's shoulder. "Says the man who grew up right in the middle of Spitalfields Market."

William sighed. "I never got used to that racket neither."

"Or the din of battle, for that matter."

William shook his head and pulled out a chair for Henry to sit. "Not 'ealthy for a man to get used to the sound of people dyin'."

"And yet most did." Henry gestured to the other chair and filled a second cup with coffee. "Sit and tell me what you found out on your rounds last night."

William folded his large frame onto the somewhat dainty chair and ladled three heaped spoonfuls of sugar into his cup, but declined the cream.

"Seems both girls are young and pretty, and both were sent to London, where they're supposed to be workin' for a friend of the earl's grandson and heir, Lord Didcomb. Lord Didcomb paid for the girls' stage tickets to London, or so the locals think, 'cause their families are poor and the girls both went on the stage."

Henry catalogued all these facts, but the pertinent piece of information still seemed to be missing.

"How old were the girls when they went? Did they work for the earl? When did they go and what do they look like; any common features?"

William straightened in his chair. "One was sixteen, the other seventeen. Both left two years ago within a month of each other, and they knew each other, but not well. They were both looking for work as domestics, and since the earl is the biggest employer around here, they most likely applied to the castle."

Henry wished he could have asked Mary if she had known either of these girls.

Meanwhile, William carried on his report. "One is blond with green eyes, the other has brown hair and eyes, and according to the men around here, they both have ample charms. Both have family in town, and I met the blond girl's father, who says they haven't seen her in two years, but she sends money home every quarter."

Henry looked out over the waves and sipped his coffee. Puffy white clouds paraded along the horizon. Perhaps he should go for a walk on the Earl of Warthon's estate in search of the abandoned abbey. This being England, the weather was unlikely to hold for very much longer.

"How does she send the money? And what about the other girl?"

"The man said it comes in a note, so I guess she gets a scribe to write the address on it, since neither she nor her father can write or read. He says he still has some of the notes and that I can have them if I want."

Nodding his approval, Henry put salt and pepper on his eggs, and cut himself a wedge of ripe Stilton. "Excellent. See if you can get a similar note from the other family too. I shall make my way up into the South Downs to see if I can find the abbey Mary spoke of."

William inspected his employer with a twinkle in his eyes. "How was Mary?"

Henry grinned from ear to ear. "Most accommodating." There was a brief pause, then Henry sobered and continued, "But she is baiting the earl and his grandson, and I think it best if I'm not seen in her company again. This may be it, William. This may well be the Snake Pit."

William could see the thrill of the hunt in his employer's eyes. "All right then, I'll keep an eye on 'er and we'll see what 'appens." He finished his coffee and pulled a folded paper out of his pocket. "I thought you might want to see the abbey, so I got you this. Told the stiff at the front desk you like to go on rambles and 'ad 'im mark some popular ones on there. Seems the abbey is a favorite destination for the more adventurous since it's said to be haunted."

Henry took the map and contemplated if he could get away with an eye roll at his age. "Good Lord, this gets better by the minute."

Then he did roll his eyes, which made William chuckle, and turned his attention back to his breakfast.

FOLLOWING THE DIRECTIONS UP WEST Street inland to North Street, Henry took the coach road out of town, then turned onto the footpath east across the Hove Parish line, and up into the Downs. Half an hour later, he passed the marker announcing he was now entering the Earl of Warthon's land, but judging by the well-maintained path, the earl had no objection to visitors to the abbey.

Henry walked through shady glades where the ground was covered in bluebells and across sun-drenched meadows filled with poppies and daisies, until he found himself in the ivy-covered Gothic ruins of the abbey. A little oak forest had grown up around the ruins, but curiously the flagstones inside were still visible despite the fact the roof was mostly missing. It was almost as if somebody swept the floors regularly; but then again, it could simply have been the wind constantly being funneled through the nave from the ruined window behind the altar to the missing double doors at the front.

The eerie sound the wind made as it whistled through the aisles also supported the rumor of the supposed haunting of the abbey, but it didn't account for the raised hair at the back of Henry's neck. The walk there had been so pretty and tranquil, it was hard to imagine anything evil could be going on amongst all that pastoral beauty, but it certainly felt like it.

Henry stood in the center of the nave and turned in a slow circle. There was no denying it: this would be the perfect location for a secret organization to have their clandestine meetings. It was remote enough to discourage people venturing there after dark. The ghost stories further deterred people and explained any noise someone traveling in the area might hear. The abbey was also far enough from the earl's residence that he could deny any knowledge of any clandestine activity there, and the fact it was a popular destination for pleasure walkers shielded him further. Come to think of it, this was a far better place for a group intent on mischief than even Astor's dungeon on Hampstead Heath had been.

If this was a meeting place for the Snake Pit, how did members remain undetected by the woman who would be the focus of any sexual display? The woman would most likely be a prostitute or a girl already destined for the trade, and fear and shame would keep her silent. Still, as proven by the secret room they had found after Astor's demise and the guests' reported use of masks, members were careful to shield their identities even from other members.

The vaulted ceiling remained intact over the altar and the two side chapels, keeping it dry enough for the purpose Henry suspected, and the side chapels were connected to the altar portion of the nave by large, low Gothic windows. The three-part windows looked like they had never had any glass in them and afforded a watcher an unobstructed view of the altar. Henry found several curiously rust-free iron rings embedded in the vault over the altar and on the underside of the altar stone. He also found several dark stains on one end of the sandstone altar. They could have been blood, but he found nothing on the flagstones. On reflection, Henry decided it would be much easier to wash blood off granite than off the porous sandstone, so he gave up on finding more on the floor and concentrated on finding out how members would get themselves to and from the abbey without attracting attention.

Checking every flagstone for hidden levers, Henry found two of them loose, but no tunnel beneath. The walls, too, turned up nothing, and the outside of the structure was mostly covered in mature ivy. In Hampstead there had been two secret tunnels leading to the fully equipped sex dungeon hidden away far below the Heath. Here there was no odd furniture, no whips, no canes, no spanking bench or chest of drawers with strange and scary toys, but somehow it felt exactly the same. Henry could not dismiss his hunch even though his search turned up no hint of a tunnel, not even a secret path.

He looked behind every tree and under every bush within a quarter mile of the abbey and still he turned up nothing beyond the stains and the metal rings. The place reeked of power and human suffering, but there was nothing further to be uncovered here without knowing when a meeting was to take place.

Henry wondered how one joined the Snake Pit, if it still existed. He was a direct descendent of one of the original Knights, and his father, as Astor had pointed out, had been a part of the group. Joining them might be the only way to find out what they were up to, but the idea left a sour taste in Henry's mouth.

Eventually, he left the abbey behind and headed toward the ocean.

CHAPTER SIX

AS HENRY WALKED AWAY FROM THE EARL'S LAND, the chilly whispers that had followed him around the abbey soon melted away in the early afternoon sun. The last of his trepidation finally blew away with the ocean breeze when he crested the last hill and reached the bluffs near Hove.

It was beautiful up here. The wildflower meadows gave way to short, intensely green grass sprinkled with tiny daisies. There were no dramatic white chalk cliffs gleaming in the sun here, like there were on the other side of Brighton, but some of the bluffs ended abruptly in sandy cliffs with rocks breaking the waves below. Others turned into sand dunes as they descended to the beach, and the sea's ever-changing waves of turquoise and blue shimmered in the sun. In the distance to the left, the fanciful domes and turrets of the Royal Pavilion rose out of the haze, and the white cliffs were visible beyond, but the hills to the right seemed unencumbered by civilization, so that was where Henry directed his steps.

Over the rise of the next bluff, Henry spotted the crown of a tree and resolved to have his lunch there. As it turned out, the tree was a huge, wind-twisted juniper, granted life by the shelter of the little dip in the cliff top. It was a beautiful tree whose dark foliage contrasted marvelously with the gold of the sandy cliff and the turquoise below. However, the blessed shade under this particular tree was already occupied most charmingly by a lady painter. To Henry's utter astonishment, the woman sitting on a three-legged stool, muttering angrily at her unfinished painting, was none other than the painter he had observed on the hill above Upavon. The very same artist whose painting he assumed he had bought in Reading.

Henry hesitated. The lady was seated about twenty paces away, and the juniper surely was big enough to shelter them both, but Henry was loath to interrupt a private moment between her and her painting. She worked at a furious pace, her movements sharp and filled with barely contained frustration, in complete contrast to the fluid competence she had displayed when Henry had last observed her. The painting was a seascape with a sandy cliff to the right in the foreground, but it was the water that seemed to cause all the trouble.

"Sweet Mother Mary! There are not two alike."

The lady briskly brushed a windswept dark curl out of her face and tucked it unceremoniously behind her ear. Henry stepped closer, and once he had reached the outer edge of the tree's shade, he sat in the grass and fished his apple and cheese out of his pocket. She was younger than he had first assumed, but most decidedly a woman. The wind must have carried the sound of Henry munching his apple away from the charming painter's ears, for she kept working and muttering to herself, completely unaware of his presence and utterly focused on her work.

"Come on . . . if Mr. Turner can do it . . . oh, for heaven's sake . . ."

Once he had consumed his meager lunch, Henry stretched out his legs, leaned back on his elbow, and observed the lady in front of him. She was in some dishabille, having discarded not only her hat and fichu, but also her shoes and stockings. Sturdy walking shoes leaned against each other in the short grass behind her, the light cotton stockings carelessly shoved into them.

Henry couldn't help but let his eyes drop to the hem of her blue dress and was rewarded by the sight of her bare toes wiggling in the short, cool grass, hinting at sensuality.

Her wide-brimmed straw hat lay flat on the ground, weighed down by a canvas bag on one side so the wind would not carry it away. The fichu rested on the painter's knee and was occasionally misused to wipe the sweat from her brow. She wore a light, short-sleeved muslin dress she looked comfortable in. The soft blue color complemented her slightly bronzed skin, while the round-cut neckline showed a pleasing amount of bosom. Henry wondered at her utter disregard for the pale-skinned fashions of the day, but admired her healthy glow.

Dark, slow-curling hair, haphazardly twisted into a knot at the back of her neck, was speared through with a paintbrush to hold it in place. Henry could see only her profile, but there was something stirring about her. Perhaps it was her passion for her art, or her perseverance in the face of a difficult task. There was also something unexpectedly erotic about the lady's naked toes, loosened hair, and barely contained temper, all displayed out here in the elements.

Henry was relatively certain the lady belonged to his class despite her dishabille, her sun-kissed skin, and her lack of a companion. Her state of dress and her skin were easily enough explained by her occupation, and really only noble-born women were encouraged to pursue the arts. Her lack of a companion was explained by her age. Surely she was married and therefore could move abroad more freely.

But Henry was now acutely aware of his own voyeuristic pleasure in watching the painter, and found he wanted to protect her from anyone else who might come along and observe her without her knowledge. It followed that he had to make his presence known, in order to protect her from himself first. So Henry stood and circled to the left a little, so he wouldn't approach her from behind.

At that moment the painter made a big huffing sound, threw her paintbrush and palette to the ground, and stood. "Oh, for all the saints, this is impossible." Then she threw her hands up in exasperation and turned away from her work, only to come face-to-face with Henry. "And what the devil are you looking at?"

She immediately clapped both hands over her mouth and stared at him in chagrined disbelief while a broad grin spread across Henry's face. Seeing his amusement, the lady turned a deep shade of red, but recovered enough to speak. "Oh dear, that was unforgivably rude."

Henry waved her concerns away. "Think nothing of it, madam. I startled you."

She cocked her head to the side and took his measure. "That's true enough. You shouldn't sneak up on a lady."

Now that he could finally see her eyes, Henry was transfixed by her gaze, deeper and more blue-green than the ocean behind her. He took off his hat and sketched her a bow. "I didn't mean to sneak, upon my word! My name is Sir Henry March. May I have the honor of knowing yours?"

She dipped into a little curtsy, a mere acknowledgement, not truly a courtesy. "I'm Isabella Chancellor."

An unwelcome thought furrowed Henry's brow at the mention of the rather familiar name. "Is Frederick Chancellor your husband, by chance?"

The assumed Lady Chancellor looked at Henry, slightly taken aback, then laughed. "Good Lord, no. He's my brother. I'm not married."

Seemingly without giving him another thought, the lady carelessly slung her crumpled fichu around her neck and shoved it into her décolletage, then spared her naked toes a dubious glance and shrugged on a little exhale, as if to resign herself to the fact it was too late to worry about her appearance now.

From the marvelously unaffected gesture, Henry concluded Isabella Chancellor was completely unaware of her charms. Wondering how she had stayed so pure, he found himself grateful, and utterly captivated.

"Well, I confess to being relieved to hear it, Miss Chancellor." Henry then chuckled at the thought of a fiery woman like her being married to a hapless puppy like Frederick Chancellor. Come to think of it, it was hard enough to picture them as siblings. "Upon reflection, he does seem a little young for you, but I do remember the good Frederick getting married not too long ago."

Miss Chancellor drew herself up to her full height, and the light of battle glowed in her eyes. She may have been unconcerned about her looks, but she was not above taking exception to comments about her age. "I'll have you know Freddy is a full year older than me, sir."

Henry, realizing his error, raised his hands in a defensive gesture. "Oh, please don't be offended, I didn't mean to imply you seem older, just more mature."

Itching the side of her slightly too prominent nose with the knuckle of her index finger so she wouldn't spread paint all over her face, Miss Chancellor regarded Henry with unveiled curiosity. Then she dissolved into a delighted peal of laughter. "I am fairly certain in the salons and ballrooms of London, old and mature are considered synonymous."

Henry acknowledged her with a little bow, glad she could laugh at herself.

"But you are right," she went on. "Freddy got married to a charming little ninny who, at eighteen years of age, has already presented him with his heir. I, on the other hand, at four and twenty am firmly on the shelf, even if my mother has taken it into her head to parade me around Brighton for the summer."

She eyed her shoes as if trying to make up her mind about something. "Would you mind turning around please, Sir Henry?" She gestured to the shoes and made a circular motion with her hand.

Feeling positively in charity with the world at the news she was looking for a husband, Henry turned and contemplated the ever-changing sea. But remembering her lack of a chaperone, he asked, "Where is your maid, Miss Chancellor?"

Miss Chancellor, having lost no time returning her feet to a state of respectability, informed him he could turn back around.

Packing up her painting utensils, she dismissed the idea of a maid with a wave of her hand. "My maid informed me two years ago she was happy to accompany me on visits and to the shops, but if I wanted to go traipsing around the countryside I could just as well take a groom. The trouble is, the grooms have even less patience than Sally, and so, for my last birthday, I granted myself the freedom of going out to paint without huffing servants to contend with."

Henry couldn't quite like it, no matter how beyond danger she thought she was. "But surely, Miss Chancellor, you should have a care for your safety as well as your virtue, especially if you are here to find a husband."

Her eyes flashed again, this time with annoyance, but there was also sadness in them. "My mother came here to try to marry me off. I only came because I'd never seen the ocean and wanted to paint it."

Henry admired her fire, but he also saw the sadness and very much wanted to find out where it came from. So, even though he knew this conversation to be unusual at best, and downright improper in the eyes of most, he asked, "Are you saying you don't wish to be married, to have children?"

Isabella was no less aware of the impropriety of the conversation; in fact, she knew well the shrieks of distress her mother would have issued had she been present, but she saw genuine interest in Sir Henry's eyes and liked it, so she tried to explain.

"It's not that I don't like children, sir. I like them very much, but I already have three nieces and a nephew and am content to be an aunt. As for marriage, I have never met a man I wanted to marry, and at my age, I don't expect to." This last was said somewhat carefully, and she peered up at Henry as if she expected him to find fault with her view on things.

Henry was suddenly acutely aware his reaction to the lady's statement mattered greatly to her and wished he knew what her sudden reticence signified. In absence of a crystal ball, Henry opted for honesty. "Finding a spouse does seem to be inordinately difficult. One wants to find, at the very least, someone one can respect. But wouldn't marriage afford you more freedom?"

Miss Chancellor laughed, and this time there was a note of bitterness in it. "If I were lucky enough to find the right man, perhaps. But it no longer matters. I now earn enough with my paintings to support myself, and soon enough I will be five and twenty. My mother will finally give up on my marrying some widower, and my father will release my dowry to me. He has promised to help me procure a cottage so I can dedicate myself to my art."

Henry felt a little disheartened by her attitude toward marriage, but admired that she had purpose and a workable scheme. "You seem to have your life well planned out."

She gave him a brilliant smile. "Oh, I had it all worked out by the end of my season six years ago. I am just biding my time."

Henry wondered what had happened during that season to put her off marriage. Eighteen seemed far too young to resign oneself to a solitary existence. "So you did have a season?"

She shrugged dismissively. "Yes, but it didn't take. The next year it was my younger sister's turn, and the year after that my grandfather died. Then it was time for my sisters Millicent and Delia to come out, and by the time they were married, the babies had started coming. With one thing or another, I have managed to avoid a second season."

She seemed to take some pride in having thwarted her mother's ambitions to marry her off, but Henry found it odd she had been allowed to stay behind in the country while her sisters had their seasons. He had many more questions, but he'd done enough prying for the moment, so he changed the subject. "May I escort you back to town, Miss Chancellor?"

SMILING UP AT HIM, SHE shrugged. Her mother would be furious, of course, but there was no need for the baroness to find out.

"I assure you it is not necessary, but I would be glad of the company."

Isabella was aware the man in front of her was attractive, and his interest in her disheveled self was flattering, but it did not explain her telling him things even her brother didn't know. Good God, Sir Henry had caught her with her feet bare and she'd had to ask him to turn away so she could put her stockings and shoes back on. She would definitely have to remember to keep her boots on from now on. And what if he had been less of a gentleman? It didn't bear thinking about.

She wanted to paint; in fact, she needed to paint; it was her purpose, her profession and her way to be independent. She would not let propriety or an awareness of danger get in her way. After all, the worst danger lay in wait in places and with people considered safe. She knew that better than anyone.

Isabella placed the board with the wet painting against the tree and dismantled her portable easel. Once everything was in her canvas bag, she jammed her wide-brimmed sun hat on her head only to realize she still wore a paintbrush in her hair. Wincing, she glanced over at Sir Henry, who had picked up her bag and watched her with bemusement. There was something utterly irresistible about the humorous warmth in his eyes.

"Goodness gracious, you must think me a hopeless heathen."

Henry only laughed as she secured the hat with the attached scarf. He picked up the board with the painting and gestured for her to precede him back toward Brighton. "After you, Miss Chancellor."

Nodding her thanks, she fell into step beside him. They strode out steadily for a few minutes before Isabella asked, "Tell me, Sir Henry, do you live in the area or are you here for the summer?"

Henry gave her an apologetic half smile. "My grandmother informed me recently it was time for me to clean up my reputation and get married to a respectable woman. So, I'm afraid, I'm here to find a wife."

Another peal of laughter escaped Isabella, her eyes sparkling with amusement. "The reluctant bridegroom and the unwilling bride! It sounds like the beginning of a rather lurid novel, the kind my mother would have hysterics if she found me reading."

Henry grinned from ear to ear, but felt compelled to elaborate. "I might be forgiven my reluctance after the season I just had."

Isabella stopped in her tracks and winced. "Oh my word, are you the same Sir Henry whose almost-fiancée caused a scandal in some duke's ballroom not long ago?"

Henry nodded and waited with some interest for any further reaction from her.

"You have my sympathies, but if you ask me, you are well out of it if it's true this woman would have mistreated your daughter."

He smiled and decided, right there on the cliffs, he would do everything in his power to change Isabella's mind about marriage. "Lady Jane indeed said several things about my daughter I found unforgivable. And you are right, I am well out of it; she really only had love for my money. However, it was still distressing to discover these things about a woman I had liked, whose opinion I had respected."

Isabella knew a thing or two about people one had liked and trusted doing things one had a hard time forgiving, so she felt for him, but didn't quite know what to say. They walked side by side in companionable silence until they reached the top of the last bluff and started to descend to the beach and the edge of town.

Henry offered his arm on the steep decline and asked, "Where have you taken residence for your stay in Brighton?"

Isabella smiled her thanks for the assistance on the path. "My mother and I are staying with one of her old friends, Mrs. Curtis, on

Broad Street. It's on the other side of the Steyne from here, just off the Marine Parade. Where are you located?"

The question was out of her mouth before she could remember young ladies didn't ask gentlemen where they lived. Henry, however, showed no sign he had noticed her impropriety.

"I have taken a suite at the Waterfront Hotel. It has rather splendid ocean views," he offered by way of an explanation.

Isabella sighed with some drama. "You are lucky indeed! All I can claim for a view are the rooftops of Brighton and a couple of the Royal Pavilion's turrets. If I want to see the sea, I have to walk a whole four minutes to the marina."

Henry grinned, rather enjoying her teasing. "Miss Chancellor, was I boasting so badly?"

Her eyes twinkled with amusement. "Rather! My beloved pater only agreed to this sojourn to Brighton because he was spared the expense of a hotel. Apparently they are rather dear during the summer months."

Henry nodded wisely. "Ah yes, I do remember the Baron Chancellor to be a rather cautious man."

Isabella laughed at that. "You must excuse him: he has a large family and a mistress to provide for."

Henry drew back in mock horror. "And how would a gently bred, unmarried young woman know about such things?"

"Just because I'm female and advanced in age doesn't mean I'm hard of hearing. You'd be amazed at what you can find out just sitting quietly reading a book."

Henry did know, all too well, but had no intention of telling his new acquaintance anything about his talent for finding out secrets, so he chuckled and resumed teasing her. They continued their banter until Isabella stopped at the corner of Marine and Broad Street.

"Thank you very much for your escort, Sir Henry. It has been a pleasure making your acquaintance, but I must strive to enter the house without attracting my mother's attention, so I ask you to leave me here."

Henry handed her her bag and bowed over her hand. "The pleasure was all mine." He then made to hand her the board with the now-dry watercolor, but paused to look at it. "You know, it isn't as good as your painting of the Avon River, but I do believe it's better than you give yourself credit for."

Isabella was stunned for a moment. She had indeed painted the Avon River, and the picture had sold, but that Sir Henry should have bought it and recognized her style was rather fantastic. "You bought the watercolor of the Avon?"

"I saw you paint it in February and later found it in a gallery in Reading. You sign your paintings 'IJC,' do you not?"

Since the gallerists preferred to hide her gender, Isabella had never met anyone who had bought one of her paintings through a gallery. "I do indeed and I must thank you. The gallerist decided to take several more of my pieces because that watercolor sold within a week."

Bowing again, Henry handed her the board with the unfinished seascape. "I'm always glad to be of service. It made a most charming gift for my grandmother and now holds pride of place in her private sitting room."

The artist in Isabella was gratified beyond anything, and she beamed with the joy of it. "I'm so glad your grandmother likes it. That day was my first day painting out in the landscape this year and everything just fell into place." She turned the painting toward herself and added quietly, "When it flows like that, it's almost like magic." Isabella studied her work for a moment, then smiled up at Henry. "Perhaps you have the right of it. I'll see whether I can get away tomorrow and try again."

Henry felt inordinately proud he'd had a small part in encouraging her. But he was reluctant to part from her, and tomorrow, all of a sudden, seemed a very long time away. "There is an entertainment tonight at Lady Carmichael's. Might I have the pleasure of seeing you there?"

Isabella rolled her eyes dramatically. "Most likely you will. My mother is not only determined to drag me there, but has threatened to fill my dance card for me."

Henry laughed, relieved he wouldn't have to wait until the next day to see her again. "In that case, will you save me a waltz, please? Preferably the one before supper."

Isabella sent him a crooked smile. "You can have whichever one you want. I'm not exactly anticipating a stampede."

Henry winked. "Oh, you never know! There are a few old rogues in this town still capable of a turn about the dance floor."

That got him another eye roll, then the lady turned her back on him, lifting her hand in a careless goodbye. "I shall see you tonight, Sir Henry."

Henry smiled and watched until she disappeared into the side entrance of one of the town houses a little ways down the street.

CHAPTER SEVEN

A SHADOW OF THAT SMILE STAYED WITH HENRY right into his hotel suite. But there, William presented him with two notes he'd obtained from the fathers of the two girls in service in London.

At first glance there was nothing amiss. The notes were written by the same hand, but the girls knew each other, so they could be employed in the same household and using the same scribe. The only problem was, Henry did not believe the notes had been penned by a scribe. A scribe usually wrote what his customer told him to write, while these notes were formal and polite. They didn't sound like they could have been dictated by illiterate girls from the province. They could have been written by someone in the house, but then they most certainly would have been more personal. Both notes contained a generic greeting to the parents, an assurance the girl was well, and no signature of any kind. They also had no sender address, which indicated the sender did not want to be found. Beyond that, William reported the missives were sent quarterly and contained two pounds each time, a generous wage for a domestic servant. That then begged the question what money, if any, the girls kept for themselves.

"Is there anybody in either family who can read?"

William shook his head. "Makes ya wonder why bother to 'ave someone write a note in the first place if there's no one to read it."

There was nothing in particular wrong with these notes, or the money they contained, but as Henry's and William's eyes met, both men scrunched up their noses as if they could literally smell the proverbial rat.

William pointed to a faint ink stamp on the outside of one of the letters and an identical one on the other. "I know that stamp, sir. The post office at Lincoln's Inn Fields uses that one. Lots of lawyers and barristers around there. Could be them notes were sent by someone's man of business."

Henry nodded thoughtfully and reached for the paper, pen, and inkwell the hotel had left for his convenience. "I'll ask Allen to go to London and investigate further. He's getting restless in Oxfordshire, and you know what scrapes our Allen is liable to get himself into if he gets too bored."

William's eyes twinkled with amusement. "Not to mention Rick getting bored right along with 'im. Do you think Miss Eliza will come down as well?"

Sir Henry dipped his quill and started to write. "I'm counting on it."

William moved to the sideboard and poured his master a drink. "Good, that'll keep Daisie 'appy for a while."

Henry didn't look up when William set a drink by his elbow. "I need my blue evening suit pressed and my dancing shoes polished."

Two hours later, the letter to Allen was posted, and Henry, resplendent in his dark blue silk evening coat, embroidered waistcoat, and white satin breeches, stood under the arch into the dining room and waited to be seated.

Lady Kistel spotted him from her table by the window and waved. "There you are, my boy, and all dressed for the occasion." Then she imperiously commanded the waiter's attention. "A second place setting for the gentleman, if you please!"

Henry reached her side and bowed over her hand. "Thank you, and a very good evening to you, my lady. Did you enjoy your day by the water?"

"Yes I did, and I saw you escorting a young lady down the esplanade. Fast work there, my boy. Who is the girl?"

Henry chuckled and took the seat opposite her. "A Miss Isabella Chancellor, daughter of Baron Chancellor. She will be attending tonight, and I was wondering if you are familiar with the baroness. I would very much like to be formally introduced to Miss Chancellor."

Lady Kistel eyed him through her lorgnette and heaved a sigh. "I hope the daughter doesn't take after the mother. That woman is an icicle. No wonder the baron has kept a mistress these past fifteen years."

Sir Henry coughed into his hand and lowered his voice. "Ah yes, the baron's mistress. I may have introduced him to his current companion."

Lady Kistel looked at him in astonishment, then barked a delighted laugh. "Handed off one of your light-skirts, eh? Don't worry, my boy, the baroness was positively relieved to be done with her duties in the bedroom when the baron took his first mistress. Besides, she takes very little interest in her husband's affairs these days, so it is unlikely she would know about the introduction."

Henry grinned, somewhat relieved to hear Lady Kistel's assessment, and wondered if her parents' indifferent marriage had influenced Miss Isabella's opinion of matrimony. They ate halibut in white sauce and veal fillets for dinner, and an hour later, Henry handed Lady Kistel into his carriage to take them to Lady Carmichael's entertainment.

THEY WERE GREETED BY CANDLELIGHT streaming out of every window and the strains of a string quartet drifting on the salty breeze.

Lady Kistel leaned close to Henry. "Entertainments in Brighton are rather lavish affairs since every hostess sends an invitation to the king in hopes he will attend, which on occasion he does."

Henry winked at the old lady on his arm. "The king is still in London and will remain there for at least another week."

Lady Kistel's eyes widened a fraction, and her aged face folded into a sly grin. "I'm almost afraid to ask how you might know that, but I'm not about to look a gift horse in the mouth."

Henry grinned right back, having no doubt she would use the information to good social advantage.

Walking up the broad shallow steps to the house, they made their bow to their hostess and strolled through a series of salons where guests engaged in polite conversation, some already playing at cards. They greeted friends and acquaintances until Henry spotted Miss Chancellor standing awkwardly in a corner. She was flanked by a hard-looking woman coldly assessing the scene and a middle-aged dumpling of a chatterbox fussing over her.

Isabella's beautiful dark hair had been ruthlessly pulled back and twisted into a tight knot at the top of her head, and her face was framed by the obligatory three tightly sprung corkscrew curls. Henry knew her hairstyle was all that was proper and fashionable, but to his mind it was far too strict to suit the free spirit he knew dwelled within her breast. As if to prove his point, at that very moment a curl sprang free from the severe top knot and resettled itself along Isabella's delicately sculpted nape, causing Henry to breathe a sigh of relief. He nudged his companion and nodded toward Miss Chancellor's group. "Which one is the baroness?"

Lady Kistel looked in the indicated direction and groaned in despair. "The ice queen on the right. Who put the poor child in that hideous gown?"

Taking a second look at the object of his interest, Henry had to admit Isabella's gown was rather arresting in its ugliness. The color was a horrid bright pink that clashed with her complexion and did nothing for her eyes. In fact, it made her look pale and washed out. But as bad as the color was, it was not as bad as the countless ruffles, bows, and flounces completely obscuring what Henry knew to be a splendid figure.

"It certainly wasn't Miss Chancellor herself. She is an artist and I feel confident she'd never pick that color. My guess is the busybody to the left is to blame."

Lady Kistel grunted her agreement. "That makes sense. I never met a woman with less taste than Mrs. Curtis. I swear to God, the woman is color-blind."

That statement was corroborated by the lady's own outfit: a yellow and turquoise gown, a bright orange feather in her hair, and a red shawl.

Henry chuckled. "That might explain the color, but the style is no less disturbing."

Lady Kistel was prevented from sharing more of her opinions.

The Baroness Chancellor had noticed Lady Kistel's approach in the company of an unknown and possibly eligible male, and did her best to rearrange her face into a welcoming smile. Stepping toward the old lady, she offered both hands to support her and guide her toward a nearby sofa, completely oblivious to Lady Kistel's resentment at the assumption she was too frail to stand at a social gathering. Lady Kistel ignored the baroness's helpful hands and greeted the ladies with regal condescension before she directed Lady Chancellor's attention to Henry. "May I make known to you my dear friend, the Duchess of Avon's grandson, Sir Henry March."

Henry bowed over Lady Chancellor's eager hand while Lady Kistel continued, "Henry, my boy, meet the Baroness Chancellor."

The baroness gushed over Henry and lost no time pulling her daughter to her side. "I'm delighted to meet you, Sir Henry! May I introduce my daughter to you? We've taken up residence with my special friend Mrs. Curtis for the summer."

As the mother rambled on about summer entertainments and the advantages of Brighton, Henry kissed Isabella's hand and smiled politely, but his eyes sparkled with amusement. "Miss Chancellor, a pleasure to make your acquaintance. May I hope to lead you out in a waltz later in the evening?"

Isabella looked painfully uncomfortable with the entire situation, but when she looked up and saw the amusement in his eyes, she managed a smile, curtsied, and pulled out her dance card. "How do you do, Sir Henry? I do believe the supper waltz is still free."

Henry was close enough to smell her now, but the heavy floral scent didn't suit her and he wondered whether that, too, had been foisted upon her. He took the card from her gloved hand and led

Isabella a few steps away to a wall sconce, under the pretense of needing more light to fill in his name. "I would love to say you scrub up well, my dear, but I confess to preferring your cliffside dishabille to this dress."

Heaving a defeated sigh, Isabella glanced down at herself. "It's beastly, that's what it is." She tapped her satin slippers against the three-tiered flounces along the hem of her gown, kicking it out a little. Then she glanced back up at Henry with a mischievous light in her eyes. "Would you mind stepping on my hem a few times during our dance so I can rip off some of these flounces without offending Mrs. Curtis?"

Henry saw the impishness in her eyes and thoroughly enjoyed it. He assessed the gown again. "Only if I get to spill something permanently staining on that unbecoming ruffle around your décolletage."

She answered his grin, warming to the idea. "Oh, do try to aim for that horrid bow just below as well. It makes me feel like the fruitcake my great aunt Millicent sends us every Christmas, dressed up with a giant garish bow to make it look more like a present."

He laughed, knowing exactly what she meant. "It will be my distinct pleasure. I shall be as clumsy as I can manage. Shame we can't do much about that color."

Isabella wrinkled her nose in distaste and confided, "Shame indeed! The only place where this particular shade of pink may seem natural is on iced raspberry cakes. But Mrs. Curtis presented the gown to me this afternoon in honor of my second coming out, and I would have offended her had I not worn it tonight. I almost wish she'd given me the gown she is wearing—at least the color would have suited me better."

Henry studied Mrs. Curtis's gown for a moment, his brow dramatically creased in thought. Turning back to Isabella, he cocked his head to the side, studying her complexion. "It would be marginally better. But not the feather, dear God, not that feather."

Henry's comical despair robbed Isabella of her composure; her shoulders shook with silent laughter. Pleased with himself for coaxing her out of her embarrassment, Henry suggested they take a turn about the salons. He applied for permission from the baroness, who granted it eagerly. With Isabella's hand looped around his arm, he led her as far away from her patronizing mama as he could without compromising her reputation.

They made their way to the refreshment table, where Henry urged Isabella to sample the deep red cherry ratafia. From there they headed toward the music, but just as Isabella stepped off the last step into the ballroom, she felt a violent tug and heard fabric rip behind her. Stumbling forward, she spilled the contents of her glass over the front of her dress, then gave a credibly shocked gasp. "Oh no, my lovely new gown."

At the same time an elderly, rather corpulent gentleman started to apologize profusely. "I'm so very sorry, miss. It's me eyesight, you know, not what it used to be."

Henry had nimbly sidestepped the ratafia and caught Isabella before she could fall. He then took the glass from her hand and handed it to an approaching footman. The servant made himself further useful by pointing out the location of the ladies' retiring room.

All the while, the old man kept apologizing, until Henry addressed him. "Would you mind finding the lady's mother, Baroness Chancellor, and asking for her assistance in the retiring room? I will escort Miss Chancellor there."

The gentleman bowed, still flustered. "Of course, of course. The Baroness Chancellor, I think I know her husband. I'll find her right away, don't you worry, miss."

With that he departed, and Henry drew Isabella away from the inquiring eyes of other guests who had gathered to watch the spectacle. Henry led her into the corridor outside the retiring room where he inspected the damage to her gown. "Well done, my dear. You managed to get the ruffle as well as the bow, and not a droplet on the rest of the dress."

Isabella stripped off her ruined gloves, her eyes dancing merrily. "That was rather too good an opportunity to pass up. And to think, you didn't even have to step on my hem."

Henry chuckled and withdrew a small pocket knife from his waistcoat. She looked puzzled, but he pressed it into her hand nonetheless. "So you can make sure the flounce is too ripped to be reattached."

Comprehension dawning, Isabella grinned conspiratorially. "I best get in there then, before my mother arrives."

Henry's answering grin was just a little wicked. "I shall stall her if she gets here too soon."

He watched Isabella disappear behind the door into the ladies' sanctuary, and marveled at how natural it felt to be with this woman.

THE BARONESS DIDN'T ARRIVE FOR some time, so Henry opted to wait for Isabella outside. She had ceased to be Miss Chancellor over the last hour or so, and was now just Isabella in his mind. It would take some time for them to officially arrive at such informality, but Henry enjoyed his private anticipation of it.

He walked out into the beautiful summer night, making his way to a stone bench from where he could see the door to the retiring room, and allowed himself to enjoy the tranquility of the garden. The bench was set against the garden wall and flanked by two potted box-wood trees, their symmetrical shapes barely visible in the hazy moon-light, while everything in front of Henry was silhouetted against the light streaming out from the house.

From his vantage point, Henry observed the baroness rushing to the retiring room, no doubt ready to deliver a lecture. Her whole person seemed to radiate annoyance rather than concern, making Henry wonder at the relationship between mother and daughter.

A couple, deep in conversation, strolled by on the seashell-covered path and disappeared out of view again around the corner of the house.

Henry was just beginning to wonder how much longer Isabella would be when another lady came into view, heading down the corridor toward the French doors. A lady alone seeking the cool of the garden wasn't unusual, but this lady looked around herself to make sure she wasn't followed, and that piqued Henry's interest. He took a closer look and was stunned to recognize his former near-fiancée, Lady Jane Castleright. He had thought her still in London, or perhaps he hadn't thought of her at all, but her behavior was indeed curious.

After assuring herself no one was in the hallway to witness her exit, she stepped outside and had a good look around. Henry stayed absolutely still, hoping the low hedge in front of him would be enough to keep him hidden. A gentleman would, of course, have made his presence known, but the lady was acting suspicious and, as Isabella had pointed out, it was amazing what one could overhear if one just remained quiet long enough.

Lady Jane, satisfied she was alone in this part of the garden, stepped to a wooden gate in the wall and pushed it open. "Diddy, are you there?"

A quiet, cultured voice came from the other side of the wall. "Yes, Jane. Keep your voice down; no need to let the whole neighborhood know we are meeting in the dark. I wouldn't put it past your mama to report it to my grandfather, and then we'd be in a pickle."

Lady Jane bristled, but lowered her voice. "Why you can't meet me in one of the salons like a civilized person, I don't know."

The man moved into the gate, but not through it. The tall wooden door obstructed Henry's view, so he had to content himself with just listening to the exchange.

There was a chuckle. "For the same reason I don't want your mama getting ideas. I'm far too young to shackle myself to one female, so I avoid all gatherings eager mamas attend with their offspring."

Lady Jane's voice rose again, this time in annoyance. "Another way in which the world is unfair to women. You and I are exactly the same age, but at two and twenty you are considered to have a decade before you have to think about filling your nursery, whereas I am considered perilously close to being on the shelf."

The answer came fast and sharp. "You might have been wed by now if you had managed to keep your overopinionated mouth shut for long enough to get the man in front of a priest. You were the one who brought this idea to us, and I stuck my neck out for you. Now we are back to Grandfather's plan, which I simply cannot like."

Lady Jane seemed unusually subdued by this outburst. "Don't scold, Diddy, it was rotten luck he overheard. You know, I actually wouldn't have minded being married to him; he's no fool."

"Precisely the reason why I still think bringing him into the fold is preferable to having him as an enemy. But now Grandfather thinks both you and me loose cannons and is back to talk of retribution and ancient rules that need to be upheld regardless of circumstance."

Henry detected a note of the sulking boy in the man's voice now. By contrast, Lady Jane was back to being sharp and combative. "And what, pray tell, do you imagine I could possibly do about it now?"

There was a little pause, then the man asked, "Well, did you allow your prospective bridegroom to sample your charms, by any chance?"

Lady Jane obviously hadn't anticipated this line of questioning and was momentarily speechless, while Henry had to stop himself from laughing out loud. It had never even occurred to him to drag her into a dark corner to do as much as steal a kiss. How he could've thought it a good idea to marry her was totally beyond him now.

Lady Jane's sharp intake of breath attested to her outrage. "What do you take me for? I'm not some two-penny whore!"

The man behind the door sighed at her outrage. "Don't be such a prude, Jane. I'm just making sure there is no way to salvage this situation."

She answered curtly, "There is not."

But her companion wasn't done complaining. "This is not good! The country is changing and the Knights have done remarkably well under the Georges. We should turn our attention to making sure we get our fair share of India and inventions like the railroad. I have no time for ancient rules and blood feuds."

Lady Jane huffed. "Well, don't let the earl or my father hear you say that; they are liable to take all your powers away. I thought you wanted to be made dungeon master and take over from your grandfather when the time comes."

The man shushed her again. "I still do. But in the meantime I have to try and stop the old guard from embarrassing us all with that Jacobean nonsense. Grandfather, and what's left of his cronies, are fast becoming a liability—even the Master agrees with me. But he also says keeping them focused on revenge will keep them out of worse trouble."

Henry concentrated on staying absolutely still and keeping his breathing even. He was reasonably certain they were talking about him, and the uncomfortable pitching of his stomach led him to believe the Knights they spoke of might well be the elusive organization he'd come to think of as the Snake Pit.

While he listened to the two argue and discuss the necessity of bringing their organization into the nineteenth century, he tried to figure out who the man was. Lady Jane called him Diddy, and Henry remembered William telling him the Earl of Warthon's grandson and heir carried the courtesy title Lord Didcomb. It all fit, and if they indeed belonged to the Snake Pit, then revenge on Henry would be for his involvement in the unmasking and killing of Lord Astor. But what the devil did Lord Didcomb mean by "bringing him into the fold"?

Henry could only assume it had to do with his family history, and possibly his father. He tucked that conundrum away to be contemplated later and concentrated on making out what the conspirators were discussing.

Lady Jane was obviously losing her patience with her companion. "Did you call me out here just to scold and rant, or was there anything you actually wanted to discuss?"

The two of them reminded Henry of Bertie and Emily in the way they quibbled incessantly. Henry hoped the hotel was equipped with a copy of *Debrett's Peerage* so he could work out why these two seemed like siblings.

The voice of the presumed Lord Didcomb dripped with sarcasm. "Actually, dearest Jane, I came to talk to you in my capacity as your friend, and to warn you not to attempt to attend any more meetings. Your father went to the earl for advice, and Grandfather was only too happy to instruct him on how to achieve discipline in his family. As someone who is intimately familiar with his methods, I implore you to keep your mouth shut and your person well away from any further meetings, no matter how informal."

Lady Jane was indignant. "I'm not about to allow two self-impor-tant old men to intim—"

Lord Didcomb cut her off with an impatient hiss. "For once in your life, heed my advice! I can guarantee you won't like Grandfather's methods."

The sound of footsteps approached from the alleyway behind the wall Henry was sitting against, and Henry heard the young man mut-ter under his breath, "Lord knows you could use a spanking. I don't know why I bother."

Inside the garden, Lady Jane slammed the gate and huffed all the way back into the house.

CHAPTER EIGHT

THE NEXT MORNING, HENRY ORDERED A POT OF tea in the public salon of the hotel, where William had assured him he would find a copy of *Debrett's Peerage & Baronetage*.

It took Henry about an hour to piece together the rather tragic Warthon family history and solve the mystery of the familiarity between Lady Jane and Lord Didcomb. Maximilian Warthon, Lord Didcomb, was the son of the earl's second son, Captain Norman Warthon, and Constance Ellis. Mrs. Warthon happened to be the Countess of Weld's first cousin, and the Warthon family lived in a manor house next to the Castleright estate in Suffolk.

The captain fell during the Battle of Waterloo, but Maximilian Warthon remained in Suffolk until the boy's uncle, the earl's firstborn, died in a hunting accident the year following Captain Warthon's death. Curiously, Mrs. Warthon remained in Suffolk. Was she not welcome in the earl's castle? Were both the Warthons and the Castlerights descended from the original knights? Henry had always assumed the traitor Astor had acted alone and out of greed, but Lord Didcomb had mentioned Jacobean leanings still existing within the group.

Of course, *Debrett's* held no answers to any of these questions. All that could be said for certain was that Lady Jane and Maximilian Warthon had grown up together until they were twelve years old, and by all appearances, they had remained close.

The man who had spoken to Lady Jane last night was indeed Lord Didcomb. Furthermore, he, the Earl of Warthon, and Lady Jane's father, the Earl of Weld, were all plotting revenge against Henry, and they were possibly involved in treasonous activities against the king. This affair had expanded well past a disgruntled maid and a couple of missing girls, but so far Henry had no evidence to take to the Old Man, and therefore nothing to report.

He ordered a fresh pot of tea and contemplated his next move. Perhaps there was a way to exploit young Lord Didcomb's desire to "bring him into the fold."

As Henry sat and ruminated over his options, Isabella made her way to Mrs. Curtis's breakfast room and found her mother already waiting for her. She inwardly groaned and wondered whether the Spanish Inquisition over the breakfast table was to be a regular occurrence. Isabella wore a simple, practical sage-green dress, and her hair was loosely held together with a ribbon at the nape of her neck.

The baroness assessed her daughter with judging eyes and turned up her nose just a fraction. "You should at least put your hair up and wear one of your new walking dresses. We are not in the backwaters of Gloucestershire here. Do bear in mind we are here for a purpose. What if we receive morning callers?"

Isabella heaved a great sigh. If her mother insisted on being at home for morning callers, she would have a hard time getting back outside to master the art of painting the ever-changing sea. "Who would come calling on us, Mother? We don't know anybody besides Mrs. Curtis."

Her mother glared at her. "We know Lady Kistel. You managed to make an impression on Sir Henry March last night, miracle of miracles, so now we know him. And if he decides to call on us, you should most definitely be in, and presentable, when he does."

Isabella bristled under her mother's scrutiny. She couldn't spend her mornings sitting in the front parlor trading barbs with her. Not only did she want to paint the ocean, she had promised two gallerists new paintings by the end of July. Aside from that, her very sanity depended on being able to get away from her mother. Encouraging the baroness to fixate on Sir Henry as a marriage prospect was dangerous, but it occurred to Isabella he could be used to get out of the house. It was devious and possibly not fair to Sir Henry, but she didn't see any other way.

"I'm planning on painting up on the bluffs, Mother. Sir Henry mentioned last night he likes to go for a vigorous walk up there in the morning. He admires a woman who isn't afraid to don walking boots and swears by the health benefits of fresh air and exercise."

Isabella thought that last bit rather too much, but judging by the scheming gleam that sparked to life in the baroness's eyes, she was well on her way to thinking Isabella's plan had merit.

"Isabella Jane Chancellor, you aren't quite as feebleminded as I thought. If Sir Henry likes a woman who traipses around the countryside, that's what he will get. And let's face it, painting is your only accomplishment, so you might as well show it off. But, goodness gracious, we have to do something about your hair."

Isabella liked her hair the way it was; besides, the wind on the cliffs would pull it apart anyhow. But if letting her mother stick pins in her scalp got her a few hours of freedom, she would gladly endure it. "Certainly, Mama, if you think it necessary. I had planned on wearing my wide-brimmed hat and securing it with a scarf since it is rather sunny today."

The baroness assessed her with sharp eyes. "The hat certainly is a necessity; we really can't let you get any darker. But you are a baron's daughter, not some barefooted heathen. Your hair most decidedly needs to be pinned up if you show yourself in public."

Isabella colored a little at the recollection Sir Henry had actually seen her bare feet. But he had liked her that way, which made her like him. She covered her blush by bending over her eggs and applying herself to her meal.

As soon as they had finished breakfast, her mother dragged her upstairs to dress her hair. Half an hour later Isabella and her maid were on their way to the Hove side of town, but long before they reached the cliffs, Isabella handed her maid her purse and sent her shopping for ribbons. She would devise a way to weave said ribbons through her hair to hold it up, rather than letting her mother pull and poke at it until it was ripped out by the roots.

HALFWAY UP THE FIRST INCLINE to the bluffs, Isabella heard footsteps moving closer behind her, and just as she turned to see who might be in such a hurry, Sir Henry took her painting board out of her hand. "Good morning, Miss Chancellor. I spied you from the salon window. Will you let me tag along for the morning if I offer my services as a mule?"

Genuinely pleased to see him, Isabella smiled and surrendered her burdens with a curtsy. "And a good morning to you! Does that offer include a ride on your shoulders?"

Henry laughed and bowed lightly. "Absolutely, my lady. Would you like to mount now or later? I promise a smooth ride." His voice dropped on the last sentence, and there was a gleam in his eyes hinting at something more than what was said.

Isabella blushed and all of a sudden didn't know what to do with her hands. He'd flirted with her the night before, but his last comment left her with the knowledge he was referring to something that eluded her, and it made her wary.

On seeing her discomfort, Henry clamped the drawing board under his arm to free one of his hands and offered it to help her up the slope. "Don't mind me, I'm an ass."

And just like that, all the tension and embarrassment evaporated. It was as if he were asking to withdraw whatever he had alluded to, and she was more than happy to oblige.

Chuckling her relief, Isabella put her hand in his. "Let's go, then, long ears!"

Henry hated that he had made Isabella uncomfortable. He had assumed her to be too innocent to pick up on his innuendo. However, she was only too innocent to know what it meant precisely, but not innocent enough to dismiss it as banter. Something had happened to her to put her on high alert the moment a sexual note was introduced; he would have to bear that in mind.

They achieved the height of the bluffs and followed the footpath along the edge between the summer meadows and the short grass closer to the water. Eager to regain their conversational ease, Henry asked, "Are you planning to paint the same scene you struggled with yesterday?"

She turned to him, one hand on the crown of her wide-brimmed hat to stop the wind from blowing it away. "I am. Mrs. Curtis's housekeeper says that juniper is the only shade tree close to the ocean for miles, so I might as well make use of it."

Letting her step ahead of him as the path narrowed, Henry admired the graceful line her body made with her arm raised to hold her hat in place, her scarf endlessly concealing and revealing her neck. "Indeed! The day promises to be rather warm, so shade will be welcome."

Isabella sighed, lifting and then dropping her bronzed shoulders. "Yes, I better not get any darker or my mother will insist I stay out of the sun altogether. How am I to master the painting of waves then?"

"You could always come and paint from the front parlor at my hotel, or you could rent one of the bathing machines," Henry offered.

She half turned back to him so he could hear her better over the waves and the wind. "Oh, that's right, you said you stay at this particular hotel for the view of the ocean." She lowered her fatigued arm, but had to rescue her hat with the other a moment later, shooting the thing an exasperated look. "I thought of finding a spot under the new pier and making a few studies of the waves from there, but I like the idea of sitting in one of the bathing machines, sheltered from the wind as well as the sun."

Henry bowed slightly. "Always glad to be of service." She acknowledged him with a small grin and then turned forward, her attention on the path again. He followed a few steps behind and imagined taking off her hat in the relative privacy of a bathing machine, removing the restricting pins from her hair, and kissing the gentle curve where her shoulder met her neck. He wondered what she smelled like without the heavy perfume she had worn the night before and imagined her melting into his arms. But then he remembered her earlier reaction, and that cooled his ardor faster than a hailstorm.

Isabella, completely unaware of the struggle within her companion, strode out toward her destination, absorbed in assessing the light over the water. Yesterday she had started with the sandy cliff, the rocks below, and the curve of the beach, then had gotten completely lost trying to fit the ever-moving sea into her painting. The waves had arrived on shore, crashing over the rocks, throwing themselves against the cliff, obscuring her reference points, and frustrating her to no end.

Today she would start with the water, get the movement right, and work on the color, and if the cliff never made it into the finished piece, so be it. Mr. Turner had exhibited several canvases capturing the essence of the ocean entirely with light and color, so maybe she should try the same. It was exhilarating to be so challenged by her work.

They had gained the highest part of the bluffs now, and before long, arrived at the juniper tree. Henry took off his coat and hat and settled in the shade, resting his back against the tree trunk, while Isabella dampened the stretched paper on her board with sweeping brushstrokes and then prepared her little cakes of color by wetting them down too.

He watched her intently as he pulled a slim volume from his coat pocket, then rolled the garment into a tight log and wedged it behind his head. "Why do you wet the paper first? Doesn't that make the colors run?"

Isabella unwound the scarf from her neck and took her hat off, her eyes still studying the waves below. "I usually sketch out my paintings before I go in with color, in a style similar to Thomas Girtin, but that approach didn't work for me yesterday because the water is so very dynamic. Mr. Turner is developing a technique of blocking out colors on wet paper and then going over it again and again with layers of color until the form of things reemerges. I quite often use this technique for my skies, but today I want to see if it improves my rendering of the waves."

Henry was familiar with both Mr. Girtin's and Mr. Turner's work. Their paintings were widely exhibited in London, and Henry had long admired the luminosity of a Turner sky, so much so that he had purchased two of his paintings. One, a view of the Thames at night, currently shared wall space with Isabella's watercolor in his grandmother's sitting room. The other was a landscape shrouded in morning mist and held pride of place in his bedroom in London. But he had never thought about what technique the artist might employ to achieve a certain effect, and marveled at Isabella's knowledge of her craft. She had studied her medium and honed her skill, and was not afraid to try something different to solve a problem. She truly was an artist and not just one of society's more accomplished young women.

Henry followed her gaze to the seascape below. "Do you mind if I sit here whilst you work? I brought some reading and I have some thinking to do. I'd rather not leave you alone up here."

Isabella shrugged with an apologetic half smile. "I'm generally not keen on having an audience, but as long as you don't huff in impatience, I suppose I can bear with your presence." She didn't wait for him to respond, but bent to pick up her palette and started to mix her first color.

Henry grinned at her bluntness. In his opinion, too many women of his class buried their resentment in polite attentiveness. Isabella clearly wasn't one of them. "I shall keep the huffing to a minimum, my dear." He watched the one corner of her lips he could still see quirk up in a little smile.

Arranging himself more comfortably against the tree trunk, Henry finally immersed himself in the history of the abandoned abbey. He had found the slim volume on the bookshelf in the hotel's drawing room and had slipped it into his pocket when he saw Isabella pass on the promenade earlier.

The book contained a rather pompous yet vague recounting of the abbey's history. The writer, Edmond Twill, asserted the entirety of the Hove Parrish had once belonged to the convent of which the abbey had been a part. According to Mr. Twill, the abbey had been built in the fourteenth century and constructed out of a mixture of local sandstone and granite. Three architects were credited with various parts of the structure, but Henry, not being particularly interested in Gothic architecture, had never heard of any of them. The writer further related the convent had built its wealth through wool, but given the area was still a smugglers' haven, he speculated the monks may have paid for the abbey with French spirits.

Smuggling accusations led to the monastery's dissolution during the Reformation. Mr. Twill reported in some detail how the land, and the abbey on it, had been gifted to the second Earl of Warthon by Henry VIII. The earl had promptly attacked the convent, chased off the inhabitants, and ransacked their dwellings. He removed anything of value from the abbey and let it fall into ruin to assert his authority in the area. The ghosts haunting the place were said to be the monks who had died defending the abbey and its sanctuary against the earl's men.

It took Henry less than two hours to read through the volume, and even less time to realize it served only two purposes: to advertise the abbey as a hiking destination for those seeking a thrill during daylight hours, and to keep everyone away from the place at night. A wailing lady in white may have attracted some adventurous souls, but slaughtered monks were singularly unappealing, even as ghosts.

The edition Henry held in his hand was printed in 1803 and included three rather lovely illustrations. One was a woodcut of the convent as it had been in its heyday, while the other two were pen-and-ink drawings of the ruins. It occurred to Henry the Earl of Warthon could have commissioned this volume to create a cover for his meetings, and he resolved to seek out Mr. Twill, if indeed he was still alive.

HENRY WAS JUST ABOUT TO put down the book when Isabella set down her palette, stretched her arms overhead as she stood, and stepped back to look at her work. Several escaped ringlets danced around her ears and neck. Henry liked the way they softened her countenance, and wished he had the right to step behind her to rub her shoulders. And then she took one more step to the left, positioning herself directly between him and the sun-bright ocean. His breath caught at the sight of the light shining through her skirts and silhouetting her slender, slightly spread legs. She had dispensed with petticoats on such a warm day, and Henry could do nothing but admire her perfect shape.

When he remembered himself, he hastily grabbed his rolled-up coat and draped it across his lap to spare her innocent eyes the sight of his growing erection.

No sooner had he taken that precaution than Isabella looked over her shoulder and inquired, "What are you reading?"

Collecting himself sufficiently, he answered, "It's just a little volume about the abandoned abbey on the Earl of Warthon's estate."

Stepping closer, Isabella warmed to the subject. "Oh yes, I heard about it from the housekeeper. It's not too far from here, I believe. Maybe I'll walk out there one of these mornings; it might make a good subject for a painting."

Henry didn't like the idea of her going to the abbey alone, but if he accompanied her, he could use the opportunity to have another look around. "I went there yesterday before I met you. The abbey itself is rather gloomy, but the walk there and back is beautiful indeed. With the meadows in bloom and the path winding up into the Downs some ways, it makes for some delightful vistas. I'd be more than happy to venture there again if you want the company. We could take a picnic."

Isabella knelt in the short grass beside his outstretched legs and took the book out of his hands. "I'd like that. Does this have any illustrations?"

Henry turned the pages to the pen-and-ink drawings of the ruins. "At the beginning of the book there is a picture of the whole convent before it fell to ruin, but this is more or less how it looks now."

Isabella studied the drawings. "These are rather nice. Hm, overgrown Gothic arches; it might be just the thing for the gallery in London."

Henry raised one brow. "You have a gallery in London too?"

Isabella's attention was still on the drawings. "I have two. One in Mayfair, just off Regent Street, and one down by the Strand, not far from the Royal Academy at Somerset House. The one in Reading you know about. I also have one in Bath, and if Freddy comes down whilst we're here, he'll help me get a watercolor or two into the little place on the Steyne where the king is said to have bought a few paintings."

Henry took a good look at the watercolor on the easel in front of him. It clearly showed Isabella had worked out, and truly understood, the dynamics of the waves. She had also achieved a luminosity of color and a lightness of touch that attested to her talent. If she had been a man, Henry would have expected her to exhibit at the Royal Academy within the decade. It was a crying shame that door was closed to her. "You did get the water right today. It's really very good."

"It's just a study, and the water is much calmer than it was yesterday, but I'm rather pleased with today's effort. If the weather holds, I'll try it from the beach tomorrow and then work on a simple composition."

Just then the light dimmed around them and Isabella looked up at the sky. "Talking of the weather holding, I do believe we're in for rain before long." She gracefully rose to her feet and busied herself with packing up her brushes and paints.

Scrambling to his feet somewhat less elegantly, Henry shrugged back into his coat, stashed the book in his pocket, and set about dismantling Isabella's easel. A quick look at the sky toward Brighton confirmed rain clouds were moving in. "We better hurry or we'll take a soaking before we can get off these bluffs."

Working quickly, Isabella seemed unconcerned. "Not to worry, it's just a little rain, and I'm not made of sugar."

Henry was all too aware she wasn't made of sugar. Neither was he made of stone, and the mere thought of Isabella rain-drenched in her summer gown had him buttoning his jacket before he turned his body toward her again. And it wasn't just physical; he hadn't been this affected by a woman in a long time.

CHAPTER NINE

ISABELLA DIDN'T BOTHER WITH HER HAT, KNOW-
ing it would only hinder her progress, and they all but sprinted back
toward town. Even so, big fat raindrops began pelting them by the
time they reached the last steep grade leading back down to the beach.

Henry had Isabella's painting bag slung over his shoulder and carried the board with the finished but still damp painting. As soon as
the rain started, he clamped it under his arm and held it out a ways on
the bottom to protect it from the rain. The other hand he offered Isabella. The wind was now blowing rather fiercely, pulling at them both
and whipping her skirts around her legs. They slipped and slid down
the rain-slick slope to the sand.

Isabella greatly valued Henry's steadying hand. Glad he had followed her earlier and stayed with her, she enjoyed his company, his
intelligence, his charm, his wit. Sir Henry was undoubtedly a good
man to have around in a situation such as this, but he was still a man
and therefore had to be viewed with caution. However, once the rain
came down thick and fast in enormous drops, drenching them to their
underthings, Isabella threw caution to the wind. She let him drape his
arm over her shoulders, and stepped into the shelter of his body.

And it was a revelation. In seven long years Isabella had not allowed more than a half-hearted brotherly squeeze or a paternal pat on
the shoulder. Not even her male cousins or her brothers-in-law had

gotten closer to her person than a handshake, but the storm literally drove her under Sir Henry's arm, and his arm was everything she had once dreamed a man's arms would be: warm, strong, comforting, and safe. His masculine chest also stirred an unfamiliar feeling of want in her, a desire to be close to him.

Isabella startled at the thought of safety in Henry's arms. Did she not know, beyond a shadow of a doubt, a man's arms could never be safe due to man's very nature? But Henry's arm around her shoulder did make her feel safe, and just for this moment she wanted it to be true.

Henry felt Isabella stiffen a moment after she had leaned into his side, and thought to reassure her. "Don't worry, my dear, there's no one about to see us."

He looked ahead through the rain at the empty beach. The best course of action was, no doubt, to take her to the Waterfront, get her warm and dry, wait out the storm, then take her home in his carriage. But when he looked down at Isabella, he was confronted with an entirely different problem. She was now soaked through, and the thin cotton of her dress clung to every one of her curves, molding to her body perfectly. She wore jumps underneath, but Henry could still see her peaked nipples clearly, could even guess at their color.

Prying his eyes away from the beautiful sight, Henry directed his gaze toward their destination once again. "Isabella, you best hold that hat in front of yourself. I can see entirely too much of your lovely form."

Isabella looked down at herself and gasped. The rain had turned her dress so shockingly sheer, she may as well have been naked. With another gasp she clutched her soggy hat to her front and stared through the heavy rain up at Henry. "Dear God."

Henry grinned, admiring the fact she could blush even in the midst of a bone-chilling rainstorm, but when he saw the worry in her eyes, he sobered. "I know you didn't mean for me to see, so rest easy."

She nodded, blushed deeper, and looked down at the barren expanse of sand in front of her feet, unable to look him in the eye again. Surely now he would be like any other male she had ever encountered and either lecture her on the dangers of impropriety or expect things from her she was never again willing to give. The whole thing was entirely mortifying.

Henry saw, as well as felt, her mortification, and although the imp on his shoulder egged him on to tease her flirtatiously, he had learned his lesson earlier that day and set about putting her back at ease. "I am taking you to my hotel. There we can get you warm and dry, and later, once the storm has let up, I will take you home in my carriage."

Isabella nodded, surprised and relieved beyond measure he was willing to just be practical. Surely a hotel full of people would be a safe place for her to shelter from the rain. But she still didn't quite dare to look at him. "Thank you. I can't let my mother see me like this. But you don't have to drive me home; I told my maid to await me in the little pie shop on Ship Street."

Henry squeezed her shoulder just a little. "Perfect, we can send someone to get her. She can assist you and I'm sure Lady Kistel will be able to provide you with a dry gown."

The mention of the elderly matron finally calmed Isabella enough to look back up at him. Wet hair was plastered to her scalp and rivulets of water were running down her cheeks and neck, but there was a tremulous smile on her face. "Thank you. That's an excellent plan."

The smile he gave her was not licentious like she had feared, nor even flirtatious as she might have expected; it was kind, and her heart skipped a beat at the sight of it.

THEY COVERED THE REMAINING DISTANCE in silence, and even before they reached the hotel, several bellboys rushed toward them with enormous umbrellas and draped a cloak over Isabella.

As luck would have it, Lady Kistel had observed the spectacle of the storm from the bay window of the guest drawing room. She took immediate charge of Isabella, ushering her upstairs to her rooms, making concerned clacking noises along the way. After Henry gave orders to retrieve Isabella's maid, he returned to his own rooms for a dry set of clothing.

Having an excellent view of the beach from Henry's rooms, William, anticipating his master's needs, had a hot bath waiting for him. As soon as Henry had sunk into the welcome warmth of the tub, William handed him a hot cup of tea laced liberally with brandy. Henry sighed contentedly, but when William tried to hang up his suit by the fire, he protested, "Not in here, for the love of God. Wet wool smells rather unpleasant."

William chuckled. "Never seemed to bother you none in Spain."

Henry took another sip and leaned back against the curled lip of the bathtub. "When needs must, but thankfully needs must no longer."

William sent a rather sly smile Henry's way. "The young lady didn't mind."

The comment earned him a quelling look. "She had more pressing things to worry about." Putting down his cup, Henry reached for the soap. "Did you find out what Lady Jane and Lord Didcomb are doing here in Brighton?"

William noted with some relief that Sir Henry felt protective toward Miss Chancellor. Apparently his employer was willing to give the women of his class another try.

"Sure did, sir. Lady Jane and 'er dear mama came down 'ere after London got too uncomfortable for them with the scandal. What's curious is Lady Jane's papa, the Earl of Weld, stopped with the Earl of Warthon instead of guardin' his womenfolk.

"Lord Didcomb came to check on 'is granddad, the Earl of Warthon, who 'ad the ague. The old man got better, and Lord Didcomb apparently left early this mornin' and took Mary, the talkative maid, with 'im. The word is 'e got 'er a position up in London."

Henry rinsed the suds off, stepped out of the bath, and took the towel William offered. The fact Mary had been spirited away in much the same way the other two girls had was not welcome news, but perhaps it was what Mary had wanted.

He vigorously rubbed the towel back and forth over his back. "It would appear Mary's gamble to get Lord Didcomb's attention paid off. Seems he's not only the reformer of the group, but also the one his grandfather calls in to clean up his messes. I wonder what else he does for this organization."

Henry drained the last of his tea and pulled a fresh shirt over his head. "How quickly can Allen and Eliza make it to town? I would really rather not lose Mary's trail." Henry pulled on his stockings and stabbed his feet into his favorite pair of buckskin breeches, opting for comfort rather than afternoon tea finery. "Finding the other two girls seems more urgent now too. This is all connected."

William smoothed the wrinkles out of Henry's coat with his hands. "I figured they might still be with Lord Robert, so I sent the messenger there first. And then this mornin' when I 'eard about Mary, I sent word to Thomas to watch that Didcomb fella's 'ouse."

Henry straightened his cuffs and reached for his watch, which seemed to have suffered no ill effects from the deluge. "Well done, my friend. With any luck the rider will get there before Didcomb, and Thomas can verify Mary arrived with him. Then we can track her from there."

"That's what I thought."

Henry absently ran a brush through his hair and took a final look in the mirror. "We will just sit tight here, then, and keep an eye on Lady Jane and the two earls. Best to stick to the social aspect of my visit since I'm already known to the group."

Clearly Lord Didcomb was not to be underestimated, and his words the night before indicated there was some kind of vendetta about to be waged against Henry. Henry had expected the Duke of Elridge to retaliate after the death of Lord Astor three years ago, but he never had. The duke had buried his son and carried on with his political life, seemingly without missing a beat or shedding a tear. As cold as it was, it had helped deflect all questions about Astor's treason away from the dukedom. All, including the king, now believed Astor had acted alone and separate from the secret society he had been a part of. But Elridge was related to the Earl of Warthon and allied in the House of Lords with both him and the Earl of Weld. The two old earls were part of the group Didcomb had called the Knights. Henry had little doubt said Knights, and the Snake Pit he had investigated after he found the snake ring on Astor, were one and the same. It was a real shame Didcomb had departed the scene, providing Henry no immediate opportunity to make his acquaintance.

Henry itched to investigate further, to call on the two earls up at the castle. But he had no reason to do so, and with Mary gone, he had no one he could have asked for assistance in getting into the castle undetected.

He headed for the door, but William called after him, "Before I forget, there's a packet from Avon on your writin' desk."

Henry paused for a moment, then continued on his way downstairs. "It'll keep. First I must see to Miss Chancellor."

ISABELLA HAD YET TO EMERGE from Lady Kistel's rooms, but Henry was informed her maid had arrived. Satisfied the social proprieties were covered, he ordered a full tea tray and sent word to Lady Kistel to join him whenever they were ready. Then he settled in to watch the storm whip up the waves.

His thoughts went to Isabella and what had happened between them up on the bluffs, and later during the rainstorm. He could have sworn she liked his company, but then there were moments when she retreated behind an emotional wall of her own making, and for a lovely, intelligent, young gentlewoman to build such a wall, there had to be a cause. Henry didn't know whether he should be patient or attempt to breach her defences. All he knew was, he wanted her in every way possible, and it was imperative to get to know everything he could about her.

ALTHOUGH IT WAS STILL RAINING, the squall had calmed considerably by the time Isabella was led into the parlor by Lady Kistel, wearing one of the old woman's gowns. It was a high-necked green and brown affair, most likely selected because it was long enough to cover

Isabella's ankles. A cream-colored knitted shawl was draped around her shoulders to cover the fact that the dress hung loose on her slender frame. Her still damp hair was held together with a light green ribbon at the nape of her neck. The colors of the ensemble did nothing for Isabella's complexion, but somehow it didn't detract from the beauty of her eyes or the quiet splendor of her delicate features. She looked warmer and less panicked, but Henry still saw the weariness in her eyes.

Lady Kistel beamed at Henry from across the room. "Henry, my boy. The tea tray is just what we need."

Rising with a smile, trying to set Isabella at ease, Henry bowed. He seated both ladies, then indicated the corner where the painting board with the study of the waves leaned against the wall next to Isabella's canvas bag. "I don't know about the contents of your bag, but the painting seems to have survived."

Isabella took the tea Lady Kistel handed her and smiled her thanks, then turned to Henry. "Thank you for keeping the rain off my painting."

The old lady turned to look at the watercolor, but having no love for the new fashion of painting as if everything was obscured by a heavy fog, she refrained from comment.

The young painter took a sip of her tea and cast a critical eye over her work. "It seems to be well enough." She then glanced at the wet patch under her canvas bag and shrugged with a little sigh. "I don't hold out much hope for my sketchbook, but my paints are in a wooden box, at least, and my brushes are wrapped in oilcloth."

Henry immediately looked for the sketchbook. He had to rummage for it, but eventually withdrew a leather-wrapped book from the soaked bottom of the bag. Back at the table, he mopped at it with his linen serviette. "I'm sorry, my dear. I should've thought of removing it from the bag before I put it down."

Isabella reached for her book and inspected the outside, almost entirely discolored by moisture. "No matter, Sir Henry. You didn't know it was there."

The sketchbook was held closed by a leather strap, and once Isabella unwound it, she peeled back the extended flap attached to the back cover of the book. The top and bottom edges of the thick paper inside were clearly damaged, but the side had been spared, and when Isabella opened the book, only a few pages at the front were unsalvageable; the rest of her sketches would dry out in time.

She breathed a sigh of relief and smiled her first real smile since she'd realized Henry had seen her nipples peek through her dress during the storm.

Seeing the smile, Henry felt a weight being lifted from his shoulders. He indicated the sketchbook. "I've never seen one with the flap extended like this. It's rather ingenious."

Isabella leafed through her work, inspecting the damage along the edges. "I know. A bookbinder in Bath makes them for me especially to protect my drawings from the elements. I use my sketches to paint in oil tempera during the winter months, so they are rather precious to me. As I mentioned, I've been rained on before, although never this violently."

She looked up to glare at the rainy beach and churning ocean beyond the bay window and got distracted by the sheer drama of it. Studying the choppy waves crashing into the pier some ways down the waterfront, she wrinkled her brow. "The dynamics have completely changed again. I can see how some painters get enthralled by the ocean. It is a fascinating subject."

Lady Kistel had looked at the sketches as Isabella inspected the pages, but now the old lady reached for the sketchbook to have a closer look. She leafed through with growing interest and appreciation. "I confess to not being too fond of your painting, Miss Chancellor, but these are absolutely lovely. You are very talented, my dear."

Laughing at the backhanded compliment, Isabella returned her attention to her companions. "I suppose Mr. Turner's methods are not for everyone."

Lady Kistel made a sour face. "I should think not. I can never quite make out what he is painting these days."

Isabella knew it was rude to argue with her elders, but couldn't quite help herself. "Mr. Turner paints the light, primarily."

The old lady snorted with derision. "That's all very well, child. But when there is a tree in the painting I would like to recognize it as such."

"All the forms are still there, it's just that they are diffused by light and imbued with atmosphere. Mr. Turner paints the way he experiences a certain place rather than slavishly drawing every pebble," Isabella defended passionately.

"Oh, posh!"

It was clear to Henry that Isabella's respect for William Turner bordered on hero worship, whereas Lady Kistel was thoroughly irritated by the man. It was also quite clear both ladies were possessed of a temper, which made him like these two all the more; but since they were in public, he thought it wise to redirect the ladies to their libation. "Miss Chancellor, could you pass me the raspberry jam, please? More tea, Lady Kistel?"

Isabella had the good grace to blush, but Lady Kistel had no such maidenly scruples. "Well, I hope you don't follow in the man's footsteps. It would be a crying shame to waste your talent that way."

Isabella's lips pressed into a thin, flat line, but before she could take the bait, Henry replied, "Oh, indeed she does not, my lady. I bought one of Miss Chancellor's watercolors in a gallery in Reading and gave it to my grandmother for her birthday last. Grossmama was so pleased with it, she hung it in her private sitting room."

"Yes, well, Ruth generally has good taste," the old lady grumbled.

In the meantime, Isabella had relocated her manners and her sense of humor, and smiled apologetically at Lady Kistel. "I beg your pardon, my lady. I didn't mean to argue."

Never one to hold a grudge, the old lady grinned at her companions. "I'm an old curmudgeon; don't mind me, children." Then she patted Isabella's hand and returned her attention to her tea cake. "So you sell your paintings in a gallery in Reading? Well done, my dear; I'm sure that annoys your mother to no end."

Across the table, Isabella met Henry's amused gaze and couldn't help the dimple growing in her cheek.

The remainder of tea proceeded peacefully while they discussed the weather, places where Isabella might paint, and upcoming entertainments. It seemed there were two informal dances and a musical planned for the upcoming week, and in a town as small as Brighton, it was a foregone conclusion they would all three be attending these events. Henry and Isabella made plans to walk to the abbey on the next fine day, and shortly thereafter, Henry ordered his coach to return Isabella to her mother before her absence during such inclement weather became worrisome.

Curiously, the Baroness Chancellor only simpered girlishly when Sir Henry delivered Isabella back into her care, thanked him for his chivalry in rescuing her daughter from the rain without asking for particulars, and ushered him back out the door with an invitation to come back and visit anytime.

Isabella was mortified. "Mama! How could you be so rude?"

The baroness let her judging eyes travel over her daughter's borrowed outfit and shook her head in despair. "You are wearing an old woman's ill-fitting cast-offs and you are asking me why I sent him away? Sometimes I despair of you, Isabella! The less time he spends in your company looking like this, the more chance you have he may call on you again, if you ever had any chance at all."

Isabella let out a resigned huff that went entirely unnoticed by the baroness and retreated to her bedchamber. There she took off the offending gown, folded it carefully, and wrote a note expressing her thanks as her maid, Sally, wrapped up the garment. Her mother may not have liked it, but the gown had given Isabella a chance to regain her equilibrium after feeling so horribly exposed in the rain. Besides, it was best if Sir Henry didn't think her attractive. She'd rather he thought of her as a friend, somebody to converse with, walk with, even laugh with, but no more than that. It just couldn't be. The devil of it was, for the first time in seven lonely years, Isabella wished she could respond to a man.

Over dinner later, Baroness Chancellor commented on Isabella's luck to have gotten stranded with Sir Henry, since bringing her to his hotel had undoubtedly compromised Isabella, and he could be brought up to scratch on those grounds.

The thought of Sir Henry asking for her hand out of duty depressed Isabella more than her mother's willingness to marry her off at any cost did. "I doubt anyone could take exception," Isabella explained. "Lady Kistel was present." She watched her mother's face fall and resolved to tell Sir Henry at the earliest opportunity to spare her a proposal based on propriety and society's strictures.

SINCE THERE WERE NO ENTERTAINMENTS planned for the evening, Henry returned to the hotel and ordered an early dinner to be brought to his rooms. Then he inquired of the concierge where he might find Mr. Twill, the author of the oh-so-charming little book about the abandoned abbey. He was informed the estimable Mr. Twill had shuffled off this mortal coil some years ago, but his widow still resided in a cottage on Church Street. Furthermore, the man had penned a number of books on other attractions around the area, and Henry returned to his rooms with a book about the Steyne and a little volume about Warthon Castle he planned to read to see what else he could glean.

First, however, Henry settled into one of the armchairs by the fire to read his letters from Avon. The missive from Grossmama was short and to the point:

Henry, mein Junge,

Julia failed to secure a proposal from Lord Proctor, so Hortense has taken it upon herself to extend Julia's season by holding a house party. But since Emily cannot be contained in the schoolroom at the best of times, and is far too pretty not to distract attention away from her cousin, we decided it would be best to visit with you in Brighton until the deed is done. Emily and I will arrive within the week, and we hope that does not interfere too

much with your plans.
Grossmama

Before he turned his attention to his daughter's letter, Henry called for William. "Be so good as to go downstairs and book a suite for my grandmother and my daughter on the first floor."

William frowned at the idea of the little miss not staying with them, but knew better then to second-guess such a decisive order. "When will they arrive?"

"Some time during the next three days, I should think." Henry gave a resigned shrug and turned back to his missives.

Emily's letter was not much longer than Grossmama's, but it made Henry smile at his daughter's view of the events and his grandmother's wily ways.

Dear Papa,

Julia, the silly widgeon, couldn't get her viscount to come up to scratch in time for a June wedding, so we are under threat of a July house party. Thankfully, Grossmama came up with the plan to escape to Brighton to see you, and we are leaving tomorrow. If you are courting someone and I'm in the way, Grossmama will take me to Charmely and we'll go for long walks on the cliffs. Grossmama says the ocean is quite stirring, so maybe I'll do some sketching. She also says Brighton has a brand-new pier and bathing machines and some fancy shops, so I'm certain we'll have no trouble amusing ourselves even if you are busy.

I can't wait to see you.
Your loving daughter,
Emily

Henry poured himself a brandy from the carafe at his elbow and wondered how much time he had before his relations descended upon him. He'd have to take their safety into consideration as he continued his investigation. Lord Astor had meant to harm him through Emily, and he had no way of knowing if the Knights were also willing to use her against him. Perhaps sending them on to his estate up on the cliffs would be best, but then he wouldn't be on hand to protect Emily.

Knowing time was short, Henry decided to do a little drinking in the local taverns. He hoped where there was one servant willing to talk, there would be others. Henry knew Brighton was the right place, but when the right time would be, and what it would take to draw out the players in this game, was another matter.

Unfortunately, tongues weren't wagging as freely that night, and all Henry could discover was that Mary had gone to London willingly.

CHAPTER TEN

THE NEXT DAY DAWNED AS WET AND WINDY AS the night had been, inducing Isabella to stay in bed an extra hour. Thursday was Mrs. Curtis's "At Home," prompting Isabella to avoid the breakfast parlor. Instead, she spent a blissful hour drawing the one exotic spire of the Royal Pavilion she could see from her bedroom window.

She wanted, more than anything, to go to the pier and look at the waves. The ocean had so many moods and she didn't want to miss this one. Isabella had little hope of escaping the horrors of a rainy day At Home, however; her mother placed too much importance on it.

It was almost comical to what lengths the baroness was prepared to go to ignore her daughters' wishes and bully them into marriage when she herself found no joy in her own. Isabella's sister Grace had had the good sense to fall in love with a wealthy baronet during her season and was happy enough in her marriage. But Isabella was certain both her other sisters had been pressured into marrying for status and had no real fondness for the men they now shared their lives with.

The only reason Isabella had withstood her mother's cajoling, and then later her tirades, was the knowledge she couldn't accept a proposal from any man. Of course no one knew that, so her family assumed she was just being difficult, or overly choosy, or both. Not being able to share her secret had separated Isabella from all those around her, but telling her mother or any of her siblings had never been an option, and the threat of the wedding night outweighed Isabella's fear of her mother's displeasure. She had refused the two offers she had received during her season, prompting the baroness to call her every name available to a lady of breeding, but in the end Isabella had gone back home to the Cotswolds to plan a life independent of marriage and her mother.

And yet, here she was, once again trying to persuade everybody involved she truly had no wish to marry, and her mother, the most unhappily married woman in all of England, refused to allow her to know her own mind. It was frustrating, but then again, the charade gave her a chance to paint the ocean.

In this spirit, Isabella donned a primrose-yellow high-waisted gown with tiny orange blossoms embroidered around the modest round neckline and the little puffed sleeves. The dress was too girlish for her, the color not strong enough for her liking, but it was pretty, and wearing it would appease her mother.

In a bid to avoid the dreaded hairpins, Isabella instructed Sally to fashion two thin braids with the hair just above her ears and twist them with the rest of her hair into a loose chignon, securing it with two horn pins. Sally then wound a pretty blue satin ribbon around the creation for added hold. It was soft and comfortable, and Isabella liked it very much, but doubted her mother would. Shrugging, she stood, grabbed a light blue knitted shawl, since the summer air had cooled considerably with the rain, and headed to the drawing room.

She found the salon already well stocked with matrons her mother's age and three unattached gentlemen who had come to look her over in the light of day. Not one of them was under forty, and two of them featured a sad lack of hair. They all bowed dutifully over her hand and remarked on the weather, lamenting the rain on account of her tender constitution, and praising it on account of their crops. Isabella had a hard time keeping a straight face as she sat beside her mother and drank her tea.

By a quarter past eleven she had just hidden her third yawn behind a dainty embroidered handkerchief when Sir Henry and Lady Kistel were announced, brightening her mood considerably.

Henry settled Lady Kistel in a chair close to the fire, and bowed over the baroness's and Mrs. Curtis's hands before he turned his attention to Isabella.

"You look lovely this morning." He assessed her and her outfit more closely. "Yellow becomes you, but I would like to see you in a silk the color of a ripe wheat field. It would bring out your coloring marvelously."

Isabella shook her head at his rather affected little speech, but had to admit a flax-colored silk gown would be to her taste as well. "So it's the fashion maven who came to visit, is it? Would you like to come along the next time I visit a modiste?"

Henry grinned at the idea. That was exactly what he wanted to do, to peel her out of her dowdy yet girlish clothes and have someone design gowns for her to highlight her assets rather than hide them. He employed his best dandy lisp. "Indeed, nothing like an afternoon spent discussing fashion."

Isabella giggled at his tone of voice, but averted her eyes, so he changed the subject.

"I hope there were no consequences to your adventure yesterday."

The dimple in Isabella's cheek reappeared. "Not even a sniffle. I told you this wasn't the first time I've survived getting wet."

"Yes, you mentioned that." He took a cup of tea from Mrs. Curtis and leaned his shoulder against the wall next to Isabella rather than taking a seat across the room. Lowering his voice, he asked, "Would you brave the elements once more? I borrowed one of those enormous umbrellas from the hotel and was hoping you might take a rainy stroll with me to look at the waves."

Isabella drew in a quick breath to tell Sir Henry she very much wanted to go, but then let it out again, knowing her mother wouldn't release her from the At Home.

Henry saw her hesitation and leaned down to murmur close to her ear, "Do come with me. I know you want to see the waves." He enjoyed the familiarity with which she leaned toward him despite the fact they were in a rather crowded drawing room.

"I can't leave yet. It'll be at least another half hour before everyone has departed, providing no one else arrives. My mother isn't likely to let me slip out whilst we still have guests." She shrugged apologetically. "These At Homes are part of her battle plan to marry me off."

He lifted his tea cup with a smile. "I don't mind waiting. I will just remain right here and keep your suitors at bay." He nodded toward the three middle-aged gentlemen who occupied chairs opposite the sofa Isabella and her mother were sitting on.

Isabella batted him away, wrinkling her nose. "They seem harmless enough. It's you my mother has set her sights on. You better not let her maneuver you into a proposal."

Henry decided to ignore her comment; she clearly wasn't ready to give a proposal any consideration, and he wasn't ready to make one. But it was never too early to take out the competition, so he lowered his voice further.

"Looks can be deceiving, my dear. The one who still has all his hair is Baron Tillister, a widower with three children under the age of ten, and a mistress in a flat in Bloomsbury. The gentleman with the many watch fobs and the bad waterfall is Mr. Wickham, an aging rake. He is too set in his ways to ever make an agreeable husband, but his brother is a viscount whose wife has failed to present him with a child in fifteen years of marriage, so it now falls to Wickham to secure the succession. He is probably trolling for a wife here because he is too notorious in London to get within shouting distance of any of the debutantes. The third one seems to be a simple country squire, but as I said, looks can be deceiving."

Isabella cocked her head at him. "And I wonder what it means that you know all this about these men."

Henry grinned. "Oh, it just means I live in London and keep my eyes and ears open."

Isabella shrugged. She had no plans to entertain any offer from any man and therefore could afford to be indifferent. "But are you not just as bad? You have an illegitimate daughter, and are rumored to have had dozens of mistresses."

Henry had the good grace to blush, but had a sudden urge to explain himself. "It's true, I'm no paragon of virtue, but all my transgressions are out in the open. I don't sneak around or try to hide the fact I'm a sexual being. My last mistress, Eliza, even lived openly in my house for three years, until six months ago when she informed me it was time for me to find a wife so I could keep my promise to my daughter. She didn't think it would be fair to my future wife for her to remain."

Isabella was startled by this speech, especially considering the setting it was delivered in. She glanced at her mother, but the baroness was involved in a conversation with Lady Kistel and the rake in need of a brood mare, and seemed completely oblivious to her hushed conversation with Sir Henry. Isabella, her cheeks burning, looked back up at Henry and wondered whether he had loved this Eliza. "She seems quite the woman, your last mistress."

"She is indeed. I wager you would like her, and she you. Eliza is independent and strong like you, has an insatiable thirst for knowledge, and loves nothing better than a good adventure." Henry's smile was full of fond memories.

Isabella saw the softness playing around his lips and felt a sudden pang of jealousy. "You love her."

Henry looked at her sharply, gauging her reaction, but ultimately decided to tell her the truth. "What was between Eliza and me never was a grand romantic passion. Our feelings were born out of friendship, and now that she is no longer with me, it is the friendship that remains."

It wasn't lost on Isabella that he didn't confirm or deny his love for Eliza. Isabella doubted his feelings were truly in the past; how could they be? He had lived with this woman for three years. She doubted anyone could turn their feelings off that easily.

"Where is she now, do you know?"

Henry could see some of Isabella's thoughts reflected in her expressive face. It was clearly not comfortable for her to talk about another woman he cared for, but he found that somewhat reassuring and had to give her credit for not shrinking from the conversation. Isabella was an unusual woman in many ways. "Eliza is staying with a mutual friend, helping him recover from an injury."

Isabella concluded this Eliza wasn't completely out of Sir Henry's life, since he knew precisely where to find her. It was irrational and quite unexpected, but she had to admit the existence of another woman in his life bothered her.

Not willing to examine these thoughts and feelings any further, Isabella was relieved when their tête-à-tête was cut short by the departure of the three gentlemen and the last of Mrs. Curtis's friends.

As soon as the other guests had departed, Henry addressed the baroness. "Lady Chancellor, would you kindly give me leave to take your charming daughter for a walk down Marine Parade to the new pier?"

The baroness was startled speechless, but only for a moment. "Goodness gracious, Sir Henry, why ever would you want to take Isabella for a walk in the rain when you can sit comfortably right here and visit with her?"

Henry smiled politely while he wondered how the creative free spirit sitting beside him could have been born to such a stiff, prosaic woman. "Indeed, madam. But the ocean makes such a dramatic display when it's churned up like it is at present, and I discovered yesterday Miss Chancellor is fascinated by the ocean, so I suspect she would like to see it."

Baroness Chancellor shot her daughter a despairing glance, but ultimately decided if the man was smitten enough to risk getting wet to please Isabella, she wouldn't stand in his way. "By all means, Sir Henry. If Isabella wants to get battered by wind and rain to watch water, and you are willing to take her, you have my blessing."

Henry bowed to the baroness and winked at Lady Kistel, who had watched the whole scene with a little knowing smirk on her face.

"May I leave Lady Kistel in your tender care until we return? I'm certain she would much prefer to remain by the fire."

"Of course, Sir Henry. We will have lunch, and Sally will accompany Isabella." Turning to her daughter, the baroness added, "You better go fetch your cloak and a sturdy hat to cover your hair. It's already falling apart, and God only knows what the wind will do to it."

Incensed on Isabella's behalf, Henry bit his tongue and led her out into the hallway. "I, for one, like the way you fixed your hair today, but a hat would help with keeping the rain off."

Isabella quirked a half smile and headed for the foyer. "Don't mind my mother; she's always like this."

Henry couldn't help himself. "Harsh and demeaning?"

She barked out a sad little laugh. "She doesn't mean to be, and I'm quite used to it."

Isabella's maid was already waiting at the bottom of the stairs. Henry took the cloak out of Sally's hands and helped Isabella into it. "I'm not sure what I object to more: that your own mother treats you like this, or that you are used to it."

She stepped to the looking glass to button her cloak and tie her bonnet securely under her chin. "It's no matter really. In a few months I'll be moving into my very own cottage, and from then on, will have to endure her disapproval only on major holidays." Turning to her maid, she inquired, "Are you sure you want to brave the rain? You don't have to come."

The maid made big round eyes. "You can't go out with a gentleman alone. It ain't proper." She then grinned from ear to ear. "Besides, Sir Henry brought one of them giant umbrellas for me, too, and I can't wait to try it out."

Isabella smiled at her maid's enthusiasm and nodded her thanks to Henry. Not many men of their class would have spared a thought for the comfort of a servant.

They headed out into the light but steady summer rain, Henry holding the umbrella aloft and Isabella stepping close enough so it might shelter them both, while Sally followed a few paces behind. However, as soon as they turned onto the Marine Parade, the wind picked up, driving the rain almost horizontally against them. But Isabella paid no mind: she was utterly captivated by the churning gray mass in front of them.

The ocean was an awesome sight, with waves taller than a man crashing onto the beach and sending up giant plumes of spray as they broke against the cliffs to their right. With the powerful swells constantly pulling at it, the pier seemed fragile, as if constructed of kindling. Isabella questioned the wisdom of walking onto it, but couldn't contain her excitement at the prospect of coming closer to the mighty waves.

They kept close to the houses along the waterfront and halted under the awning of one of the hotels fronting the pier.

"Can we get any closer?" Isabella asked.

Sally looked at her mistress as if she'd lost her mind, but Henry rather admired Isabella's spirit of adventure. He smiled at the worried servant. "It's safe enough, but you can watch over your mistress from here, Sally." Then he offered Isabella his arm and stepped onto the wooden quay. Isabella eyed the structure with some uncertainty, but having Henry by her side made her bold enough to follow.

The closer they got to the surf, the louder grew the roar of the crashing waves. Once they came abreast with the water's edge, Henry led her to the railing and they watched the foamy waves race over the sand, escaping the confines of the ocean only to be pulled back into the brutal undertow. Isabella longed to stick her toes into the water there, just to feel its sheer power.

Eventually they ventured farther out onto the pier to contemplate the massive swells as they broke in big crystalline rolls. At the end of the pier they were surrounded by foam-capped peaks reminding Isabella of an etching she had once seen in a book. The artist had turned the foamy caps into racing white horses galloping toward the shore. The whole spectacle was so full of mystery and drama, it was spellbinding.

They stood there for a long while, huddled under the umbrella and watching the storm-whipped waves rolling and crashing into shore. Eventually Henry turned to her. "Does it help you paint the ocean, to see it in this wild state?"

She continued to watch the drama just below them, but a smile played around her lips. "Of course it does. It's akin to painting a portrait: the more sides to a person's character you get to know, the more of their personality comes through in the finished painting."

Pulling her hand through the crook of his arm, Henry gently urged her back to the shore. "Have you painted many portraits?"

Isabella glanced up at him. "Not lately. My sisters used to sit for me during the winter months before they got married, but I am more interested in painting landscapes and am starting to make a name for myself with them. Now I mostly paint oils from studies during the colder months, unless there are interesting views to be had from the windows."

Henry looked thoughtful. "My cousin's castle has some charming views of the snow-covered woods in winter, and my ancestral estate in Norfolk has very dramatic views of the sea at any time of the year."

"Oh, is that where you live?" Isabella inquired.

Henry shrugged; he had no love for the gloomy medieval pile in Norfolk, but knew there were those who thought it romantic. "I grew up there, and have to visit three times a year to attend to my lands, but I live mostly in London and visit frequently at Avon, where my daughter lives with my grandmother and my cousin's family."

Isabella turned to have one last look at the angry waves. "Yesterday Lady Kistel mentioned an estate not far from here. Do you own that too?"

The rain had let up some, but the wind battered them fiercely.

"Yes. Charmely is rather lovely, with a bluebell wood and the cliffs on the far side, but I don't spend much time there. It was my great-grandmother's summer seat and has only enough farmable land to grow vegetables and grains for the estate's use. The land above the cliffs is grazed by sheep, and they don't take much managing."

Isabella looked at him with surprise. "I didn't realize you were so involved in the management of your land. Most landowners hire a man for that."

Henry grinned down at her. "I inherited four crumbling estates, but I have managed to make all four of them profitable, two of them very profitable indeed. It turns out I'm a dab hand at figuring out what will grow where, and whether there is a market close enough to make it worth the while to grow it."

Isabella smiled. This was one more thing to like about Sir Henry: he was not one of those self-important, self-indulgent fribbles who thought their estates ran themselves. "My father constantly struggles with the profitability of his crops despite our having the best soil you could possibly want, but perhaps he doesn't consider the markets he delivers to."

Henry thought Baron Chancellor's estate to be somewhere in the Cotswolds. "Where exactly is your father's estate? And how does he sell his crops?" He hoped he hadn't offended her by assuming such knowledge from a gently bred female, but she answered without hesitation.

"I believe he sells his grains to an agent, and we only grow enough vegetables and fruit for our own consumption." She wrinkled her brow in contemplation. "Perhaps that's the problem: my father's estate is just outside of Bilbury, close enough to Gloucester and Cheltenham to sell vegetables at market there, if we had any to sell."

Considering Isabella's obvious interest, Henry warmed to the subject. "Despite food shortages in some of our cities, growing grain is barely worth the trouble at present. I do better with the potatoes I grow in Lincolnshire on nothing but rocks than I did with the corn I grew in Berkshire before I built my glasshouses there."

They were almost back at the Marine Parade now, and Isabella was starting to look forward to a hot cup of tea, but the mention of glasshouses stopped her in her tracks. "You have glasshouses? As in glasshouses, plural, more than one? Are they not horrendously expensive and difficult to maintain?"

Henry urged Isabella toward the hotel where Sally huddled under the awning. "Yes, well, the initial investment was quite considerable, but when I inherited the estate from my mother fourteen years ago it was barely profitable despite the rich soil. Luckily my mother also left me a small amount of money, and I decided to spend it on two glasshouses in an area clearly too wet to be used for growing grains. I spent a month building raised beds before the glasshouses were constructed on top of them and then went back to the Peninsula to fight Bonny. By my next visit home, my head gardener had grown a crop of strawberries in January and earned enough money with it to build the next two glasshouses. Now I have eighteen of them on four fields and can harvest berries, herbs, and green vegetables all year round. The estate is in the Thames valley near Reading and close enough to London to get my produce there fresh and sell it at a premium to people who can afford the luxury."

Isabella was fascinated. "So it's largely about knowing what the people you can reach are willing to pay for your produce and producing what they want." She cocked her head in thought while Sally fell in step behind them. "It's not unlike me painting watercolors because they are in fashion and letting the gallerist decide on the price since they know better what their clients are willing to pay. That painting you bought in Reading would've cost at least a third more in my Mayfair gallery."

Henry laughed and gave her hand resting in the crook of his arm a little squeeze. "And so it should be. Those are the principles of supply and demand, and if people are fool enough to think they are getting a superior example of your work because they are purchasing it in a fancy London gallery, they deserve to pay more for it."

"My sentiments exactly." Isabella winked, and Henry's whole body warmed in want of her despite the chilly weather. He tucked her closer so he could feel the swish of her skirts against his leg as they walked. Rather than protest, Isabella wound her arm tighter around his and smiled up at him.

CHAPTER ELEVEN

UPON THEIR RETURN, HENRY STAYED ONLY LONG enough to fortify himself with a hot cup of tea, then escorted Lady Kistel back to their hotel. There, Henry changed into plainer garments and took himself on a visit to the widow Twill.

The rain had stopped, and the heavy cloud cover blanketing the South Downs was breaking up in places, letting the occasional ray of sunshine slip through. Mrs. Twill's cottage, on a quiet lane in North Brighton, was set behind a low hedge with a white-painted wooden gate leading into a small garden, fragrant from the earlier rain. The whole picture was so wholesome, it should have been a million miles away from anything nefarious, and that very idea set Henry's instincts ablaze and his teeth on edge.

Henry knocked on the door and was admitted by a pretty young maid in a starched white apron. She led him into a small but well-appointed parlor, where he was welcomed by a rotund matron in her sixties. She greeted him with a far-too-friendly smile and cunning in her eyes.

"A visitor, how perfectly marvelous!" Mrs. Twill stood and offered Henry her hand, the local brogue evident in her voice.

"Forgive the intrusion, Mrs. Twill. I'm Sir Henry March. I've come to inquire about your husband's books." Henry saw just the slightest hint of a widening of her eyes as he took her hand and bent over it.

He wondered if she recognized his name and had been told to expect him. Looking around at the exceedingly tidy abode and spying the extensive and well-kept back garden, Henry also wondered how she afforded a maid and a gardener. The woman certainly did not seem the type to exert herself if she could help it. Surely her husband's obscure little books didn't provide an income large enough for the upkeep.

Mrs. Twill indicated for Henry to sit in an armchair directly opposite the sofa she occupied. "Of course you have, dear. Will you have some tea?"

"My thanks, Mrs. Twill, but don't trouble yourself. I just came to ask a few questions."

She simpered up at him. "Oh, it's no trouble. I have so few visitors now, and it's always so gratifying to talk about my dear Mr. Twill's work." She then leaned toward the open doorway and hollered, "Miny, bring us the tea tray."

To Henry's surprise, the girl hollered back, presumably from the kitchen, "Won't be but a moment, Mrs. Twill."

Henry's twitching lips threatened to give away his amusement. The widow Twill may have had more than average funds for her station, but she clearly was not as genteel as she wished to appear.

"So which one of my late husband's books have you read, Sir Henry?"

Convinced the widow had her own agenda, Henry decided to keep his inquiries about the abbey for later. Sometimes one gleaned more from the questions others asked than from the answers they were willing to give. "I found his book on the Steyne most informative and his volume on Warthon Castle charming. I've never had the pleasure of meeting the earl, but am almost tempted to call on him just to get a good look at his abode."

Mrs. Twill heaved a rather affected sigh of regret. "The earl is sadly getting on in years and not as welcoming to visitors as he once was. But he still maintains the footpath to the abbey. Have you read my dear Mr. Twill's book on that?"

And there it was: someone had surely told her he might come asking questions about the abbey. Henry wondered if Mrs. Twill could be induced to communicate with that someone. "Indeed I have. I suppose I wasn't quite as interested because I had already seen the abbey. But it was fascinating to find out what a part it had played during the Reformation. As Gothic ruins go, it's most impressive, but a little gloomy for my tastes."

She watched him carefully as he talked, then relaxed back against the sofa. "Oh dear, yes, ever so gloomy. But the walk there is lovely, don't you agree?"

"Absolutely charming! In fact, if the weather is sunny tomorrow, I plan to take my painter friend there."

Mrs. Twill was suddenly very interested again. "Oh really, will he be painting, do you think?"

Henry smiled at her eagerness. "Quite possibly. She seemed to think Gothic ruins would be just the thing for her gallery in Mayfair."

Mrs. Twill's eyes grew round. "Goodness gracious! A lady painter who sells her pictures in a gallery in Mayfair. Whatever next."

Henry enjoyed the woman's antics and felt only vaguely guilty for involving Isabella.

"She is very good. But of course she wouldn't sell any paintings if people knew her to be a woman, so I rely on your discretion." He gave her a conspiratorial smile, and she looked as if she wanted to pat his hand, but just then the maid entered with the tea tray and, thankfully,

Mrs. Twill turned her attention to pouring tea instead.

Henry took a cup of tea and a biscuit from her. "How many books did your husband write? He seems to have done rather well with them." He let his eyes sweep across her cozy parlor, and she preened with pride.

"He wrote seven of them in all, and he did do rather well with them. Two are still making money for me to this day."

Henry feigned surprise. "Indeed? How could that be?"

She tittered. "Why, they are being reprinted every year, that's how. The one about the abbey and the Smugglers Cove one. The one about the Smugglers Cove is my favorite; you should read it." She got up and walked to a small ornate bookcase standing against the wall and pulled a little volume from it. "There we are, I knew I had an extra copy. Why don't you take it."

"That's most kind of you, Mrs. Twill. I shall return it to you forthwith." He stashed the book in his coat pocket and stood to take his leave.

This time Mrs. Twill did pat his hand. "No need, Sir Henry, no need."

As Henry stepped into the hallway, the maid appeared and walked him to the door. She curtsied very properly, but he could feel her eyes on him as he walked down the garden path and then turned left into the lane, as if to walk back to his hotel.

The moment he was certain he could no longer be seen from the cottage, Henry hopped over a low wall and doubled back, cutting through neighboring gardens, vaulting over fences, and pushing through hedges until he had a clear view of Mrs. Twill's cottage and into her parlor.

The woman was writing a letter on a little desk by the window.

She finished the missive and called out for the maid, but then added a postscript before she closed it up, addressed it, and handed it to the maid with a coin. The girl placed the letter in her apron pocket and seconds later emerged from the front of the house with a blue shawl wrapped around her shoulders.

Evidently she was headed to the posting inn on North Street, so Henry, rather than follow her, made his way through the neighboring garden to the lane running parallel to Church Street. He walked to North Street at a leisurely pace and, turning the corner into the busy thoroughfare, was just in time to see the girl enter the inn through the front door. Henry, meanwhile, walked into the stable yard, and from there to the back entrance. The yard entrance lay a half story higher than the street entrance. Henry cautiously made his way to the end of the corridor, where six steps set at a right angle to the hallway led down to the lower level. From here he overlooked the taproom to the left and the front entrance with the postmaster's desk to the right.

Mrs. Twill's maid stood at the desk, but the postmaster was nowhere to be seen. Just then a matron bustled from the kitchen into the taproom, her arm stacked full with steaming trenchers, and halted briefly when she saw the other woman by the desk.

"If you have the right change, love, you can just leave it, and Mr. Pratt will see to it in a bit."

Henry stepped back into the shadows as the maid turned to smile at the proprietress. "I've got a halfpenny for a letter to London."

"One sheet?"

"Yes."

The landlady indicated the writing table with her head. "Then leave it right there."

The maid placed the letter and money on the desktop. "Thanks ever so much."

Pushing open the door to the street, the maid disappeared into the bustle outside while the matron continued on her way to the taproom.

Henry stepped out of the shadows, walked down the steps, and crossed the entrance hall. Since there was only one letter with a London address, he took a furtive look around, slipped it and the coin into his pocket, and left through the front door. He immediately crossed the street and stepped into the closest store with a display window so he could check the maid hadn't seen him leave the inn. She was in the butcher's shop next to the inn and deep in conversation with the man behind the counter.

"Good afternoon, may I help you, sir?" The female voice came from behind Henry.

Henry looked around himself and realized he had wandered into a modiste's establishment. Making a show of inspecting fabrics and fashion plates, he tried to come up with a plausible reason for his presence, when he recollected Emily's impending visit. He smiled happily at the modiste.

"My fifteen-year-old daughter is about to pay me a visit and will be in need of a few new gowns. Have you anything suitable for a very young miss?"

The modiste smiled politely and directed him toward a display by the second window on the other side of the door. "I have some lovely sprigged muslins for the mornings and outdoor activities, and some brushed cotton in case the young lady is allowed to attend small gatherings."

Henry stepped closer and studied the fabrics, touching them, holding them up in the light. He finally picked out three bolts. "This white sprigged muslin will be lovely for a summery day dress, the rose pink for a gown she can wear for dinner, and the blue-gray cotton for a new riding habit. Will you put these aside for her, and I'll bring her in to be measured? She grows rather rapidly at the moment—in all directions." The last came out on a little exasperated sigh.

The modiste smiled at him warmly now, sympathizing with the plight of a father watching his daughter grow into a woman. "I would be happy to, and look forward to meeting your daughter."

Henry smiled back and was about to leave when he caught sight of the most marvelous softly glowing straw-colored silk. It was exactly the shade to bring out Isabella's coloring. But he couldn't bring her here, and he couldn't give her any presents other than flowers and sweets until she had accepted his suit, and even then, buying her fabric would be frowned upon. Still, it was just too perfect. Henry took down the bolt from where it stood on the shelf. "Can you sell me enough of this silk to make a ball gown with a short train?"

The modiste hesitated for a moment, probably gauging whether she could talk Henry into letting her make the gown, but ultimately decided to humor a new client. "Isn't it beautiful? It's called Duchess Satin and comes straight from Paris."

She took the bolt from Henry and unfurled the softly shimmering fabric onto her cutting table, where it rippled like ripe wheat in the wind. The modiste measured out ten yards, folded the precious silk, wrapped it in a square of linen, and tied it with a blue ribbon. Then she named a sum high enough to make a Bond Street modiste proud. Henry paid her, inclined his head in thanks, and departed the dressmaker's shop contemplating how to convey his gift to Isabella without arousing her mama's suspicion—or hopes, as it may be.

Flowers were not an option as a means to hide his offering; the precious satin would be too easily damaged by water. But a confectioner's box had possibility, so he directed his steps down North Street toward the Royal Pavilion in search of a shop specializing in sweet treats. Finding such an establishment in one of the side streets, he asked the rosy-cheeked matron behind the counter whether she had a large box with her store's name and address on it that he could buy from her. The woman looked at him with a degree of uncertainty, but then placed three differently sized wooden boxes on top of the glass display case holding an enormous selection of candied fruits and flowers.

Taking the large box off the counter, Henry opened it and placed his packet with the satin inside. It fit perfectly.

"Ah, sending your lady a secret token."

His eyes snapped up, and he was confronted with the confectioner's knowing little grin.

"You know, when she sees this box, she'll be expecting sweets." She gestured around the shop. "Better not disappoint her."

Chuckling, he checked the small box would fit on top of the packet inside the bigger box, handed the container to the matron behind the counter, and winked. "I strive never to disappoint a lady, so you better fill this with your most exotic candied fruits."

Smiling, the woman started placing slices of candied orange and lemon, whole cherries, chunks of pineapple, and ginger into the box. Then she added a neat row of almonds, sprinkled a few candied violets on top, and finally held the selection out for Henry to peruse.

Taking a deep breath, Henry appreciated the mixture of sweet and spicy fragrances. "She will love this! And if she doesn't, I will."

The woman nodded sagely while Henry pulled an elegant silver case from his breast pocket and selected a gold-framed visiting card. "Do you have something I can use to write the lady a note?"

Again the matron smiled knowingly and produced a pen and inkwell from behind the counter, as well as a piece of foolscap to note down the lady's direction.

After finishing his note, Henry set the small box on top of the packet with the silk, added his card, and secured the lid. He wrote down Isabella's address, paid the confectioner, and left a shilling for the box to be delivered that day. A satisfied smile played around his lips as he headed back to his hotel.

ONCE BACK IN HIS ROOMS, Henry shed his coat and went about the tricky business of opening a letter without breaking the seal. A sharp knife and a steady hand were required. If the seal broke or the paper ripped, there would be no covering the fact the letter had been tampered with.

The missive was addressed to a solicitor in Lincoln's Inn Fields, located within easy walking distance of the very post office from which the letters from the two girls in service in London had been postmarked. The pieces of the puzzle were starting to fall into place.

Henry heated a slim blade in the flame of a gutted candle. It was always a near thing to get the metal hot enough without blackening it. Gauging the right moment to take it out of the flame, Henry wiped the blade on his handkerchief to ensure there would be no soot transfer onto the wax seal, a sure sign for anybody checking whether the seal had been compromised.

Once the blade was ready, Henry's practiced fingers inserted it carefully between the seal and the paper and separated the two with one swift move. He unfolded the letter, mindful not to disturb the creases in the paper, and read.

Esteemed Sir,

I am sending you word through Mr. Harcourt, Esquire. As you predicted, Sir Henry March came to visit today, but he seemed more interested in the castle than the abbey. He has already visited the abbey and found nothing of interest, but voiced his wish to pay his respects to your grandfather. I tried to direct his interest toward Smugglers Cove, but am unsure as to my success in this, or whether it was indeed necessary, since he had already dismissed the abbey.

Your humble servant,

Mrs. Twill

Postscript: Sir Henry mentioned a painter friend who sells her paintings in galleries wanting to paint the abbey. Apparently Gothic ruins are in vogue. Perhaps you are unconcerned by this, but I thought you ought to know.

There was no doubt the letter was meant for Lord Didcomb, and that the young lord was hiding something. The letter also confirmed Didcomb suspected Henry had come to Brighton to gather information.

Henry needed to take a closer look at the abbey as soon as the weather permitted, and Isabella would have to do as his cover. It wasn't right for him to involve her, but what was done, was done.

Henry refolded the letter along the existing creases and retrieved a wooden box containing a dozen different shades of sealing wax. He selected the shade most like the color of the seal on the letter and heated the wax stick. He also held the underside of the seal to the candle to warm it, and when the wax stick was ready to drip, he let one singular drop fall on the back of the now malleable seal, then gently pressed the seal back into place. He let the whole thing cool for a few minutes, inspecting his handiwork with a critical eye. Satisfied not even he could see the seal had been tampered with, he set the missive aside, setting the coin he had swiped with it on top.

Sitting back down at the writing desk, Henry pulled a fresh piece of writing paper out and wrote a brief message to Thomas in London, instructing him to put a man on Mr. Harcourt, Esquire, obtain a writing sample from the same and his clerks, and send them to him posthaste. Then he wrote another note to Allen, asking him to find out whatever he could about Lord Didcomb, but cautiously. The young man had secrets that could well make him dangerous.

When William appeared a few moments later, Henry pointed to the letters. "We may just have found the man of business who wrote the letters for the missing girls. Take those to the posting inn on North Street and make sure they get onto the next mail coach."

William took the letters and looked at the addresses, then stashed them in his coat pocket with a nod. "Thomas'll find out. Anythin' else whilst I'm out?"

Henry handed him the stump of the wax stick he had used earlier. "I could use another stick of this shade."

William took the stump and grunted in the affirmative. Matching wax was clearly not one of his preferred chores. "I polished them Hessian boots of yours. Figured you might need them tonight."

Henry nodded. "Good. Order me a bath on the way out, would you?"

William's mood lightened and he grinned at his employer's enthusiastic tone. It looked like Sir Henry was looking forward to showing off for Miss Isabella. Things were decidedly looking up on that front.

CHAPTER TWELVE

AT THAT MOMENT, ON THE EAST SIDE OF BRIGHton, in Mrs. Curtis's cozy town house, Isabella was washing her hair in preparation for the musical that evening. Not a fan of cooling bathwater, she rinsed off quickly and climbed out of her tub as Sally bustled into the room, a large wooden box tucked under one arm, and Isabella's freshly pressed gown over the other.

"Seems you have at least one admirer who knows better than to send you flowers, miss."

Discarding her towel, Isabella slipped into her dressing gown, but looked up with mild curiosity. "Oh, and which admirer would that be?" She picked up her hairbrush and stepped to the fire to dry her hair.

Shrugging, Sally placed the box on the little table next to her mistress and went to lay out the gown alongside Isabella's underthings. "Don't know, miss. There are two bouquets of flowers waiting for you downstairs, but George the footman says this box came from the best confectioner in town, so I brought it upstairs before Her Ladyship sees it."

"Oh, good thinking, Sally. She would probably tell me I can't afford to gain any weight whilst we are here and confiscate my treats." Isabella grinned at her maid, knowing how much Sally loved sweets. She wrapped her hair into a towel and twisted it all up into a turban. "Let's see what's in the box." She flipped the catch to the side and lifted the lid, only to find a similar smaller box inside. Intrigued, she read the card lying on top.

Dear Miss Chancellor,
I know I have no right to send you this, but I couldn't resist. I believe it to be the exact right shade for you, so please accept this token of my friendship.
I hope to see you tonight at the Landover musical.
Your friend,
Sir Henry March

Sally had stepped behind Isabella to read the missive over her mistress's shoulder. Now she lifted the smaller box out of the bigger one and exclaimed, "Look, there is a package underneath."

Isabella sat on the sofa with the parcel and pulled off the ribbon. Once the linen cloth fell away, she caught her breath at the sight in her lap. It was simply the most beautiful, softly shimmering satin she had ever seen. It was the color of ripe wheat, and Sir Henry was right, it would suit her beautifully.

"Oh, miss," Sally breathed. "That's going to look so pretty on you."

Isabella lifted the richly glowing material out of its packet, and the modiste's card fluttered to the ground. She picked it up and went to the mirror over her dressing table to see how the satin looked against her skin. "Oh, Sally, it's terribly wicked to accept it, but look, it's absolutely perfect." She draped the fabric around her shoulders and turned to her maid, who studied the effect, nodding approvingly. The silk set Isabella's eyes to shine blue-green like the ocean in the sun. It also contrasted beautifully with her dark hair, and complemented her lightly tanned skin.

Sally contemplated the silk. "Remember the dresses you drew before you had your coming out? You could make some drawings of how you want the dress and then have it made for you."

Isabella turned back to the mirror, stroking the material lovingly. "Yes, Mama wouldn't even let me show my designs to the modiste and stuffed me into all those frilly pink and white things instead." She shrugged off her dressing gown and let the material fall down the length of her body, admiring the way it molded to her every curve. "I would keep it simple. All the lines clean, perhaps just a little gathering across the bosom and the sleeves short and slightly puffed. The waist should be lower than empire, but the skirt narrow, like we saw in that magazine in London on the way here."

Stepping up behind her mistress, Sally's eyes gleamed with professional zeal as she fingered the satin reverently. "There is enough there for two gowns, miss."

"Or a gown and a spencer and maybe even a shawl too. What's in the other box?"

Sally, still holding the small box, flipped the catch and opened it. Both mistress and servant looked down and gasped in unison.

"Candied fruit, however did he know?" Isabella had expected a few icing-covered cakes or chocolates, but instead the box was brimful of exotic candied fruits, the likes of which she had only ever admired in a London shop window. She had tasted most of the fruits contained within fruit cakes, but displayed like this they looked and smelled entirely different. Delicately lifting one of the little flowers out, Isabella examined it more closely. "Candied violets. The only time I've had one of these, it was drowning in the icing on top of a fancy tea cake, so I couldn't really taste it."

She placed the rare treat on her tongue and closed her eyes to better concentrate on the taste. "Mmm, it's exquisitely delicate and melts on your tongue. And the color, so deep and rich, like the satin. Perhaps we should embroider the shawl with violets." She furrowed her brow as she lifted the satin to study the effect of the two colors next to each other. Then she pushed the box toward her maid. "Try one, Sally."

Sally, who had stared at the selection with round, covetous eyes, needed no further encouragement. She took one of the violets and placed it on her tongue, then took a slice of orange and pointed to the chunks of ginger. "I know I like the orange and the lemon slices, but what's that one?"

Isabella grinned and took one of the amber-colored pieces. "Ginger, I think. They were my grandmother Chancellor's favorite and she always tried to give them to us when we were children, but I didn't like them back then." She nibbled on the piece, her eyebrows pinched together, then her face cleared. "Oh, that's rather good. Spicy but sweet, and it doesn't have the fibrous texture my grandmother's had. Maybe it's one of those adult tastes, like caviar and oysters."

Sally looked at the rather substantial slice of candied orange in her hand and grinned. "I'll try that tomorrow. So, I take it you're keeping Sir Henry's lovely gift?"

Isabella read the challenge in her maid's eyes loud and clear. Sally knew she loved all things beautiful, including fabrics and laces, and the gowns that could be fashioned from them. Sadly, the wardrobe her mother continued to foist on her in the name of propriety and wanting to attract the right sort of husband ranged from the uninspired to the downright ugly. Checking herself in the mirror once more, Isabella sighed at the marvelously sensual feel of the satin on her skin.

"Whatever will I tell my mother?"

Sally snorted derisively. "Tell her you saw it in the window and just couldn't resist. She'll understand that one; does it often enough herself, she does."

Isabella sent her maid a warning glance, but there was no heat in it, for they both knew she was right. She heaved another sigh. "But will she believe I paid for such a costly dress with my painting money?"

A calculating gleam stole into Sally's hazel eyes. "She just might. She might believe you paid for it to spare your papa the expense, and when she sees you bought such a fancy gown, she might also conclude you do want to catch a husband this time. That'll get her off your back so you can go painting."

Trust Sally to figure it this way. "I don't want to encourage Mother in her zeal to marry me off, but I did something similar yesterday when I told her I was going to paint up on the bluffs because Sir Henry told me he walks there in the mornings." She giggled at her own wickedness, then stroked the satin again and turned to the mirror, admiring how it brought out her eyes. "Oh, I'm not sending it back, it's simply too beautiful." She looked at the modiste's card in her hand and turned to her maid. "We'll go see this tailor tomorrow." Then she put away the satin carefully and started dressing while Sally set the curling tongs near the fire.

Sally regarded her mistress's back for a moment, pity clearly written in her eyes. "Maybe you should think about marrying Sir Henry. He's not a bad-looking gent, and he likes you."

Isabella's shoulders slumped, but she didn't turn around. Her voice was barely above a whisper. "You know I can't."

Sally made an impatient noise at the back of her throat. "Just tell him. He's got an illegitimate daughter, and he's kind. If there's one gentleman in all of England who might not judge you, it's him."

Isabella just shook her head and got on with the business of rolling on her stockings. Sally had been there that fateful day. She'd cleaned up her distraught mistress and burned the evidence of her downfall, but even she didn't know the whole of it. Perhaps Sally was right and Sir Henry wouldn't judge her, would continue to treat her with respect and kindness, but for that very reason he deserved better than her.

Sally stepped up behind her mistress and started to lace her stays. "You like him, don't you." It was a statement, not a question.

Isabella nodded, but said no more, and Sally was wise enough to know when to stop pushing. Still, it killed her to see her lovely mistress languishing alone, shriveling into spinsterhood while her mother griped at her, and her sisters exploited her good nature at every turn.

TWO HOURS LATER, CLAD IN a simple light-blue silk gown, Isabella entered the fashionable town house where the musical was to be held. Her dark hair was piled loosely on top of her head and held in place with the help of several tiny braids and two blue ribbons. A moderate string of pearls graced her throat, and teardrop pearl earrings dangled from her ears. Pearl-white satin gloves covered her arms, a crocheted seed-pearl-encrusted reticule hung from her wrist, and a painted fan was clasped in her hand. In short, Isabella had made an effort. Not that she would have admitted it to a living soul, but she wanted to look good for Sir Henry, especially after he had seen her in the horrid pink gown and sent her the marvelous satin. Her blue gown was slightly out of fashion—it had been purchased for her coming out seven years prior—but she knew its simplicity flattered her trim figure, and the color suited her.

Isabella made her curtsy to her hosts, the very fashionable Lord and Lady Landover, and followed her mother and Mrs. Curtis into the throng of guests. They wandered through a smaller side chamber, where people who chose not to attend all the musical performances could converse, and continued on to the large salon at the back of the house where the pianoforte was set up.

The event was already well attended, and Isabella had only just crossed the threshold when Mr. Wickham charged their little group with the single-mindedness of a man on a mission. "My dear Baroness Chancellor, Miss Chancellor, and Mrs. Curtis. How fortunate I am to encounter such grace and beauty twice in one day." After the rather flowery greeting, he turned his particular attention to Isabella. "May I inquire whether we will be favored with a performance from you tonight, Miss Chancellor?"

Isabella had been assured it would be her choice whether to offer her mediocre skills or not, but one look at her mother and the matrimonial gleam in her eyes cured her of that illusion.

"Isabella will be delighted to sing and play for us, won't you, dear?"

Isabella forced a smile and conceded. "I might sing a song in a little while."

Mr. Wickham bowed over her hand, his breath hot and encroaching even through her satin gloves. He held onto her hand as he straightened, and she caught him staring at her bosom. Sir Henry's warning came to mind, and Isabella knew with a flash of certainty it would be ill-advised to ever be alone with this man. She was almost relieved when Baron Tillister approached. Tugging her hand out of Wickham's possessive grip, she smiled at the newcomer.

"Baron Tillister, I bid you good evening. Thank you so much for the lovely roses."

The baron bowed over her hand very properly, released it immediately, and stepped back, smiling at her. "You are most welcome, Miss Chancellor. I trust you had a good day since last I saw you."

He then turned to make his bows to the baroness and Mrs. Curtis, and Isabella let her eyes travel across the busy salon and found the squire, who'd been the third in Mrs. Curtis's salon that morning, waving to her from a sofa near the piano.

Eager to escape Mr. Wickham's attentions, Isabella nudged her mother. "Look, Mama, Squire Gardener is holding a sofa for us. How very thoughtful."

With some satisfaction, she noted Mr. Wickham glaring daggers at the poor man while her mother led the way to the squire and the sofa he guarded. The baroness may have preferred a titled gentleman or the aging but still dashing Mr. Wickham as a son-in-law, but a sofa was always preferable to the hard chairs set up in rows in the middle of the room. On those grounds the squire deserved their attention and the pleasure of their company.

"My dear Squire Gardener, you must have read my mind. This should be big enough for at least the three of us."

The good squire looked like he had hoped the sofa would be big enough for at least four, but bowed graciously, invited all three ladies to sit, and pulled one of the hard chairs toward the end of the sofa where Isabella had settled. "Did you receive my flowers, Miss Chancellor?"

Isabella turned her attention toward the stout little man and noted his smile held genuine kindness. Out of the three men dancing attendance to her, he was most likely the safest to converse with; possibly the best choice for a husband, too, had she been at all interested in matrimony. She inclined her head in lieu of a curtsy.

"I did. Thank you so much. It is always such a pleasant thing to see blue and white bellflowers paired with hollyhocks, especially on a rainy day."

The squire's chest swelled with pride at her praise. "They grow in my gardens, and I'm so pleased they brightened your day. Perhaps one afternoon you'll do me the honor of letting me show you my home."

Isabella made a mental note not to encourage the man any further, for surely it wasn't kind. She smiled pleasantly, but said nothing, and was grateful when she spotted Sir Henry leading Lady Kistel toward them before her silence had sufficient time to grow awkward. She stood and greeted the old lady with a kiss on her cheek. "Take my seat on the sofa, my lady. Sir Henry will bring me a chair."

Henry's eyes met hers in silent greeting as he led Lady Kistel to the seat on the sofa. "It will be my pleasure, Miss Chancellor." But before he could go on his errand, Baron Tillister moved a chair into position for her so she would be seated between the good baron and the squire.

Henry took one look at the scene before him and decided to extricate her from her gaggle of suitors. He bent over her hand as she curtsied. "Would you like to take a turn about the room before the music starts, Miss Chancellor?"

Isabella, mindful of her need to say a private *thank you* for the costly present he had sent, agreed readily. "That would be just the thing, Sir Henry. Do you enjoy music?"

Henry offered his arm and led her away from the group. "I do indeed. I usually get asked to play a little Beethoven at these occasions. Do you play or sing?"

Isabella groaned, remembering her mother's coercion earlier, then glanced over her shoulder to make sure the unseemly noise hadn't carried back to the baroness. "I sing passably and play some. What gets me into trouble is doing both at the same time."

Henry chuckled. "You sound as if such a fate were about to befall you."

Rolling her eyes heavenwards, Isabella was confronted with the cherubs playing harps over their heads. She wrinkled her nose in distaste. "I do hope the music is better than that fresco." She shuddered for good measure and turned her attention back to Henry. "My mother took it upon herself to announce to all and sundry I would perform tonight."

Henry smiled at her wrinkled nose in honor of the mediocre fresco and wondered whether she would enjoy singing if she didn't have to play the piano. "What are you thinking of offering? If I am familiar with it, I could accompany you."

Her expression was so unabashedly hopeful, he almost laughed out loud.

"I like the old English folk songs. They sound better on the harpsichord, but that can't be helped. Do you know 'Through Bushes and Briars'?"

Henry nodded. It was a rather sad song, but very beautiful, and somehow it suited her. "It's settled then; I shall accompany you. And I do think there is a harpsichord hidden in the corner behind the pianoforte."

"Thank you, Sir Henry." Isabella let out a relieved sigh and, recalling the other reason to be grateful to him, turned to beam up at him. "I must also thank you for my treasure chest. You truly shouldn't have sent the satin, but it's perfect, so I'm keeping it, even if it makes me a wicked person."

Henry grinned. "It doesn't make you wicked, just sensible. And since it's cut and I can't return it, you would insult me for nothing if you insisted on giving it back."

"That's what Sally said. She is vastly in favor of keeping it too."

"She's a smart woman, your maid. Listen to her."

Isabella blushed and lowered her eyes, remembering what else Sally had suggested she should do. "I know, and I frequently do."

Henry wondered what had triggered her discomfiture and deflected so she could regroup. "Let's go see if we can find the sheet music to Beethoven's 'Piano Sonata No. 27 in E minor.' I think it will go with your song, but I haven't played it in a while, so I'd best have the music in front of me."

Isabella was grateful to have a moment to gather herself while they leisurely walked over to the pianoforte. Until Sir Henry made the comment about listening to Sally, Isabella hadn't realized her maid was quite literally the only person she could trust completely, and the only person she actually did listen to, her only true friend. Of course she had other friends, and enjoyed cordial relationships with her siblings, but no one else knew her as well as Sally did. She was also the only one who would be moving to her cottage with her when the time came. That thought at least was comforting.

It didn't take long to locate the sheet music for the Beethoven sonata, but by the time Isabella handed it to Henry, she was back in control of her emotions.

Henry placed it on the piano next to the open lid, where it would be easy to find later. "Thank you, my dear. Shall we go in search of our hostess to tell her what we each will be performing? Or would you rather I take you back to your mother before I seek out Lady Landover?"

Isabella took his arm again. "I've no plans to return to my scheming mother's side until I absolutely have to." The dimple in her cheek made an appearance as she looked up at him with a naughty little grin. "I'm sorry to use you in such a way, but my mother is rather excited at the thought of me marrying all those piles of money you are rumored to have, and as long as you show interest and I reciprocate, she won't get carried away with the idea of my marrying a title or me becoming the mother of a viscount—I hope." Isabella shrugged.

Henry laid his gloved hand over hers, resting on his arm, and lost himself in her gorgeous blue-green eyes for a moment. Should he tell her he was serious about courting her? It would be the honest and decent thing to do, but he was almost certain she'd draw away from him. And if he couldn't spend time with her, there was no chance of changing her mind, or at least finding out what troubled her. So he gave her hand a friendly pat. "I am glad to be of use, my dear. I do rather enjoy your company."

That earned him a radiant smile, making him feel just a little guilty, but not enough to confess his intentions and risk their easy camaraderie again.

"Thank you, Sir Henry. I do so appreciate your friendship."

Henry and Isabella found their hostess still greeting guests. She was bathed in refracted light under the chandelier in the foyer. It took but a moment for Henry to whisper their plans into Lady Landover's attentive ear, and then he directed Isabella to the refreshment table in the smaller salon. There he instructed a footman to take drinks to the three ladies on the sofa in the music room and furnished Isabella with a glass of berry ratafia. He himself opted for claret and saluted Isabella. "You look lovely tonight, my dear. No need to spill any of this on any part of you."

Isabella burst into a helpless fit of laughter. "Oh, you are wicked."

BY THE TIME THEY HAD consumed their libations, the last expected guests had arrived, and Lady Landover made her way through the smaller salon into the music room, clapping her hands to attract everyone's attention. "Come along, my dears. Let's begin!"

She herded four young ladies to the piano, while Henry led Isabella to her chair between the squire and the baron and stood behind her, letting his hand rest on the chair's back, not two inches from her shoulder. Lady Chancellor noticed, her eyes gleaming with excitement, prompting Henry to smile at his unlikely ally.

The young ladies opened the concert with their quartet, a four-handed piano accompaniment lending it weight. Then came a fine performance on the harp, followed by a string of young men and women singing and playing instruments with varying degrees of skill. When Lady Landover motioned for Isabella to come to the front, Henry followed her and settled at the harpsichord.

Her voice was strong and clear, and perfectly suited to the simple yet powerful song, but by the time she concluded with the lines "If I show him my boldness / He'd ne'er love me again," Henry was certain the song had meaning for her. He could feel her sadness over her self-imposed loneliness, and he took heart; surely he would be able to change her mind if she didn't wish to be alone.

Taking their bow amidst steady applause, Henry brought Isabella's gloved hand to his lips. "That was lovely, my dear. You'll have to sing for me again soon." He then took his place at the pianoforte, and a hush fell over the assembled guests while Isabella took her seat.

It was obvious a number of people in the audience had heard Sir Henry play on other occasions and were in expectation of a treat. It felt special to Isabella that he should smile at her at this moment, almost like he played for her alone.

The sonata began with a few strong chords and a brief introduction to the melody, building quickly in intricacy. Isabella recognized Sir Henry not only played with considerable skill but possessed the talent to imbue the music with emotion, to bring out the sheer lilting beauty of the piece. Lady Landover turned the pages for him, but he barely glanced at the sheet music. Once he progressed beyond the initial chords, the music his fingers created on the keys of the piano wound itself around him and took him to a place where only the music itself existed, and the audience willingly followed. It was indeed a treat, and after the last note floated through the room, applause thundered in its wake.

Everyone then agreed it was time to take a break and go in search of refreshments.

Henry made his way back to Isabella's side, and she instinctively reached for both his hands. "That was simply marvelous. I could listen to you all day, but I'm decided you shall never hear *me* play that particular instrument."

Henry laughed and gave her hands a little squeeze before he reluctantly let go of them. "I'm quite content to accompany you while you sing. However, I'm no virtuoso. I can play a few pieces well, but never did practice enough to be truly good. It's my grandmother who is the musician in the family."

Lady Kistel leaned over the squire to get Isabella's attention. "I hear his daughter, Emily, is following in her footsteps." She then grinned up at Henry. "Ruth tells me she is the best student she's ever had, including you."

Henry chuckled. "Ah, Emily's twin obsessions: horses and music. The little dervish is about to overtake me on both counts." He smiled down at Isabella and added, "You will meet both of them soon. My grandmother, the Dowager Duchess of Avon, is bringing my daughter to Brighton for a visit."

Smiling, Isabella took the champagne Henry had plucked off a passing waiter's tray. "I'd love to meet your daughter."

Taking a sip from his own glass, Henry contemplated his fair companion. There was not a single thing he disliked about this woman and quite a few he liked very much. Now he just had to find out the reason for her reluctance to wed.

CHAPTER THIRTEEN

THE NEXT DAY DAWNED BRIGHT AND CLEAR, SO Henry sent word he would pick Isabella up at ten o'clock and drive them to the footpath leading to the abbey. Sally was of course disappointed not to be visiting the modiste, but soon reconciled herself to the delay when her mistress pointed out she wouldn't have to trudge to the abbey, since there would be no room for her in the curricle and a groom would be present for propriety's sake.

Isabella answered that she would be delighted. It was no small thing to be spared the walk through town and beyond to get to the path, not to mention having the pleasure of Sir Henry's company.

Promptly at ten o'clock Henry appeared at Mrs. Curtis's door, bowed politely over the beaming baroness's hand, and got permission to take Isabella on a picnic at the famous landmark. Once at the footpath, Henry swung Isabella off the high seat, pulled a picnic hamper and a blanket from the box, and instructed his groom, Roberts, to return for them in the late afternoon.

Isabella wondered for a moment if her mother would have agreed to the outing had she known Sir Henry wouldn't bring his groom, but then dismissed the thought. Miraculously, she trusted this man. She had a day of freedom and painting ahead of her; why trouble herself with details?

Both thoroughly enjoyed their ramble through the Downs. The

rain had added new vibrance to flowering meadows, and once they reached their destination, they spread the blanket in the shade of a gnarled old oak tree and ate their lunch amidst the lush green of an English summer.

Isabella declared the abbey a subject Gothic and gloomy enough to satisfy even the most romantic art patron. She made several sketches to work from on rainy days at home, then spent the afternoon painting a watercolor of the overgrown, doorless front portal of the ruined church. The pointed arch and ivy-covered masonry seemed to promise mysteries, even to a habitually rational young woman like herself.

Henry stayed close by as long as Isabella sketched in the ruins, remembering the unsettling sensations he had felt while wandering through the Gothic structure by himself. Today these sensations were compounded by the feeling they weren't alone in the abbey. However, out in the open the impression dissipated, so when she settled under the oak tree to paint, he left her side. Henry was now positive the abbey held mysteries and set about searching the area within a half-mile radius of it as thoroughly as he knew how. Last time he had looked closely at the ruins and the immediate surroundings, but now he walked outward in a star-shaped pattern, coming back to check on Isabella every half hour or so.

Isabella liked painting by herself, but in these strange ruins, she was glad to see Henry every time he came wandering back. She'd had the oddest feeling of being watched while sketching in the abbey. The sensation wasn't as prominent out under the oak tree, but still, it was good to know Henry never ventured far. To her mind, Gothic ruins were overrated, and the quicker she finished with her painting, the better.

Henry's search of the area confirmed there was no secret tunnel into the abbey unless it originated from Warthon Castle. From the hill behind the Gothic ruins the castle was clearly visible. Surrounded by parkland, it stood about a mile to the north. The castle was moated by a man-made lake as square as the structure itself. That made a tunnel from the castle unlikely, but not impossible. There were other structures in and around the park from which a tunnel could originate, but it was also entirely possible there was no tunnel, and everyone taking part in a meeting of the Knights simply walked or rode to the abbey.

In Hampstead their meeting place had been underground and accessible by tunnels, but Astor's dungeon had also been on common land in a fairly populated area. This was private land. Who would notice a few men heading out to the abbey late at night? Thanks to the rumors of the haunting, if the locals saw them, they would just assume them to be ghosts.

Still contemplating the issue, Henry sauntered to where Isabella stood back from her easel, appraising her day's work. He studied her painting for a few moments. "I think I like this ruin better in your picture than in real life."

Isabella nodded thoughtfully. "I know what you mean. There seems to be something a little disturbing in the air around this place. I admit to being rather anxious to depart before the sun sets."

Henry leaned a little closer, but refrained from draping a protective arm around her. "I'm quite satisfied with my day's exploring, so if you are finished painting, we can pack up and leave right now."

Isabella let her eyes travel between the scene in front of her and her painting one more time and sighed. "Yes, I am indeed finished. There is something not quite right about it, but I can't work out what it is."

Henry looked between her, the abbey, and the painting, and shook his head. "I can't see anything wrong with it. In fact, I think it's very good, even if the subject is a gloomy Gothic ruin."

Isabella patted his arm and grinned. The compliments he paid her skill as a painter always made her a little giddy. "It's the Gothic ruin that troubles me."

"How so?"

She stroked her middle finger back and forth along her chin in a thoughtful gesture, her eyes on the painting. "There is something wrong with the proportions, but I can't work out what."

Taking the board with the painting pinned to it off the easel, she leaned it against the oak tree and folded up her easel. "Do you still have that little book about the abbey?"

Henry was curious himself now. If her trained painter's eye detected an abnormality, perhaps there were stairs contained within the walls of the abbey after all.

"Yes, it's back at the hotel."

Isabella turned to him and smiled. "Can I borrow it for a day? It had a rather good drawing of the ruins in it. Perhaps it can shed light on the proportions mystery."

Henry folded the picnic blanket and returned her smile. "By all means, I seem to recall the drawing of the portal had far less foliage obstructing the walls than there is now."

"Precisely," Isabella agreed.

THEY PACKED UP IN COMPANIONABLE silence and headed back the way they'd come. Isabella bore the now-empty hamper with the blanket folded inside, while Henry carried her much heavier painting bag over his shoulder and held her board under his arm like he had done the day they got caught in the rainstorm. They were starting to work as a team, developing routines, feeling comfortable in each other's company. Henry loved the ease of their interactions and the lack of formality.

For her part, Isabella walked alongside Henry and wondered why it was so much easier to be with him than with any of her friends or siblings. She reasoned it to be their shared appreciation of nature and all things beautiful, but if she was honest with herself, she knew there was more to it. Walking next to Sir Henry, being at ease with him, enjoying his company, she asked herself for the first time in almost seven years why, precisely, there couldn't be anything more.

Neither wore gloves due to the heat, so every time Henry took Isabella's hand to help her over some obstacle, she felt the intimacy of his physical proximity. His hands were warm and dry, as well as manly and strong, and although that combination would have unnerved her with any other man, she had to admit she liked his touch. Henry was an uncommonly attractive man, and what she felt was visceral, and physical, and entirely new to her. Could it be that other, more intimate things might be different with him too? But then, what did it matter? Her path was set; safe, predictable, and entirely hers. Best to just enjoy his friendship and avoid daydreams.

They walked in the late afternoon light, mostly in silence, lost in their respective contemplations, sharing a smile and a touch here and there. A little less than an hour later, they arrived at the road, where Roberts awaited them. It was roughly an hour until dinnertime, so Henry offered, "The Waterfront is almost on our way to Mrs. Curtis's house. We could stop off and send one of the bellboys to retrieve the guidebook from the salon."

Isabella directed a tired smile his way as he helped her into the curricle. "I would appreciate that. The quicker I take another look at the drawing, the more likely I am to recognize the problem. I feel I am missing something important about the building."

Henry waited for her to arrange her skirts and then handed up her painting and her bag. "It's settled, then."

BUT, LIKE MOST PLANS, IT didn't account for the unexpected. Not that the arrival of the dowager duchess and Emily was unexpected per se; Henry just hadn't foreseen it for that very evening. They had just pulled up outside the Waterfront, and Henry had instructed one of the boys to fetch the book, when Emily appeared in the open doorway and shrieked, "Papa! Papa! You're finally here."

Pure delight suffused Henry's face when he caught sight of his daughter, but her shriek elicited a sigh. "And now the whole of Brighton is aware of that fascinating fact."

Henry hopped off the high seat just in time to catch Emily, who had launched herself into his arms. Using her momentum, he swung her in a full circle, earning him a squeal in his left ear, prompting him to set her down with a grimace. "I'm glad you are here, Poppet. How was your journey, and where is Grossmama?"

Emily, completely immune to her father's discomfort, beamed up at him. "Grossmama got too hot in the carriage today, so she's resting in our rooms. Will and I sent her up some soup. I don't think she'll come down for dinner, you know how she is about eating late."

The pageboy returned with the book, and Henry handed him a

penny for his troubles, but kept his focus on Emily. "Indeed, Poppet. I'll visit her just as soon as I've escorted Miss Chancellor home."

Emily didn't register the latter part of her father's remark. She stood there, her head cocked to the side, her hands set on her hips, ready to do battle. "Papa, you really have to stop calling me Poppet. I'm getting much too old for it." She accompanied the comment with an exaggerated eye roll, oddly contrasting her battle pose. Isabella had to bite her lip in order not to laugh out loud.

Henry tried his best to contain his own amusement, and pulled her forward. "I'm sorry if you don't like it, Poppet, but you're my daughter and therefore will always be my Poppet. Now, can you stop being a heathen so I can introduce you to my friend?"

"Oh!" was all Emily could manage as she assessed the stranger in her father's curricle, but once she caught herself, her manners took over. She curtsied and smiled and waited to be introduced.

Isabella sensed she was being evaluated as to her suitability and worthiness of Sir Henry's attention. She almost wanted to tell the girl they were only friends, but that would've been wholly inappropriate.

Henry, unaware of his daughter's critical appraisal, handed the book up to Isabella, then motioned to Emily. "Miss Chancellor, this is my daughter, Emily." Turning back to Emily, he added, "Emily, this is my friend Miss Chancellor."

Emily curtsied again and kept the polite smile in place, but it had warmed a little. "How do you do, Miss Chancellor?"

Isabella felt a sense of relief at the subtle change in the girl's expression and reached down to shake hands with Sir Henry's beautiful daughter. "I'm pleased to make your acquaintance, Miss March."

Emily's smile warmed a little morc at the use of her formal name.

The girl really was stunning. Isabella estimated her to be about fifteen, with the too-slender long arms and legs of an adolescent. But her breasts were already well developed, and she was drawing attention from the male hotel guests. Emily had the most beautiful skin, showing none of the blemishes usually marring girls her age. Her blue eyes were wide and expressive, her hair silvery blond and shiny, and her face exquisitely fine featured. However, she showed none of the fragility that afflicted some blondes and which was carefully cultivated by some of the fashionable misses. Her whole being was imbued with energy and determination, and Isabella had the distinct feeling young Emily was a force to be reckoned with.

Isabella smiled. "I regret not being able to stay and become better acquainted, but I'm sure we will meet again very soon."

Henry waved at Lady Kistel, who had appeared in the bay window of the salon a while ago. She had followed the meeting between Emily and Isabella with interest, and now waved back at Henry, indicating she would look after Emily. Henry nodded his thanks and turned to Emily. "Poppet, why don't you keep Lady Kistel company whilst I take Miss Chancellor home? Then we can dine together."

Emily grinned and in that moment looked the very spit of her father. "That's what Grossmama said when she begged off for the rest of the day, only she told me to keep Lady Kistel company till you got back, and not to call her for dinner."

Emily curtsied to Isabella, who inclined her head in a polite farewell. "Until we meet again, Miss March."

Henry watched his daughter until she disappeared into the foyer in the direction of the salon, and climbed back into the driver's seat.

He couldn't contain the smile on his face; it had been so very long.

First the season, then the measles, the scandal, and finally the Brighton mission. It was good to see Emily, hold her, know she was still his little girl, but he was also nervous about Isabella's reaction to his almost grown and boisterous daughter.

"I'm sorry about the delay, but I'm glad you met my daughter. She is a very big part of my life."

Some of Henry's worry must have reflected in his face, for Isabella answered him with a reassuring smile. "She's absolutely beautiful, your Emily. You must be so proud."

Henry beamed. "She is, isn't she? She takes after her mother more and more, now she is growing into a woman." He cringed a little at the thought of Emily growing up. "She'll have to get used to having a maid or, better still, a footman with her. I didn't like the way she was being ogled just now. She is an heiress too. Double trouble, as far as keeping her swains at bay will be concerned."

Isabella frowned at the thought. "You should plan a few outings with her. She doesn't strike me as the kind of young woman who is content to sit and embroider handkerchiefs."

Henry laughed out loud. "You don't know how right you are. In fact, that's why she's here: to keep her out of the way so her cousin can catch a husband." He contemplated the calm ocean sparkling before them in the golden evening sun. "If the weather is sunny again tomorrow, I shall hire one of the bathing machines. Would you like to join us? You could take the opportunity to make more close-up studies of the waves. What do you say?"

Isabella didn't have to think at all. "I would be delighted and most appreciative of the opportunity. I may even do some bathing myself."

"It's settled then. We'll go swimming tomorrow."

CHAPTER FOURTEEN

AS HENRY TURNED THE CORNER INTO BROAD Street, a lone rider approached Warthon Castle at a fast clip from the north. The castle was an impressive gray granite structure, square and bold, set into the lake surrounding it on all sides. It had guard towers on all four corners, and a parapet ran along its roof, but the windows were too large for a medieval structure. And indeed the castle had been built by the second Earl of Warthon in the sixteenth century.

The rider, however, paid no mind to the majestic building, nor to the genteel parkland surrounding it. He had dispensed with a hat, leaving his blond mane wild and uncovered, but his dark blue riding coat and buckskin breeches were exquisitely cut and molded to his athletic body like a second skin. He reined in his dappled gray gelding just before he reached the drawbridge and cantered into the courtyard, where a smartly dressed young man hurried from one of the lesser buildings to greet the new arrival. He did not bow, but smiled warmly and held the horse's head. "Pleasant journey, my lord?"

The blond gentleman dismounted with easy grace, but remained next to his horse and grinned with a familiarity suggesting they were friends, not just master and servant. "Rather. The coach will arrive after dark. Make sure the ladies are accommodated in the usual fashion."

The young man nodded his dark head. "The east tower is ready. Do you want one of them to be sent to the hall later?"

The young lord patted the steed's neck and shook his head. "Not unless the earl asks for one. I would rather they were rested and unmarked for tomorrow. How are things here?"

"The same. Your Sir Henry is busy in Brighton courting the Chancellor girl. Moses saw them at the abbey today, but they only came so she could draw. And your grandfather is busy with his guests." The man started to lead the horse toward the stables, but was held back.

"Guests, Ben? I thought it was only Weld?"

Ben shrugged. "Don't worry, Max, it's just Lady Jane driving everyone crazy. Bradshore came a day early to brag about his title, and that cretin Ostley arrived this afternoon. Has the old men all excited about something."

Max, Lord Didcomb, heir to the Warthon earldom, ran his hand through his wind-tousled hair. "Cretin indeed. He was one of Astor's creatures and has a longstanding grievance against the good Sir Henry. I do hope he doesn't intend to interfere with my well-laid plans."

Ben's clear blue eyes sparkled with mischief. "I doubt he has the brains, or the power, to prove much of an obstacle. How are your well-laid plans? Am I a rich man yet?"

There was a matching spark in Lord Didcomb's jade-green orbs. "You are, my friend. I told you I'd take you with me, didn't I? The *Enterprise* came in last week, laden with silks and tea, amongst other things, and once we know exactly how much money we made on the venture, I will invest some of it into the railway project. With a little luck the railway will be the way to travel, thirty years from now." Lord Didcomb grew thoughtful. "I wonder whether I could draw Sir Henry into the fold with it. An agent of his caliber snooping around is decidedly uncomfortable; better to have him on the inside." The last was said more to himself, so Ben took it as his cue to take the horse to the stable. Max, lost in thought, made his way across the courtyard.

Whoever had designed the castle had decided to dispense with the medieval theme on the inside. The interior was entirely Tudor. Dark polished oak paneled the walls and dominated the grand staircase leading from the foyer to the upper floors. Lord Didcomb waved the ancient butler aside and made his way past the staircase to the back of the castle and into the hall. There he found his grandfather, the Earl of Warthon, huddled together with the Earl of Weld, the newly minted Viscount Ridgeworth, and Baron Ostley. They were silhouetted against a fireplace big enough to roast an ox in.

All four men looked up at the sound of Max's approach, but it was the old man with the unrelenting ice-blue stare who greeted him. "About time you graced us with your presence, boy."

The young lord's shoulders tensed almost imperceptibly as he bowed. "My lords." Then he turned to the baron and fixed him with a stare not unlike his grandfather's. "Ostley, I hope you had a pleasant journey. I take it you're here for the feast and the display?"

Ostley looked rather proud of himself and was about to say something when the old earl banged his ivory-carved cane on the oaken floorboards and snapped, "Of course he is, boy. What else would he be doing here?"

Lord Didcomb's eyes were still on the baron, whose mouth snapped shut. Max had lived long enough in his grandfather's formidable shadow to know something was afoot and decided to probe further once his grandfather had succumbed to his gout and gone up to bed. He turned to the Earl of Weld and addressed the other issue on his mind. "My lord, am I correct in the assumption Lady Jane has seen fit to remain here?"

The earl heaved a put-upon sigh. "She's got it into her head I need her here."

Max had known Lady Jane since birth and was positive she had no concern for her father's health, but rather wished to make herself indispensable to the Knights. What she failed to appreciate was that to flout eight hundred years of tradition was to put herself in danger. "She needs to be gone by the time I come down for breakfast tomorrow."

The Earl of Weld looked chagrined, to say the least, but tried to explain. "She keeps insisting she needs to speak with you, that she is waiting for you."

Max could barely hold on to his temper. "Why would you allow such nonsense? There is a good reason why our women are not allowed anywhere near these meetings, have you forgotten?"

The earl flashed him an annoyed look. "Indeed I have not. And if you ask me, a claiming might be her only chance to catch a husband now."

Lord Didcomb snorted in disgust. So that was the plan. Not if he could help it. "I'll see Jane now, so there will be no obstacle to her speedy departure in the morning."

Max turned back to his grandfather, who had watched him throughout the exchange with a curious mixture of pride, disapproval, and affection. He kissed the back of the old man's outstretched hand. "I shall convey all news over dinner, sir. I still have a lot to prepare."

The old earl waved him away with an impatient "Bah," but then addressed his departing back. "Just make sure the display is more interesting than the last one. At the very least, chain them to the altar so they can't hide behind their hair and such. The Knights come from all over the country for this, you know."

Max gritted his teeth and continued to make his way to the door. "Yes, sir, I am aware of your preferences."

And thanks to Mary and her big mouth, he was now also aware of the good Reverend Bradshore's rather disturbing tastes. For a girl like her to run out on a lucrative arrangement, things must have gotten very rough indeed. He would have to watch the man, especially now he'd gained a title. It would be just like his grandfather to use his former lapdog's new status to block reforms long overdue.

Max made his way back to the foyer, where some commotion heralded the arrival of another player in this continuous game he engaged in with his grandfather. Ever since the last dungeon master, Lord Astor, had so spectacularly died in his own dungeon, Max had taken it upon himself to forge a new direction and purpose for the organization, one that was more closely aligned to its medieval origins. He considered his grandfather's generation's political leanings as pointless, since there were no Stewarts left to restore to the throne.

Lord Jennings, the present dungeon master, was an intricate part of Max's plans, but not someone Max trusted. He plastered a pleasant smile on his face, greeted the new arrival with a handshake, and got right down to business.

"Jennings, I'm glad you're here already. The earl just admonished me to offer a display more to his taste this time and at least to chain the women to the altar so they can't hide their charms. We will have to shift some equipment to the abbey after all. I'm not well pleased with having to use manpower for that instead of for securing the surrounding area."

Jennings returned the smile. "Well, my boy, we might just have to pack the ladies and some equipment into a hay wagon and drive out there, set it up well in advance, and then return to dinner."

Max shook his head. "I don't dare go out there before dark with Sir Henry on our scent. He found out about Mary; Ben saw him at the Red Lion. And he paid a visit to the Widow Twill. The man is too smart for us to ignore his presence in the area. Besides, all the footmen are needed to serve dinner, so we would have to rely solely on Ben. Although he knows about it, I don't think he could operate the pulley system by himself and chain the ladies before we get there with the crowd."

Lord Jennings slapped his riding crop into his gloved hand a few times, mulling the problem over in his head. "I could leave when the cognac is served and help Ben chain the girls. It's almost expected of me to have to prepare. Who will I have to work with?"

Max nodded. "That might work. I would do it, but I can't leave the newer members alone in the wolf's den. You have Patsy, Marie, and the new girl, Jenny." Max indicated the crop with his head. "Apropos, go easy with the whip. Some of the new gents haven't even been to the club yet, so we should leave off the more acquired tastes."

Jennings had an evil little grin on his face, reminding Max of his grandfather's just before he would tell him to bend over and hold on to the desk.

"Well, I have to at least crop them, or the old guard will have me replaced."

Max grunted a grudging acknowledgment. "Perhaps you should crop Marie; at least she doesn't mind. Then we force them all to take our cocks down their throats and fuck Patsy together. We could suspend her with the pulley system, her arms high above her head and her legs spread wide. This year's honoree can have Jenny, whom we'll tie to the altar stone. Does that sound debauched enough for you?"

Jennings laughed out loud. "For someone professing not to care for any of our games, you have quite a talent for staging them. Have one of the girls try to escape—that always gets them going. And have them all tied up in the corner. We can chain them when we get there and use the pulley system for the second half of the display."

Max grinned and nodded his approval of the amended plan, then headed for the stairs. "Oh, I like the power and submission games! It's the whips and chains I'm not overly fond of."

WITH THE PLANS FOR THE display settled, Max turned his attention to the task of saving his childhood friend from being forced into marriage with one of the attending Knights. There hadn't been a claiming for over three hundred years, the practice too medieval even for the Knights. But Max had observed the Earl of Weld in his club, and didn't doubt him capable of such cruelty toward his daughter.

A claiming, as it was recorded in the old documents, was an archaic practice, designed to keep all the wealth within the circle of the Knights. His grandfather had forced Max to study those documents after he'd decreed he should live at Warthon rather than with his mother.

Max made it to his friend's door without coming up with an explanation why Jane had to leave so urgently. He would have to risk his grandfather's wrath and tell her some of the truth. Knocking, he entered almost before he heard her muffled response.

Lady Jane Castleright stood up from behind her writing desk by the window, shook out the folds of her unassuming taupe walking dress, and beamed at her visitor. "Diddy, I've been waiting for you." She stepped toward him with a conspiratorial glint in her eyes. "I knew you would come for the Knights' dinner, and I just have to talk to you."

Max walked over to buss her cheek, and led her to the sofa by the ornately carved but empty fireplace. "Whatever for, Jane? I told you to get out of Brighton and to stay away from my grandfather. And what do you do? You move less than five miles out of town and sit yourself right into the hornet's nest."

Lady Jane smiled with complete confidence in her own assessment of the situation. "Oh, Warthon is just an old curmudgeon. His gout improved since I told Cook to stop serving pork, and he has warmed to me considerably in the last couple of days. Papa even stopped asking me to return to Weld."

Max turned his eyes to the ceiling, seeking strength, and tried his best to address her various misconceptions. "Jane, you need to leave, and I mean without delay. The women of our families haven't attended gatherings like the one tomorrow for more than three hundred years."

Lady Jane interrupted him in her usual abrupt manner. "That's precisely why I have decided to stay. It's utterly ridiculous to keep us from these functions, and it's about time there were some changes made. How am I to take an active role if I can't attend the functions where decisions will be made? But I'm about to change all that, and you'll help me."

Max ran both hands through his hair in frustration. Perhaps he should just let her stay and go through with the claiming; it would certainly solve all his problems with her. But she was his friend, and he would end up feeling sorry for her, and then he might end up claiming her himself, and he had no desire to be married to the little harpy.

"Jane, you need to stop deluding yourself and listen to me. The reason my grandfather is reasonably nice to you is not that he has warmed to you. He is gleefully awaiting your humiliation, which will come tomorrow if you don't leave in time. I can't tell you any of the hows or whats, but I can tell you the why. He has convinced your father that after the Sir Henry disaster, your only chance to get married is to be offered to a member of the Knights. He might even hope I'll feel sorry for you and offer. I suppose he thinks matrimony would make me more controllable."

Jane looked at him as if he'd gone mad. "I'm over twenty-one. My father can't force me to marry."

Max just shook his head and stood. "He wouldn't have to. You wouldn't dare to object after what they'd do to you."

Lady Jane looked at him for a moment longer, then burst out laughing. "How wonderfully dramatic of you. You should suggest that to Mrs. Radcliffe for one of her novels."

Max had always known Jane was stubborn, even bullheaded, but this was the moment he lost his temper and took his childhood friend by her shoulders to give her a good shake. "Pack your things and be gone from here by the time I come down for breakfast or, so help me, I'll carry you out of here and throw you in the coach myself. Is that clear?"

With that he turned on his heel and left her standing there, open mouthed and indignant.

CHAPTER FIFTEEN

THE SUN SHONE BRIGHTLY ON AN AZURE BLUE sea, beckoning bathers to come dip their feet in the gentle waves. It was a pull most strongly felt by the young, resulting in a certain young lady being rather impatient. Henry had yet to emerge from his bedchamber when Emily stormed into his sitting room, where William was laying out breakfast.

"Good Lord, William, he hasn't broken his fast yet?" She picked a rasher of bacon from the breakfast platter, took a bite, and threw herself into one of the chairs by the empty fireplace. "Honestly, how can he sleep this long? It's past eight already. Grossmama and I have been up for hours. Can't you wake him? I want to try out these bathing machines." The whole speech was one continuous flood of words, lasting until the speaker finally ran out of breath.

A grin tugged at William's lips as he carried on setting the table. "Your papa will wake soon enough."

Emily lounged in her chair, impervious to the still-chilly English summer morning, her pose in contrast to her impatiently jiggling foot. "He better, or I will go in there and pull his covers off." The last bite of her bacon disappeared into her mouth and she made as if to rise, prompting William to step between her and his master's door in some alarm.

Breaking into a delighted peal of laughter, Emily slumped back into the chair. "You should see your face, Will."

Her laughter turned into a snort when William rolled his eyes and muttered under his breath, "Should've known."

"Don't pout, Will, I got you fair and square."

At that moment, Henry emerged from his bedchamber, walked over to his daughter, and bent to kiss her cheek as she raised her torso up to meet him halfway. "Good morning, Poppet."

"Good morning, Papa. Can we go swimming now?"

Chuckling, Henry made his way to the table. "May I eat my breakfast first?"

A big put-upon sigh slumped Emily back into her chair. "If you must, Papa. But for the love of God, hurry."

Amused, Henry sat and spread his napkin with deliberate leisure before he poured his coffee. Then he turned and winked at his mulish daughter. "I see your aunt still hasn't broken you of taking the Lord's name in vain."

Emily couldn't help the smile, banishing the pout from her beautiful face, and when the dimple appeared in her cheek, Henry knew it wouldn't be long before she joined him at the table to indulge in a second breakfast.

"Oh, but she thinks she has, and that's all that counts, according to Uncle Arthur. He is quite devious really. He constantly lets her think he is agreeing with her, then goes and does the opposite. She never even notices." She wrinkled her nose in thought. "I don't think I would like my husband to tell me what I want to hear just so I leave off harassing him. Come to think of it, I don't think I want a husband who lets me harass him. I want someone who will talk to me and I can trust to make the right decision."

She had strolled over to the breakfast table during her little speech and taken a cup of coffee her father had poured for her. Stirring liberal amounts of sugar and cream into it, she helped herself to another piece of bacon before she took a seat at the table.

Henry set down his coffee cup and smiled at his daughter. She wasn't just growing up physically, she was maturing in other ways, too, and he liked the woman she was becoming. "That's what I want for you, too, Poppet. Someone who loves you and appreciates you for who you are as a person, not just your pretty face or your money."

Emily preened, having zeroed in on the comment about her appearance. "You think I'm pretty?"

His mouth full of eggs and mushrooms, Henry winked at his daughter, but then grew more serious. "Yes, Poppet, I think you are very pretty. And so does half the male population of this hotel, and no doubt the town, once they lay eyes on you." All amusement vanished from his expression as he remembered the ogling she'd been subjected to the evening before. "This town is full of bachelors on the lookout for amusement, so no trips down the road to the shops or strolls on the beach without either me, William, or Grossmama; understood?"

The playfulness melted from Emily's face, and she looked at her father in some distress. Henry didn't issues orders very often, but there was no question he expected his decrees to be obeyed when he did resort to giving them. She searched his eyes, trying to gauge how serious he was, and seeing the resolve, lowered her gaze with a quiet "Understood."

They sat and ate in silence for a while until Henry inquired, "Does Grossmama intend to come down to the beach with us?"

Grateful for the change of subject, Emily nodded eagerly while she swallowed the last bite of her scone. "She said she would have them carry a chair down to the surf for her, but that wild horses wouldn't get her into a bathing machine."

Henry smiled at his daughter repeating his grandmother's phrasing. "Why don't you go and organize the chair for Grossmama? And have them put one into the bathing machine for Miss Chancellor so she can paint the waves from there. I'll go fetch her."

Emily looked at him thoughtfully. "You like Miss Chancellor, don't you? And not just because she's suitable and available. You like her."

Henry brushed a strand of silky blond hair out of his daughter's face, then let his hand rest on her shoulder and met her gaze with equal sincerity. "Yes, I like her. Miss Chancellor has purpose, an independent spirit, and is a very talented artist. She is smart and funny, and I very much hope you will like her too."

Emily patted his cheek in a gesture that would have been patronizing had she not been fifteen, and his daughter. "If you like her, I'm sure I will."

Henry pulled her into his arms for a quick squeeze, kissed her rosy cheek, and turned to shout for William: "Will, help Emily and my grandmother down to the beach with the chairs and organize the bathing machine. I shall meet you there in half an hour."

BY THE TIME HENRY RETURNED with Isabella, their party had claimed a sizable portion of the beach directly in front of the hotel. Several chairs had been brought down to the water's edge, and Henry was pleased to see Lady Kistel had joined their group. He was less pleased, however, to find a gaggle of young men attached to the ladies, no doubt to ogle Emily. The object of all this inappropriate attention was blissfully unaware of it and fully engaged in driving the owner of a bathing machine to distraction.

Henry handed the reins to Roberts and instructed a page to unload Isabella's painting kit from the box. With the practicalities taken care of, he jumped off with a graceful turn of his body and lifted Isabella down, enjoying the opportunity to hold her for a moment. Isabella didn't believe in corsets on a hot summer's day, and Henry felt like blessing the inventor of jumps, for they allowed him to feel the warmth and weight of her breasts against his thumbs when she bent forward to steady herself against his shoulders. Of course he let go of her the instance her feet were firmly on the ground, but Henry found himself increasingly affected by Isabella's physical presence. He reached for her hand to pull it through the crook of his arm, and led her down to the beach.

Isabella wondered at the strange giddiness possessing her whenever Henry was near. Why was she in a near swoon when his strong arms lifted her down from the curricle? If anyone had told her a fortnight ago she would soon relish the play of a man's muscles under her hand, she would've told them they had taken leave of their senses, but relish the play of Henry's muscles she did.

Walking down to the beach, Henry's attention was drawn to the young bucks. The presence of Mr. Wickham among them caused him a twinge of distaste.

"One of your admirers seems to have attached himself to our group. I suggest you stay close to Emily and me, especially when we go bathing."

"I'm planning on doing so in any event." Isabella smiled up at him, and Henry's heart did a little somersault. He returned her smile, but she had already turned back to the spectacle in front of them, the brim of her rather ridiculous poke bonnet obstructing his view of her beautiful face. Henry resolved to flout convention once again and replace the ruined wide-brimmed hat. Apart from affording him a better view of her face, it also seemed far more practical for painting; the poke brim of the current fashion obstructed her peripheral vision.

"Whatever is Emily so excited about?" she asked.

Following Isabella's line of sight, Henry found Emily waving a wildly accusing finger in a bemused-looking local's face. Henry deduced the man was the driver of the machine next to the one William had hired for them, which William was currently equipping with a chair. Their machine was a boxy sort of carriage with tiny windows and a door on the side of it as well as double doors and a platform with stairs that would lead into the ocean in the back. It had been pulled onto the sand and the horse was happily munching oats from a sack of feed around its neck. But the horse next door was forced to stand in the waves and was obviously miserable. It seemed the machine was occupied and the driver had decided not to unhitch the horse while the occupants were bathing. Emily no doubt was incensed by the driver's disregard for the horse's well-being. Henry knew without a shadow of a doubt he would have to intercede on the horse's behalf, and lengthened his stride to get there before the situation escalated. He noticed with pleasure that Isabella matched his pace before he could ask her to; he patted her hand in approval, earning himself a grin from underneath her voluminous brim.

The commotion had attracted the attention of the young bucks, one of whom seized the opportunity to make himself known to the young lady. Henry and Isabella came into hearing range just as the young man inquired, "What is this great oaf doing that has you so upset, miss?"

Emily turned toward him, face flushed, eyes flashing with anger. "If you have to ask, you are as stupid as he is."

The young man colored with embarrassment.

Emily, however, spotted Henry. "Oh, Papa, tell him to unhitch the horse! It's obvious it doesn't like standing backwards in the surf."

Henry noted with relief Emily was about as impressed with the local bucks as she was with her ducal cousins and smiled reassuringly at his daughter. "Take Miss Chancellor over to Grossmama and introduce her, Poppet." With that, he turned to the driver and handed him a crown, while Emily, her cause championed and her head held high in triumph, took Isabella's arm and led her toward the group around the dowager duchess.

What was said between Henry and the driver was drowned out by the sound of the waves, but within seconds the driver jogged to the horse and unhitched it without the slightest hesitation or delay.

Isabella watched the interchange over her shoulder. "I wonder what your father said to change the man's mind."

Emily chuckled, no longer interested in the man or his horse, now she had achieved her objective. "I haven't the foggiest idea. But my father can be downright scary when he takes command." Emily's grin was so easy, Isabella concluded Henry's daughter had never been taught to fear her father, and she was glad of it. In fact, Emily seemed to consider him her very own secret weapon.

"So he just commanded him?"

Emily laughed. "Of course he did, but the crown he handed him may have helped motivate the man to comply."

Isabella laughed too. In Emily she saw the same easy bravado she had admired in Henry on a number of occasions. The woman and the girl looked at each other, and everything seemed to still for a moment as they recognized within each other the free spirit trying to plot its way in a world governed by social rules.

Emily broke eye contact first as she took in the pale violet-lined brim of Isabella's hat and crinkled her nose in distaste. "That bonnet is atrocious."

A new peal of laughter stopped Isabella in her tracks. "Oh, please don't let my mother hear you say that. She thinks it *de rigueur* and insisted I should have it for our stay here."

Emily's grin was open and utterly irresistible. "Come shopping with me and Grossmama tomorrow, and we will find you something that suits you better." She then took Isabella's hand and pulled her unceremoniously through the throng of young men to her grandmother, throwing over her shoulder, "Come on, the sooner we get into the bathing machine, the quicker you can take that monstrosity off."

Still grinning when she found herself face to face with the Dowager Duchess of Avon, Isabella hastily sank into a curtsy of the appropriate depth. But Emily only laughed, bobbed the briefest of curtsies to Lady Kistel, and introduced Isabella with a flippant, "This is Miss Chancellor, Grossmama. Papa likes her."

Isabella blushed, sank a little deeper into her curtsy, and promptly forgot she was meant to wait until spoken to by such a great lady. "Your Grace, I'm honored to make your acquaintance."

Lady Kistel cackled her amusement. "They indeed made beautiful music together the other night."

The heat rising in Isabella was more annoyance than embarrassment now. Why did people always have to assume marriage to be a woman's only objective? She was just about to reply something to that effect when the dowager stepped in.

"Oh, hush, you two." The duchess then turned her attention to Isabella. "It's a pleasure to meet you, Miss Chancellor. Do come and sit down before your legs cramp up."

Isabella rose from her curtsy with as much grace as she could manage in the sand and smiled at the old lady with the slightly windswept steel-gray curls and the youthful blue eyes. Eyes just like Henry's, sparkling with the same mischief and *joie de vivre*. The old lady patted her hand and indicated the painting board and bag being loaded into the bathing machine. "You are planning on painting rather than bathing?"

Isabella let her eyes travel to the horizon and shrugged. "I was hoping to do both."

The dowager laughed. "In that case, I better organize a picnic on the beach for lunch." Then she leaned a little closer and added in a conspiratorial voice, "I believe I'm the proud owner of one of your paintings."

Isabella beamed, pleased to be acknowledged as an artist. "The watercolor of the Avon Springs Sir Henry bought?"

"Indeed. It's lovely and holds pride of place in my sitting room. I never could do much with paint and brush, but I appreciate art."

Isabella warmed to the topic and Henry's grandmother in equal measure. "Oh yes, Sir Henry mentioned your great talent on the pianoforte. And Lady Kistel teased him that Emily is following in your footsteps, already having surpassed him in skill. I find that hard to believe; he plays so very beautifully."

The dowager looked at her great-granddaughter with pride. "I love to play, and Emily is indeed my best student so far. But you are quite right, she lacks maturity, so she hasn't yet overtaken her father in expressing the music."

Their conversation was cut short when Henry called Isabella and Emily to the edge of the water, declaring the bathing machine ready for them to embark. He helped them into the dark interior of the little cabin on wheels, then flagged down one of the small boats allowing male bathers to strip down to their smallclothes and jump into the water farther out so they wouldn't offend the delicate sensibilities of the ladies present.

Inside the bathing machine, Isabella and Emily helped each other out of their dresses and stripped down to their chemises, holding on to each other and the walls to keep their balance as the cabin was maneuvered into the waves. Emily's enthusiasm for the whole adventure was so infectious, even being tossed into a corner when a wave hit the wagon from the side seemed like splendid fun. By the time they had stored all their valuables in the wooden boxes provided for the purpose, the machine was in place and the attendant, whom they had largely ignored, opened the back door for them.

They emerged just in time to watch Henry jump head first into the sparkling sea, in nothing but his drawers. Isabella had to admit his form, well-muscled and lean, was pleasing to the eye, but the prospect of bathing with him in such a state of undress was unsettling. Still, what harm could there be in looking?

Emily lost no time getting into the ocean. She didn't even consider the stairs, jumping right in, leaving only billowing cotton and hair on the surface, but immediately shot out of the water with a shriek of delight. "Holy hymns, it's cold! Use the stairs, Miss Chancellor. I'm going to swim to Papa to warm up, but we will be right back."

Isabella had progressed to the third step, where the cool water rose and sank around her calves and knees. "I think it's a little too late for formalities, don't you agree, Miss March? Call me Isabella."

Emily, who had already covered a quarter of the distance between herself and her father, turned and let a swell take her back toward Isabella. "I quite agree. Call me Emily."

Turning toward the open sea again, she employed the powerful stroke her cousin had taught her and swam to her father.

Left to her own devices, Isabella eased herself into the ocean for the first time in her life and reveled in the physical experience. The water was cold indeed, so she followed Emily's example and swam as vigorously as she knew how. However, she wasn't nearly as strong a swimmer as Henry's daughter, so she stayed close to the bathing machine and the attendant, who kept a watchful eye. She repeatedly swam a few strokes out to sea, then turned and let the swell of the next wave take her back. It was a marvelous game. Not only did it allow her to see how the waves started and then rolled into shore, but she could also feel the power of the water, note the currents flowing all around her, and taste the salt on her skin. Behind her, some ways off, she could hear Henry's reassuring baritone and Emily's excited chirps, but the words did not carry all the way to her. The water soothed her and exhilarated her all at the same time. She had seen the sea in such turmoil just days before, but now it was calm and felt smooth except for the sand that scraped her toes when the waves dipped.

Before long, Henry and Emily joined her in her little game. They bobbed in the waves for a good hour, easy banter flowing between them and their friendship growing. But eventually their skin pruned and the game grew old, so Isabella decided to climb back into the bathing machine to dress and get her sketchbook out.

CHAPTER SIXTEEN

HENRY CHALLENGED EMILY TO A RACE TO THE boat and back to give Isabella a moment of privacy as she got out of the water. The race also served to get him closer to the pier. A gentleman had been observing them rather intently for the past hour. The man had moved to the end of the pier and back a couple of times, but always returned to his observation of their game. There was something familiar about the figure, niggling at Henry's memory.

Bertie had taught Emily well: Henry had to exert himself to not let her win too easily. He lengthened his strokes as they neared the boat and used the opportunity to have a good look at the man on the pier. His face was in shadow under a brown top hat, and his clothes were befitting of a gentleman but worn without care. His hair was long and grayish blond, and even at this distance Henry could tell it was greasy. As Henry watched, the man turned to walk to the end of the pier again. But in that moment, the sun backlit his profile, and Henry's hunch was confirmed. The beaked nose and too-generous lips belonged to a man Henry hadn't crossed paths with in a very long time, and his presence in Brighton could mean all kinds of trouble. The profile belonged to none other than Baron Ostley, husband to Emily's mother, and Henry's bitter enemy.

Ostley's presence threw up a multitude of questions, but Henry doubted it was a coincidence. Father and daughter touched the boat at almost the same time, and as he raced Emily back to the bathing machine, Henry went through all the possible reasons for Ostley's presence. Several facts struck him as inescapable: the Earl of Warthon and his grandson, along with the Earl of Weld, were high-ranking members of the Knights. Both either resided in the area or had been seen in Brighton in the last fortnight. Ostley had been part of Astor's organization, but not at a high rank. His presence seemed to indicate a gathering of members. Henry had kept track of many of Ostley's associates in an attempt to avoid running into the man, but didn't know which of them were Knights.

And then another possibility made its ugly debut in Henry's head: the man could have come to the area in order to exact some kind of fifteen-years-overdue revenge on Henry. It was an unsettling thought, and Henry resolved to tighten security around his daughter. Life had taught him it was always best to be prepared.

That settled in his mind, Henry let Emily beat him to the bathing machine by a mere handspan, instructed her to get dressed for lunch, and made his way back to the boat to do the same.

Once back on the beach, he waved William behind the horses and out of the line of sight of the baron on the pier. "Will, I need you to follow the disheveled-looking fellow with the long greasy hair and the brown top hat once he leaves the pier. I'm pretty certain it's the Baron Ostley, and he has been looking at our group for over an hour."

William looked at Henry with a measure of alarm. "Not that Ostley?" William was familiar with his employer's story and immediately comprehended what this could mean for Miss Emily's safety.

Henry nodded in the affirmative and let the news sink in while William rubbed his forehead, trying to come up with an explanation for this turn of events. Eventually Will lifted his head and continued his thinking out loud. "Ostley is one of the Knights?" Henry nodded, so William continued, "And I just over'eard that Wickham fellow talk about some shindig at Warthon Castle tonight. Do you think it's a meeting?"

Henry clapped his old comrade on the shoulder. It was one of William's most useful qualities: he could always be relied upon to re-call an overheard conversation when it mattered. "Wickham is one of them too? Well done, Will. Who was he talking to?"

Will looked briefly in the direction of one of the young gentlemen who still milled about their group. "The blond one in the burgundy coat who looks like 'e caught the sun. He's somethin' or other in the city and was invited by Lord Didcomb, so I figure he'll be there too."

Henry grinned at his longtime companion and confidant. "Looks like we'll be able to observe the Knights in action sooner rather than later. I admit to being excited. Finally we are close enough to find out who the members are and what the objective of the organization is exactly. But Emily's safety must be assured, especially with Ostley tak-ing an interest."

William rubbed his hands together in anticipation of an adven-ture, but he also recalled the danger they'd all faced the last time they dealt with the Knights. This was no time to let their guard down. He spared his pristine gentleman's gentleman outfit a brief glance. "Right, I better get changed. I'll go up with the next batch of servants from the hotel and watch the good baron from the sittin' room window."

"And send Roberts down to help guard Miss Emily."

William nodded and headed over to tell the driver of the bathing machine to bring it in for lunch.

Henry assured himself the baron was still on the pier before taking up his place at his grandmother's side. Lunch was an impromptu affair, and afterwards Isabella climbed back into the wheeled cabin to spent the afternoon sketching in pencil and watercolor. The rest of the party amused themselves with countless innings of horseshoes and a noisy game of tug-of-war. The baron left his vigil in the early afternoon, when it became clear the party intended to spend all day on the beach, and Henry observed William following the man at a discreet distance once he regained the street.

The old ladies retreated to the hotel for their naps around three in the afternoon, and Isabella emerged from the bathing machine an hour later. Henry rushed to help her down the narrow steps and was admiring her watercolor of the waves when a fresh-faced, dark-haired young man, who had joined their group sometime after lunch, loped toward them. "Izzy, what a pleasant surprise. I didn't know you were in Brighton."

At the sound of the young man's voice, Isabella's head snapped in his direction, so Henry couldn't see her face, but her hand on his arm started to shake. Instantly on high alert, Henry put his hand over hers protectively, and she stepped closer to him. Something was clearly wrong, but she answered the man with the familiarity of an old friend.

"George, what are you doing here?"

George grinned broadly. "I'm staying with the Earl of Warthon for a few days." He then turned to Henry. "My apologies, Sir Henry. Let me introduce myself: I'm Viscount Ridgeworth."

Isabella was stunned. "Viscount? When did that happen? I thought you were fifth in line?"

George's hazel eyes spewed venom, but he gifted Isabella with a condescending smile. "Evidently no longer."

Henry had been aware of the viscount and the tragic accident allowing him to ascend to the title during the London season. The men exchanged small bows, but since Isabella's hand still shook under his, Henry was unwilling to let go of it. "How do you know Miss Chancellor, my lord?"

The young viscount preened at the use of the courtesy address. "We practically grew up together. My father held the living in Bilbury." He turned to Isabella again. "So where are you staying, Izzy? You are still unmarried, are you not? I better pay my respects to the baroness."

Isabella's fingers dug into Henry's arm, but she answered the viscount. "We are staying with Mama's friend Mrs. Curtis."

It wasn't lost on Henry she neglected to give the address, so he intervened. "Will you excuse us, Ridgeworth? Miss Chancellor has been working for the past few hours and is in need of refreshment and rest."

George tittered and rolled his eyes. "I see you're still painting. Well, I better get back to the castle. We shall meet again." He bowed and smiled, then turned and stalked through the sand toward the promenade.

Isabella's hand under Henry's slowly relaxed, until she finally turned to him with a smile. "Thank you, I am rather tired."

Henry knew there was more to it, but this was neither the place nor the time to press her further, so he led her to a chair and handed her a drink. Before long, Emily dragged her off to play horseshoes, and Isabella seemed back to her usual self.

EVERYONE LEFT THE BEACH AROUND five, exhausted but happy. Emily had made several friends among the young men in the group, ordering them about with the same careless efficiency with which she ruled her cousins. She was thoroughly unimpressed by one and all, and had nothing but contempt for Wickham. Henry was most pleased with his daughter's display of common sense and healthy skepticism.

As Emily skipped upstairs to wash the salt off her body, Henry escorted Isabella home. She and the baroness had a prior engagement for dinner, so Henry planned on a quiet evening meal with his family.

By the time he returned to the hotel, a tub of hot water was waiting for him, and William informed him a regular who-is-who of prominent members of society had descended on Warthon Castle throughout the day. Curiously, there were no women among them. Lady Jane had departed early in the morning, but had only gone as far as the next inn along the road to London. That particular bit of gossip had been volunteered by a very happy coach driver at the Red Lion. He'd been hired and paid the day before to take a lady all the way to Somerset, only to be dismissed by said lady a scant eight miles away at the next coaching inn. This all seemed very curious indeed and made Henry more hopeful than ever he was about to witness a meeting of the Knights, or perhaps even a ceremony. Without knowing what they actually did, he had nothing to report, and no way of stopping their nefarious activities.

ISABELLA SHUT HER BEDROOM DOOR behind her and collapsed against it. Closing her eyes, she tried to catch her breath as her whole body shook uncontrollably.

Sally dropped Isabella's freshly pressed gown on the nearest chair and rushed to her mistress. "What happened, miss?"

Isabella gratefully leaned on Sally, letting her lead her to the bed.

"George Bradshore is here." Isabella's voice was flat and barely audible.

Sally's heart sank. "Here in the house, or here in Brighton?"

"In Brighton. Sally, he is the viscount now."

The maid helped Isabella onto her bed and stroked her back to calm her. "How do you know?"

A sob escaped Isabella. "He came up to me at the beach and talked to me as if nothing had ever happened. If Sir Henry hadn't been there, I don't know what I'd have done."

Sally shook her head grimly. "We haven't set eyes on the blighter in seven years and now he shows up?" She lay down next to her crying mistress and gathered her in her arms.

Isabella wailed into Sally's shoulder, "What am I to do? I can't go out painting by myself any longer, and what if my mother decides to encourage him, now he is a viscount?"

Sally brushed the hair out of Isabella's face and looked into her panicked eyes. "Hush. I can always come painting with you, and Sir Henry seems to enjoy taking you, so let's not worry about that. And as for your mother encouraging him, just make it clear you've set your cap at Sir Henry. He might not have a title, but he has lots and lots of money, and his grandma's a duchess. That has to count for something with the baroness."

Isabella calmed a little. "You think that would work?"

Sally shrugged. "It will with the baroness. And with any luck, George Bradshore won't want to marry you."

Isabella wasn't shaking like a leaf any longer, but the tears were still flowing freely. "Oh, Sally, I wish I could simply go home. I'll be afraid of seeing him everywhere now."

GEORGE BRADSHORE, VISCOUNT RIDGEWORTH, ENTERED the great hall at Warthon Castle and poured himself a brandy. He still had to change for the big dinner, but first a little private celebration was called for. Isabella was even prettier than he remembered, notwithstanding that dowdy hat. The season had been a disappointment. Apparently his cousin's financial woes were well known, so the heiresses had been off limits to him. But not all was lost. In fact, things were decidedly looking up. George savored his first sip of the earl's most excellent brandy.

"You look chipper, Ridgeworth."

George turned and met the Earl of Warthon's calculating eyes. He had assumed himself alone in the hall at this hour, but perhaps it was just as well. He would need help putting his plan into action. "I just ran into my future wife! We grew up together. She is a baron's daughter and comes with just enough money to cover the dratted mortgage on the estate. The only problem is she won't want to marry me."

The earl barked a harsh laugh. "Sounds like just your type. What will you do?"

A sly smile crept across George's deceivingly boyish face. "Make myself agreeable to her mother, I think. Isabella herself seems to be quite partial to Sir Henry. He is courting her."

The earl's jaw clenched, and his cold eyes flashed with hate. "Don't waste your time on the mother; she's most likely blinded by March's money. Take my advice, boy. Get a special license and bring the girl here. The new curate will marry you and I will witness the consummation, so there won't be a damned thing anyone can do about it."

The plan had merit. Once he had a special license with Isabella's name on it, surely the bank could be stalled with the news of his impending nuptials. George grinned his approval. It was good to have powerful friends, even as a titled gentleman. He raised his glass in salute and drained it. "I best get dressed for dinner."

The Earl of Warthon rubbed his arthritic knee and contemplated this newest development. George Bradshore, now Viscount Ridgeworth, was a fool, and possibly a dangerous one, but it was always better to have two ways to strike at the enemy rather than just one. It looked like his wait for vengeance was finally coming to an end.

CHAPTER SEVENTEEN

HENRY AND WILLIAM RODE OUT IN THE DIREC-
tion of Hove, jumped the hedgerow onto Warthon land by the light
of the moon, and carried on about a mile before they left the horses
in a stand of trees southwest of the abbey. As they reached the grove,
Henry spotted an owl swooping down on some poor unsuspecting
field mouse in the meadow ahead and pointed to it. William nodded his agreement. On the Peninsula, they had spent countless hours
learning to imitate the call of various birds and animals. The true skill,
however, lay in spotting an animal or bird present in a locality at the
time so the call would blend into the place.

William surveyed the terrain in front of them and pointed to a
large oak tree standing on a small rise about halfway between them
and the thicket bordering the back of the abbey. The oak, once climbed,
would afford an excellent view in all four directions, and made a perfect spot for William to watch over Henry's progress.

The two men waited for a cloud to move in front of the almost-
full moon and then slipped soundlessly into the meadow, William
toward the tree, and Henry toward the thicket beyond. On the other
side of the meadow, Henry paused to listen and let his eyes adjust to
the gloom amongst the trees. There was no path to the abbey from
here, and the brambles were too thick for him to walk through without making a lot of noise. But his previous visits had revealed a cart

track located some ways to the left. It led from the castle past the abbey and continued on in the direction of Hove. Just as Henry decided on the cart track, two owl hoots sounded the all-clear behind him, but a third hoot after a short pause indicated activity ahead. Henry could barely contain his excitement at the prospect of finally learning something concrete about the Knights. They had eluded him for three long years, but no longer; Henry could feel it in his very bones. He stayed under the cover of the thicket until he reached the path, passed behind a sentry posted there, and crept up to the abbey undetected.

A few torches burned in the abandoned church, making it glow from within. Henry circled the ruin, counting three more guards strategically placed to notice anyone approaching. Armed with that knowledge, Henry made his way to the abbey itself, just as a cart approached from the castle side. Three scantily clad women were handed down and led into the abbey by a well-dressed young man, who seemed to be on familiar terms with the ladies. One of the women was a rather young-looking blond, the second a pretty brunette, and the third a curvaceous redhead who looked to be the most confident of the three and walked into the abbey as if she had been there before.

Henry managed to get to one of the windows and peered in. The dark-haired young man led the women into a windowless corner behind the low altar Henry had examined on his first visit, and pointed to a rope hanging from an iron hoop anchored into the wall. "We have about half an hour, ladies. Make sure the bindings look real, at least from up there." He indicated the arches above them, and Henry wondered if there was some kind of observation platform overlooking the altar. Both the thickened wall Isabella had detected and the feeling of being watched inside the abbey made sense if there was an observation platform above and a staircase leading there hidden inside the wall.

The young man stepped into the light of a torch, and Henry recognized him as the same man who had spoken to Mary, and upset her, in the Red Lion. As he lit and placed torches into wall sconces around the abbey, Henry got a good look at his hands. He wore no ring, suggesting he wasn't a Knight. The man turned back to the three women and grinned winningly. "I best get back to the castle. The gentlemen were getting rather inebriated last I checked, and Lord Didcomb might need help getting them into the tunnel." He then stroked the youngest girl's cheek. Now that Henry could see her face clearly, he noted she was remarkably pretty and seemed to enjoy the young man's attention. The man winked a clear blue eye at her. "Try to look suitably scared when they arrive, you are meant to be the virgin sacrifice."

All three women giggled, and the curvaceous redhead with the luminous, pale skin waved him away. "Not to worry, Mr. Ben, we know how to put on a show."

Ben blew her a kiss and turned to leave, but then thought of something and pointed to the altar. "Oh, and there is extra oil in a bowl on that little ledge, should you need it." He winked again and disappeared into the night.

HENRY PAUSED FOR A MOMENT, then slipped away from the window, sure of two things: a sexual display was about to take place for the enjoyment of the Knights, and the women to be used for the purpose were willing participants, like Mary had been. Henry wondered if these were changes implemented since the Astor fiasco, or if Astor had been the only one deranged enough to torture and kill women as part of the displays.

Due to his earlier reconnaissance, it took Henry less than ten minutes to get to the top of the hill between the abbey and the castle. This side of the hill was densely populated with oaks that gathered the darkness beneath them, providing excellent cover for Henry's ascent. Right on top, however, was a bald spot, and there Henry found another sentry. The man was completely preoccupied with the torchlit spectacle below, so Henry had no trouble ducking behind a bush and crawling around the top so he, too, could observe the activity around the castle.

The castle was brightly lit, even the towers and parapet illuminated with numerous torches. It was a most impressive sight. But what had the guard on the hill so transfixed was the procession of lantern- and torch-carrying gentlemen moving over the castle drawbridge to a Gothic chapel right below the hill, where the lights and the gentlemen disappeared one by one.

Henry watched until the last light had gone into the chapel and, he presumed, into the aforementioned tunnel. Only two men hadn't followed the crowd. Instead they mounted their horses and rode toward the abbey. Henry scanned the area one last time. Finding nothing further to concern himself with, he thought it prudent to go back to his spot by the window. He got there just in time to see Lord Jennings and a tall, blond, well-built young man, presumably Lord Didcomb, ride up and shed their dress coats by the cart. Jennings was middle aged, with silver-sprinkled dark hair and dark eyes. He was well known to Henry as an associate of the Duke of Elridge. The two of them picked up several items from the cart, but didn't immediately enter the abandoned church.

Seemingly inside the wall beside him, Henry heard shuffling and scraping, winding higher and higher. The secret staircase, he concluded.

Once the shuffling up into the Gods subsided, there came a strange, long mournful sound, the kind a shepherd might make with a ram's horn, signaling the start of whatever ceremony was about to commence. The two lords took the sound of the horn as their cue to enter the abbey, Didcomb with a flogger nonchalantly flung over his shoulder and Jennings slapping his riding crop menacingly against his boot.

Henry watched spellbound as the three women, now tied to the iron ring in the wall, started to whimper and pull on their bonds. Each girl had her hands tied to her sides, and their waists were bound together and to the iron ring. From the viewing gallery above came appreciative comments regarding the unfolding spectacle. So encouraged, the women whimpered and pulled on their bindings ever more desperately as the two men with the whips approached.

Once the lords reached the chapel area, Didcomb stopped and Jennings stepped forward, bowing to the gallery.

An ancient-sounding voice croaked from above, "What have you for us tonight, dungeon master?"

Jennings indicated the women in the corner with a theatrical gesture. "These three captives shall be despoiled to celebrate our victories and the anniversary of our union."

At that moment, the brunette managed to unravel her bonds and started to run like a panicked hare for the great open portal. The excited shouts from the gallery bore witness to just how much the move electrified the whole atmosphere of the proceedings. Henry mentally congratulated the ladies on their theatrics. In reality, the girl had no hope of escape, but she made a valiant effort while Jennings eyed her menacingly and nodded his chin for Didcomb to go get her, then he went to secure the other women's bonds.

Didcomb barely had to exert himself to catch up with the runaway. He grabbed her by her luscious dark mane and dragged her unceremoniously back to the altar. There he pulled out a knife and sliced the lacing off her corset, letting it fall to the ground, then ripped away her chemise to a smattering of applause from the gallery. Now she was completely naked, and he maneuvered her onto the altar and manacled her wrists, knees, and ankles so she lay in a prone position, with her legs folded beneath her but spread apart so her bottom and her sex were completely exposed to the eyes of every man present. The murmurs of appreciation and excited exclamations from above were now constant.

Jennings returned to the altar and made a complete circle around the girl, letting his crop follow all her curves, touching her with it wherever his eyes wandered. All through this inspection she did not make a sound, but when his crop struck her for the first time she yelped, more out of surprise, it seemed, than any pain he inflicted. But that changed quickly, and Henry realized the girl's unusual position exposed her most sensitive parts to Jennings's crop, which he began to apply with great enthusiasm.

Had Henry not known the girl was a willing participant, he would have been tempted to give up all hope of remaining hidden to come to her rescue. As it was, he flinched every time the crop connected with the brunette's pretty derrière with an audible thwack. But he was here to confirm he was indeed watching a ceremony of the Knights of the Snake Pit, and to that end, he searched both Didcomb's and Jennings's hands. There was a glint of gold on the pinky finger of Jennings's left hand, but in the ever-changing light the design was hard to make out. Didcomb, however, was now mere steps away from Henry, and when his left hand came into view, so did a gold ring with the hissing snakes, identical to the one Henry had taken off the dead Lord Astor.

Henry's heart pumped with excitement. This was it. This was the organization he had sought for three long years. But there was no Astor here, there was no treason, no torture, and certainly no murder. A few disgruntled old men perhaps, bemoaning a time gone by, but the most he could accuse of anyone gathered here was fraternizing with prostitutes. It was all theatrics.

He turned his attention to his surroundings outside the abbey to make sure he was still unobserved. The next step would be to get up onto the platform to see who was present.

As he let his eyes sweep over the open spaces around the abbey, Henry became aware of a figure approaching through the shrubs and trees. The closer the figure got, the more certain he became it was a woman; also that she was being followed, and unaware of it. Once she stepped into the moonlight, he was stunned to recognize Lady Jane Castleright.

Henry may not have had any love for the conniving harpy, but surely this was no place for a gently reared virginal female. One look inside the abbey confirmed the proceedings had turned decidedly sexual. The girl on the table was emitting a continuous wail now, her bottom streaked with red welts. Lord Jennings's placket could barely contain his erection, and Didcomb had freed his cock completely, forced the redheaded beauty to her knees, and was making her service him with her mouth. There was really nothing for it; he had to stop Lady

Jane from walking into this.

Henry had retreated from the window and was about to step out from behind the rhododendron when he saw the man following Lady Jane wave away one of the sentries and then step swiftly behind the lady. The man put his hand over her mouth and grabbed her by the waist, lifting her off the ground so he could swing her around and carry her back in the direction she had come from. Henry was reasonably sure it was the same young man who had brought the three women to the abbey earlier.

It may have been useful to find out more about the ceremony and the men on the platform, but it was entirely possible he would find out more by following Lord Didcomb's childhood friend. By the looks of it, a very annoyed childhood friend. The young man the ladies of the night had called Mr. Ben kept his hand firmly on Jane's mouth to keep her protests quiet as he carried her back down the path through the thicket. Henry made his way around the other side of the guard as quickly as he dared and tried to get parallel with Lady Jane and her captor once the darkness amongst the trees allowed him to move faster.

As soon as they were out of sight and earshot of the abbey, Ben set Lady Jane on her feet and turned her to face him, still keeping his hand over her mouth. When Lady Jane recognized him, she started to attack him with renewed fervor, but Ben was strong and held her tightly pressed against him so she couldn't kick him too hard. He also pinned her hands behind her so she couldn't scratch him, and his other hand remained over her mouth. Henry wondered why it hadn't occurred to her to bite the man, but then was glad she hadn't, for Ben started to speak in a barely contained whisper.

"You stupid woman. Couldn't you listen to Max for once in your life and go to your mother where you belong?"

Henry had stopped behind a tree close enough to hear, but couldn't make out the expressions on their faces. However, the exasperation in the man's voice was clear enough.

"I'm going to take my hand from your mouth, but you need to remain quiet. I just saved you from being raped by your friend in front of a crowd of the most depraved men in England. But we are not safe yet and I can't carry you all the way to Hove, do you understand?"

Henry had known the abbey and the ceremony was no place for a lady, but Ben's assertion was far more serious than he had suspected. It would appear there was more to this meeting than just a celebratory display.

Lady Jane was understandably subdued, and nodded in the affirmative. Removing his hand, Mr. Ben let her go enough so she could take a half step back. The lady took a deep breath. "What are you talking about? Max would never do that to me." Her words sounded confident enough for the average female, but Henry had never heard her sound less sure of herself.

"He would have done it to spare you from worse." It was said as a mere matter of fact, making the statement all the more chilling. "Where is your carriage? We need to get you away from here."

Lady Jane turned to carry on walking toward Hove. "On the other side of this wood."

Ben kept his arm around her to steady her as they walked. "What did you do with the guard there?"

Lady Jane shrugged in that uniquely belittling way of hers. "I gave him some money and told him to go visit his girl."

Ben chuckled darkly. "Well, he is in trouble. He was specifically told not to let you through."

There was genuine surprise in Lady Jane's voice. "Why would you expect me after I left this morning?"

Ben urged her to walk faster. "I've known you since we were twelve years old, love. Besides, I live here; the locals tell me things. I knew you'd only gone as far as the Downs Inn, and I couldn't just let you walk into this."

"You couldn't? You know, you are the only person who ever could stop me from doing things." Though astonishment colored her voice, she didn't sound displeased.

They had reached the other side of the thicket now, and Henry could make out the coach in the moonlight. "Should have taken you over my knee and told you what's what a long time ago. Come, we can talk about all this once we are safely in the carriage."

Henry couldn't help but wonder whether a thorough spanking would indeed improve Lady Jane's disposition. She surely deserved one for the way she had treated him.

Lady Jane ignored the spanking comment. "And I want to know why Max would ever contemplate raping me."

Opening the coach door for her, he lifted her in without letting the step down. "Yes, I'll tell you, and Max can take my head off later. Keeping you in the dark is putting you in danger." He instructed the driver to take them to Hove and hopped up into the coach, shutting the door behind him.

Henry waited until the coach set off, then sprinted after it and swung himself up onto the empty back seat. He crouched low and let his fingers wander over the wooden panels until he found a peephole and pressed his ear to it so he could hear more clearly what was said inside. But the first thing he heard was a few slaps sounding suspiciously like someone's bottom being smacked through a few layers of petticoats, while the lady shrieked her indignation.

"What did you do that for, you brute?"

Ben sounded much more relaxed now. "That was for disobeying Max's direct order and giving me the fright of my life, my beloved highborn idiot."

Lady Jane sounded a little less annoyed, but also a little less sure of herself. "I'm not your beloved."

"Yes, you are." It was a simple statement of fact. It appeared Ben wasn't the sort to sugarcoat things or hold back when he felt something needed to be said. "And I think you feel the same way about me."

There was silence for a few moments, then Lady Jane's reply came so low, Henry could barely make it out. "It makes no difference what I feel. My father would never agree to it."

Ben sounded far more hopeful. "Jane, after the way you ruined things for yourself in society, he has no further illusions about your chances at a grand marriage. That's why he agreed to the claiming."

There were a few more beats of silence. "What on earth is a claiming?"

Ben took a deep breath. "The thing Max was trying to spare you from. It's an ancient ritual, so depraved it hasn't been performed in more than two hundred years, and the last time it was done, it was used to provide the impoverished widow of a former Knight with a new husband and home."

"You're speaking in riddles, Ben. What ritual, and what has it got to do with me?"

Ben sighed. "For someone who's grown up within this organization, and is so proud of it you want to play an active role in it, you know remarkably little."

Lady Jane made an impatient little noise. "Well, enlighten me then. I've lost all patience with Max telling me to stay out of it. He is modernizing the organization, is he not? Making it more about economic gain than all the outdated political maneuvering Elridge and Warthon continue to plot."

"You've been eavesdropping on the wrong people, Jane. Elridge has long since resigned himself to Hanoverian rule and has become very powerful in the House of Lords. Jennings is aligned with Elridge, and all the other members of the old guard have died and left younger, more progressive members in their stead, or retired to their estates and only venture out for the big events like tonight's festivities. The only two still hankering after Jacobean glory are Warthon and your misguided father."

Ben took a deep breath and continued, "Max is getting more powerful through the money he makes for the Knights, and he's won over many a member by providing them with a clubhouse, but Warthon is still officially the leader of the Knights and very much clings to that power. You, my dear, have stepped inadvertently into a brutal power struggle betwixt Max and his grandfather."

Lady Jane sounded confused. "What do you mean? Max is the heir!"

"He is indeed, and Warthon did his best to create him in his own image, I'm sure you remember. But Max has become his own man despite all the earl's efforts, and Warthon doesn't like it one bit. You see, this is a very old organization, with rules and rituals dating back to the Dark Ages. Warthon is a true disciple of the old ways. As far as he is concerned, there can only be one leader, and since he is that leader currently, everyone should follow him unquestioningly or face the consequences. Max's ascension looks like rebellion to him and therefore needs to be quelled. Max, however, is already far too powerful for the earl to simply discipline him, hence the power struggle."

Again there was an impatient huff from the lady. "Yes, yes, I see. So they are posturing about like prize fighters. How very male of them. I still don't see why I can't be part of this ritual you speak of."

Henry could feel the waves of frustration emanating from the young man in the coach, but he answered Lady Jane with remarkable patience. "The original Knights came over with William the Conqueror. They were all younger sons with no hope of inheriting land and had pledged themselves to William in the hope of earning land through their service. They proved themselves in battle, and when they were given their reward in England, they were also given carte blanche in how they wanted to handle taking over the land. They were Norman, and everyone else on the land was Saxon, so not only did they have trouble communicating with the people who worked their land, the populace tended toward rebellion. So the twelve original Knights, who were all unmarried when they arrived, decided to pacify the land by marrying either the widow or the daughter of the disposed Saxon lord. They killed the men, then literally claimed the women, publicly, with a priest in attendance.

"Two of the Knights who were given land found no lady of marriageable age left on their new property. They called for a meeting and asked their friends to bring marriageable women they were now responsible for so they could choose from amongst them. The Knights claimed wives at the meeting and thereby pacified their land. And as new Knights joined their secret pact to protect the king and claim

England, and as their daughters grew to womanhood, they performed claimings at their annual meetings. Two generations later, they no longer needed to pacify the land, but marriage amongst their children made the bonds between them stronger."

Lady Jane snapped impatiently, "So my father decided to offer me to the Knights to find me a husband. Why is that so bad? I'm of age; all I had to do was say no."

Ben let out a bitter little laugh. "You haven't been listening. The Knights never gave the women a choice. If a father offers his daughter at a meeting, he presents her naked, and the Knight with the highest rank who wants her, claims her by taking her virginity right there in front of all those present."

Henry could hear Lady Jane drawing in a sharp breath, then there was a long pause. When she finally spoke, she sounded much younger, almost vulnerable. "Oh Lord. I never would have thought my father could be so cruel."

Ben's voice gentled. "To be fair, I don't think it was your father's idea. The old earl was behind it. Warthon is desperate to find some way to bring Max back under his control, and he knows about your friendship with him. He banked on Max doing everything in his power to shield you, but the only thing he could have done would have been to claim you himself. You see, a ritual claiming in this day and age would have been a clear victory for Warthon. All the younger, more progressive members would have gone along with it because they're already drunk on spirits and the sexual display they're watching. The ones less familiar with the ancient rules would probably have assumed it to be part of the display. Max can't openly challenge his grandfather in such a meeting without losing all he has worked for, and you know how important guiding the Knights into a new era is to him."

"So my oldest friend and confidant would have claimed me, raped me, in front of a crowd of drunken men, and then forced me to marry him." The words were bitter, but Lady Jane sounded so lost, Henry actually felt sorry for her. The coach shifted in an odd way and Henry surmised Ben had moved to sit beside her.

"Jane, my love, there would have been no other choice. He can't go against the rules of the Knights, Warthon, and your father without incurring the wrath of the entire assembly. In this organization you do not publicly defy your elders, and most certainly not those with higher rank than you. Warthon would've stripped him of his membership and named a new successor, then the next-highest ranking Knight would've claimed you. Do you see now why you really couldn't be there?"

Jane's response was muffled, as if she had buried her face in his lapels, and he made a humming sound, presumably to soothe her.

Henry, from his perch behind the coach, noticed the lights of Hove and decided to leave the two lovebirds to their own devices. As the coach passed the next bush, he jumped down from the high seat and immediately rolled behind the bush in case someone in the carriage noticed the movement and looked out the window. But the vehicle carried on along the tiny lane, and so, after a suitable interval, Henry got up and headed back to check on the three women taking part in the display. But by the time he reached the abbey, the three ladies of the night were climbing into the wagon, happily chatting, so Henry returned to where he and William had left their mounts in the little stand of trees.

CHAPTER EIGHTEEN

HENRY REACHED THE HORSES WITHOUT INCI-
dent, sounded two owl hoots separated by three beats to tell William
it was time to retreat, and freed the animals from their tethers. By the
time William joined him, Henry was in the saddle, eager to get back
to the hotel. An hour later, they made their way up the back stairs to
Henry's apartment.

William gave the rooms a quick inspection, then took a glass of
brandy from his employer and sat opposite Henry by the fireplace.
"And?"

Henry took a sip of his brandy and grinned at his companion. "It's
the Snake Pit, all right. Didcomb wears the ring, and I could swear
Jennings had one too. There is no conspiracy against the crown to
speak of, or anything like we found in Astor's dungeon, but they are
still as active as we suspected, and some of their rituals are rather bar-
baric. Warthon is the leader, not Elridge as we thought, and the rather
ingenious Lord Didcomb is changing the organization from within.
He is sidelining the old warriors by recruiting young, like-minded
people and providing them with a clubhouse. He is also making them
all rich with his forays into the world of commerce. I have a good
mind to invest a little money with him just to see how he does it. No
way to know for sure until Allen finds the house, but I think Mary
and the missing girls are employed at Didcomb's club, and if the three

women I observed this evening are anything to go by, they are quite happy with their lot."

William whistled through his teeth and raised his glass to salute his employer. "Quite the night's work. So what will we do now?"

Henry contemplated the amber liquid in his glass. "Keep an eye on the Warthon estate, since Warthon is the one who wants to take revenge on me, and he is the leader. We also need to identify all the members and make sure Ostley has no opportunity to harm Emily in any way." Henry smiled at his old comrade. "Beyond that, I intend to enjoy the summer by the sea."

William couldn't resist teasing, "And carry a certain young lady's painting bag about the place."

Henry grinned and drained his glass. "A worthwhile occupation, I assure you."

THE FOLLOWING MORNING FOUND ISABELLA on the first-floor landing, about to descend the stairs to attend Mrs. Curtis's At Home, when George's voice stopped her short. Knowing he was near disturbed her no less than it had the day before. All the blood seemed to drain from her brain, and she had to hold on to the banister to steady herself.

There was a short exchange with the footman at the door, then George was led to the drawing room.

"My lady, Viscount Ridgeworth to see you."

Isabella, still frozen in place, could hear her mother's excited greeting through the open drawing room door.

"George, hello! What do you mean, Viscount Ridgeworth? Since when?"

"Since April, Lady Chancellor. A tragic accident."

There was a pause, and Isabella imagined him bowing and smiling that ingratiating smile everyone thought kind. He continued, "I ran into the lovely Isabella on the beach yesterday and simply had to come pay my respects before I have to return to London. A viscountcy doesn't run itself, you know, so my stay here is short."

Isabella noted for the first time how affected his speech was. It certainly wasn't an improvement on the impulsive boy she had known. Sally had come up behind her and put her arm around her waist as the drawing room door closed, and they could hear no more.

"At least now you know he isn't staying long."

Isabella nodded, but made no move to go down.

Sally gave her a little nudge. "You best get in there before he puts a flea in your mother's ear. Remember what we talked about."

Isabella remembered, but didn't trust her voice. She was still contemplating her wobbly legs when another knock sounded from the front door, and the squire was admitted, carrying a big bouquet of daisies and cornflowers.

Sally nudged her again. "Go in with the squire. It'll be easier."

Her friend had a good point: it would be easier to enter the room on another man's arm. Still not easy, but easier. Isabella squared her shoulders and descended the stairs.

"Good morning, squire. Are these for me?" She smiled at her unsuspecting savior. "They are lovely!"

The squire smiled back and came forward to offer his hand as she stepped off the last stair. "Good morning, Miss Chancellor. You look pretty in blue. I'm so glad you like what grows on my land."

"Thank you, squire, I'm indeed partial to wildflowers." She took the flowers and put her free hand on the squire's arm so he could lead her to the drawing room, addressing the footman as she went. "Eddy, would you bring me a vase?"

It was unusual to arrange flowers during an At Home, but it would give her something to do, and that would make it easier to face George once again.

George jumped up as soon as she entered the room, but she only greeted him with a short, "Hello, George; you found us, then?"

George bowed. "Indeed I did, Izzy. I couldn't leave without ascertaining if I would still find you here in a fortnight or so, when my affairs may allow me to return."

Isabella took the bouquet to a small table by the window, so overcome by the news of his planned return that she forgot to reply.

The baroness answered for her. "Oh goodness, of course you will! We plan to remain here till the second week of September. Do come back. You two must have so much to talk about."

Isabella cringed at her mother's enthusiasm, but managed a weak smile. "We shall expect you then."

George happily took that as his cue to leave. "I shall hurry back." He made another bow. "Until we meet again."

Isabella's eyes followed George to the door and stayed there even after it had closed. It was as if she needed to know he had left the house before she could breathe again. Her hands shook as she arranged the flowers in their vase, but the squire helped her and made pleasant small talk, and bit by bit she calmed again.

A quarter hour later, the squire took his leave, and as soon as the door closed behind him, the baroness swung around to face her daughter.

"You could've been more welcoming to an old friend like George, especially now he is a viscount. He asked for your hand once, and he isn't married yet. I'm sure he could be persuaded to offer again."

Isabella was not surprised at her mother's way of thinking, nor that she knew he was unmarried. Remembering Sally's advice, she pulled a sour face. "Mama, George was Freddy's best friend when we were children; he put bugs in my hair and soap in my tea. How could I ever think of him in that way, especially with a man like Sir Henry about."

Isabella conveniently blushed at this point, because, after all, it was true. Both Lady Chancellor and Mrs. Curtis looked at Isabella in stunned silence for a moment, then Mrs. Curtis excitedly tittered into her handkerchief. "Oh, Lydia, I do believe our Isabella has a *tendre* for Sir Henry."

The baroness's eyebrows rose in astonishment. "Is that so, Isabella?"

Isabella lowered her eyes to the floor and shrugged. "I do like him."

Mrs. Curtis smiled with the enthusiasm of a woman who knew love and wished such happiness upon every other female. "Look at her, she's shy about it." She nudged her friend conspiratorially while the baroness assessed her daughter from head to toe.

"Well, if you want him, we better all do our part to bring him up to scratch."

Isabella, realizing what hornet's nest she'd stirred up in her zeal to draw her mother's attention away from George and his title, racked her brain for a way to halt her mother. "Please, Mama, keep in mind Sir Henry had a rather unpleasant experience during the London season. I don't think he would react well to any sort of pressure."

Mrs. Curtis cocked her head to the side in thought. "Lydia, dear,

I do think the child is right. And he is already very attentive. No need for feminine wiles just yet."

THE NEXT FEW DAYS WERE spent in the kinds of pursuits both a fifteen-year-old and a lady of four and twenty could enjoy. They went shopping for a new painting hat for Isabella and dresses for Emily. Isabella used the trip to the modiste to order a dress made from the silk Henry had given her. She brought in her own design, and Emily was so enamored with it, she asked Isabella to design a dress for her as well. They spent a very pleasant rainy afternoon working on it.

Other outings included a walk in the grounds around the Royal Pavilion, another beach day, tea with the baroness at Mrs. Curtis's house, and a drive into the countryside in an open landau. The dowager duchess chaperoned them wherever they went, firmly establishing Henry in the number-one spot among suitors, in Lady Chancellor's mind.

The baroness was made aware of Mr. Wickham's less-than-desirable reputation, which, much to her daughter's relief, prompted her to give the man the cold shoulder. Isabella's other two suitors still hung round, but Henry's presence and continued interest relegated them to the background.

Lady Chancellor was clearly not happy with the presence of Henry's illegitimate child, but couldn't hide her pleasure at making the acquaintance of the legendary Dowager Duchess of Avon. That Emily was beautiful and the dowager doted on her reconciled the lady somewhat to the prospect of having to accept her into the family. After all, marriage to Sir Henry would bring some major advantages. He had no need for an heir since he had no title and already had a child to spoil and love, therefore there was a good chance he might spare Isabella the marriage bed and return to his long-term mistress immediately after the wedding night. She communicated these conclusions to her stunned daughter and was gratified to find her child rather sensible on the matter for a change.

What Lady Chancellor didn't realize was that Isabella agreed Henry would seek solace in his former mistress's arms—in fact, she assumed he would do so as soon as he discovered her secret. She spent a dismal night in contemplation of her future because of it. There was only one consolation in this situation: Henry was her friend and knew her thoughts on marriage, so there was no danger of him proposing. And with his daughter and grandmother constantly in attendance, he posed no danger as a man either.

CHAPTER NINETEEN

A COUPLE OF WEEKS AFTER EMILY'S ARRIVAL IN Brighton, and in the midst of the July heat, the dowager announced to her grandson that all was in readiness for them to enjoy a weekend excursion to his estate above Brighton. Lady Chancellor, Mrs. Curtis, and Isabella were invited, and several horses hired so they could go riding along the cliffs.

When they reached the town house on the appointed day, however, they were greeted by a harried-looking maid and, behind her, the male members of the staff rushing in and out of the morning room, while a continuous wail of despair emanated from that direction.

Alarmed, Henry flung all decorum to the wind and ran to the little salon at the back of the house. There he found Isabella wafting smelling salts under Mrs. Curtis's nose while her mother paced the floor, wringing her hands. Henry knelt next to his Isabella—having started to refer to her as his in his mind. He took the smelling salts out of her hand and asked quietly, "What in the world is going on?"

Isabella helped the wretchedly crying Mrs. Curtis to sit up so her maid could loosen her corset. "We just got word Mr. Curtis died two days ago of a heart attack. Poor Mrs. Curtis is in complete shock."

Henry covered the distraught woman's hands with one of his. "I'm so sorry for your loss, my dear Mrs. Curtis. Whatever you need, please don't hesitate to ask."

Mrs. Curtis looked up at him miserably. "He's never had anything worse than a cold in his life." She sobbed between hiccups, "I'm so sorry to spoil your weekend, but I don't think I can make it to Surrey all by myself. I need Lydia to come with me."

Isabella rubbed the distraught woman's shoulders and met Henry's gaze, her eyes full of sadness and regret. Surmising Lydia to be the baroness, Henry nodded his understanding. "Of course we can't let you make the journey by yourself."

Just then the dowager entered the room, prompting Lady Chancellor to stop pacing and turn to her, "Oh, Your Grace, I am desolate to have to spoil your plans for the weekend, but Mr. Curtis died suddenly. I have to escort my friend Mrs. Curtis home and help her with the funeral arrangements."

The dowager's sharp eyes surveyed the scene in front of her and found those of her grandson. She had no trouble seeing the silent plea in them. Henry had fallen in love with the delightful young artist, and Grossmama was all for the union. The solution to this particular problem seemed obvious.

"My dear Lady Chancellor, of course you do." Grossmama led the baroness to a sofa to calm her. "Do you need your daughter's assistance during the journey? Or would it be helpful if she stayed with us on Henry's estate, under my chaperonage of course, until you return from your mission of mercy?"

Lady Chancellor squeezed the dowager's hands with a warmth she normally reserved for her titled married daughters. "Oh, Your Grace, that is a wonderful suggestion." She lowered her voice in a rare moment of discretion. "I would hate to break up the young people at such a delicate state in their acquaintance."

Grossmama whispered conspiratorially, "I do believe we want the same thing here. You may leave your daughter in my care, and we will expect your return within a fortnight. Will that give you enough time, do you think?"

The baroness nodded. "Ample, I should imagine."

With her daughter's chances with Sir Henry restored, perhaps even improved, the baroness stood to address Isabella. "Daughter, Her Grace has graciously invited you to stay with her and Sir Henry at his estate until I return from taking Mrs. Curtis to her family. Please remember to make yourself agreeable." Believing the subject closed, she marched into the foyer and hollered for Isabella's maid. "Sally, you are going to Sir Henry's estate after all, but for a fortnight, so repack your mistress's trunk accordingly."

Isabella, embarrassed by her mother's high-handedness, took Mrs. Curtis's hand. "I hate to leave you like this, Mrs. Curtis."

Mrs. Curtis was a good-natured woman and, despite her obvious grief, would have none of it. "Oh, no, no, don't mind me." She waved a weak hand, then rallied a little. "You know, my Timothy used to say 'Life is for the living.' Do go and live, dear."

Isabella embraced the dear lady and then allowed her mother to hustle her out to the foyer, while Henry expressed his gratitude and said his goodbyes.

OUT BY THE STAIRCASE, EMILY heard the baroness's commands. Having never met the deceased and therefore untroubled by his demise, she whipped up and down on the balls of her feet with excitement. "I think this means we are staying out at Charmely until your mama returns," she told Isabella. "We can ride every day, Grossmama can give you piano lessons, and you can teach me how to paint with oils."

Seeing Isabella wrinkle her nose at the thought of piano lessons, Henry intervened. "Isabella prefers to sing. And I don't mind accompanying her, so we might have a concert one of these evenings."

Isabella's thoughts were still with Mrs. Curtis, her smile not quite reaching her eyes yet. "That would be fun. And I'll be happy to teach you a few things about oils. That reminds me, I need to make sure Sally packs all my painting supplies."

Isabella perked up considerably at the prospect of unlimited painting time. Glad to see the sadness lift, Henry watched her hips sway as she ran up the stairs with more energy than decorum, and pondered which of the lesser salons at his house had the best light so it could be turned into a studio.

Half an hour later, William handed Sally into the coach holding all their luggage while Isabella's trunk was secured to the top. Lady Kistel and the dowager had made good use of their time while waiting for Sally to pack. Notes had been sent to hostesses regarding previously accepted invitations. They cancelled everything except for a luncheon at the Royal Pavilion on Tuesday next. One simply did not cancel on the king.

THEIR PARTY RODE OUT OF town in rallying spirits. Isabella's heart broke for Mrs. Curtis, but she couldn't deny her relief at not having to escort the lady home. The road climbed up into the Downs, and at the first fork in the road, the little procession of two open vehicles and the coach veered east onto a quiet country lane. Once they had reached the height of the plateau, they doubled back toward the sea again. As the crow flew, Henry's estate was a mere seven miles from Brighton, but the journey took them the better part of two hours. They passed through a couple of hamlets and finally came to a turnoff on the right. It led them through tall, lion-topped sandstone pillars supporting a wide-open wrought iron gate. The gate, with the oak-tree-flanked lane beyond, already beckoned Isabella to paint.

As they drove up the gentle incline, the sea came into view, stretching endlessly to the horizon. From the lookout on top of the rise, the drive curved to the left and down to Henry's two-story house. It wasn't a castle or even a mansion, but a generously proportioned country home, built out of a light-colored sandstone, like the gate. It was surrounded by flower strewn summer meadows and grand old trees. Behind the house, protected from the sea winds, was a garden, but from the front of the house the focal point was the ocean beyond the enormous white cliffs. About a third of the way to those cliffs, a low wall hemmed in the wild meadow, and beyond that wall, the hills were dotted with sheep. Out there, the grass was the dense, short kind generally found on the Downs.

Isabella turned to Henry. "I love the wild meadows around the house. It is, however, an unusual choice for landscaping."

Henry grinned. "You want to know why I let the front lawn grow wild?" He paused for dramatic effect and when he saw the spark of amusement in her eyes, he continued. "As it turns out, they built the house right onto the best, most fertile land I have here. The field by the gate we use for corn, oats, and barley in rotation, and the walled gardens behind the house are full of fruit trees and vegetable patches. Out here we harvest some of the best hay in the county. All those flowers you see are herbs that are particularly nutritious for our cows, and the milk and cheese are tasty because of it. The cheese fetches a pretty penny down in Brighton and is prized by my cook in London."

Isabella's grin matched Henry's. "Is this another lesson in how to turn a profit with agriculture? I would've thought your cash crop here to be wool."

"Oh, it is, but it never hurts to be self-sufficient. With the grains, the vegetables, the fruit, and the milk products, the people on my land eat well, and because I let them keep half the profit from the dairy, it has become a very successful sideline."

Isabella was genuinely surprised. "You let them keep half the profit? That truly is unusual."

"Well, it makes sense to me. I pay them to plow the fields, tend the sheep, and look after the house and gardens. Running a dairy is above and beyond. It was my housekeeper's brainchild, at first. She hates sheep's milk and asked if we could keep a cow. I bought two because one of my neighbors was selling them cheaper as a pair, and the next time I came to visit, Mrs. Bennett presented me with a delicious cheddar she had made herself. I bought another two cows and suggested they take some of the cheese to market. As soon as the others found out there was extra money to be made, they were more than happy to help out."

Isabella tilted her head in thought. "Sally grew up on our home farm, and they make very nice little fresh cheeses wrapped in herbs. Perhaps Mrs. Bennett would like the recipe."

Henry smiled at her as he drove into the stable yard next to the house. "I'm sure she would. She already makes a passable Gloucester and a marvelous Stilton."

They stopped in front of the stable, where Henry handed the ribbons to his groom. After jumping off the high seat, he walked around to place his hands around Isabella's waist and swung her down.

It was the closest Isabella had let any man get to her since George, and she wasn't entirely sure why she allowed Henry the liberty, but she had come to like it. It was always the same: He walked around to her side and waited for her to scoot forward and turn toward him. He placed his hands firmly on her waist, and she put hers on his shoulders to steady herself. Then he swung her down, and while she found her feet, he looked deep into her eyes and smiled. There was a moment of infinite possibility then, and even though she knew they could never truly be together, she cherished those moments.

"I do like a good bit of Stilton with a ripe pear," she remarked.

Henry reluctantly let go of her waist and pulled her hand through the crook of his elbow. Again, no corset—he loved that. "We might have pears by now. I hope you don't mind going through the side entrance. I let the front drive go to seed in favor of the meadow."

Isabella smiled at the play of words. "It looks like the seeding was successful; there is barely a footpath left. But I don't mind the side entrance. It seems practical to step into the house from the stable yard; I do it all the time at home."

Their tête à tête was interrupted by the arrival of the dowager's landau. Emily jumped down without waiting for the step to be lowered and strode toward the stables. "I'll just go take a look at the horseflesh."

With an almost imperceptible shake of his head, Henry muttered, "Here we go," then called after her, "The tall dark bay hunter is a little too spirited, but take your pick from amongst the others."

Emily turned to her father, but kept walking backwards while bobbing him a cheeky curtsy. "Why, thank you, Papa." She turned back to the stables, but Henry was fairly certain her eyes were rolling, and he couldn't help smiling.

Isabella had watched the exchange with a little frown, but when she saw his smile, it cleared from her brow. "I take it you got the hunter for her."

"Very astute, my dear. I'm hoping my telling her the hunter isn't safe will make her pick him, and keep her from choosing the white stallion. The two are about comparable in quality, but the hunter has a much better disposition."

Isabella crinkled her nose as they walked to the back door. "I know you told me she is a superb horsewoman, but still, a hunter? Are you not worried she will fall?"

Henry shrugged, not because he didn't care, but because he knew his daughter well enough to know there was nothing he could do to stop her. "She will jump over walls, hedges, and gates; she might as well be on a horse that knows how."

Reaching the door, they were welcomed by a middle-aged woman with a comfortable face, framed by soft brown hair pulled under a tidy white cap and the figure of someone who appreciated good food.

She curtsied and held the door open for them. "Welcome home, sir!"

"Good day, Mrs. Bennett. May I present Miss Chancellor? And I need to inform you, we will be staying two weeks rather than the planned two days."

Mrs. Bennett smiled broadly. "Oh, that's grand. It will be a pleasure to have guests in the house."

Henry let go of Isabella to help his grandmother up the steps.

"Grossmama, are you sure you won't want the master suite after all? It has the most wonderful view of the ocean."

The dowager patted his arm affectionately. "*Ach lass nur, mein Lieber.* It will be much quieter out to the garden. I do so like my windows open at night." She turned to the housekeeper, who had sunk into another curtsy. "Hello, my dear. You must be Mrs. Bennett. Would you be so good as to show me where I might wash the dust off my face?"

"It'll be my pleasure, Your Grace." The housekeeper led the company down the broad corridor to the foyer at the front of the house and up the main staircase.

THE HOUSE WAS LESS THAN a hundred years old, with spacious rooms and high ceilings. Tall, multipaneled sash windows framed the outside world to best advantage, and polished wooden floorboards gave the place warmth. It was a comfortable house built into the most wonderful setting.

There were eight bedrooms on the second floor, and the one Isabella was given boasted a view of the ocean as well as a small sitting room where she could spread out her painting supplies. It also sported a bookshelf holding a few novels and poetry. Isabella perused the choices and selected one of Lord Byron's epic poems, which contained some of Isabella's favorite musings on nature. Everyone had retreated to their rooms to settle in and rest before lunch, but the summer meadow below called to her, so she took the book and headed downstairs.

Right outside the front door was the head of a little path leading to the sheep wall, the grass-covered cliffs, and the ocean beyond. It seemed Isabella wasn't the only one who found walking through the meadow appealing. She meandered along the tiny uneven path, letting her hand skim over the heads of the hip-high flowers and grasses along the way. The meadow played a symphony of bees buzzing, cicadas chirping, and different birds singing, all set to the distant roar of the ocean crashing against the cliffs.

It was a pleasant stroll. The midday heat was tempered by a mild ocean breeze, but the wind wasn't strong enough to threaten Isabella's new wide-brimmed hat, and so she sat on the low wall. The cliffs were truly magnificent. She had, of course, seen them from Brighton and admired the white chalk gleaming in the sun, but this was much more impressive. The short, dark green Downs grass apparently grew right to the edge of the cliffs. They seemed high right in front of her, but to the left, where a brook ran down in little cascades toward the sea, there was a dip in the cliffs and one could walk right down to a small sandy beach and a few whitewashed cottages. Boats bobbed in the ocean and fishing nets hung from poles. Beyond them the cliffs rose once again with all the majesty nature was capable of. This view would most certainly make for a grand painting, and Isabella decided to beg off any afternoon entertainment to try her hand at it.

With the buzzing and chirping behind her, the thunder of the ocean in front of her, and the heat of summer upon her, Isabella opened her book and looked for a verse to suit the scene. She read a few lines, then let her eyes find the horizon to test how the words went with the grandness of the view. When she found the right lines, the words described what she saw, and the beauty around her gave the words wings. It was a lovely way to rediscover a treasured poem.

HENRY WAS STANDING BY THE open window of his bedroom

when he heard the front door shut below. Looking down, he watched Isabella take the path through the meadow. Carrying a book in her right hand, she spread the left to touch the tall grass, and Henry had never seen a woman look more alluring. He knew Isabella didn't set out to entice anybody, but, believing herself unobserved, she didn't bother to deny her urges. It gave the moment a potency all its own. She was sensual by nature, and he so wanted to nourish that quality in her. Henry watched Isabella until the bell calling them to lunch provided him with a convenient excuse to follow her out to the low stone wall.

Once Henry got to the meadow, he spread his hands and brushed them over the grass like Isabella had done. He wanted to touch what she had touched, breathe the air she had breathed. The thought of sharing a breath through a kiss, the anticipation of one day holding her in his arms and watching her find her pleasure, made him tingle all over.

Isabella was seated on the stone wall, alternately reading her book and looking up to let her eyes wander over the landscape. Henry had surmised she was reading poetry, but he was still a little surprised to find *Childe Harold's Pilgrimage* on her lap. Of course every library in England held a copy of Byron's work, but to think the rather prud-ish Lady Chancellor would let any of her daughters read it was un-imaginable. Then again, Henry had seen Isabella do, and enjoy, several things the baroness would have objected to. The passage she was read-ing proved she was intimately familiar with the text; it was perfectly matched to the scene before them. Isabella looked up and smiled as he read the beautiful words aloud.

"There is a pleasure in the pathless woods, / There is a rapture on the lonely shore, / There is society where none intrudes / By the deep Sea, and music in its roar: / I love not Man the less, but Nature more."

Henry had stopped reading and started reciting with his eyes on the horizon about halfway through the verse. The words trailed off and his eyes sought hers, to find the blue-green pools moist with sentiment. His left brow hitched up a little in question, but she only shook her head no, prompting him to stroke her cheek in silent comfort. Once he was sure her emotions had steadied, he offered her his hand to help her up and across the wall.

Isabella didn't know how to close her heart to this man. He saw the beauty in the world like she did, felt it in the words of a poem, heard it in the sound of the waves, and created it with the music he played. And then, when he knew her to be overwrought with the impact of it, he offered tenderness and companionable silence. The tears she had almost shed, however, had not been for the poem, nor for the beauty of nature, but for the life she would not be sharing with him. At moments like this it was so very hard to remember just why it could never be. She took his offered hand and preceded him wordlessly back to the house, where luncheon had been readied.

Henry watched Isabella's hips sway, admired the straightness of her back and the purpose in her step, and felt his heart sing "I love you." The words tumbled to his lips and almost spilled out, but at the last instant he held back, not wanting to overwhelm her, now she was in his house and couldn't leave until her mother returned.

CHAPTER TWENTY

BY THE TIME ISABELLA SAT DOWN TO LUNCH SHE was perfectly composed once again and able to converse freely. They discussed the various options for entertainment, from a walk along the creek further inland, to bathing in the sea, to going to the village for buns and pies. Emily was eager to go for a ride along the cliffs, but Isabella, having already found her motif for the afternoon, begged off. Soon after lunch, she collected her painting bag and a cushion, and went back to her spot on the wall. The afternoon sun brought different light, but also brought out the turquoise of the sea, a lovely contrast to the white cliffs.

There were no trees out on the cliffs, so Isabella could see Henry and Emily for quite some time, and it turned out to be rather distracting. They rode a race and jumped walls, and sometimes Emily's shrieks of delight carried to Isabella on the wind. It was lovely to see a father and daughter simply enjoy each other's company, not something she had thought possible with her own kind but indifferent father.

Once the riders had turned into dots on the horizon, Isabella turned her attention to her painting and imbued it with all her pent-up longing and the sadness she felt at the thought of leaving Henry and his delightful family behind. The summer would come to an end, and then it wouldn't be long before her birthday. She would move into her cottage and devote her life to painting. It was what she wanted;

she had defied conventions and fought many a battle to get to this point.

Then why did she feel this devastating loneliness just thinking about it?

HENRY AND EMILY WERE THE first to return to the house and found both Grossmama and Lady Kistel snoring softly, reclined in armchairs in the shade of a lovely old oak. The garden, though not particularly large, was unconventionally charming. It ran the length of the house and was walled on all sides, and shaded by an oak, three cherry trees, and several walnut trees. Ornamental arches supported grapevines as well as peas and beans, and along the tall back wall, apple trees and tomatoes were supported by wire so they could carry more fruit. The roses shared space with gooseberries and red and black currants, and at their feet strawberries filled in the gaps between. Carrots, spinach, lettuce, and cabbage were discreetly tucked behind rows of lilies and lupine, and the square patches of herbs were surrounded by borders of verbena, lavender, and daisies.

Henry stopped Emily from waking Grossmama and boosted her up to pick some cherries before he went inside to order the tea tray. From a window in the foyer he could see Isabella painting out on the wall. He had watched her carefully over lunch and had seen the unsettled look in her eyes. With any other woman, he would've concluded she missed her mother, but that clearly wasn't the case with Isabella. He hoped it had nothing to do with him, but suspected it did. Henry could tell Isabella liked him; it was evident in her every look and in the measure of trust she placed in him, but she was completely dedicated to her painting and thought marriage incompatible with her profession. With any other man it would be, but he admired her sense of purpose. Perhaps it was time to reassure her regarding his expectations of his future wife.

High above the ocean, a cliff jutted out farther than the others. From there, both sunset and moonrise were quite spectacular in summer. The cliff was within sight of the house, and the moon would be close to full that night. A walk to see it rise might create the right occasion to speak to Isabella about marriage and her plans, and whether the two could be reconciled so they might spend their lives together.

Henry found an almanac in the study toward the back of the house and calculated that, with only a little over a week remaining in July, the sun would set just before nine and the moon would rise about forty minutes later.

He'd had a stone bench placed on the cliff the year he inherited the estate and had discovered the moonrise for himself. They would be able to watch the sun set, linger in comfort to enjoy the waning of the last light of day, then watch the moon ascend out of the sea. Of course they would have to invite Emily along, but with any luck, she would tire of the spectacle as soon as the sun set.

With the plan made, Henry went in search of Mrs. Bennett. When he stepped back out into the garden, he found the old ladies still asleep and Emily sitting cross-legged on the lawn with a large quantity of beheaded daisies in her lap.

Henry crouched down next to her. "What are you doing, Poppet?"

Leaning close, Emily whispered conspiratorially, "I'm making summer wreaths for Isabella and me." Then a note of uncertainty shadowed her face. "Do you think she will like them, or is it too childish?"

Henry considered for a moment. The notion that Emily cared

about someone else's opinion enough to feel insecure was encouraging on many levels. "I think Isabella would look lovely with daisies in her dark hair. Are you weaving in any other flowers?"

"Cornflowers would be nice, but there are none in the garden, so just daisies. I think that will look best on her anyhow." Emily picked up another flower and focused on weaving it into her wreath.

The old ladies woke up one after the other as the servants set up tea. Isabella joined them shortly thereafter, elated with a good day's painting. She stood the board with her work still tacked on it against the oak tree, and everyone agreed she had rendered the ocean perfectly.

"I do believe it's passable." Isabella smiled at Henry as she accepted a cup of tea from one of the footmen. "I need to send some of my completed paintings to my gallery in Mayfair. May I ask for some cloth to roll them in, and could you frank it for me, Henry? The mail always tries to tell me they can't take it unless it has some important person's seal on it." She drained her cup in one gulp and handed it back to be refreshed. It was such an easy, comfortably domestic moment; Henry could see his life unfold with Isabella by his side. All he had to do was convince her to accept his suit.

Emily, having finished her wreaths, put one on her own head and stood to place the other on Isabella's. She made a full circle around Isabella, inspecting the effect, and cocked her head to the side. "It doesn't look right with your hair all tied up in a bun. Here, hold it for me." Pulling the wreath off Isabella's head and handing it to her, Emily stepped behind her.

Looking at the wreath in her hand, Isabella smiled. "I haven't worn a daisy crown since my youngest sister got married. Thank you, Emily."

Emily beamed, pulling pins out of the simple knot at the nape of

Isabella's neck, and finger-combed it until it fell in cloudy waves down her back, then put the wreath back on.

With her daisy-crowned soft brown curls cascading to her waist and her simple mint-green painting dress, Isabella looked like a medieval princess. Henry wanted nothing more than to bury his hands and face in her luscious mane. He had to turn his attention to practicalities so he wouldn't embarrass himself in front of the ladies. "Mrs. Bennett is sending a cart of cheese and fruit to my house in London. You can send the paintings along. Write a note where to deliver it, and my man, Thomas, will take care of it."

Isabella, having no idea about Henry's predicament, laid her hand on his arm and smiled up at him in the most innocently beguiling way. "Oh, that would be wonderful. Then I don't have to worry about the paintings being crushed or lost." She thought on it for a moment and added, "I know some of my pictures sold. Do you think your man could collect the money for them from the gallery? And could you hold it for me until I come through London in September? I usually have my brother deal with the business part of things, but since the birth of his son, he hasn't been able to travel as much."

Henry stroked his thumb lightly over the back of Isabella's glove-less hand resting on his arm. He relished not only the softness of her skin, but also the chance to help her with her paintings. "Does the gallery on the Strand owe you money too?"

"Yes, but not as much as the one in Mayfair."

"Write down the addresses and the amount both places owe you; Thomas will collect it for you. He can then bring it down here when he comes with my mail next week."

Isabella sighed in relief. The gallerists in the capital sold the bulk of her work, but were the least willing to deal with her because of her gender. The money she earned there, however, was critical to the success of her plans to make herself independent of her father's household.

The dowager and Lady Kistel watched the exchange between Henry and Isabella with matching sly grins on their faces.

EMILY, TOO, SAW HOW HER father looked at Isabella Chancellor, and noted with relief how Isabella reacted to him. She'd been heartsick for her father when he told her he'd left Eliza to find a suitable wife. Emily knew she was illegitimate and what it meant. She had heard the servants whisper and seen visitors stare all her life. She knew she needed all the help she could get in order to have a successful coming out. However, she didn't want it to mean her father had to give up on love.

But now, her beloved father looked happy holding Isabella's hand. And it wasn't just that, or the fact he gazed at her with longing whenever he believed himself unobserved; it was who Isabella was. She was older than the average miss, and although she was from a very good family, she earned her own money with her painting. It made her seem a much more suitable partner for her father than any other woman Emily could think of. Besides, Isabella was nice. Emily liked her. She could see her father wanted Isabella for a wife, and she decided to do her best to help him achieve that goal. She was quite sure Grossmama was in favor of the match, too, so Emily resolved to follow her lead. But she would also have to keep an eye on them to make sure all progressed the way it should. Nothing was going to come between Papa and his happiness this time, not if Emily could help it.

EAGER TO SHOW ISABELLA THE moonrise, Henry disclosed his plan to take them all out to the cliff after dinner, and was gratified that all except his grandmother were enthused by the idea. They stayed in the garden until the bell told them it was time to dress for the evening meal, and reassembled half an hour later in the dining room.

Isabella had donned a simple salmon-pink silk dress with a round neckline. Her hair was in a braided knot at the nape of her neck and she had finished her toilet with small teardrop pearl earrings and a matching pendant nestled in the little hollow between her breasts. Henry noted how exquisite her taste was whenever she chose her own attire.

He had opted for a bottle-green coat with large lapels and carved mother-of-pearl buttons, a vertically striped cream vest with matching buttons, and tan breeches. His feet were in Hessian boots, but he had forgone the customary tassel adornments.

Dinner was a simple but well done country affair, cauliflower and cheddar cheese soup followed by pan-fried trout from the stream and lamb with minted peas. For dessert they had ripe pears and Stilton, which made Isabella smile. Henry was evidently a thoughtful and attentive host. He even peeled a pear for her so she wouldn't get its sticky juice all over her hands. Marveling at the two perfect pear halves he presented her with, she laughed at the stories he and Emily told of Emily's various adventures, and gladly took his arm to walk out to the cliffs once dinner was done.

It was a marvelous evening, the low sun painting the country in shades of gold. Isabella wondered if, one of these days, she could excuse herself from dinner to capture the fleeting splendor on canvas. It would have to be canvas and oils; paper and watercolor would not be vibrant enough for this. Or perhaps she would just sketch and commit the colors to memory, then paint it in her sitting room later. Walking up the cliff, it felt as if they were stepping into the flaming orange sky, and the ocean's roar was a constant reminder of the power below.

Once they reached the top of the cliff, the sea spread before them, shimmering in aqua shades of silver and deepest turquoise. The waves were capped with white foam as the wind drove them against the cliffs, where they shattered into a million sparkling droplets. The sun hung low and huge in all its fiery glory, and the horizon was painted in orange and purple, while the sky to the east was the palest shade of green. Isabella had never seen anything like it. It was so moving, she felt the tears burn behind her eyes as she took in the beauty all around her.

Emily ran ahead, yellow ribbons fluttering and white sprigged muslin billowing behind her in the evening breeze, then she sat right at the cliff's edge with her legs dangling over the ocean, or so it seemed.

Isabella gave a start, concerned the girl might fall, but Henry reassured her. "There is a ledge right there; she is quite safe."

Isabella walked over to where Emily sat, and when she realized what a perfect natural perch it was, she joined her new friend. Henry sat beside her, leaving the bench to Lady Kistel, who brought up the rear on William's arm.

They watched the sun sink into the ocean and the deep shadows turn into twilight. It was a profound thing to see the day bleed out in such splendor.

But then the wind picked up a little, prompting Emily to scramble to her feet. "Aunt Kistel, we better go back, or Grossmama will call it a night and I won't get my chance at victory."

Lady Kistel allowed William to help her off the bench and took his arm for the walk back to the house, but there was a youthful spring in her step. She, too, it seemed, was keen to get back to their ongoing game of whist. "Come along, darling, we better talk strategy or she will get us both. The woman is a whist demon."

Emily skipped after her, ready for the next adventure. "She is, isn't she. Maybe we could . . ."

Whatever Emily thought they could, or should, do to beat the dowager at her favorite game blew away with the wind. Henry smiled and turned to Isabella. "Would you like to stay and watch the moon rise?"

Isabella looked after the three departing figures blending into the twilight as they got farther and farther away. Propriety demanded she go back to the house with them, but she had never seen the moon rise out of the ocean before. And although the sunset had been spectacular and soul nourishing, she so wanted to stay.

"I have a lantern under the bench in case the moonlight isn't enough to light us home." Henry smiled encouragingly and raised a single questioning brow.

Returning his smile, Isabella pointed at his mobile brow. "How do you do that? Try as I might, I always end up raising both brows, or neither at all."

Henry raised the other brow and grinned. "It's a rare talent, my dear. Will you stay?"

Isabella knew it was a risk to linger with him into the night, but this was Sir Henry. She simply couldn't believe he would ever take advantage of her.

Henry saw her hesitation and decided to play his trump card early.

He stood and held out his hand to help her up. "I was hoping you could commit the scene to memory and paint it for me. I think you are every bit as good a painter as Mr. Turner, and I would be proud to call one of your paintings my own."

How could she refuse such a request? In her opinion, William Turner was the most interesting painter of their time, and to be compared to him was simply beyond flattery. "Of course I'll stay." She took his offered hand and they strolled to the bench. Henry pulled the lamp and a couple of leather-covered outdoor cushions from under it. The lamp he set aside where it would be easy to find in the dark and put the cushions on the bench before gesturing for Isabella to be seated.

"I heard the light in a north-facing room is best for painting. Do you agree?"

Isabella appreciated Henry's thoughtfulness. The cushions would certainly improve the experience of sitting on a cold stone bench for an hour or more. "I do. The light in such a room is even throughout the day, and even light is very important, especially when painting in oils."

Henry took his seat next to her. "Perfect. The little salon at the back of the house faces north. I had it cleared for you. Feel free to set up in there whenever you want; it's all yours."

Isabella couldn't help but feel gratified to finally have someone's support for her painting. Her brother helped her sell her paintings, but mostly because he had no wish to pay her an allowance once the estate was his. Everyone else merely tolerated her artistic bent, while complaining incessantly about the smell of her oils.

"Thank you so much, Henry, but will you not mind the odors?"

"The salon in question is tucked away, and it's summer, so we can always air the place out. Make use of the room, I beg of you. I really admire your sense of purpose and your resolve to go your own way. A talent like yours shouldn't be belittled by relegating it to female accomplishment, where it is easily hidden from the world by small-minded relatives."

Isabella was speechless for a moment. It was getting harder and harder to remember why she couldn't possibly marry this man. But she couldn't, so there was nothing to be done except watch the moon rise and paint him the best painting she could.

Twilight was turning to night when a silvery glow over the horizon heralded the moon's glimmering ascent into the sky. A companionable silence settled over them as they watched. The moon was big and the palest shade of gold, rather than the silver she expected. The shimmering disk was surrounded by a foggy halo, making it appear even bigger, its light reflecting on the waves below, whispering of magic. The night around them was the deepest, darkest blue, but the higher the moon rose, the paler the shade became until the landscape was almost monochrome.

Henry watched Isabella as she drank in the ever-changing scene before them. The moon reflected in her eyes, its pale light making her skin glow like marble, her hair a dark cloud around her head. She let her eyes wander from the moon, to the sea, to the cliffs, and back; and before his gaze could make her uncomfortable, Henry turned his attention back to the moon, now hanging low and full in the sky. But as the night breeze coming off the ocean got more brisk, he noticed her drawing her arms around herself and realized she had neglected to bring a wrap. Henry contemplated putting his arm around her, offering the warmth of his body. But on top of a cliff on the first night at his home was likely not a good time or location to make his first move toward a physical relationship with Isabella. Instead, he peeled himself out of his dinner jacket and draped it gently around her shoulders.

Isabella stiffened in alarm, but once she realized it was just his jacket, she smiled gratefully. "Perhaps it's time to head back to the house."

"Only if you have seen your fill, my dear."

Isabella smiled and stood, her gaze still fixed on the moon. "I have for now. I would like to go back and make a sketch before I forget."

Henry had risen with her and busied himself putting the cushions away and lighting the lamp. When he straightened, he noticed his jacket, much too big for her, was about to slip off her shoulders, so he stepped closer to button the top. Realizing his intent, she allowed him the intimacy with a smile. So encouraged, Henry leaned in to kiss her cheek tenderly and brushed his lips briefly over hers, then picked up the lamp and offered her his arm for the walk back. He could hear, as well as feel, the relieved breath she let out, and was glad he had shown restraint. He was certain now: this was the woman he wanted to marry, and she was worth waiting for.

ISABELLA CHOSE TO BELIEVE THE moonlight was to blame for the kiss, and her acceptance of it. The strange thing was, she had enjoyed it, and felt a pang of sadness that it couldn't happen again. Back at the house, she hurried to fetch her sketchbook, hoping to drown those feelings in her art, determined to prove to herself all was as it should be. She found a small table in the drawing room where Emily had claimed Henry for a fourth at whist, and listened to their banter while she worked.

An hour and a half later, when the dowager declared herself ready to retire and even Emily had to admit she'd had a full day, Isabella put the finishing touches to her drawing, and the whole company gathered behind her to admire her work.

It truly was an inspired drawing: the charcoal she'd used was the perfect medium to render the dark jagged shapes of the cliffs as well as the shimmer of the waves in the moonlight. There was little fine detail, but she had captured the atmosphere perfectly.

Henry was the first to comment. "This is quite wonderful. I can't wait to see what you'll make of it with your paints."

The two old ladies exchanged looks, and Emily jumped up and down, clapping her hands. "You commissioned Isabella to paint the moonrise for you? That's a marvelous idea—these walls are nearly bare."

Isabella smiled at Emily's enthusiasm and stood the drawing on the mantelpiece to inspect her handiwork from a few steps away. She looked forward to getting her oils out and painting Henry's moonrise. This way he would always have something of hers; she liked that idea.

Only that morning Isabella had feared she would never see Henry again if she left with Mrs. Curtis. Of course she'd have to say goodbye at the end of summer, but was it so much to ask of fate to let her enjoy his friendship for a little while longer?

Fate, or the dowager, had intervened, and now she was staying with Henry and had all the time she wanted to enjoy his company. He had even commissioned a painting, not to mention he had kissed her.

And then there was Henry's family. They, too, understood her need to paint, and embraced her art. Isabella had never had much contact with other artists of any kind before, excepting the reverend who had taught her to paint. It was entirely new and wonderful to be part of a group of people who understood the need to create.

CHAPTER TWENTY-ONE

ON TUESDAY MORNING THE FOLLOWING WEEK, the ladies boarded the landau, dressed up in their finest day dresses to drive down to Brighton on the invitation of the king.

The dowager, magnificent in dark blue silk with matching hat and the most marvelous string of pearls Isabella had ever seen, nodded at the ostrich feather in Lady Kistel's hair. "Are you sure that's wise in an open carriage?"

The good lady only shrugged. "No more foolish than a hat, when the wind gusts."

The younger women, both in muslin as was customary, giggled at the banter as they took their seats. Emily was in pure white due to her age, and Isabella wore a pale aquamarine gown that brought out her ocean-hued eyes. Diamonds and aquamarines graced her neck and winked from her earlobes.

Henry, splendid in a midnight-blue tailcoat, embroidered vest, and dove-gray pantaloons, a top hat jauntily perched on his head, surveyed his companions with a sense of pride and took the rear-facing seat next to Isabella. The week she'd had away from her domineering mother had done wonders for Isabella's sense of self. She made good use of the salon he had cleared for her, producing three paintings and several drawings, and best of all, there was always a smile on her face.

The king's luncheon was a relatively relaxed affair in John Nash's lovely gardens surrounding the Royal Pavilion. They had arrived in good time and took a stroll through the flower beds before they settled on the lawn with the rest of the company. A string quartet flavored the breeze with skillfully rendered melodies, and a large tent, mirroring the turrets and cupolas of the Pavilion, shaded the ladies from the midday sun. The dowager duchess introduced Isabella and Emily to the aging monarch before they settled down to lunch. The food wasn't as delicate or refined as one might expect from royal kitchens, but Emily declared herself well pleased with the mountain of strawberries served with cream. Due to the relaxed nature of the affair, most guests stayed in the gardens beyond lunch and whiled away the afternoon talking with friends and acquaintances.

Emily was bubbling over with the excitement of her first completely adult engagement. She declared herself delighted with her introduction to the king, even if she intimated to Isabella that his multiple chins and rotund midsection reminded her of a walrus. But bit by bit the excitement caught up with her, and settling on a blanket spread at Grossmama's feet, she soon dozed off in the afternoon heat.

Some time later, Grossmama's voice, in a rare state of agitation, penetrated the fog of Emily's slumber.

". . . that's why I told the boy he had to make other arrangements for the child. Hortense would make her life a living hell, were I not there to prevent it. She is not to be trusted with the task of bringing Emily out, and I'm too old to do it right. A stepmother is really Emily's best option. I just hope Lydia Chancellor unbends enough to accept the child. Henry is head over heels for Isabella."

Emily was fully awake now, but stayed perfectly still so as not to alert her elders to it. What was that about Aunt Hortense? She knew the woman was a stickler and always found fault with her, but it had never occurred to Emily that Grossmama continually intervened on her behalf.

Lady Kistel did her best to calm Grossmama. "Oh, Ruth, don't worry so. The Chancellor girl seems to like Emily well enough. Henry will marry Isabella, Emily will have a home, and before long, there will be brothers and sisters. She'll be just fine."

Emily must have inadvertently moved, for Grossmama's next words were hushed. "Shh, I think the child is waking. No sense in worrying her pretty little head with any of this. As you say, it looks like it will end well enough."

IT WAS PAST FOUR O'CLOCK in the afternoon by the time the ladies climbed back into the landau to begin their journey back to Henry's estate.

As they drove through the streets of Brighton, Emily looked around, trying to imagine what her life would be like without her great-grandmother's protection or her father's money. Would she be a servant girl, ordered about by a less-than-kind mistress? Lost in her ruminations, Emily caught the eye of a rather unpleasant but somewhat familiar-looking individual in a hand-me-down suit. He stood outside the posting inn on Main Street, and as recognition dawned in his eyes, he grinned at her with glee, revealing a large gap in his front teeth. But before Emily could react in any way, he tipped his hat at her in a mock greeting and ran into the inn.

Emily spotted the same man later on the road behind them, but he never came close enough to worry her, so once safely back at Charmely, she promptly forgot about him.

The man on the road, however, took careful note of the driveway they went down and turned his mount back toward Brighton with the air of a man who had a plan and news to sell.

FOR THE REST OF THE week Henry and his company were blessed with glorious weather, but on the following Monday, the wind picked up, making the top of the cliffs a little uncomfortable, so Henry suggested a walk to the chapel further into the Downs. The ancient sanctuary would make a lovely motif for Isabella to teach Emily more about painting, and would provide shelter for the ladies if needed. It was an easy and pleasant walk along the little stream, with a ripe cornfield to the left, barley on the other side of the brook, and the Downs in front of them. Soon enough they left the fields behind and climbed higher into the hills until they reached their destination.

Henry saw Isabella and Emily settled under a grand old oak tree, then opted to climb the hill ahead of them while the women painted. The oak they sat under and the little stand of trees behind the chapel were the only trees on the sheep-dotted grassland for some distance, so he could see them and they could see him. Once on top of the hill, he sat to enjoy the unobstructed view of the cliffs. The ocean below sparkled to the horizon in the summer sun, prompting contemplation. Henry remained there for some time until he saw his daughter pack up her painting gear, wave to him, and head back down the path to the house, no doubt in search of lunch. Isabella continued her work, and Henry took a detour on the way down to another lookout to give her plenty of time to finish what she had started.

When Henry made it back to the chapel an hour later, the painting stood finished against the tree trunk, and Isabella was stretched out on her back in the tall grass. At first Henry thought she was looking up into the crown of the tree, but her eyes were closed and her chest rose and fell with the regularity of sleep.

She was adorable in her repose, all soft and relaxed, so Henry decided to let her rest for a few minutes more. He settled down next to her in the grass, his left arm folded under his head barely ten inches from hers. It was lovely to share this intimate moment with her, even if she was unaware of the sharing. He watched the sway of the branches above them and listened to the wind in the leaves and the steady rhythm of her breathing, but when he caught himself dozing off, he thought it better to wake Isabella before they missed lunch altogether.

Henry lifted up onto his elbow and picked a long-stemmed purple flower to brush along her nose and cheeks in an attempt to wake her gently. "Isabella, my love, wake up, it's time for lunch." Her nose twitched where the blossom tickled, and she sighed in her sleep, but didn't wake. After a few attempts, Henry abandoned the flower on her breast and allowed his fingers to caress her face. He kept his voice low, not wanting to startle her. "Wake up, my love. Time to head back to the house."

She leaned into his touch, smelling of hay and sunshine. So encouraged, Henry moved closer and used his nose to caress along her hairline, then placed a chaste kiss on the crest of her cheekbone. Her lips were slightly parted and she made a tiny sound of pleasure in the back of her throat when he placed his cheek to the side of her face, so he whispered in her ear, "Will true love's kiss wake you?"

A barely audible sigh of contentment was his answer, so he kissed both her closed eyelids and trailed kisses down her nose till he captured her lips in the gentlest of kisses, breathing in her breath, brushing his lips against hers. She turned toward him like a flower to the sun, making him think she had indeed awoken, and he deepened the kiss just a little, touching his tongue ever so lightly to the inside of her parted lips. Isabella sighed with what he interpreted as longing, prompting him to cup her face with his hand, and keeping his lips soft and gentle, he continued to kiss her with a fervor he had rarely experienced before. True love's kiss indeed.

But amidst this most perfect kiss Isabella suddenly stiffened. Her eyes flew open, and before Henry knew what had gone wrong, she had pushed him away, jumped to her feet, and fled down the path toward the house and the safety of female company.

Henry was stunned at first and called after her to wait, but when she didn't slow, he thought it best to let her go. She may have some maidenly objections to being kissed, but she seemed to have reveled in his touch, and that knowledge made him confident he would be able to make this right as soon as he could talk to her and assure her his intentions were entirely honorable.

HALFWAY DOWN THE PATH, ISABELLA calmed enough to slow to a walk. She knew there'd been no need to run from Henry. He had not pinned her to the ground, hadn't groped her or forced her legs apart . . .

Quite the opposite, Henry had let her go immediately, and his kiss had been gentle, lovely actually. But the old panic had gripped her, making her bolt. Now her heart raced as much from running as from the panic, and she even felt a bit of remorse that she hadn't been able to enjoy Henry's most perfect kiss. Isabella touched her fingertips to her lips and felt the tingle of Henry's gentle touch once again. She'd have to give him a reason and tell him it couldn't happen again. But she'd treasure the memory of his lips on hers, of his hand cupping her face, of knowing beyond a shadow of a doubt that he cared for her.

Isabella entered the house through the garden and headed straight upstairs to wash her hands. She'd been keeping secrets for close to seven years and had learned that as long as you ate regular meals, no one asked too many questions regarding your well-being; so she freshened up and went downstairs to eat.

Lunch was served as a cold buffet in the breakfast room, and when Isabella entered, Henry was already there filling his plate. The only other person in attendance was a footman, ready to serve them tea or coffee.

Henry turned to her and smiled, presumably to put her at ease. "We are late for lunch, my dear. The others have already eaten. My grandmother and Lady Kistel have settled down for their naps, and Emily is in the stable. It's just you and me, I'm afraid."

Isabella gave him a crooked smile and selected some cucumber and tomato slices to go with her chicken breast. "That's quite all right, I don't plan to make a long affair of it." She sat down opposite him and they ate in silence.

Finishing first, Henry waited for her to swallow her last bite before he asked quietly, "May I speak with you in private for a moment?"

It seemed Henry had come to the same conclusion she had: the kiss needed to be discussed. Holding his gaze, she nodded somberly.

Moving her chair back, Henry offered his arm. "Excellent, my dear. The study should do."

Isabella placed three very proper fingers on his arm and walked beside him, but left a foot between them. She didn't want to be rude, but had to make it clear in every way: there could be no physical intimacy between them. She noted the tiny crease between his eyebrows and knew he hated this new distance. Truth be told, so did she, but it had to be. No good would come from deluding herself, and even less from giving him hope.

BOTH HENRY AND ISABELLA WERE so thoroughly occupied with their own thoughts, they didn't notice Emily stepping into the shadow of an alcove under the stairs.

The girl had seen Isabella return on her own without her painting or her bag. Then, when she saw her father come back a few minutes later, carrying all Isabella's things, she figured they had quarreled. Concerned, Emily decided to find out what the problem was so she could tell Grossmama. Their polite distance over lunch worried her even more, and prompted her to follow them to Henry's study. She slipped into the adjacent salon, where she knew a connecting door would make it easy enough to hear what was said if she pressed her ear to the keyhole.

HENRY LED ISABELLA INTO THE room and shut the door. Leaving it ajar may have put his friend at ease, but what he had to say was for her ears only, and her answer was for him alone. Isabella looked nervous, but didn't object, so he guided her to a chair by the empty fireplace and waited for her to be seated before he spoke.

"My dear Isabella, let me begin by offering my apology for startling you." Rubbing the crease between his brows, he added, "That was not the reaction I had hoped for."

Isabella blushed furiously, but held his gaze and took a deep breath. However, before she could answer, he raised his hand to stop her. "Please let me say my piece." He cleared his throat. "I enjoy our friendship very much, and it makes me happy you are getting to know my daughter and my grandmother. They are both very important to me, and it warms my heart to see all of you getting along so well."

Isabella smiled for the first time since the incident under the oak tree, relieved Henry steered things into the realm of friendship. "Thank you. I do too."

Pausing to enjoy the moment, Henry mirrored her smile, then continued, "But, my dearest Isabella, what I feel for you goes far beyond friendship."

The smile died on Isabella's face. She lowered her eyes and shifted uncomfortably in her seat.

Henry saw her reaction, but took it for nerves and pressed on. "I'm in love with you, my darling, and it is my fondest wish you should become my wife."

Isabella jumped up, startling both of them, and walked to the window in agitation, fighting back the sudden tears behind her eyes.

"Please don't." She turned to Henry, and her voice broke as she repeated, "Please don't ask me."

Henry had moved to her and pulled her into his arms before he knew what he was doing. "Shh, darling, if it causes you this much anguish, I won't ask."

There was no panic this time, just the comfort of his arms. Isabella rested her forehead on his chest and let the tears flow. "I can't marry you, Henry. I wish I could, but I can't." With that, she extricated herself from his embrace, knowing it wasn't fair for her to rely on his kindness, and quickly left the study to seek refuge in her room.

Henry let her go, momentarily lost for words. Eventually he let out a heartfelt "Damn it!" and stormed off to the stables. He needed to clear his head, and a gallop along the cliffs might just do that. Something was very wrong and he needed to figure out what, for both their sakes.

ON THE OTHER SIDE OF the connecting door, Emily let out the breath she'd been holding ever since she'd heard Isabella say "don't." She slumped down into her billowing skirts and shook her head sadly. She knew they loved each other, any fool could see that, and she thought she knew why Isabella wouldn't even let her father propose. Isabella was a good person, and they had become friends. Emily had seen the Baroness Chancellor's disdainful looks. She hadn't paid much attention to them, but after hearing that not even her own aunt wanted Emily in her family, there was no doubt in Emily's mind the baroness would raise objections to Isabella's marriage if she, Emily, was part of the bargain. And since Isabella knew how much her father loved her, Isabella had stopped him from proposing. There was only one way to solve this so Papa could be happy with the woman he loved: Emily would have to leave so there was no need for him to choose.

She sat there for a while, pondering how to go about things. Eliza was in London, William had told her. Eliza didn't care that she was illegitimate; high society didn't approve of her either. Eliza would take her in. It might end up being a grand adventure for them both, and Papa could come visit her. Grossmama, of course, wouldn't be happy, but everyone would know she was safe, and Aunt Hortense would be ecstatic to see the back of her. There would be no grand marriage for Emily, but with the ton full of people like the baroness and her aunt, what chance did she have anyway? She might as well go and stay with Eliza till Papa saw reason and gave her the estate she was to have for her portion. Then she could raise horses, or maybe she would become a concert pianist. But first things first, she needed to write some notes.

Propelled by the optimism of youth, Emily pulled herself up and went through the connecting door into the study.

ISABELLA RAN UPSTAIRS, THREW HERSELF onto her bed, and gave herself up to a good cry. She cried for herself and for Henry, for the family she would never have and the companionship she would miss, and finally she cried herself to sleep. Sally heard the crying, and knowing it was best to just leave her mistress be when she felt like this, waited an hour before she came back upstairs with tea. She noticed a letter addressed to Isabella on the hall table, so she added it to the tray in the hope it might cheer her.

Placing the tea tray on the bedside table as Isabella woke from her nap, Sally poured her puffy-eyed mistress a steaming cup. "Here, that will make you feel better."

Isabella doubted it, but there was no point in wallowing in self-pity any longer. She'd made her choice and she'd had her cry; time to get on with the business of life. She sat up and took the cup, and seeing the letter, broke the seal and read.

Dear Isabella,

I accidentally overheard your conversation with Papa, and knowing you love each other, I cannot let myself be the obstacle to your happiness. Please don't concern yourself for me, I will stay with friends in London, and as soon as my father and Grossmama realize I've completely ruined my reputation with this action, they will give up on wanting to bring me out in society. You will no longer be faced with the embarrassment of having to play mother to Sir Henry's bastard, and your family will no longer have any reason to object to your marriage to my papa.

I hope we can remain friends, away from the eyes of the ton, of course. I do want to be able to see my father, but I will be quite beyond the pale.

Sincerely,

Emily

Isabella had to read the missive a second time to understand all the implications of what Emily communicated, but once she fully understood, she jumped off the bed with a most unladylike scowl on her face. "Sally, go to Miss Emily's room and see if she's there. If not, check if she's with the dowager. Then come find me in the stables."

She slipped her feet into her walking shoes, then thought better of it. "Hand me my riding boots first, and you better get my habit ready, and a cloak."

Sally handed her the boots and looked at her with some worry. "Whatever's the matter, miss?"

Isabella pulled her boots on and headed to the door. "Miss Emily misunderstood something, and I have to stop her from doing something she'll regret. Go make sure she isn't still here. And if you see Sir Henry or William anywhere, send them to the stables." With that she pulled the door open and headed for the stairs without bothering to close it.

Sally stared after her in consternation for a second, then rushed to do her mistress's bidding.

CHAPTER TWENTY-TWO

ISABELLA CROSSED THE STABLE YARD, JUST AS A horse-drawn cart rambled along the drive toward them, but in her haste she ignored it completely. Henry's head groom was coming down the outside stairs from his room above the stable.

"Roberts, have you seen Miss Emily?"

Roberts looked at her with curiosity. "No, miss, it's me afternoon off."

"Who is in charge then? Who would know?" Isabella did her best to remain calm and rational. She itched to throw herself onto the next horse and chase after the dear, stupid girl, but there was little sense in doing that until she knew Emily had actually left.

Roberts pointed to a lanky youth pulling a water bucket up from the well. "Eddie over there should know."

Isabella turned to address Eddie. "Has Miss Emily taken any of the horses out this afternoon?"

"Why yes, miss." The youth scratched his head under his cap, then remembered himself and pulled the cap off. "Harnessed the grays for her about an hour ago. Said she was going to the village to get buns, she did. She wanted to go all by herself, but we told her how Sir Henry wouldn't like it, so she took Tim along."

Isabella felt her agitation rise. Emily had an hour's head start and she was driving a team of horses not likely to tire anytime soon. The only bit of good news was that she wasn't alone, although the boy in question was no more than fifteen himself. "I need a fast horse saddled. Have you seen Sir Henry, by chance?"

The groom obviously liked the attention he was getting. "Sure did, miss. He took the white hunter for a ride along the cliffs. Looked like a storm cloud, he did."

Isabella cursed herself inwardly. The storm cloud on Henry's face was her fault too. "Saddle the other hunter for me." She turned to go don her riding habit, but was blocked by the cart she had seen earlier and a concerned Roberts.

"Anything wrong, miss?"

Isabella was weighing whether to tell Roberts what had occurred when William came rushing out of the house.

"Sally sent me to tell you Miss Emily is neither in her room nor with her grandmother, and she has your riding habit ready. Now what is this all about?" He then acknowledged the man in the driver's seat of the cart with a familiar nod. "Thomas."

Thomas jumped down and planted himself next to William, facing Isabella. "What's this about Miss Emily?"

William saw the hesitation in Isabella's face and indicated his friend. "You can trust Thomas, he's one of us."

Isabella took a brief look at the young man beside William and concluded he must be the one bringing Sir Henry's mail. He was tall and muscular, had more than average good looks, and was remarkably neat for someone who had just traveled from London. Seeing concern in his hazel eyes, she pulled Emily's letter from her sleeve and handed it to William. "She took Sir Henry's grays about an hour ago. Tim the stable boy is with her, but I have to go after her and tell her she has it all wrong, that she is doing this for nothing and needs to come back before anyone finds out."

William read through the note quickly, Thomas reading over his shoulder. "Miss, you stay here; Thomas will go after her, and if he can't persuade her, he will take her safely to London. In the meantime, I'll go find Sir Henry."

Both men started toward the stables, but Isabella put her hand on Thomas's arm. "I'm coming with you. She is doing this because of me. I have to tell her why I did what I did, or she will find some other way to ruin her reputation. And she will need a woman with her to make the journey respectable."

Aware the young man was taking her measure, Isabella held his gaze. Finally he nodded. "We leave in ten minutes."

TIME WAS OF THE ESSENCE; they both knew it, and neither of them wasted any of it on the unnecessary. Thomas was already mounted on the hunter when Isabella got back to the yard. She was boosted into the saddle of a sprightly gray, and off they went. But not to the road, as Isabella had thought: Thomas led them out the back of the stable yard and directly north through the fields.

"We're taking a shortcut to the London road."

Isabella only nodded and followed Thomas across fields and over a couple of sheep walls. They rode up the little vale where she had painted earlier. Trotting alongside the young man, all thoughts of Henry and his kiss banished for the time being, she urged her horse into a gallop whenever the terrain allowed.

Their path took them through a narrow pass from which Isabella could see the road snake around a large hill to the west; she assumed the village lay on the other side of it. They made excellent time and joined the road just where it finally turned north into flatter terrain. They kept the horses to a steady light gallop, both well aware of the speed and endurance Henry's grays were capable of. The afternoon turned into evening, and although the long summer days would allow them to carry on for a good three hours yet, they hoped hunger and concern for the grays would prompt Emily to stop soon.

Passing through several hamlets before they encountered the first inn, they stopped only long enough to water the horses and make inquiries. Emily, too, had stopped there, and the groom had taken care of the horses while she had used the facilities. According to the innkeeper, they'd come through about half an hour ago, giving Isabella hope they would be able to catch up before nightfall. It was imperative for Emily's reputation she wasn't observed frequenting an inn alone by members of the ton traveling between London and Brighton.

Back on the road, Isabella turned to Thomas. "If we catch up with Miss Emily at an inn, I'm going to say I'm her stepmother and that her father will be arriving shortly. I'll go inside and talk to her. You wait for Sir Henry and tell him the plan."

Thomas thought about it and then nodded. "Simple and believable. We will use that as our cover story. And we got separated because she challenged you to a race." He chuckled. "No one who knows her will doubt she did."

The thought of Emily challenging her to a race did coax a little smile onto Isabella's face. "It's not very ladylike behavior, but she is young enough and we are remote enough from London to get away with it. Certainly better than the truth." With that she urged her horse back into a gallop.

The road merged with one coming from the southeast, and traffic got heavier. With an inn in every hamlet and village now, they had to be mindful not to overshoot their target, so they stopped wherever a weary traveler might rest himself and his horses. It seemed they were gaining steadily, despite their frequent stops.

Around seven o'clock in the evening, they turned into the busy stable yard of a postal inn and finally got some good news. The ostler attending them reported he had just put up the grays, and the miss had gone into the taproom to order her evening meal. He also related her groom had gone into the inn with her, despite her objections. This piece of information prompted Thomas to mutter "good man" under his breath, and the ostler to nod wisely. Isabella slid off her horse and made her way into the inn as fast as she could without breaking into a run.

The inn's combined taproom and dining room occupied most of the ground floor. The wooden bar ran the entire length of the room to the right, while a large fireplace dominated the opposite wall. A staircase to the upper floors was at the back. The room was filled with smoke and surprisingly enticing food smells, prompting Isabella's stomach to growl. But before she could think about food, she had to find Henry's daughter and clear up this misunderstanding, and she had to do it without causing a scene. Isabella let her eyes travel over the guests in the room, noting the locals seemed to be grouped around the bar while the travelers occupied the tables filling the rest of the room. Emily wasn't amongst either group.

Just then, a rotund woman in a starched pinafore bustled into the room with a large tray full of steaming goodness. She distributed the fare to a group of men sitting around a table by the large front window and then stepped toward Isabella standing in the door. "Can I help you, ma'am? We got a nice bit of lamb, chicken pot pie, beef stew, and lentil and pork soup."

Isabella smiled at the woman's enthusiasm for her food. "Oh, chicken pot pie sounds lovely, but I should find my stepdaughter first. She beat me fair and square to your doorstep, but she didn't wait for me to arrive as we agreed. I better find her before my husband gets here or he will be most upset. She is blond, pretty, young, and just a little shorter than me."

The woman made a grimace as if to apologize. "Dearie, you better brace yourself. Your husband is here and none too pleased. He marched your stepdaughter upstairs as soon as he saw her. She looked worried, so me husband tried to calm him down, but he told him to mind his own business, and the little miss didn't say nothing, just looked a bit scared. But I'm glad you are here and can help her explain." She winked at Isabella and pointed to the stairs. "Top of the stairs, third door to the left."

Isabella didn't know what to make of the story, but it was possible Henry had known an even better shortcut and reached the inn ahead of them. No matter; it was her mess, and she had to tell Emily the truth. She headed for the stairs, a sense of foreboding quickening her step.

GEORGE STOPPED AT THE INN on the recommendation of a friend and found the food every bit as palatable as promised. He was about to order his team be hitched up again when Ostley entered the taproom, and on a hunch, George stayed where he was in his shadowy corner. Before long Sir Henry's pretty young daughter arrived and was forced upstairs by the baron. Aware of the Earl of Warthon's ultimate plans for Sir Henry's daughter, George contemplated going upstairs to take the girl off the baron's hands and deliver her to Warthon himself, when Isabella entered the scene, and George's plans changed abruptly.

Here was his chance. He wouldn't even have to go into Brighton and announce his presence to all and sundry; he could snatch her right here and now, and before anyone knew what had happened, she would be his wife.

Isabella scanned the room from the stairs one more time to see if she could locate the stable boy, to no avail. Something was definitely wrong. Following the landlady's directions, she quickly found the room the good woman had indicated and stopped for a moment to listen, in case the man in the room with Emily was Henry. She didn't want to intrude on a heart-to-heart between father and daughter. But the angry male voice from within did not belong to Henry, and as soon as she comprehended that fact, Isabella threw open the door and rushed inside. The sight greeting her made her exceedingly glad she still held her riding crop.

Emily had been thrown onto the bed and an older, greasy-haired man in an ill-fitting brown suit stood over her. He was wiry and menacing, and had his hand pressed over her mouth. Emily did her best to fight him, but he'd tied her wrists with a leather strap and was securing her to one of the bedposts with it. He took his hand off her mouth for a moment to backhand her and shouted right in her face.

"That's what you get for scratching, you trollop! You'll learn to treat your betters with some civility." The man spoke with a clipped upper-class accent, and his voice dripped with entitlement. He smacked Emily again, unaware there was another person in the room. "Doesn't matter where you were brought up, you are still a bastard, and since your fine father saw fit to take my wife, I'll have you in payment."

Old fears crept up Isabella's spine, threatening to paralyze her with memories she had done her utmost to lock away. But fury at the cretin mistreating her young friend, and the knowledge she was the only one present to prevent worse, gave her strength. She rushed forward, the riding crop raised high. "Get away from her, you fiend!"

Emily's attacker turned, his overgenerous lips set in a cruel smile, as her riding crop connected rather harmlessly with his cloth-covered arm. "Ah, Sir Henry's new bint. Don't worry, I have enough for both of you, so wait your turn."

Isabella's next strike found its target, instantly raising an angry red welt on the man's cheek and filling her with a satisfaction she had never known before. She raised the crop again, and again found her mark. Astonished by her own savagery, but also empowered, Isabella raised her arm once more. Every wrong she had ever been done and had never dared tell anyone about seemed to flow out through her hand, and the crop, to paint the man's face in red.

With the man busy fighting off Isabella, Emily scurried to the other side of the bed and screamed for help at the top of her lungs. Unfortunately, the man soon got over his surprise at Isabella's attack. Hatred burned in his eyes, and his fist slammed into her stomach, doubling her over.

"You fucking bitch! I'll teach you to strike a man with a crop." His voice just added to the dull roar in Isabella's ears. But when he threw her over the side of the bed and placed a knee in the small of her back to hold her down, there was no way she could stop the panic from rising. Isabella thrashed as hard as she could, but couldn't dislodge the knee in her back, and then his hand connected painfully with her behind. But despite the sting, it was a relief: he couldn't spank her and force himself on her at the same time. She stilled and tried her best to breathe through the pain. She had to think of a way to get both Emily and herself away from this madman. As the man continued to thrash her bottom, Isabella's vision blurred with helpless tears. And then, through the haze of pain, panic, and fury she heard an unfamiliar voice.

"Ostley, cease!"

The command went unheeded, and after some shuffling a terse voice instructed, "Out of the way, miss."

There was an almighty crash, water splashing all over Isabella, and then the full weight of her attacker slumped onto her. Panic engulfed her, but before she could lose all sense of reality, her attacker was pulled off her and unceremoniously dumped on the floor. Isabella scrambled off the bed, compulsively pulling on her skirts, and retreated to the corner behind the door. Her impulse to run was almost overwhelming, but even amidst the panic, she was still aware she couldn't leave Emily alone with yet another man, even one who had just come to their rescue, so she slumped against the wall and tried her best to collect herself.

EMILY STARED AT THE GOLDEN god who had just smashed the water jug over the odious creature's head. Thanks to him, the disgusting vermin was now crumpled in a heap on the floor. She still didn't quite understand how she'd come to be in the room with the horrible man. He had cornered her in the taproom and told her her father would suffer if she didn't come quietly. Then he had knocked out poor

Tim, who'd tried to stop him in the corridor, dragged her into this horrible little room, and railed against her and her mother. He'd even had the audacity to tell her this was only fair, considering her father had stolen her mother from him.

Emily looked up at her rescuer, who was using his pocket knife to free her from her bonds, and thanked her lucky stars he had come to their aid. Once free, she took his offered hand and even found a smile.

"Thank you so much for helping us." Her voice broke, her mistreated cheeks burning, but she managed to smile through it.

The young man smiled back reassuringly. "You are safe now, Miss March."

Despite the ghastly circumstances, Emily couldn't help but notice just how beautiful he was, tall and manly, with lovely green eyes. Her golden god helped her gently off the bed and brushed the wild tangle of blond hair out of her face. The caring gesture prompted Emily to topple straight into his arms and sob on his shoulder.

MAX HAD FOLLOWED OSTLEY FROM Warthon Castle. His grandfather's new confidant had departed rather suddenly, raising Max's suspicions. He entered the inn through the kitchen door, trying to keep an eye on the demented bastard without his noticing, then heard a woman scream from upstairs. They weren't the lusty screams one might expect in a roadside inn, but shrill, frightened screams for help. Taking the stairs three at a time, Max only stopped long enough outside the room to ascertain that one woman screamed in pain, the other for help, and the man's voice was Ostley's. He opened the door to a scene he might have arranged for the edification of his guests at the club. Only this was real, and he found absolutely nothing titillating about it. Ostley had one woman pinned over the side of the bed and was spanking her while Sir Henry's young daughter, trapped on the bed between Ostley and the wall, tethered to a bedpost, kicked at him desperately and shouted at the top of her lungs.

"Help! Stop it, you fiend, stop it! Oh please help, someone, help!"

Max raised his hand to silence the girl and commanded, "Ostley, cease."

When Ostley ignored his command, he scanned the room for something he could use to subdue the baron. The water jug seemed his only choice, so he grabbed it, ordered Miss March out of the way, and smashed it over Ostley's idiotic head. Then he pulled the imbecile off the woman on the bed and dug the tip of his boot into Ostley's side to make sure he was knocked out.

That was when Max took his first close look at Sir Henry's daughter. Emily March was the very picture of female perfection, even in her frightened, disheveled state. Of course she was entirely too young and too innocent for his taste, but he could not deny her beauty.

Max searched his pockets for his knife to cut her bonds. Once she was freed, he held out his hand to help her off the bed and watched the smile bloom on her lovely face. The smile was guileless and open, and spoke of nothing but trust. And then she proved that trust by walking straight into his arms and sobbing her relief into his chest. The gesture made him feel ashamed to ever have entertained a thought of using this girl to exact revenge on Sir Henry. As he folded his arms around her to return her embrace, Maximilian Warthon swore a solemn oath that nothing ugly would ever again touch her life.

Then the door crashed open, and Max just knew Sir Henry's pistol was squarely aimed between his shoulder blades. He thought of raising his arms in surrender, but before he could, Emily March lifted her head off his shoulder and addressed her father with clear reprimand in her voice. "Papa, you are pointing that thing at the wrong man. The golden god saved us."

Max took that as his cue to step away from the girl, but couldn't help chuckling at her irreverent naivety. He turned so he might face both of them. "I think I'd better introduce myself. Lord Didcomb, at your service."

HENRY WAS NOT AT ALL pleased with the scene in front of him, especially considering what had happened the last time he'd had the opportunity to observe Lord Didcomb. But he lowered his pistol when his daughter stepped into his arms and pointed at the unconscious Ostley on the floor. "That horrible creature over there said he would hurt you if I didn't come quietly. Then, once we were in here, he went on and on about you and my mother. He tied my hands and even hit me."

Henry reluctantly admitted to himself he would have to shake the young lord's hand in gratitude. However, Emily's next words pushed Lord Didcomb and his proclivities to the back of his mind.

"And when Isabella whipped him with her riding crop to get him off me, he beat her."

Isabella was here too? But where? And she had been hurt. The blood froze in Henry's veins. "Isabella. Where are you?"

Emily pulled the door closed to reveal Isabella behind it. She stood propped up against the wall, her eyes shut tight to stop the tears from escaping, doing her best to control her breathing.

Henry took one look and pulled her into his arms. She shook from head to toe and felt stiff and brittle. Speaking in low tones, he hoped to reassure her. "Isabella, my darling, my love. Where are you hurt?"

She relaxed a little when she recognized his voice, but her teeth still chattered when she answered. "My stomach, he punched my stomach, and then he hit my, my . . ."

Emily explained for her. "The fiend hit her bottom so hard his hand must sting. Papa, can we shoot him, please? I bet he beats his horses too. And I really don't like that my mother has to live with this cretin."

Henry stroked Isabella's back and felt her slowly relax against him. He spoke to Emily over her head. "No, Poppet, unfortunately we can't just shoot him. He is a baron. We'll have to find a magistrate willing to prosecute him for kidnapping, but even then he'd probably just pay a fine."

Lord Didcomb stepped a little closer and offered, "If you would allow me to deal with Ostley, I can offer you my personal assurance that no further harm will come to you and yours, or I will kill him myself."

At that moment Ostley groaned from the floor, and Henry, mostly concerned with taking care of his daughter and the woman still shaking in his arms, fixed the young man firmly in his sight. "I will hold you to your word, Didcomb."

Didcomb bowed and turned to pick up the sorry excuse for a human from the floor, but Henry added, "We will continue on to London to avoid any kind of talk. Will I have an opportunity to meet with you there to properly express my gratitude?"

Didcomb bowed again. "I look forward to it."

CHAPTER TWENTY-THREE

THE THREE OF THEM STOOD EMBRACING ONE
another after Didcomb had manhandled Ostley out of the room. Isabella gradually calmed; Emily shed a few more tears, but soon blew her nose noisily and declared herself all right; and Henry offered a silent prayer of thanks that things hadn't gone any further than they did.

Eventually Isabella, still huddled into Henry's shoulder, turned to Emily. "Emily, dear, you shouldn't have run away. My not being able to marry your father has nothing to do with you."

Emily looked at her quizzically. "If it's not me, then what is the reason?"

Isabella swallowed hard. Aware Henry was at least as interested in her answer as Emily was, she hoped a half-truth would be enough explanation for both of them. "I'm not fit to be a wife. I'm no longer a virgin."

Henry's response would have been reassuring if that had been the entire issue. He gently stroked her shoulder and placed a kiss to the crown of her head. Emily looked at her for a moment as if that possibility had never occurred to her, then nodded wisely. "Aunt Hortense keeps telling us how important one's virginity is." She thought about it, then asked her father, "Do you really care about Isabella not being a virgin?"

Henry weighed his words carefully, not wanting to give Emily the impression her innocence didn't matter, but also very aware Isabella had tensed while waiting for his answer. "No, it would be very hypocritical of me to condemn the woman I love for an indiscretion when all the world knows I've had so many. But most men would, Poppet, so I understand why Isabella didn't want to tell me."

He again kissed the crown of Isabella's head and murmured into her ear, "It doesn't make me love you any less." That elicited a sob, prompting Henry to hold Isabella closer still.

Emily, however, took the sob to be one of relief and patted both her father and her presumed stepmother on the back. "There, you see, all's well that ends well."

Henry's chuckle at her use of Shakespeare served as Emily's cue to extricate herself from the three-way embrace. The nervous energy still coursing through her after the attack made it impossible to stay still any longer.

At that moment Thomas knocked on the door frame and announced, "The Dowager and Lady Kistel just arrived, sir."

Emily brightened considerably. "Oh good. I don't know why I thought I could live without Grossmama, she always knows exactly how to feel about things." Heading for the door she added, "And I better find Tim. That nasty baron hit him too."

Relieved his grandmother was on hand to take care of Emily, Henry smiled his approval and called to Thomas. "Go with Miss Emily. And tell the landlady we'll be staying the night."

Thomas rushed after Emily, who could be heard excitedly calling out: "Grossmama, Grossmama, the golden god smashed a water jug over the nasty baron's head."

CLOSING THE DOOR AFTER EMILY, Henry pulled Isabella close once more. They stood like this for a while before Henry asked, "Do you still love him?"

The mere suggestion she might love another shocked Isabella. She slowly shook her head against his shoulder.

Henry let out a relieved breath. "Will you tell me about it?"

Her shoulders slumped and she stepped back half a step. "It seems I owe you that much." She finally looked up at him, and his heart sank. There was such profound sadness in her eyes, he suddenly lost all confidence that the obstacle between them could be overcome.

"You don't have to tell me now, or in this place." He gestured to the remaining evidence of struggle in the room.

But Isabella shook her head, walked to the window, and opened it. "No, I think this is the perfect time and place to tell you." She leaned her upper body on the broad windowsill, supporting herself on her elbows, and looked outward.

Realizing she couldn't sit on her ill-treated bottom, Henry went to lean out the window next to her. The field the room overlooked was bathed in golden light from the low-hanging summer sun. They couldn't see the sunset from their vantage point, but the long shadows cast by the inn and the trees around it told them there were mere minutes remaining in the day.

Watching the lengthening shadows, Isabella observed, "There is such peace and beauty in this world, yet man is capable of such ugly violence."

"Indeed. That's why you like Byron."

"Yes."

When she said nothing more, Henry decided to prompt her. "Did he force you?"

A visible shiver went down her spine, but she kept her eyes firmly on the beauty outside. "Not the first time."

Her words reverberated in his head and filled him with dread at what she would reveal, but he kept still and waited for her to continue.

"I'd known George all my life; he was the vicar's son and my brother's best friend. We dug for worms together when we were children and later occupied the same schoolroom at the vicarage. I joined my brother there after I overtook our governess in skill with my painting. The vicar was an accomplished artist, and I was eager to learn. On the day it first happened, I walked to the vicarage by myself because Freddy had come down with a fever, and since I was to go to London for my season soon, I didn't want to miss my lesson.

"As it turned out, the vicar, Mr. Bradshore, had come down with the same malady as my brother, but George was there and working on the problem his father had set him. I'd been set a task too. I set up and worked until I became aware of George staring at me. I wondered whether I had a smudge on my nose and made a face at him. He just grinned, told me I'd turned out very pretty, and asked if I'd been kissed yet. I shook my head no, but I'd been wondering what it would feel like, so I let him when he bent down and kissed me. I didn't mind it at first, but then he pried my lips open with his tongue and stuck it so far in my mouth I could barely breathe. Next I felt his hand on my breast. I was still curious, so I didn't push him away or tell him to stop. We were in the back parlor, away from the kitchen, visitors, and any other distraction, so there was little fear of discovery. Before I knew what was happening, I was on the floor and George was pushing inside of me. It hurt, but his tongue was still in my mouth, so I couldn't cry out, and then it was over before I could gather myself enough to even think of what to do. George got up, closed his placket, grinned at me, and said, 'That was brilliant, Izzy.' Then he walked out, leaving me lying there on the floor."

Henry hissed out between clenched teeth, "The disgusting vermin."

But Isabella only shook her head, indicating he needed to let her tell her story, and kept her eyes on the peaceful scene in front of them.

"I cleaned up as best I could, using my petticoats as rags, and then walked home. By the time I got to my room I was in hysterics. Sally helped me bathe and burned my soiled clothes so no one would know about my shame. She's been my confidante ever since, but even she doesn't know what happened two days later."

Henry clenched his fists and braced himself to hear it.

"The next day I was in the upstairs parlor when George came to call. My mother assumed he had come to visit Freddy, but he had come to call on my father. Papa came up a while later to announce George had asked for my hand in marriage, and he'd given him his blessing. I was in complete shock. Of course I'm aware most would consider it the only thing to do, marrying the man they had allowed to take their virginity, but I had spent all night thinking about the situation. To my mind, the one bright spot was that George likely wouldn't want to get married, so at least I wouldn't have to endure him again. Now I was confronted with a lifetime of encounters like the one on the rectory floor, and all I could do was burst into tears and flee the room. I heard later my father had excused me to George after my mother had put her foot down and told Papa my season was already arranged and I was sure to attract a better prospect than a mere vicar's son, no matter he was fifth in line to a viscountcy."

Henry had a sudden recollection of the Viscount Ridgeworth startling Isabella on the beach in Brighton. She had called him George. He felt sick with trepidation remembering how she had trembled the entire time she had talked to the man.

"My father bowed to my mother's wishes, but made it clear at dinner that night he was very much in favor of the union. I was mortified, but assumed as long as I didn't give George an opportunity to propose, I would be able to escape his physical attentions."

Isabella took a deep breath to steady herself before she recounted the rest of her tale. "Freddy remained abed for the rest of the week, and I used that excuse not to go back to the vicarage. But it was spring and I wanted to paint, so I took my board and my stool and looked for motifs around my father's estate."

Another shudder went through her body, but with her eyes fixed on the horizon, she continued. "George found me in one of the far meadows, where I'd set up to paint. But he didn't propose like I had imagined he would. Instead he dragged me into the forest. I told him to let me go, but he wouldn't hear of it. He said it didn't become me to play hard to get, and reminded me of the pointlessness of shutting the barn door after the horse had bolted. Besides, I had raised no objection the first time, which he took as permission to do it again. When I told him I didn't want to and that it hurt the first time, he laughed at me and asked if I didn't know it always hurt the first time, and not to be such a ninny."

Henry knew what she was about to tell him and wished he could take her in his arms and tell her he didn't need to hear it, that she could spare herself the telling. But he had also known, since she had started the confession, that she had to get it out. He had seen it enough times with his soldiers on the Peninsula: the telling was part of the healing.

Isabella's hands shook, but she carried on. "I told him I didn't want to do it again, but he trapped me between a tree and himself, and told me to stop worrying, that he would marry me and it wouldn't hurt this time. I knew it wasn't true the moment he pushed inside me, and begged him to stop, but he just told me to relax, and then he didn't respond to my pleas at all and just kept rutting into me. It took him longer this time and it hurt far worse. By the time he was done and was pulling his breeches back on, I was crying and telling him I never wanted to do it again and to stay away from me. He looked at me as if I was a carnival freak and said, 'Jesus, Izzy, you are frigid like your mother. I'll marry you if I have to, but you better get used to it. I guess I can always get myself a mistress like your father did.' Then he stalked off again and left me crying in the forest."

Isabella pressed her lips together tightly and willed the tears back behind her eyes. "I didn't leave the house again until we left for London and my season. I made up my mind: if I was like my mother, then marriage was not for me. I was in London by the time my monthlies arrived, and I sent him a letter explaining there was no need for him to marry me, and then I went about the business of rejecting every suitor that ever came my way."

She turned to Henry for the first time since she'd settled in the window to tell her story. Tears were streaming down her face, and Henry reached out to brush them off her cheek with his thumb. She caught his hand, held it to the side of her face, and looked at him with apology in her eyes. "You see, Henry, I love you, and that will make it even worse when you get tired of me crying every time you take your conjugal rights and go back to your mistress. It would break me to know I can't give you what you want and need from me as your wife.

So please understand, I can't marry you."

Henry's voice was hoarse with his own unshed tears. "I'm so sorry for what you had to endure. He treated you abominably, there is just no excuse, and I'm sorry for every time I made you feel uncomfortable, especially the kiss earlier." He pulled her up from the windowsill and turned her toward him so he could see her eyes better, his hand still holding the side of her face, his thumb caressing her cheek. "But I can't believe you are frigid, Isabella."

Now that he said the word back to her, Isabella couldn't hold his gaze any longer, and her face flamed scarlet.

But Henry continued. "There is passion in you, I see it every time you paint, and I have felt it every time I've touched you. That kiss this morning: you responded before you knew it wasn't just a dream. Then here, when I pulled you into my arms and you knew it was me, you calmed at my touch—you responded to it." Henry paused, unsure of whether to name the evil that had been visited upon her. But he had to make her see her attacker was at fault, not her body, so he continued. "You're not frigid, you were raped."

Isabella drew in a sharp breath and looked up in confusion. How could George have raped her? She had known him all her life. Rape was something that happened to women during war. But Henry held her gaze and nodded slowly. "That is the correct word for what he did to you, my love. The first time, he took advantage of you, which is unforgivable in and of itself. But the second time, he forced himself on you despite you telling him you didn't want to, and that is rape. No woman enjoys being taken against her will—that always causes pain. When a woman is willing and relaxed, it's entirely different."

Isabella looked at him in disbelief, but there was also a glimmer of hope. It was strange to have a word for what George had done to her. Rape. It kept echoing in her head. An ugly word, but it would explain her lack of responsiveness. But then, hope was dangerous. Hope led to disappointment. And yet . . .

Henry could see the internal war between what she believed to be true of herself and the hope that he might be right. She needed time. All he could think of doing for her at this moment was to lead her down to dinner, so he took her hand to thread through his arm, but she held him back, a question in her eyes.

"He robbed me of my first kiss. It should have been tender and imbued with innocence and it should have gone no further than a kiss." She held his gaze and took a deep breath. "Would you give me such a kiss?"

Henry's heart jumped in his chest. If she allowed him to express the tenderness he felt for her with a kiss, perhaps there was hope for them after all.

Isabella searched his eyes, teetering between hope and mortification. How could she have asked such a thing of him? But oh, to have his kiss! Just one, consciously and with the promise it would be just that, a kiss for her to enjoy. A memory to treasure. A chance to know she could reclaim that much of what was stolen from her.

Henry's eyes were full of love and concern as he nodded solemnly, then smiled the most beautiful smile she had ever seen. "True love's first kiss."

She answered his smile and stepped back into his arms, but he didn't embrace her. Instead he stood very close and used his fingers to trace tantalizing little circles around both sides of her face. Lowering his gaze from her eyes to her lips, he focused on the one part of her he was about to love with all his physical being.

Isabella closed her eyes when he touched his nose to hers and let his breath caress her lips before they made contact. He slowly and ever so tenderly brushed his lips against hers in the lightest of kisses, then withdrew an inch. Her mouth followed his to taste his kiss again, and he repeated the light brush a few times till she kissed him back. Then he embarked on a more prolonged sweep against her lips from one corner of her lovely, wide mouth to the other and back. Her responses were halting and unsure, but there was nothing clumsy about them. Henry let himself sink into the experience and deepened the kiss.

Isabella didn't know what to do with the feelings flooding her as Henry's fingers moved from tracing circles at the side of her face to threading into her hair and holding her gently in place to receive his kiss. His lips brushed more firmly now; they nibbled and sucked too, but he didn't use his tongue like George had. His kiss was all about giving himself to her, not demanding anything in return. It was a beautiful kiss. A kiss that made her want to melt into him with the sheer pleasure of it. And when he finally lifted his lips from hers and rested his forehead against her brow, she felt bereft at the loss of them. Henry had gifted her with a kiss more wonderful than even her most daring teenage dreams had conjured.

He saw the transfixed expression on Isabella's face and smiled. "I hope you enjoyed that as much as I did."

She blushed a lovely shade of pink and took his arm to go downstairs for dinner.

BOTH THE DOWAGER AND LADY Kistel declined dinner, but ordered Emily's to be brought to their rooms once they were ready. One on each side, they led Emily upstairs for a hefty dose of fussing and scolding. Emily followed with the air of one being led to the gallows, but just before she reached the stairs, she turned and winked at her father and Isabella. Henry laughed, and Isabella, sitting gingerly on her seat, remarked, "She seems to take the events of today in stride. I only hope she doesn't suffer any ill effects later from the attack."

Henry reached across the table and caressed her hand, uncaring of who saw them. "I think you took the brunt of the attack. That swine scared her, but she seems more angry than hurt. My grandmother and I will take care of her and double our efforts to keep her safe."

Isabella nodded and took another bite of her deliciously flaky chicken pot pie. It was after ten of the clock and the dining room was fairly quiet now. There were still a few locals at the bar, surrounding a man singing folk ballads, but the tables around Henry and Isabella were empty, so they could speak freely. Henry pulled a jar out of his pocket and pushed it toward his fair companion. "Have Sally apply this later. My housekeeper in London makes it. It works remarkably well on bruised skin. I wish I could spare you the trip in the coach tomorrow, but we will all be safer and more comfortable in London."

Isabella blushed furiously, but took the jar and smiled her thanks, then kept turning it in her hands while Henry ate the last of his lamb, and refilled her glass with the excellent house ale. Eventually she took a deep breath. "Henry, can I ask a favor of you?"

Henry observed the fidgeting and Isabella's deepening blush with concern. "Of course, my darling, whatever you need. Are you well?"

Isabella waved a dismissing hand. "Yes, yes, it's just. You see, I truly enjoyed our kiss earlier. In fact, it was wonderful."

Henry smiled. "It was indeed. I will never forget it."

Moving uncomfortably in her chair, Isabella continued, "Henry, I keep thinking about what you said about me responding to you. I know I did when you kissed me earlier, and I'm wondering . . . if I responded to you then, could I possibly enjoy your physical attentions?"

He reached for her hands. "I would give anything to find out."

"I know, but I'm not brave enough to marry you without finding out first." Her embarrassment was obvious, but she held his gaze. "Can we, please?"

Isabella looked at him with such a mixture of trepidation and hope, Henry almost laughed. But instead he stroked his thumbs over the back of her hands reassuringly and asked, "Will you please stay with me and Emily when we get to London?" He paused to work out how they might achieve this objective. "My grandmother hates summer in town and will be more than happy to hand you officially into the care of my godmother. Lady Greyson will neither judge nor comment if you choose to stay at my house instead. If I ask her, she will even cover for you when the baroness arrives in town."

Isabella held on to his hands for dear life. With a workable plan before her, the physical connection between them seemed the only thing capable of holding the panic threatening to grip her at bay.

Henry could feel her tremble. "Isabella, nothing will happen you are not ready for, I promise. I know this will be difficult for you, but you are right: we owe it to ourselves to try."

She had suggested it, and it was the only way for her to find out if she could marry him, but could she do it? And wouldn't she feel even worse about herself if she couldn't? Furthermore, there were practical considerations.

And all the while his incredible kiss still burned on her lips and she craved for him to kiss her again. Her eyes drifted to his mouth, and he smiled knowingly. Isabella's eyes snapped back up to Henry's. "What if you get angry because you are aroused and I can't continue?"

Henry lifted her hand to his lips and kissed it. "I was very much aroused earlier and I didn't get angry."

"And what if I fall pregnant?"

He considered the question. "Then, of course, we would have to marry for the sake of the babe. But if we get that far, I can wear a French letter."

Isabella nodded her agreement and pushed back her chair.

Standing, Henry offered her his hand. "Come, it's late, let me escort you to your room."

She placed her hand in his and let him lead her upstairs, and when they stopped to say good night outside her room, she tilted her head up to offer her lips without thought. Henry felt like a king to have gained her trust so quickly.

This kiss was brief but tender, leaving Isabella wanting more, and that feeling gave rise to hope: they were doing the right thing.

ISABELLA ENTERED HER ROOM AS if walking on a cloud. She closed her eyes and leaned back against the whitewashed wall.

"Sally? I'll need your help with this ointment."

She held the jar out in front of her when she heard movement and a muffled noise in the room, but when a hand was placed over her mouth, her eyes snapped open and her heart sank right through the cloud she had been on, free-falling toward the ground.

"Sally is a little tied up right now. But don't worry, my dear, you can send for her once we're married."

That George should materialize tonight of all nights was horrifying. It was as if talking about what he had done to her had conjured him. Isabella wanted to rail against the gods and scream for Henry, but most of all she wanted to get away from George. She hit and kicked and scratched at him, but the more she fought, the bigger his grin got and the harder he pushed her into the wall.

He shook his head. "Oh, Izzy, you don't understand, do you?" He leaned close and whispered in her ear, "The more you fight, scream, and beg, the more I like it. Funny, isn't it? Turns out you are my perfect mate."

Then all the demented playfulness disappeared. He forced a knotted scarf into her mouth and pulled it painfully tight at the back of her head. Isabella barely had time to think before he spun her away from him and tied her hands with practiced moves.

"But first things first. I have to get you out of here and to the castle."

Isabella took heart at the realization he didn't plan to rape her right then and there, but she also recognized how important it was to alert someone to her plight. She looked all about her to try and find something or someone who could possibly help her and met Sally's terrified eyes across the room. Sally, too, was gagged and tied to a chair. Clearly, Isabella couldn't expect any help from her friend, but George had stepped away to pick up a cloak from the bed. Trying her best to contain her rising panic, Isabella used her momentary mobility to step to the door and kick it with all her might as fast and often as she could. Then there was a sharp pain to the side of her head and all went black.

CHAPTER TWENTY-FOUR

HENRY KNOCKED ON GROSSMAMA'S CHAMBER door to apprise her of the plan to quarter Isabella with Lady Greyson. The dowager immediately declared herself much relieved not to have to spend more than a night in the sweltering capital, and Henry was admitted to find Emily and Lady Kistel still with her.

During one of Lady Kistel's amusing stories about her various daughters' and granddaughters' adventures in search of married bliss, Henry heard a strange rapping sound, but it stopped, so he thought nothing further of it. The stories continued for some time, and eventually Henry bid Grossmama good night and took Emily with him.

"Come, Poppet, I'll take you to your room. Susie will sleep with you tonight. Wait for me, William, or Thomas before you leave the building. I know Didcomb gave his word to take Ostley to Oxford-shire, but that's no reason to let our guard down, understood?"

Emily nodded and followed Henry into the corridor. The ordeal of the day had subdued her enough to follow her father's rules without protest. They were headed to the end of the corridor when booted feet climbed the stairs behind them in some haste. Both turned to see who it was, and Henry stepped in front of his daughter to shield her. But as soon as the head of the man became visible between the slats of the banister, all anxiety dissolved.

"Allen, what the devil are you doing here?"

Allen's somber expression lightened the moment he saw his friend and Emily, who rushed past Henry with a shriek and threw herself into Allen's arms.

"Uncle Allen, where have you been?"

Allen caught her, but had to steady himself against the wall. "Good Lord, sweet pea, you have grown." He set her down and stepped back half a step so he could get a good look at her. "In every possible way."

He took in Henry's pained fatherly expression and grinned apologetically over Emily's head. Then he sobered. "I only have a few moments, Henry. But I thought since you are here, and know the lady in question, I should let you know before I carry on."

He looked down at Emily, then met Henry's eyes again. "Can I speak freely in front of the sprout, or should we send her to bed first?"

Emily shook her head vigorously, and Henry sighed. "Well, you've done it now. You better just tell us."

Allen grinned, but his eyes remained serious. "I'm hard on the heels of a Viscount Ridgeworth. I came across him in Lord Didcomb's establishment, where he was bragging about being on the verge of wedding a Miss Chancellor."

Henry stepped closer at the mention of Isabella and Ridgeworth.

Allen continued, remembering another piece of information: "Your Mary is there, by the way, and she doesn't like Ridgeworth one bit. She sends her regards and bids you not to worry about her, but she wants you to know Ridgeworth is the perverted reverend—she said you would know what that meant."

Henry's lips pinched into a tense line. This was most unwelcome news. He nodded for Allen to continue.

"You mentioned enjoying the company of a Miss Chancellor in

one of your letters, so Ridgeworth's claims piqued my interest. At first I dismissed him as a delusional fop, but then he used the news of his betrothal to stall his creditors in the city. Whilst following him around, I ran into an old acquaintance. He works for Bow Street, and it turns out they're after Ridgeworth for murdering his cousin and his cousin's two sons to gain the title. My friend, Deeks, was about to arrest Ridgeworth when he rushed off toward Brighton, with Deeks right after him. I tagged along, not least because I thought you should know."

The color had drained out of Henry's face. His Isabella was in danger, from the man who had raped her, and who was, moreover, a murderer. Panic threatened to overpower his reason, but grim determination steadied him. Then the army training took over: get all the information and take the next logical step.

"Emily, go knock on Isabella's door and make sure she is safe and well."

Emily knew an order when she heard one and took off down the corridor to do as her father had asked. There was no answer, so she opened the door and slipped inside.

Henry turned to Allen. "You followed Ridgeworth here? I didn't see him."

Allen had seen Henry's face turn pale and knew the news he brought to be the worst possible kind.

"Yes, we stopped to make sure he wasn't staying here for the night. Turns out he put up his horses and had dinner in the taproom around seven o'clock. But he had his horses hitched up again and his carriage brought to the back of the building about an hour ago. It's no longer there, so I need to get on the road after him."

Henry had already turned and was running toward Isabella's door. At the same time Emily could be heard from within.

"Papa, Papa, come quick!"

What Henry found in Isabella's room made his blood run cold. Sally lay on the floor, her hands and feet tied to a chair she had toppled in an attempt to draw attention. Emily knelt beside the crying maid, desperately trying to remove the gag from her mouth. Both Allen and Henry produced pocket knives to cut her bonds, helped her to sit on the bed, and rubbed one arm each to get the circulation flowing again.

Despite the urgency of the moment, Henry noted Allen moved with speed and agility. There was no hint of the broken man who had returned from the Crimea, and Henry was exceedingly glad to have his friend by his side.

The moment Emily got the gag out of Sally's mouth, Henry demanded, "Where is your mistress?"

Emily added a pleading "What happened?" when Sally couldn't answer through her tears, and pressed her handkerchief into the maid's hand.

Drying her eyes, Sally resolutely blew her nose and straightened her spine before she spoke. "George Bradshore took Miss Isabella. He wants to marry her, but I can't for the life of me work out why now."

Allen supplied the answer. "The viscount needs an heir. He is also in considerable debt and needs to marry a woman of means."

Sally turned to Henry. "You have to go after her. You don't understand, she can't marry him, it would kill her."

Henry looked into the soft brown eyes of Isabella's maid and saw the real worry there. "I do understand, Sally. We will stop this. Did he say anything about where he was taking her?"

"He said something about a castle. Since he's the viscount now, it could be the one in Wales."

Henry shook his head. "Why would he do that? Allen, see if you can find out in which direction they left."

Allen lost no time carrying out his former captain's order. "I'll have them saddle a fast horse for you too."

As Allen's footsteps descended the stairs, Henry returned his attention to Sally. "Can you remember anything else that might help us find Miss Isabella?"

Tears welled up in Sally's eyes again, but she shook her head. "He hit her when she kicked the door to make noise."

Henry drew in a sharp breath and balled his fists.

"Please, Sir Henry, this isn't the first time he's hurt her. Find her, and quickly, please."

Henry nodded grimly and ushered both Sally and Emily out toward Emily's room. "Stay with my daughter. I'll bring your mistress back, Sally, I promise."

Once in her room, he kissed Emily's brow. "Stay here till I come back with Isabella. Don't even go downstairs without Thomas or William, understood?"

Emily hugged her father. "I hope you have your gun, and I hope you shoot him."

Henry quickly checked for his gun and nodded. "Tell Grossmama what happened, should I not be back by morning, and wait for us here."

All the bluster left Emily. "Bring her back, Papa."

HENRY RAN INTO THOMAS AT the bottom of the stairs and

ordered him to organize a watch, then hurried outside to mount the horse Allen held for him.

"The coach was seen heading toward Brighton less than an hour ago."

Henry adjusted his stirrups. "How fast were they going?"

"A sedate trot, according to the man who saw them. We can ride much faster, even with the limited moonlight. I sent Deeks ahead to check they didn't turn west at Bolney. Ridgeworth could double back toward the Brighton road and Wales, or London, from there."

Henry tightened the reins and urged his horse into the night. "Good thinking."

The road was well maintained for summer travel and the night clear. It took them less than half an hour to make it to the crossroads just south of Bolney, but waiting for the Bow Street runner to confirm they were headed in the right direction proved excruciating. Allen dismounted and made several attempts to draw Henry into conversation, but all Henry's focus was on getting to Isabella, and self-reproach. He'd been so certain they were safe for the night, arrogant fool that he was. The horse danced nervously beneath him as Henry worried about the miserable swine raping her again.

After five minutes of waiting and ruminating, Henry couldn't stand the inactivity any longer and turned to Allen. "He's taking her to Warthon Castle. Ridgeworth is one of the Knights and allied with the earl. I'll ride ahead."

Allen had to grab the horse's reins to stop Henry from galloping off. "And what if the maid is right and he's taking her to Wales?"

"Then we'll have days to catch up with them, but he'll be at Warthon in less than two hours. I simply have to get to her in time."

Allen saw the anguish in Henry's eyes, heard it in his voice, and refrained from pointing out a coach was a good secluded place to hurt someone. Clearly Henry was in love with Isabella and George Bradshore had done worse to her than hitting her over the head to keep her quiet. But as emotional as Henry was at present, it wouldn't do to let him go alone.

"Henry, you say this cretin is allied with the Earl of Warthon, and you wrote in one of your letters the earl has it in for you for some reason. If the situation were reversed, would you let me walk into this half-cocked?"

Henry knew his friend was right and, for the second time this evening, was glad to have him by his side. He relaxed the reins and nodded in resignation. "It's just the thought of Isabella being at his mercy." Sighing deeply, Henry eased himself off his horse. "Might as well let them rest for a moment."

Both men busied themselves with checking their guns were loaded and their knives secure: Henry's in his boot and Allen's under his shirtsleeves. Harnesses and saddle straps were checked and rechecked in tense silence, but despite all his efforts to keep himself busy, Henry had never lived through a longer quarter hour.

The return of the Bow Street runner was heralded by the sound of his galloping horse. Henry mounted immediately and demanded of the night, "Where to, Deeks?"

The answer carried on the wind: "To Brighton."

Henry urged his stallion into a gallop, consumed by the need to get to Isabella before irreparable damage was done. "Follow me! To Warthon Castle!"

Isabella woke to a sharp pain in her head and the consciousness that that was not the worst of her troubles. Her body ached, and tense voices, one of them George's, argued nearby. The viscount was having words with the driver over their speed.

"Look, my good man, the moon is almost full and there is not a cloud in the sky. Surely you can risk a light gallop, or at least a trot."

"Beggin' your pardon, sir, but we lost the second lamp a half mile back."

Isabella could hear the agitation in George's voice.

"Well, relight it, man!"

Coachy sounded like he was talking to a toddler who had broken his new toy. "If the wick gets drowned with all the jostlin', I can't relight it. I told you after the first one went."

The disrespect in the driver's voice evidently infuriated George. "Just get us there before the sun comes up, you fool."

Isabella's arms were numb right up to her shoulders; in fact, she couldn't move them at all. She concluded her hands were still bound and tried to pull herself upright so she wouldn't have to smell the grubby seat her face rested on, but thought better of it the instant George fell back into his seat with an exasperated huff. If he was traveling in the coach with her, surely it was safest to pretend she was still asleep. She closed her eyes, and relaxed her body as best she could.

Meanwhile her companion muttered viciously to himself. "He will regret talking to me like that. I know just the madam who'd be happy to introduce one of his daughters to the trade."

There was something wrong with George, something Isabella couldn't put her finger on, but knew not to be right nonetheless. He had always been excitable and impulsive, but now there was true cruelty in him, covered by a thick veneer of genteel pride and fake concern. She needed to get away from him. George had said something earlier about liking her screaming and crying. If that was the case, he would leave her alone as long as he thought her unconscious, but it was hard to keep still when her whole body shook with dread.

Isabella tried her best to think of other things, but George's persistent impatient huffing from the opposite bench made it impossible to ignore his presence. Luckily all his ire was directed at the driver. Eventually, offering a ten-guinea bonus convinced Coachy to do his passenger's bidding. He urged the horses into a trot, bouncing Isabella painfully about on the worn leather bench. Not too long after, they went over a rut in the road, and a groan escaped her despite her best efforts.

George was at her side in a flash. "Aha, my pretty bride is coming to."

Isabella shrunk into the musky seat as far as her bound hands would allow, doing her very best to keep her galloping heart and shaking body from giving away too much of her fear.

"Where are we?" It seemed imperative to find out where exactly they were and where he was taking her.

George smiled almost kindly. "We are in a coach, on our way to our wedding, dearest." He stroked her cheek tenderly. The pretense was more chilling than if he had turned into a demon in front of her very eyes.

Her breathing became more labored as she fought down the panic. "Why are you doing this, George? Why abduct me? Why insist on marrying me now?"

George sat back on his haunches, leaning his back on the opposite bench, his hand still resting on her cheek. "So many questions, dearest!" He considered the matter, then fixed her in his unsettling stare again. "You're quite right; I should've insisted on us marrying after I took your virginity. It would've been the honorable thing to do. But you seemed violently opposed to the idea, and I didn't know myself then as I do now. I had no idea your resistance was the very thing inflaming me most."

The forced smile made another appearance. "As to why now? It's simple: I need an heir, and your dowry will keep the wolves from the castle steps until I can collect for the next harvest. Providence dropped you in my lap, don't you see?"

Isabella was stunned. George Bradshore, her childhood playmate, her rapist, and now apparently the Viscount Ridgeworth, had lost his mind. Even worse, she was bound and stuck with him in a coach, traveling to an unknown destination in the dead of night, and no one knew of her plight. She wondered whether there was any hope he might respond to reason, but considering how he had applied reason to his justification of her abduction, Isabella decided she'd be better served finding out where he was taking her. Perhaps she could raise the alarm there.

"You'll need my father's consent to obtain a marriage license. Are you taking me home?"

George pulled up onto the opposite bench and chuckled as he patted his breast pocket. "Oh, dearest, your father gave his consent seven years ago, and my bishop wrote out the marriage license on my word of it. Did you know I followed in my father's footsteps? I had the living at Hove for nearly four years before my cousins so conveniently died and I became the viscount."

Isabella could only shake her head in dismay. Apparently he had thought of everything. But how had he known where to find her? She herself hadn't known she'd be at the inn. Had he followed her and taken the opportunity as it arose? The whole thing boggled the mind.

In the meantime George continued: "I might as well tell you, we're going to Warthon Castle, and the earl, my mentor, will be our witness. He has his own reasons for wanting to see you married to me, but enough of that; suffice it to say, we'll be his guests."

Isabella had no idea what to make of George's little speech, so she didn't try. The important thing was, they were headed to Warthon Castle, and that was only a few miles from Brighton. If she managed to slip away from there, she'd be able to make it to Mrs. Curtis's house. Isabella was relatively sure the servants would be there since the house had been rented for the entirety of the summer. How she would get away, she didn't know, but it was reassuring to have some kind of a plan.

HENRY LED THE WAY, SPURRING his horse through the night, visions of Isabella in torment urging him on. Allen and Deeks kept pace with him. The moon still stood high enough in the sky to light their way, and Henry was anxious to reach the turnoff toward Warthon Castle before it set. The idea of missing the road and having to extend the journey by half an hour through Brighton sent cold shivers down his spine.

An hour and a half later, they reached the still moonlit turnoff, set their horses to the east Downs, and descended toward the earl's property.

CHAPTER TWENTY-FIVE

THE JOURNEY TO THE CASTLE GATES HAD SEEMED endless, stuck as she was in a moving carriage with the worst company imaginable. But when Isabella was handed out of the coach, the position of the moon in the sky was not nearly as advanced as she had assumed. A sleepy footman led them into the bowels of the castle, then left them unattended to notify his master. George appeared to be a frequent visitor. He marched right to a table topped with several carafes and poured himself a generous amount of what looked like brandy. Neglecting to offer Isabella a drink, he threw himself into a wing chair and stared impatiently at the door. Isabella opted to stand in the narrow semicircle of light by the cold fireplace, her hands still bound behind her. She felt surrounded by menacing shadows in the enormous hall and waited with trepidation for the earl to appear. He never did, even as the hour of the night was revealed by a clock striking one, but he did send word eventually to call the preacher.

When George realized the earl had no plans to leave his bed until the reverend was present and ready to perform the ceremony, he let out a black string of curses, grabbed Isabella's arm, and dragged her to the foyer, where he hollered for someone named Ben.

A dark-haired young man appeared almost immediately and bowed politely, but Isabella didn't think him a mere servant. There was surprise in his eyes when he first saw her, and she fancied distaste fluttered briefly across his countenance when he turned to George.

"How can I be of service, Viscount Ridgeworth?"

"Ben, my boy, we need a second witness. As soon as the new reverend arrives, get your master and come with him to the chapel. In fact, get his sedan chair ready so we don't lose any time. I'm anxious to have the deed done."

Ben's brow knitted together as he tried to make heads or tails of what George had said. "I take it there is to be a wedding?"

Isabella blanched at the fate George had planned for her, and it seemed the young man noticed. He smiled at her and she fancied there was kindness in it.

But George scoffed. "Of course, man. What else would I be talking about? Now snap to it; we need to ready the chapel for the occasion."

Ben squared his shoulders. "Fresh candles are in the candelabras, they just need to be lit. And there is a pleasant arrangement of roses in front of the altar. We can send a maid to cut some for the bride's bouquet. Are we expecting the bride's kin?"

George waved a dismissive hand. "I certainly hope not. They can toast our health later, once we are settled into matrimony."

Ben made to ring for a maid, but George raised his hand to stop him. "Miss Chancellor doesn't need flowers. Is the flint still in the same place?"

"It is."

As George went to grab a torch off the wall, Isabella cast her troubled eyes around the foyer for someone who might take pity on her plight. Her gaze collided with Ben's. He took a cloak off a hook in an alcove and dropped something into the left pocket, then stepped behind her. "The night is rather cool; best wrap this around you."

It was just a cloak, but to Isabella it felt like armor against George, and when she twisted her bound hands around to surreptitiously examine the pocket from the outside, her fingers found a pocket knife. She barely had time to smile her thanks before George grabbed her arm once again and dragged her out the door and toward the drawbridge into the night. But for the first time in hours, Isabella had hope.

THE CHAPEL WAS ABOUT TEN minutes' walk away, the path crossing a cart track about halfway. As far as Isabella could make out in the dark, blinded by the torch George carried, the track led to the south around the bottom of a hill. She was almost certain it would lead to the ocean and decided to make her way along it once she got free of George. She was glad the knife was in the cloak pocket; George's handling was so rough, she would have dropped it many times over had Ben placed it in her hands. Her fingers were numb from being bound for so long, and she tripped more than once trying to keep pace with her captor.

When they got to the chapel, George pushed her into one of the pews. "Stay there while I light the candles."

Isabella didn't say a word; she just waited until his back was turned. George made himself busy with the flint to light the taper. He could have spared himself the effort and lit it on the torch he'd brought, but Isabella wasn't going to point that out. She carefully twisted the cloak around her person until she could reach her hand into the left pocket to pull out the knife. It took her a few minutes of concerted effort to open the blade and then several more to find a way to insert the blade between her bound hands. Cutting the rope proved even harder. She ended up wedging the knife between the bench and her back, and moving her hands up and down along the blade instead.

All the while George grumbled. "Servants. Will they ever do a decent job at anything? How hard is it to clean the wick after you snuffed the flame?"

The man found fault with anything and anybody, except his own behavior. Isabella was now certain he had lost his reason.

It took her quite some time to free herself, but by the time George had cleaned the wick of every candle and lit them all, the rope holding her hands had snapped. The muscles in her shoulders and arms screamed after being forced into one position for so long; it took all Isabella's willpower to keep them behind her back. George was much stronger than she, and the element of surprise was her best ally, should she gather the resolve to use the knife against him. She knew from their childhood games she couldn't outrun him unless she dealt him a serious handicap. But could she stick a knife in a living being? Boys learned such things as they hunted at their father's side, but she abhorred the blood sports so popular in the English countryside. Still, she held on to the knife, determined to get away from George before he could hurt her again.

George had meticulously arranged every item in the chapel to his satisfaction before he turned his attention to Isabella once again. "Come, Izzy."

It was clearly a command, but the ingratiating smile was back on George's face. Isabella almost dropped the knife in fright and immediately admonished herself for letting her mind drift. She stood to join the madman at the altar, her hands clasped firmly around the knife. When she got to within five feet of George she stopped, but he wouldn't allow it.

"I said come here, Isabella." He pointed to the spot right before his feet.

Taking a deep breath, Isabella took the remaining steps to stand in the spot indicated, but making sure space remained between them.

"Why so shy, my lovely bride?" George raised both hands to her shoulders to pull her closer, and in that moment something inside Isabella snapped. Before she knew what she was doing, the knife was at George's throat, and he stepped back against the altar. She watched with a savage satisfaction as shock wiped the ingratiating smile off his face.

"What the bloody hell do you think you are doing?" Fury burned in George's eyes, but there was also a sick excitement.

Isabella had seen that mad fire in his eyes once before, and pushed the knife harder into his skin to stop her hands from shaking. "I will cut your miserable throat before I let you touch me again."

IT MUST HAVE BEEN CLOSE to two in the morning when they finally reined in their horses at the gatehouse and passed through the side gate. However, all hope of slipping through undetected died when a man stepped out of the gatehouse and into their way.

"Who goes there?"

It took Henry a second to place the speaker's voice, but once he recognized it as the young man's who had rescued Lady Jane at the abbey, he decided to make himself known in the hope Mr. Ben would see the wisdom of helping him rescue Isabella.

"Sir Henry March. I travel with a Bow Street runner, and we have reason to believe the Viscount Ridgeworth has abducted a young lady and brought her here." The whole thing sounded gothic and far-fetched even to his own ears, but to Henry's astonishment, Mr. Ben raised his lantern a little higher and let out a relieved sigh.

"Oh, thank God! I just sent a man to your rooms at the Waterfront. Ridgeworth arrived an hour ago with an obviously frightened and unwilling Miss Chancellor. The viscount insisted on waking the earl, and the earl sent word to fetch the vicar from Hove."

Henry's horse reared up, sensing its rider's impatience. He had to take a moment to calm the steed. "Where are they now?"

"Ridgeworth and Miss Chancellor are waiting at the chapel. There is a path leading directly there, not five hundred yards along here on the left." He indicated the driveway to the castle.

Henry pointed his horse in the direction indicated. "Thank you! Mr. Ben, is it?"

The young man looked a little surprised. "Ben Sedon, at your service. Whatever the earl is up to, I'm certain Lord Didcomb wouldn't approve."

Henry and Allen were already on their way to the indicated path, but Dccks, his horse dancing beneath him, held back long enough to answer, "I take it he will like it even less when he finds out George Bradshore is accused of murdering the previous viscount and his family."

Standing in the middle of the drive, Ben let out a low whistle. "By thunder, not even the earl will be thrilled to be associated with a murderer." He then pulled his horse from under a lean-to at the side of the gatehouse, mounted, and rushed back to the castle.

THE MOON PERFECTLY ILLUMINATED THE path and the chapel at the far end of the meadow. Henry sped through it with only one thought in mind: to get to Isabella. The hour was desperate, but Henry had tasted hope in the kisses they had shared, so hope spurred him on now.

There was light in the little church. Henry slowed his grunting, foaming steed, jumped off, and ran into the chapel, pistol drawn.

Behind him, Allen brought his horse to a skidding halt. "Wait, Henry! You don't know what you are walking into."

Allen was right, of course, but Henry's need to get to Isabella was greater than his ability to rationalize, so he crashed through the doors. He was amazed at the sight greeting him. His gentle damsel in distress held a short pocket knife to the obviously furious viscount's throat. She had him trapped against the altar stone, but at the noise of Henry's entrance, she turned to see who had come, and in that split second of inattention, George knocked the knife out of her hand and grabbed her by the throat, forcing her between himself and the barrel of Henry's pistol. With the other hand he brought forth his own pistol and forced its mouth directly against Isabella's temple.

Having his target obscured by the woman he loved and her so gravely threatened, Henry came to an abrupt halt.

"Isabella, are you unhurt?" As he spoke, he moved farther into the chapel and around the pews toward the altar, hoping to keep George's attention on him and away from the door so Allen could get a good shot. He himself didn't dare attempt the shot for fear of injuring Isabella. The viscount's pistol wasn't cocked, but just then the vile man used his thumb to force open the lever and commanded, "Halt right there, March! You may stay and witness our nuptials, but only the preacher and the earl will be permitted to come closer. Is that clear?"

"Perfectly." Henry recognized there was nothing he could do for the moment, and thought to appease the viscount, especially as noises could be heard from the chapel door. Allen had company out there, and not just from the Bow Street runner. Words were exchanged, but the three inside the church couldn't make out what was said.

George, however, gloated. "There comes the earl with the reverend. We are on his land, and even you won't get away with shooting a peer on another peer's land."

Isabella, George's unforgiving arm holding her in a vise grip and the cold steel of his pistol jammed into her temple, nearly wept with joy and relief upon seeing Henry. He had come for her. When George had dragged her from her pew and trapped her against the altar stone, she'd had no choice but to reveal the knife and hold it to his throat. But Isabella wasn't sure she would've been able to use it. However, now they were both in danger, and she needed to warn Henry about George's state of mind.

Unable to take a shot, Henry found Isabella's frantic gaze. She clearly was terrified, but to his surprise, he also read relief there, and concern—concern for him. Her eyes repeatedly flicked up to the viscount, so Henry took a closer look at the man he knew to be a rapist, a kidnapper, and most likely a murderer.

The condescending smile was firmly in place on the viscount's face, so Henry tried to draw his eyes, but found the man focused always just above his gaze. It was rather disturbing, but not as troubling as the unhinged light in his eyes. All at once, Henry realized what Isabella was trying to warn him about: the man had lost his mind. And Isabella was more worried about what George would do to Henry than she was about her own future. That part was gratifying to know, but dealing with a madman was ten times more dangerous than arresting a murdering rapist. With a cunning murderer you could at least count on his self-interest: in this case, that he would need Isabella alive in order to marry her and claim her dowry to pay his creditors. But given the circumstances, self-interest could not be relied upon. Henry had to put Isabella's safety above all else. He lowered his gun and stepped back slightly, although still away from the door.

George beamed with triumph. "Very good, March. Now lay your pistol on the ground."

Isabella gave Henry an almost imperceptible nod as George eased the gun away from her temple, and they both started to breathe a little easier. All three turned their attention toward the growing commotion in front of the chapel.

The door at long last opened, and the earl, leaning heavily on a carved ivory cane, and flanked by Allen and Deeks, walked in. Henry took in the Earl of Warthon's wild white mane and steely blue eyes and knew at once nothing would happen from here on out the old man didn't decree to happen. His gaze fell on the cane, and another thought formed in his mind. He felt certain to be in the presence of one of the men who had watched from the antechamber three years ago as Henry and Robert had confronted and ultimately killed Astor in his dungeon. The old man's eyes came to rest on him, and there was such hatred in them, Henry had to ask himself who Astor had been to this man. The earl's hatred felt entirely personal.

George, of course, took no notice of the exchange between his former employer and Sir Henry, laid his gun behind him on the altar, and cheerily proclaimed, "Splendid! Now that you are here and you brought more witnesses, we can get on with the ceremony. I'm rather anxious to get to the consummating part. Where is the preacher?"

Warthon didn't even look at the viscount. "Your idiocy surprises even me, Bradshore."

George looked affronted and was about to protest, but the earl's eyes snapped to him as he raised a small silver gun and fired at the stunned George.

"Not another word!" thundered the earl, and a second shot followed almost at once. The first went through George's open mouth, the other straight through his heart. A bloodstain pulsed outward over his white shirtfront even before his legs collapsed beneath him.

Isabella scuttled backward, convulsively trying to catch her breath as bile rose in her throat. One moment he had held her in an iron grip, the next he lay unnaturally still, a blood puddle forming under him, and bits of grayish matter stuck in his hair. Isabella couldn't tear her eyes away. She had held herself together during the entire ordeal, watching, planning, waiting for the moment to act. But now that she was free of George, suddenly and permanently, seven years of dread and the last three hours of terror combined to paralyze her. Darkness hovered at the edge of her vision, and all that kept her from blacking out was the cold stone beneath her hands. How could George be so alive and terrifying one minute, and dead the next? It was incomprehensible.

Henry had no thought except getting to Isabella and shielding her from whatever the hell was happening. He vaulted over the pews and straight through the line of fire and pulled her farther back with him, down behind some prayer benches to the right of the altar, rubbing her back, silently encouraging her to breathe.

Behind Henry, Deeks was clearly annoyed. "He was to be tried in the House of Lords."

Warthon turned toward Deeks and Allen. "My apologies to the

crown, but I couldn't let the man get away with the murder of a peer."

Henry suspected the earl of covering his tracks rather than avenging a fellow peer, but there was no way to prove it. Besides, Isabella was rid of George Bradshore for good, so he was willing to let the earl's actions go.

Deeks evidently figured his job would be considered done whether he brought the suspect back dead or alive. He simply picked up George's body off the ground, threw him over his shoulder, and walked out of the chapel with him. "I'll be making a report. I expect the Lord Chief Justice will send for you if he has any further questions."

"Give him my regards and tell him not to bother," was all the earl grunted before he turned to Allen. "Can I rely on you to restore Miss Chancellor to her family?"

Allen bowed and stepped toward the bench where Henry stood now, his arm wrapped around Isabella's shaking shoulders. "Absolutely, my lord, that's why we came."

The earl's and Henry's eyes met once more, and Henry saw such rage and malice in them, he was surprised to be unscathed when the spell broke and the earl turned away.

"You better get on with it, then." To Ben, holding the chapel door for him, the earl added, "Get this mess cleaned up and send word to the reverend to get back to his bed." Then he was gone, leaving Henry to puzzle over where he had seen those eyes before. It was a true mystery, since he was certain not to have crossed paths with the man previously.

"TAKE ME AWAY FROM HERE, please." Isabella's words called Henry back to the present. The woman trembling in his arms had been through so much in the past day, he could barely conceive of it. He turned her to take a good look at her. She was pale and exhausted, and when he lifted her hands to kiss them, he found red welts and cuts on her wrists. "You were bound. Did you cut them?"

Isabella nodded, her eyes so full of trust and gratitude, they made Henry want to be a better man. "Yes, the young man, Ben, slipped a knife into the pocket of the cloak he draped around my shoulders before we left the castle."

"Ah yes, the helpful Mr. Ben." He didn't elaborate any further, but made a mental note to find out more about the man. There were so many odd aspects to this scenario, it might take him a while to untangle them all. But he had found his Isabella in the nick of time, so he chose to rejoice for the moment. He led her outside where Deeks was making arrangements with Ben Sedon. The night was still dark, but George's lifeless body had been flung over a spare horse, head and arms dangling as the animal scratched the dirt in front of it in search of a snack.

Henry pulled Isabella's face into his chest. "Don't look, darling."

She made no answer, but leaned into him and let him guide her to his horse, where he boosted her into the saddle, then mounted behind her.

Allen climbed into his saddle as well. "Where to?"

Henry hesitated, as he considered the impropriety of the situation. "The Posting Inn on North Street in Brighton. We can rent a carriage there. Neither the horses nor Isabella are in a fit state to make it all the way back to the inn this night, but reach it by morning we must, if we are to preserve Isabella's good name."

Isabella shook her head at the conventions of her time. "I've been kidnapped by a madman and watched him get shot and die, yet the thing I have to worry about is to get back to my chaperone before anyone finds out?"

Henry pressed a soothing kiss into her hair and chuckled. "It's absurd, I know."

PERHAPS HALF AN HOUR LATER they trotted into the deserted yard of Brighton's second-busiest posting inn. Once a grouchy stable master had been roused from his bed, it was a matter of minutes before Isabella, Allen, and Henry were ensconced in a light chaise pulled by four swift horses, and breathed a collective sigh of relief.

Henry drew Isabella against his shoulder. "Rest, darling. Sleep if you can; nothing else will happen tonight, I promise."

Allen smiled at his friend and the lovely Miss Chancellor in his arms. "Do you think you could finally introduce me before we all settle down to sleep?"

Henry looked up in some consternation, but when the sleepy woman in his arms fell victim to a fit of the giggles, the penny finally dropped, and he burst out laughing. "Good Lord, it never occurred to me you don't know Isabella." He straightened a little and gestured toward his friend. "Isabella, meet Allen Strathem, one of my two best friends. Allen, meet Isabella Chancellor, the bravest woman I know."

Isabella blushed at the praise. "Pleased to make your acquaintance, Mr. Strathem."

Allen bestowed his best smile on the woman who had so clearly captured his friend's heart. "Call me Allen, and we shall be the best of friends."

Isabella smiled, but it was clear it took effort to keep her eyes open. "I would like that." Then she settled back against Henry's shoulder and gave in to the urge to close her eyes.

Henry's and Allen's eyes met, and all that needed to be said passed between them silently. Allen now fully understood what had driven Henry this night. He couldn't have been happier for his friend, particularly since it also removed the last remaining hurdle to his own complete happiness. He smiled, stretched out on the rear-facing bench, and pulled his hat over his eyes to catch some sleep.

Henry took a little longer to close his eyes. He knew there were still obstacles to his happiness with Isabella, but there was hope. Surely there was hope.

CHAPTER TWENTY-SIX

THEY REACHED THE INN SHORTLY AFTER DAWN. Henry sent Thomas ahead with a message for Lady Greyson, explaining his need for a little subterfuge, and the whole company set off at a leisurely pace. Isabella's dreams had been full of corpses and childhood friends turning into demons, but now that she was back amongst her friends, she felt remarkably calm, considering the ordeal of the previous night. Sitting was obviously still uncomfortable, and she wore a long-sleeved dress to cover the welts at her wrists. But she laughed with Emily, conversed with the old ladies, and met Henry's gaze openly and with a smile in her eyes just for him.

They arrived in London in the late afternoon and descended on Lady Greyson for tea. Henry's godmother took the invasion in stride and declared herself delighted to get to know a female painter. Her sharp eyes immediately determined Isabella to be Henry's choice for a bride, and that the girl was in love with him. She pledged her support as soon as Henry detailed his plan.

TO ENHANCE THE FICTION THAT she had been dropped off at Lady Greyson's, Isabella said an elaborate goodbye to Henry, Emily, the dowager, and Lady Kistel on the front steps of Lady Greyson's town house. Then she went back inside and was led to a bedroom upstairs where she took the time to change out of her serviceable light-brown traveling costume into a simple but elegant blue muslin walking dress with little mother-of-pearl buttons and puffed sleeves. She also had Sally dress her hair in a Greek style, piled loosely on top of her head and secured with two ribbons. Once ready, she was ushered through the house and down to the end of the garden, where Thomas waited to take her to Sir Henry the back way. Sally was to stay behind at Lady Greyson's to front for Isabella, should her mother arrive in town while she was still at Henry's house.

They arrived through the mews. She was again led through a garden and entered Henry's house through the music room. From there she was ushered to the library, where she could hear Henry talking to Allen and his daughter even before she reached the open door. The moment she entered, Emily jumped up from the sofa and rushed toward her.

"Allen is getting married to Eliza, and everyone is going to be happy. Isn't it wonderful? I'm to be a bridesmaid!"

Isabella was pulled into an exuberant embrace, then the girl twirled away, swooning over the role she was to play in the wedding of her friends. Isabella could only marvel at Emily. She seemed to have put the events of the previous day behind her, but it also occurred to Isabella that Emily might be putting on a performance for the sake of her father. Isabella herself was still shaky inside, but as soon as Henry took her hands and kissed them in greeting, all the apprehension in her stomach seemed to settle, despite the reason for her presence in his house. This was Henry; he loved her. He had come to her rescue. If there was one man in the whole wide world she could trust, it was him.

"Welcome to my house, dearest."

The smile on Isabella's face was so open and trusting, it was like the benevolent rays of the sun. Isabella had come to his house despite all that had happened to her in the past twenty-four hours, and now it was up to them to find a way to their "happily ever after." Allen evidently had already found his with Eliza, and Henry couldn't have been happier for them.

Isabella smiled at the dark-haired man with the youthful grin, Allen, who had helped Henry rescue her the previous night. She marveled at how a shared experience such as theirs had the power to bond them in such a short period of time. "Congratulations, Allen, I hope you will be very happy."

Allen winked and bowed. "I already am." Then he grabbed Emily for a polka around the room.

Still smiling at their antics, Isabella had a quick look at her surroundings as she moved farther into the library and toward the tea tray by the empty black marble fireplace. There were two fireplaces in the cavernous room, and both had splendid landscapes hanging above them. The room ran the entire depth of the building from the front bay window to the open windows into the garden, and the walls were covered from floor to ceiling in bookshelves. A long uncovered table big enough for one to lay down a large book and study it occupied the middle of the room, and by the back windows stood a huge desk and a wingback chair. Most of the other comfortable seating in the room was grouped around the back fireplace, obviously a spot much in use for informal gatherings.

Emily, laughing and slightly out of breath from the wild gallop around the room, remembered herself as the hostess in her father's house and urged Isabella to sit with her on the sofa. "Let me pour you a cup of tea, and we can talk bridesmaid dresses. Papa and Uncle Allen still have matters to discuss, so it might be best to just let them get to it."

Isabella lowered her voice to a stage whisper. "From what I witnessed yesterday, your papa and Mr. Strathem make quite the formidable team, so by all means."

Allen smiled his approval at Isabella and winked at Emily before he turned to Henry. "Would you like that report now? I know you were preoccupied last night."

Henry watched his daughter and the woman he loved settling in for a cozy chat, then led Allen to the two seats by the bay window at the front of the house. He poured his friend a brandy. "You said you found the girls? What exactly are we dealing with here?"

Allen took a sip of Henry's excellent brandy, leaned back in his armchair, and crossed his legs at the knee. "Both women, as well as Mary, are well and in Lord Didcomb's employ. As to what we are dealing with? Well, that is a little more complicated. Emily's 'golden god' is not only the heir to the Warthon earldom, he is also doing rather well for himself in trade, has his fingers in all sorts of pies in the City, and runs a very exclusive gentlemen's club. In fact, it is so exclusive, the only way I got any information at all was by hiring on at the wine merchant who supplies Lord Didcomb's residence. Lucky for me, Didcomb is a loyal sort, and the merchant also supplies the club. I figured out from the accounts which house was the likely candidate and crept in through the cellars. The girls are there to entertain the club members, and on the night I was there, I counted fourteen."

Henry leaned back in his chair, steepled his hands before his face, and frowned. "So the 'golden god' is a glorified pimp."

Allen grinned. "Aren't you going all proper on us in your old age."

Henry was pleased to see his friend back to his carefree old self and grinned right back. "You will recall my general dislike of pimps. So how bad is he?"

"According to the women in his employ, Lord Didcomb is a good master even if the requirements are sometimes strenuous. They are all there of their own free will, have everything they could possibly want, and their families are supported with a London upper-servant wage, paid out by the barrister in Lincoln's Inn Fields. Apparently Didcomb does his best to match members to what he knows the women like, and he never uses one for a display who doesn't appreciate what's being done to her. They all have oils in their rooms to ease the way and ointments for after things get rough. That's much better than what the average madam provides or even allows."

"A smart pimp with a heart, then. At least he is not following in Astor's footsteps."

Allen sat up a little. "You said something last night about the Earl of Warthon being part of the Snake Pit. So this is the same secret society you've been tracking ever since Hampstead?"

Henry nodded gravely. "Indeed, Didcomb is trying to wrest control over it from Warthon, and, due to his efforts, it's now more of an economic alliance. But I still can't like that Emily and I owe the man a debt of gratitude."

Allen considered the situation for a moment. "You wanted to get on the inside. Here is your chance."

At seven o'clock sharp Mrs. Tibbit had William and Thomas serve an elaborate meal in the formal dining room. Isabella,

Emily, and Henry ate at a table designed for twelve where they were so widely spaced they practically had to shout at each other, which caused much hilarity and teasing from Emily. In all the fifteen years of her life, she had never eaten a meal in the dining room and assumed, quite rightly, Mrs. Tibbit had robbed them all of their comfort in the breakfast room to impress her future mistress. So once she had wolfed down three of her favorite eclairs for dessert, Emily lost no time herding Henry and Isabella to the music room. She urged them to sit on the little sofa opposite the piano and, noting the fading light outside the window, lit a few candles around the room.

Isabella leaned back against Henry's arm resting along the back of the sofa, and shyly placed her left hand on his thigh. Henry caressed it gently, glad for a chance to get her used to his touch in the comfortable setting of his house.

Emily delighted them with an exquisite rendition of "Rondo Alla Turca," and Isabella had to smile at Henry's fingers playing along on the back of her hand. He was a dear friend, her hero, and a man of his word. Perhaps she truly could give herself to him.

Emily excused herself after the rondo to seek her bed, citing her desire to say goodbye to her great-grandmother before her trip to Avon in the morning. After she had kissed both Henry and Isabella good night, Henry opened the door to the terrace and held out his hand to Isabella. "Come dance with me."

Taking his hand, she followed him into the warm summer evening. "But we have no music."

He twirled her into waltzing position. "I'll sing for us." Humming a popular waltz, he swayed them back and forth until Isabella joined the singing, and Henry led them in a slow, sensuous dance around the terrace. By the time the waltz ended, their bodies were flush against each other. Neither of them stepped out of the embrace, even though Isabella could feel his erect member against her, and the sensation filled her with trepidation.

Henry knew she could feel his excitement and stroked her back in silent praise for her bravery. "Are you ready for another kiss?"

Isabella's mouth was as dry as she imagined a desert would be. Licking her lips and swallowing did nothing to alleviate the arid discomfort. She nodded nonetheless.

Henry admired her more every minute. He brushed his lips against hers and then swept his tongue along her mouth to moisten her lips. It startled her, but she didn't pull away.

"Isabella, nothing will happen here that you don't want. I know my excitement makes you nervous, but just because I'm excited by your nearness does not mean I will fall upon you like a wild beast." Henry stroked his left hand from the small of her back to the nape of her neck and back down again. His right hand caressed the side of her face as he leaned in for another kiss. He massaged her lips gently with his, but her body was still rigid with tension. "My darling, my objective is only to make you feel pleasure. You have absolutely nothing to fear."

She nodded and leaned her head against his shoulder while he stroked her hair and cuddled her close. She was half a head shorter and fit perfectly against him, a fact not lost on his wayward organ. He felt himself twitch, and mindful not to frighten her any further, he stepped back. "Come, my love, let's order tea to my sitting room, and I'll show you where you will sleep."

Henry took her hand to lead her upstairs and into what was clearly a gentleman's sitting room. Several brightly colored Persian rugs covered the polished parquet floor, and generously sized upholstered leather furniture was grouped around the fireplace. The candelabra on the mantel only partially illuminated the room, but Isabella could make out a great many books stacked on the floor, even though there were several bookshelves along the walls standing ready to receive them. "Are you principally opposed to housing your books on shelves?"

Henry laughed. "This is my private room and I read here for pleasure. I like to have my favorites on hand." He shrugged. "Mrs. Tibbit wants to box my ears and tell me to clean up every time she comes in here, so I mostly keep the servants out."

Isabella tried to imagine the kindly matron who ran Henry's household boxing his ears, and burst into laughter, relieving some of her tension.

The sound of Isabella's laughter was pure joy to Henry. "Oh, you have no idea! Tibby boxed my ears and told me to tidy up a great many times when she was my nursemaid. She didn't think it healthy for a boy to grow up without chores and responsibilities."

Isabella thought the fact a grown man would deliberately flout his former nursemaid's rules even funnier, and Henry reveled in her unencumbered mirth. Draping his arm around her shoulder, he steered her toward a door next to one of the three sash windows. He led her into the adjacent chamber, lit the candle on a small table just inside the room, then took the key out of the lock and handed it to Isabella. "This is your room, if you're uncomfortable, or need time to yourself. If you feel things have gone too fast or too far, or you simply want to retire for the night, this is where you can come." He kissed her brow and gave her shoulders a reassuring rub. "I will not follow you in here unless you specifically invite me in. The key you hold is the only one to this door, so you can be assured of your privacy."

Isabella closed her fingers around the key and took a good look around the room. The dark turned posts of the four-poster bed were draped with white lace, and the white bedspread and pillows embroidered with a flower motif she couldn't clearly see by the light of a single candle. The armoire, chest of drawers, and privacy screen in the corner were made of the same dark wood as the bed and exquisitely worked. Rose-pink velvet draped the tall sash windows, and Isabella suspected there would be lace over the windows once the drapes were pulled back. The crown molding and skirting was kept brilliant white while the walls were covered in cream brocade, and a cream-and-beige carpet covered most of the gleaming floorboards. At the foot of the bed a pink-covered chaise longue invited rest, and an armchair stood by the fireplace. The whole room was cozy, airy, and light, even at night. She walked into the center of the room and held her candle high, imagining what a marvel it would be with the morning sun streaming in. "This room belongs to the lady of the house."

Henry smiled at the genuine wonder in her voice. "I very much hope you will be. The furniture belonged to my mother. I had it cleaned, and the room decorated, after we became friends in Brighton."

Isabella was incredulous. "But I told you I had no wish to marry."

"I'm afraid I set my heart on winning you all the same." Accompanying his statement with an unapologetic grin, he held out his hand to her. "Will you spend some more time with me?"

Isabella swallowed. She was still nervous, but trepidation no longer shadowed her eyes. Holding his gaze, she walked back to him and placed her hand in his. Her throat momentarily too dry to speak, she gave him a nod, and he brought her hand to his lips for a lingering kiss.

"Thank you, my darling."

Placing the candle back on the side table by the door, she put the key back in the lock, then took Henry's arm. "No tea, please. Just show me."

CHAPTER TWENTY-SEVEN

THE TRUST SHE PLACED IN HIM MADE HENRY feel ten feet tall, and by all that was holy, he would not let her down.

They passed through his sitting room toward a door directly opposite the one to her room. Isabella expected to feel dread at what was surely to come, but all she felt was nervousness. She had chosen to do this, and apparently that made all the difference. She was in control and she trusted Henry to listen to her. Isabella even felt hopeful. She had enjoyed Henry's kisses and his arms around her; perhaps she would be able to enjoy other things about lying with a man, even if the sexual act itself remained daunting.

Holding the door for Isabella, Henry was overcome with pride at her willingness to face her fears. He had loved twice before in his life, but never like this. The woman before him was strong and independent, needing nothing and no one to make her way in this world. Still, she needed to be loved, and he was more than willing to give her that. They would clear this hurdle together, and then they would be able to build a life uniquely their own.

Isabella halted a few steps into the room, taking in the distinctly masculine surroundings. Henry's room sported lit candles on every surface. The bed, clothes press, and chest of drawers were made of oak, the bed and windows draped in a forest-green velvet, and the wooden floor covered with a blue rug. An armchair and ottoman by the fireplace were covered in Gobelins depicting medieval courtly scenes, and so was the privacy screen in the corner. But what drew her eye was the painting above the mantelpiece.

"You have a Turner."

Henry took the opportunity to remove his jacket and waistcoat while she admired his favorite painting. He spent a good amount of time dreaming into it himself, but at present he was far more interested in the gentle slope of Isabella's shoulders and the graceful curve of her neck. Stepping behind her, he unwound the ribbon holding her coiffure in place. Isabella glanced over her shoulder with a smile, and thus encouraged, Henry liberated her hair from its pins until it fell in dark luscious waves down her back.

"I like waking up to this one," he explained while running his fingers through her hair. "It reminds me of fog in a morning meadow."

"That's exactly what it is. It must be spectacular in daylight."

Henry massaged her scalp where the pins had dug into it, eliciting an appreciative hum, then gave in to his urge to kiss her neck. "It is. And you are beautiful by candlelight."

Isabella tilted her head to the side to give him access, emboldening him. He traced kisses up her delectable nape and along her hairline to just behind her ear. His hands found their way around her waist, over her ribcage, and to her breasts and explored her fullness there, caressing her gently through the soft muslin of her dress. She stiffened at first, but then relaxed into his touch and leaned into his embrace, turning her face up to him. He kissed her mouth slowly and with great care, introducing his tongue into the play of their lips, while his thumbs brushed lightly back and forth over her hardening nipples.

"May I remove your dress so I might see more of you?"

Isabella was momentarily taken aback by his request. Both her previous encounters had left her clothing in disarray but had not required the removal of any of it. Perhaps that had been the very problem. Both occasions had been rushed and violent, and had lacked any of the tenderness and consideration Henry bestowed upon her now.

His hands caressed her breasts, then moved along her ribs to her back to open the three buttons holding her blue gown together. He placed three kisses down her spine, one for each button he opened, and allowed his tongue to flick out to taste her skin. It was an entirely new experience to feel someone's lips and tongue against her spine, sending pleasurable shivers down the length of it. Closing her eyes in bliss, Isabella held her arms out to the sides to assist Henry in taking off her dress, but he waited for her nod of consent before he moved it off her shoulders.

Nerves still fluttered in Isabella's stomach, but she could feel love in his every touch. His lips and tongue traveled the slope of her shoulder, down her arm to her wrist, and back toward her now eager mouth. This time Isabella not only opened her mouth when Henry brushed his lips to hers, but tentatively touched her tongue to his.

Henry's heart soared at the tiny caress. Her active participation meant everything to him. He turned her in his arms so she would face him, took her hand to place it on his cheek, and rejoiced when her fingertips stroked him ever so lightly and then traveled to his hairline to splay into his hair. His tongue slid a little deeper into her mouth to invite her tongue to dance with his. Stepping closer so their bodies touched head to toe, he encircled her in his arms, enjoying the warmth and softness of her.

Isabella's body was slender and firm, and as he caressed her, she melted further and further into their embrace. The more her body yielded to him, the more confident he became in his ability to give her pleasure, but it also made him aware of how affected she was by her previous experiences. If she had denied herself for seven years for fear of being raped again, then it was his responsibility to make sure no echoes of those encounters intruded on their time together.

Henry placed kisses on every inch of exposed skin, enjoying the little sounds of pleasure beginning to escape her. First she hummed; then, as her breathing deepened, she opened her mouth and the hum became a sigh. He leaned back enough to see her face, using his fingertips to continue caressing the swell of her breasts. She wore short stays and a chemise underneath, but there was still a petticoat in Henry's way before he could unlace her. He pulled the string and loosened the undergarment until it slipped over her hips to pool on the floor. She opened her eyes at the feeling of the falling fabric and met his gaze smiling down on her.

"I like the way you touch me." Her words were accompanied by a dreamy little smile, and hope soared between them.

"Good. I want you to enjoy it. All of it. My eyes on you, my hands, my kisses and eventually my body, all of me."

"I've been afraid to enjoy you looking at me."

"I know, love. It was obvious that day in the rainstorm." He held her close and buried his nose in her hair. She smelled like summer rain. "Are you brave enough to let me see all of you now?"

Isabella nodded into his shirt. "Yes."

"And may I take off my shirt? I want to feel you skin to skin."

Again she nodded.

Henry removed his carved ivory cufflinks and placed them on a little side table within arm's reach. Then he made short work of his neckcloth, pulled his shirt from his waistband, and lifted the garment over his head. Isabella watched him and had to smile at his boyish eagerness to get the shirt off. She had seen her brother do the very same thing when he was about to go swimming in the pond. But once the shirt was off, Isabella's throat dried at the sight of Henry's manly chest. He was lean but well muscled, suggesting endurance. There was a smattering of sandy blond hair on his chest and forearms, but the rest of his torso was smooth. In short, he was beautiful. Isabella itched to draw him, even more so to touch his skin, but she wasn't quite sure how to go about either.

Henry smiled at her studying him. He took her hands gently once more and put them on his chest this time. "I would love for you to touch me."

Her hands trembled where he had placed them, but she took a deep breath and spread them wide to brush them over his pebbled nipples like he had done to hers earlier.

"Mmm, that feels amazing," he hummed.

Isabella let her hands wander where her eyes admired, over his pectorals and shoulders, and down his arms. When she reached his hands, he captured hers and brought them to his lips one by one, never breaking eye contact. "Turn around, love, so I can unlace you."

This time Isabella did not swallow or lower her eyes to hide her nerves; she held his gaze as she turned. Her pupils were enlarged, the first sign of arousal and a reward for his efforts. He brushed her luscious dark hair over her shoulder, then trailed his fingertips over her shoulder blades down to where the laces of her stays were tucked in, and pulled them free. While loosening the corset, he kissed her again, sliding his tongue against hers with all the fervor of his love.

Now that Isabella had had time to get used to the sensation of Henry's tongue against hers, she relished it. It felt loving, but it also stirred something primal in her, something she had never felt before. The feeling of Henry's bare skin against hers fanned that flame even higher. The corset slid to the floor, leaving her in nothing but her short chemise. She turned to him and he lifted the garment over her head.

Isabella stood before Henry as naked as the day she was born except for her shoes and stockings and marveled at how natural it felt to be with him like this. She was still shy, a blush creeping from her chest upward, but Henry smiled lovingly and enfolded her in his arms. The skin-on-skin contact created a closeness Isabella had never experienced with anybody before, and she began to trail her fingertips over his shoulders and down his back. At the small of his back, she laid her hands flat against the warmth of his skin and hugged him. She hadn't anticipated the move would press her breasts against his smooth chest, and the lovely pressure made a little moan rise in her throat. But the hard length of his member, although encased in his pants, still made her nervous, and so she moved her hips back while hiding her face in his neck.

Henry kissed her brow. "Remember what I said earlier: just because I'm excited doesn't mean I will fall on you like a wild beast." He let his hands roam down Isabella's back over the curve of her bottom, and gently brought her back into contact with his lower body and his manhood. "I love the way your body feels next to mine."

The words were whispered into her ear, sending pleasurable shivers down her spine. She hummed her agreement into his neck and let herself sink further into the embrace, but whispered, "Please don't be impatient with me."

"Never, my love. I only want you to get used to how our bodies feel together. My breeches will stay on until you tell me you are ready for me."

Isabella was grateful to know the last step would be up to her, too, and finally allowed herself to relax. They stayed like that for a while, swaying back and forth in tiny increments and simply enjoying the feel of each other.

Eventually Henry stepped back to lift her onto his bed. He sank to one knee to pull off her buckled shoes and neatly roll down her stockings, giving every inch of skin he revealed his full attention. Where his gaze caressed, his fingers and lips followed. Her smell, her taste, the smoothness of her skin, drove Henry half mad with want. Still, he kept a tight rein on his passion. Once she was divested of every last stitch of clothing, he smiled up at her and motioned for her to scoot into the middle of the bed, then followed her up. She was spectacular: her breasts firm and full, her belly flat, her limbs long and lean. She didn't have the rounded softness so in vogue in the salons of London and Brighton, but rather the healthy, nubile body of a woman who was not afraid to exert herself. Henry found her physique utterly desirable, just like he found her sense of purpose attractive, even provocative.

Isabella smiled, lay back, and raised her arms to welcome him back into them, warming Henry's heart and assuring him she was ready to be touched. He took the time to pull all her hair out from beneath her and fanned it out around her head; such a lovely contrast against the white bed linens. Her blue-green eyes were dreamy with desire, her skin glowing with health where the sun had kissed it, and milky smooth where it had been covered by clothing. He brushed his lips against hers, enticing her into another deep kiss, but leaving enough space between them to caress her breasts and run his hands all over her alluring body.

Henry imbued every touch, every kiss, every caress with the love he felt for Isabella. He let her feel every ounce of gentleness and care he possessed and felt her enjoyment blossom. Her breath deepened, and the blush of arousal spread over her lovely breasts as he kissed his way from her mouth down her neck to the pebbled peaks. His tongue brushed over her deliciously hard nipples before he suckled them deep into his mouth, as his hands traveled down her stomach, over her hips to her inner thighs. Isabella's reactions to his touch were so full of wide-eyed innocence, he felt certain she had not yet discovered the joys of self-pleasuring.

Spreading her thighs gently so he could reach the apex, he brought his lips back to her mouth to reassure her with a kiss, then asked, "May I?"

She nodded just before a startled moan broke from her when he first brushed his fingers against the lips of her sex.

"Let yourself sink into the feeling. Let go of everything you think it should be and just feel what is: my hand on your sex, caressing you, bringing you pleasure."

Isabella had heard women whisper behind their fans about the pleasure a man's hands could give, and had envied them because she had thought herself unable to experience those pleasures. But now her whole body tingled, her back arched to encourage Henry to suckle her breasts, and she was breathless with anticipation, wondering what his hand between her thighs would do next. The fluttering in her belly was no longer anything to do with nerves; instead it was a growing need for something just out of reach, an event she knew instinctively would change everything. She did not yet know what it was, only that she wanted Henry to give it to her.

When Henry first parted her thighs and touched her there, she could barely stand it, the feeling was so intense. But his words guided her into relaxing into the sensation. His fingers gently parted her folds and found some moisture there, allowing them to glide easily back and forth. He stroked from a spot hidden deep within her folds that seemed to be the center of the tingling sensation, to her opening now throbbing with a feeling she could only describe as hunger. When his fingers circled around her opening she wished for them to push inside, and when one of his digits finally did, there was such a feeling of rightness about it, she let out a long moan of carnal longing.

When Henry heard that moan, elicited by sliding half the length of his index finger into her sheath, he could barely contain himself. She was coated in her arousal, primed and ready to receive him; he wouldn't hurt her if he slipped off his pants and pushed inside her. But if he did, he would destroy the trust they had built between them. Henry held her tight for a moment while he called his body to order, then threaded one of his arms under her shoulders and held her close. With her face buried in his neck, Henry used his other hand to pleasure her. His index finger set up a gentle rhythm sliding in and out of her, and his thumb stroked tantalizing little circles around her clitoris, flicking directly over it after every rotation.

Before long, Isabella could barely draw breath, the feelings Henry stirred in her were so intense. Her whole being seemed to race toward some kind of precipice, but instead of using her muscles to get there, all her focus was on Henry's finger brushing over that magical spot.

She wanted to urge him to rub it faster or harder, but seemed to have lost the power of speech, so she had to surrender herself to the tingling numbness until she went rigid with tension. Just when she thought it impossible to take any more of his teasing, Henry ground his thumb more forcefully into that magic spot and she felt herself liquefy into a starburst of bliss. Isabella cried out her orgasm into Henry's neck, even bit into his collarbone in the heat of her passion.

Henry grinned at her savagery and welcomed the pain; it helped him control his now near-overwhelming urges. His cock throbbed relentlessly behind his placket, but the only relief he allowed himself was to press his arousal against her thigh. He kept up his caresses until every last orgasmic spasm had wrecked her body and she rested limp and spent in his arms. Stroking his hand up her belly and over her breast to her shoulder, he lay back and settled her onto his chest to rest. She had come beautifully, proving once and for all she was far from frigid, and Henry felt a pride he had never known before at the accomplishment.

An indescribable peace had come over Isabella in the aftermath of her first orgasm. Her body felt boneless as she rested in Henry's protective arms, and she hummed her contentment as he stroked her hair, her shoulder, her hand on his chest. Slowly she floated back to earth and became aware that loving as his touch was, it still held tension, and when she opened her eyes, she was confronted with the straining bulge in his pants. She knew it was unfair; Henry had just proved she could feel pleasure. She also knew he wouldn't hurt her, or force her in any way. He most likely deserved a reward for his patience with her. But all of a sudden it became imperative to know she could indeed leave without allowing him to take his pleasure with her. She lifted her head and met his gaze. "I think I want to go to my room."

It was impossible for Henry not to be disappointed, but he recognized her statement as the test it surely was.

"I'll miss you, but if you think you will sleep better in your room, then by all means, my love." He kissed her forehead and then her lips to show her he understood and didn't hold it against her.

Isabella kissed him in farewell, scooted off the bed, and slipped her chemise on. Then she balled up the rest of her clothes and left the room with one last smile.

PROPPED ON HIS ELBOW, HENRY watched her go. Once he heard the door to her room close, he stood to pour himself a brandy. He drained the glass and sighed deeply. He had to give her time.

CHAPTER TWENTY-EIGHT

IN THE BEAUTIFUL CHAMBER HENRY HAD FUR-
nished for her, Isabella stood in the center, listening to the house and
the city beyond. The door behind her was open, but Henry did not
follow her. Again he was true to his word, and all she wanted was to
be back in his arms.

Being alone was all wrong!

Dropping her bundle of clothes, she turned on her heels and hurried back to Henry.

HENRY'S HEART SKIPPED A BEAT when he heard the door open.
He turned to meet Isabella's tentative smile, her eyes shining with
what he hoped was love.

"I don't want to sleep alone. After all, my mother may well arrive
in town tomorrow." A deep blush heated her cheeks, underlining the
subtext of her statement. Henry was next to her in two long steps,
kissing her tenderly, caressing her face, and making her feel as if she
were the most precious thing in the world.

"Sleep in my arms, my darling. Be mine tonight."

She nodded, but Henry could see her swallow and soothed her
with gentle hands. "My promise still stands. I won't enter you until you
tell me you are ready."

His breath smelled of brandy, and she could see the spirits sparkle in his eyes. However, there was love reflected in them, too, and his hands and lips were gentle. "Yes, Henry, I'll be yours tonight."

Henry kissed her again, deeper this time, holding her close as she sank into him and stroked her tongue against his. He lifted the shift over her head, once again leaving her completely naked. To his surprise, Isabella reached for the buttons on his placket. He helped her without breaking their kiss, and pulled her back into his arms as soon as there was no stitch of clothing left between them. He lifted her so she knelt right on the edge of the bed, and feeling her skin next to his from their thighs to their necks was simply glorious.

Kissing his way to that magical spot just behind her ear, he whispered, "I love you, Isabella Chancellor, body and soul."

The warmth of his skin all along her front, his arms encircling her, his hands and breath caressing her, all combined to create a sense of well-being in Isabella she hadn't thought possible. Even Henry's erect penis nestled against her mount didn't unnerve her; on the contrary, it added to her arousal. Henry being so excited by her nearness flattered her, and his consideration endeared him to her. Presently, he lifted her with one arm to scoot her into the middle of the bed and laid her down. He opened her legs so he could kneel between them and devoured her with his eyes as he stroked his hands over her body with long, smooth movements, further heightening her sense of well-being. But no matter how much she liked his hands on her, his looking right at her open sex felt less comfortable. She tried to cover it with her hands, but when his eyes pleaded with her to let him see, she let her hands fall away.

Henry could barely contain his pride in her. "Thank you, my brave darling." He ran his long fingers through the curls between her legs and stroked one between the lips of her sex. "You are beautiful here too." Henry collected some of her sweet-smelling moisture on his finger and sucked it off. "You taste good, as well."

Isabella gasped, blushing furiously at the intense carnality. Laying a calming hand between her breasts, Henry soothed, "Easy, my love. I will kiss you there sometime soon, but since it makes you uncomfortable, we won't do that tonight. You will like it, though, I promise. It's another way to give you pleasure."

Isabella was shocked by his words. It had never occurred to her he might want to kiss her there. Nevertheless, his words and the thought were so arousing, things inside her seemed to liquefy, and her breathing grew heavy.

Her lips opened in obvious invitation and Henry entwined their tongues in a lush kiss, then trailed his lips down to her nipples as he settled in, lying half on top of her, his left arm threaded under her shoulder and his cock excitedly nudging against her upper thigh. He could hear her breath changing, see the passion rising in her, and couldn't remember ever being this affected by a woman. He laved her nipples with his tongue and then sucked them into his mouth one by one, eliciting a pleasured moan. His hand returned to gently stroke her sex, wanting to give her everything he was capable of giving.

Grabbing fistfuls of the sheets beneath her, Isabella lifted her hips a little. Everything in her hummed with anticipation, and she hoped fervently Henry would bring her pleasure like he had done earlier. Only this time she wanted his member inside her, not just his finger; she now knew that to be the ultimate goal. It was also her biggest fear, but it was a fear she meant to face this night.

Henry's fingers on her sex, stroking back and forth over that magical spot, made her feel she was racing toward a precipice again. Every time he passed over her clitoris, she seemed to climb higher on the mountain of desire. Isabella's breath escaped her in long drawn-out sighs of pleasure. And then he started to dip his finger into her entrance, and that hunger came over her again.

"Henry, I'm ready, I think."

He let his index finger sink deep inside of her drenched sheath, drawing a moan from her, and raised himself over her.

"You are, my love." The words, whispered into her ear, made Isabella tingle with need.

Henry kissed her neck, sliding his shaft through her folds to coat himself in her delicious wetness, and pushed halfway in. But as he did, Isabella let out a cry that sounded like all the air had been forced from her lungs. Henry stopped immediately and searched her face to determine what was wrong. Her eyes were wide, her pupils huge with arousal, and her expression not pained exactly, but stunned.

"Did I hurt you?"

Isabella at first didn't realize he had spoken. She was too busy feeling all the amazingly wonderful, primal things having Henry inside her made her feel. She loosened her grip on the sheets to stroke his face and shook her head almost desperately, afraid he would stop now.

"No! No, you didn't hurt me. You just seem to have displaced all the air from my lungs."

Henry chuckled at her reaction and nudged a little deeper, making her gasp again. "And I'm only halfway in."

He brushed the hair off her dampening brow and pushed in deeper still. This time he swallowed her gasp with his kiss.

Isabella held on to his shoulders now, doing her best to open herself wide enough to accommodate him. Evidently Henry's member was big, or at least it felt that way to her. It amazed her that what he was doing didn't hurt, but it truly did not. So she relaxed into the experience, and then Henry's fingers found that magic spot again, and the tingling sensation took hold of her entire body.

"Wrap your legs around my hips."

Isabella heard his voice as if in a dream, but lifted her legs and slung them around his middle. That seemed to open her wide enough to take all of him. He began to move in and out in smooth strokes, driving not only the air from her lungs, but all thought from her mind. She was nothing but carnal pleasure, and then the tingling turned into waves of ecstasy, utterly consuming her. She heard herself cry out in helpless surrender, felt her sex clench around him, and knew she would be forever changed.

Henry felt, heard, and watched her orgasm and let himself fall over the edge just as she started to calm down. He poured all the love he felt for this woman into her, and it turned the simple sexual act into a profound experience. Hope, love, and pride mingled as he kissed her through the aftershocks and then settled her into his arms to sleep.

HENRY WOKE TO A COOL breeze running up his side where Isabella's warm body should have been. Someone had extinguished all the candles in the room, and for a moment he feared she had left. But then his eyes found her standing in the moonlight by the open window. Henry watched Isabella as she watched the night, her lovely body beautifully outlined by the silvery light. It must have been the early hours of the morning, for the moon was almost full and bright, setting to the west on the other side of the square.

Henry slowly rose, pulled the blanket from his bed, and gathered it around himself, intent on sharing its warmth with the stunning naked woman before him. He moved closer, but stopped short to admire her for a little longer.

"She walks in beauty, like the night / Of cloudless climes and starry skies; / And all that's best of dark and bright / Meet in her aspect and her eyes."

Isabella looked at him over her shoulder with a soft smile. "Byron again."

"Yes, it seems apt, seeing you standing there." He closed the gap between them and wrapped the blanket around them both.

Leaning her back to his chest, they enjoyed the beauty of the night together.

Isabella eventually broke the silence. "He was wrong, wasn't he?"

Henry instantly knew who she was talking about. "Yes, he was."

"It's like my body is finally mine again, and it's a good strong body, complete and all woman." Her voice was quiet but powerful, in the same way her body felt soft as well as strong in his arms.

Henry kissed her neck and stroked his hand over her belly where he had planted his seed earlier, and hoped it had already taken root. He wanted everything with this woman, a lifetime of doubled joys and halved woes.

"Marry me, please."

Isabella turned her head to look up at him and offered her lips for his kiss. He bent down to her, but let his mouth hover right above hers, waiting for her answer.

"Yes."

Smiling his pleasure, he kissed her tenderly to seal the bargain.

They stood there for some time longer admiring the night, until Henry draped the blanket over Isabella's shoulders to go get the armchair. He placed it right behind her and settled them both in it, she on his lap and both of them covered by the blanket, to watch and rest in warmth and comfort.

THE NEXT TIME THEY WOKE, it was to the sound of a coach arriving in the square, and the first rays of dawn lighting the sky. The coach stopped outside Henry's house, and soon the sound of insistent voices confirmed the presence of visitors.

"I believe your mother just made her entrance on the scene. And by the sounds of it, she's brought your father along. Shall we give them the good news now, or would you prefer the back door, and I bring them to Lady Greyson's in an hour or so?"

Isabella giggled into his neck, unwilling to give up her comfortable spot in his arms. "The back door, I think. No point in giving my mother an apoplexy. She would never understand why we did what we did."

Henry grinned and snuggled her close for a little while longer before he helped her into her shift and rang for William.

THE END

∽◦∽

THE STORY CONTINUES IN...

THE MEMORY OF HER

∽◦∽

CHAPTER ONE

THERE WERE STARS ABOVE HIM, CLEAR AND bright in the velvety night sky. Why could he see stars? How come he was no longer in Henry's breakfast room, watching the morning sun on her dark curls?

Cold air made him shiver. Christ, they'd taken the lid off the hole.

Allen hastily tucked the memory of her into the furthest corner of his mind. They could never know about his love; they would use her against him, threaten her with harm, and that would surely break him.

Above him the ladder appeared and was secured against the rocks, then the customary bucket of water hit him square in the face. It was meant as a prelude to the horrors to come, but Allen had learned to anticipate and use the clean spring water they threw down on him. His Russian captors tossed down a loaf of bread once or twice a week, too, but never bothered to actually give them water. They had the rivulets of water skipping down the rocks to the soft bottom every time it rained, and it rained frequently in winter on the Crimea. Not as much as in England, but enough to make an abandoned well a miserable place to live. Luckily, the water they caught in the two buckets they had in the hole was enough to survive on. Allen had no reason to believe the Russians had brought down the buckets for their prisoners to collect water with. It was far more likely they had gotten drunk before deciding to interrogate one of their captives, and had flung the entire water-filled bucket into the hole. Be that as it may, there was now clean water in the drinking bucket and he was wet from head to toe. He rubbed his mangled hands together as best he could. Best to get as much of him as clean as possible before they inflicted more wounds. Hygiene was not the most pressing concern, but it was a concern, right after their weakened state and the demented demons above.

Judging by the stars winking down at him, four days had passed since the Greek had been thrown back into the hole, and left to die. It had been horribly cold since the poor soul breathed his last. It occurred to Allen he should refer to himself in the first person singular, since he was currently the only live prisoner in the hole.

One of the Russians must have climbed down while Allen was busy cleaning his hands. He was roughly yanked up by the scruff of his neck and hauled out of the hole. Once above ground, he was dragged to a fire further down the hill. The light was almost blinding after the almost-complete darkness of the hole, and Allen rejoiced for a moment, thinking he would be able to warm up while he took his beating. But then he recognized the tall figure of the Russian colonel and knew today would be more than just painful. Allen didn't actually know the man's rank, he never wore uniform and none of the others addressed him as such, but he was clearly in charge and everything about the man spoke upper crust and military training.

One look into the man's cold pale eyes and Allen also knew today would be the last time, his last chance to earn himself a quicker death by telling the Russian what he wanted to know. But his tormentor didn't understand Allen's objective. He would face death on his terms, back in the hole, where he could remember her one more time.

The ogre who had dragged him out and down the hill dropped Allen on the dirt by the fire and kicked him viciously. Allen heard the rib crack, all breath wrenched from him, and wondered how many more would break before they left him to die.

"Why are you in Sevastopol?" The colonel wasn't just an aristocrat, he was cultured. His French was flawless and his English only slightly accented. He was tall, blond, clean-shaven and wore a gentleman's suit that looked like it may have been tailored on Bond Street. By contrast, his men were in local garb consisting of breeches, wool shirts, fur vests and heavy boots. All of them wore their hair long in various shades of dirty blond, their beards were unkempt, and they smelled no better than their prisoners. The two holding Allen down periodically passed a bottle containing strong spirits back and forth.

Allen breathed heavily through the pain. "Business," was all he got out between his teeth.

"Who do you work for?"

The questions weren't exactly original. Allen had been asked the very same ones several times a week for three months now and his answers were always the same. "Myself. I import fine leather."

Allen knew he had made a mistake the moment the words were out of his mouth.

"I didn't ask what you did, spy. Spare me your rehearsed answers." He ordered in Russian, "Left hand."

It was a Herculean effort not to react. Letting on he understood Russian would further convince the man he was a foreign agent. Allen's arm was yanked to the side and his hand placed on a flat rock. That alone was painful enough with all the broken fingers. Allen panted with the panicked anticipation of having yet more bones broken in his hopelessly mangled hand.

The colonel placed his boot on top of Allen's hand and applied some of his weight as he ground his heel. Allen whimpered when half-healed bones broke once again, his eyes streaming hopelessly.

"What were you doing on the hill above Sevastopol?"

Allen had to focus to answer the question. This was not the time to slip up. "Walking."

The colonel lifted his foot and a moment later his heel smashed down onto his prisoner's hand. Allen's agonized screams tore through the frigid mountain air, his whole being an inferno of pain. Eventually the wave of agony subsided and he sobbed: "Just walking."

The kick to his head was swift and painful, but nothing compared to the throbbing in his hand.

"Stop lying to me!" the Russian thundered. Then in Russian he added, "Take off his boot, let's see how much he likes his toes."

This was new. So far they had left his feet alone, and none of the others had ever had any missing boots after an interrogation. None of the others had lasted a whole three months either, but that was all the more reason for the Russian to want to crack him before he died. This was it. This was where he finally proved himself as an agent. This was where he gave his life for the sake of the mission. If he cracked now, then three months of agony would have been in vain and Rick would be next in that miserable hole. Rick didn't know all he had uncovered, but enough so the Old Man would be able to draw the right conclusions, enough so the Russians would kill him for it. There was a chance his man and friend had sent a report to England, but there was no chance whatsoever he had taken that report home himself while his master was missing. Rick was still looking for him. Just like Allen would be still looking for Rick if the situation had been reversed.

Allen's continued sobbing convinced his tormentors he was still fully occupied with the pain in his hand as the colonel's two hellhounds held him down and pulled off his boot. The wool socks he had carefully washed and dried after each rain to avoid foot-rot were next. One of the brutes joked in Russian how his pretty little toes were the cleanest part of him, wondering if he kept his cock whore-ready, too. That got a big laugh from his companion and the two guards who were supposed to watch the woods in case someone stumbled upon them. They were instantly admonished to keep their minds on their respective tasks.

The colonel pulled a short sword from his dainty mahogany walking stick and tested the blade against the tender part on the inside of Allen's foot.

What came out of Allen's mouth could only be described as a shriek. The Russian smiled, satisfied with the sharpness of his weapon and wiped the blade against Allen's pants.

"Lets try this again. Who do you work for?"

The gush on his foot stung horribly, but Allen did his best to breathe through it. "Independent merchant. D-don't work for anyone."

The colonel shrugged, then motioned to the man holding the bottle. "Let's set the cut on fire."

The demon with the bottle grinned and tipped the liquor over the injured foot. Allen had little time to brace for the hurt to come and hissed frenzied pants until the wave of pain subsided. He was reaching the limit of what he could take. His mind was beginning to wander and there was no guarantee on what he would tell the bastards if he didn't keep himself under control.

The colonel motioned for the two brutes to hold him down "Again, English. Who do you work for?"

"Just me," Allen insisted, knowing it was not what the Russian wanted to hear and therefore would mean more pain. The two helpers held him down so tightly, he couldn't move a muscle, but he had an unfortunate full view of the colonel's hate-filled eyes as he raised his sword-arm, and the incredible speed with which it came down on his big toe.

The howl Allen sent into the night was barely human. Then the pain overwhelmed his brain and he fainted.

ALLEN AWOKE TO SOMEONE HEAVING him onto a donkey and cried out as his foot hit something, probably the donkey's belly. The man tying him to the donkey instantly put a firm hand over his mouth.

"Allen, sir. If you have any sense left in that brain of yours, use it to keep quiet. The Ruskies only left about half an hour ago so they aren't far in front of us going down the trail, but I've got to get you to the doctor, you're bleeding out."

Through the haze of pain and a profound weakness, Allen registered two things: the person talking to him was Rick. And he wasn't in the hole. His mouth was as dry as a desert wind, so it was hard to get the words out.

"Did I tell them anything?"

A reassuring hand came to rest between his shoulder blades, and Allen had never before been so glad for a kind touch from another human.

"No, you didn't."

Allen breathed a sigh of relief and drifted back into unconsciousness.

THE MEMORY OF HER

COMING 2022

ACKNOWLEDGEMENTS

Whenever it comes to writing my acknowledgments for a book I'm reminded of how writing really isn't the solitary activity we are led to believe. Yes, I write my stories by myself, but you wouldn't be reading them without all the people who support me.

I'll be forever grateful to Michelle Halket at Central Avenue Publishing for taking on the *Gentleman Spy Mysteries* and letting me tell this story my way.

My profound thanks to Molly Ringle for editing *The Gentleman's Daughter*. Thanks for gently prodding me in the right direction and corralling my wayward commas and word choices.

A huge thank you goes to my writer friends. Let me begin with my lovely friend Carmen Chancellor whose surname you will no doubt recognize; thank you for all your support and story advice.

This book and the whole series might not exist if it wasn't for the encouragement from my Book Besties: Kelly Cain, Cathie Armstrong, Jamie McLachlan and Amanda Linsmeier. Thank you for always being there when I need you and for your spot-on suggestions for *The Gentleman's Daughter*. You truly are the best.

A shout-out to Annemarie Levitt. I miss bringing you pages and sharing a glass of Adams wine.

I also want to acknowledge my husband and son who share me with my stories. Thank you for understanding how important writing is to me.

Bianca M. Schwarz was born in Germany, spent her formative years in London, and now lives in Los Angeles with her husband and son. She has been telling stories all her life, but didn't hit her stride until she started writing books she would want to read for fun. *The Gentleman Spy Mysteries* are those books.